ROMASANTA
FATHER
OF
WEREWOLVES

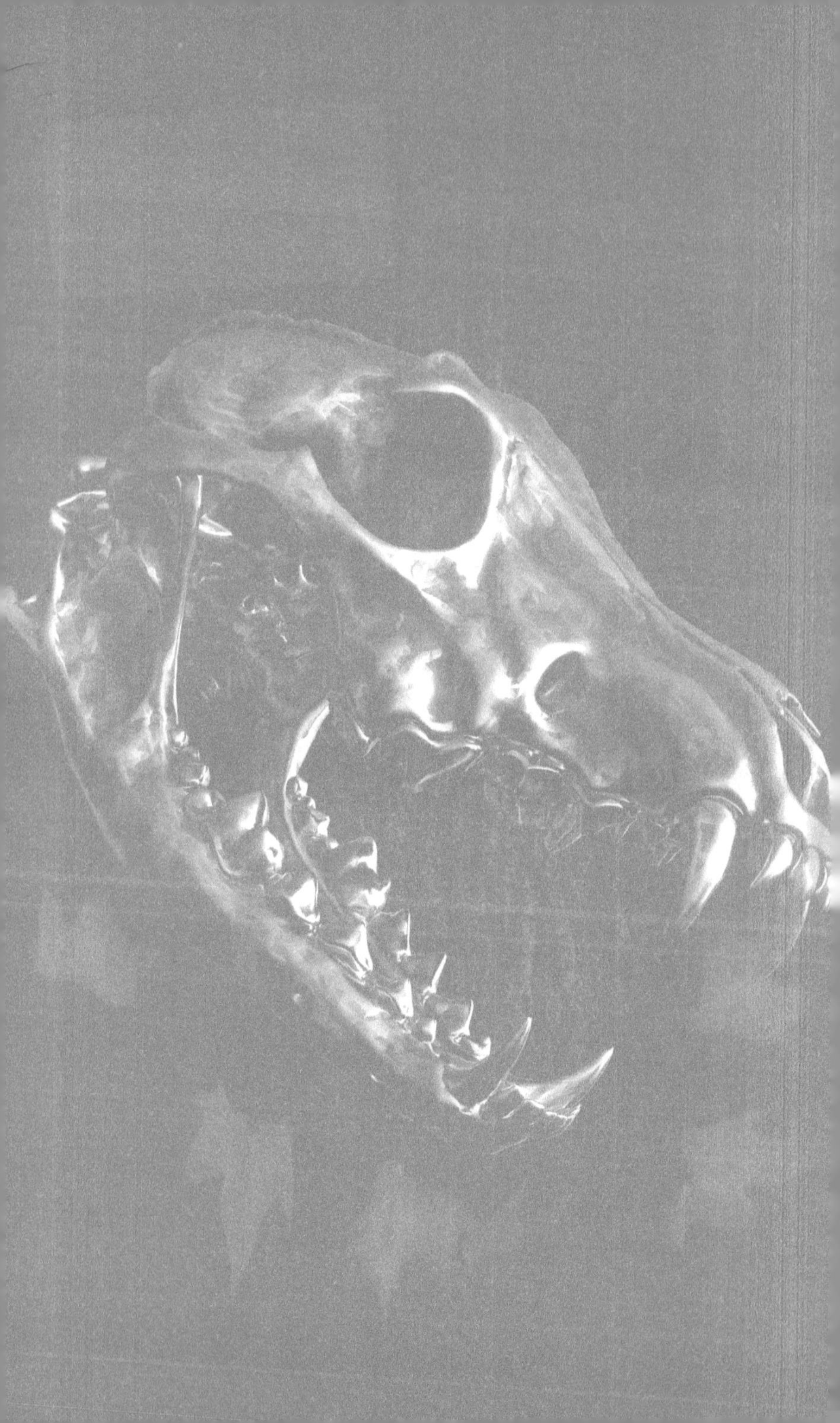

THE CEDRIC SERIES

ROMASANTA
FATHER
OF
WEREWOLVES

AWARD-WINNING AUTHOR
VALERIE WILLIS

Dedication

Thank you to Mr. Justin Willis—my amazing, wonderful, super sexy, Mr. Fix-it-all husband—who threatened that he better be in every dedication here on out … or else! I am not allowed to just say, Husband! He also thinks that all my readers should thank him for not insisting I go to bed every night by midnight.

I Love You, Mr. Justin Willis.

Table of Contents

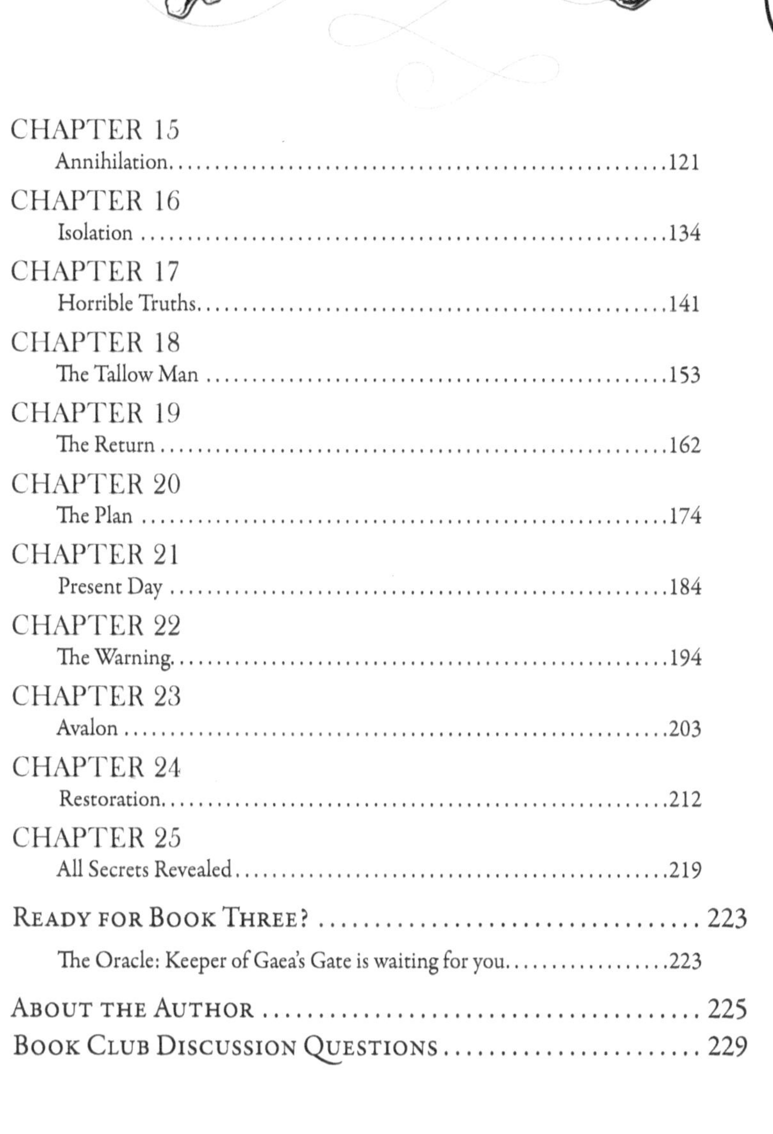

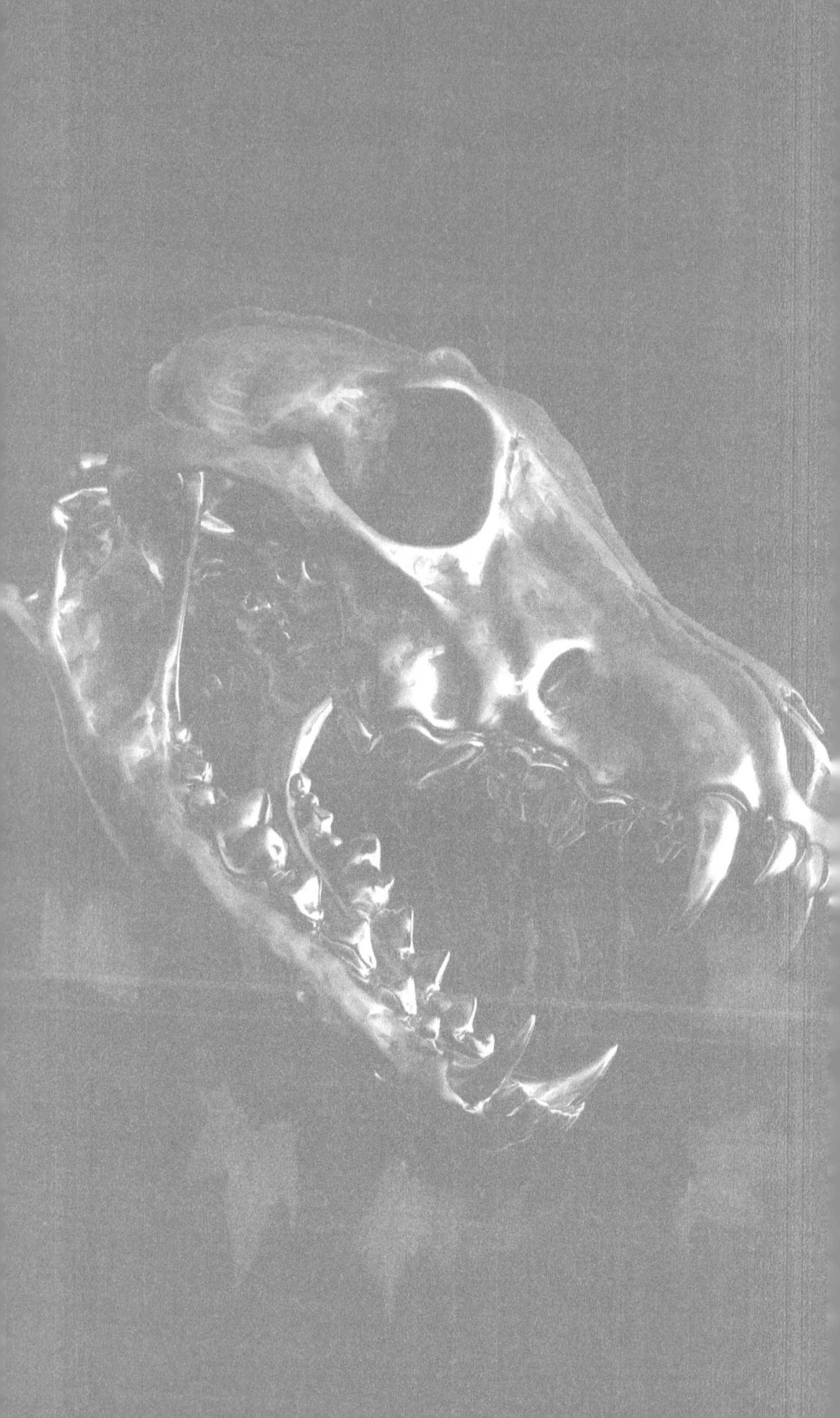

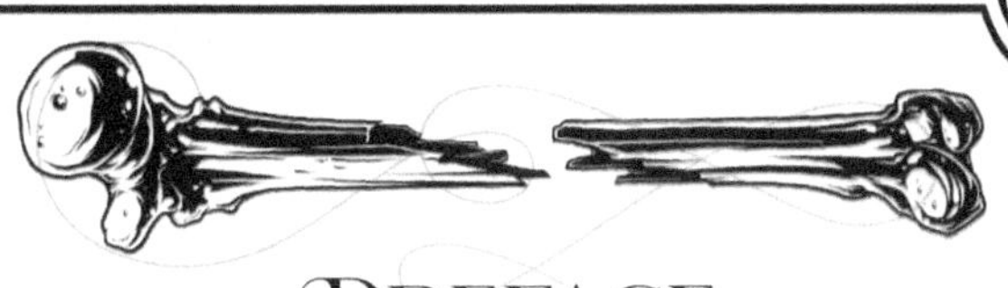

PREFACE

It was brought to my attention that I should take a moment to talk to the readers and fans of *The Cedric Series*.

I wish to share my inspirations for writing this story. This will explain a lot about how I came about creating these amazing ideas, characters, creatures, and events as a fictional work with heavy fantasy and romance elements in the mix. If one really wanted to drag out all its genres, I could label this a historical fiction, mythology, or even an occult and paranormal series. So far, fantasy romance has done this work the most justice for my readers' expectations.

Historical fiction can be applied to several parts throughout the series, whether it's a scene, event, or even a reflection of a character and their on-goings. What do I mean by this? Well, a lot of you might get the Vladimir Tepes, or Vlad the Impaler references, but it dove deeper than that. King Frederic was the First King of Germans and the lepers in those times did indeed have to ring bells and seek refuge in colonies, Cerdanya was a real trade town, and so on. There are a ton of subtle hints here and there because I wanted to bring the unseen, untold side of the history during the Medieval Times to a tangible state.

As far as the mythology side of this series, I wanted to teach you all my versions of forgotten lore, legends, and mythology. I did my best to not use anything that was newer than the 12th century as I dug deep. Some of the concepts woven in with my own perception were hard to obtain and justify. There was a lot of book buying, digging through a Medieval-age bestiary, and though I scoured the internet, it failed me often in my journey for research. As I created and developed each character, I did my best to tie them into one or more myths so that I may weave a wondrous story without limits. At the same time, I wanted some of you to get caught in a conversation or to be sitting in class and have that moment of, "Oh! I know how this myth goes!"

Let me enlighten you all on some of the tales, history, legends, and myths stitched into some of these amazing characters you have experienced so far:

- Cedric takes after a very forgotten and neglected epic legend from the Medieval Times of the Russian knight hero, Ilya Muromets. Search him, check it out, and feel free to compare what you unknowingly learned about this amazing legend. You'll be excited to see a red-haired knight on a black horse as one of the images in the mix. Included in this were some really obscure Romanian beliefs involving early vampire-like stories. The off-shoots involving the strigoi showed less fear toward these vampire creatures, but held a tone of sorrow and remorse. People who became these creatures had not finished living their lives (Including not ever getting married) and met the insane stipulations to come back as one of the undying. Truly interesting, and I can only hope to capture that same empathetic tone I had discovered in my digging.

- Barushka combines a few tales as well, starting with his name drawn from the Russian knight hero tales. Other than that, I focused heavily on the shag foal lores. I was intrigued by the first few variants I stumbled on and found that the internet proved void of information. Amazingly, the hairy phantom horse tales started so long ago. There was no exact date as to when they began. The folklore was mysteriously always there. Adding to my wonder about this lore was the fact I stumbled on a 1927 naturalist journal that devoted a section to them. Even this far forward, it was believed it may be an undiscovered species of horse! Despite that, the one thing I saw reflected in all the writing was that a shag foal approaches lone travelers and scares them so much that they run off to their deaths. Never once did the research say the horse actively killed someone.

- Morrighan, Badbh, and Nemaine were derived from the tales involving the evil sorcerer Calatin. This was an older tale involving them that did not mix the three as one entity. There are no words to describe my frustration and disappointment at how many times Badbh and Nemaine were labeled as alternative names for Morrighan.

Especially when the story of the Legendary Cuchulainn made it clear that they were three sisters, each with unique powers. Seeing that Badbh and Morrighan had earned the title of goddess at some point through the passing of time, I felt the need to give Nemaine her own placement as a goddess as well.

- Romasanta is the most complex of all my characters. His name is taken from a man in history who is not as common as he once was, Manuel Blanco Romasanta. He was the first serial killer to be trailed and as you read book two of the Cedric Series, you will see a lot of that history drawn upon. Feeding off the tragic aura, I pulled in both werewolf and wolf-related myths and lores, wanting to show a more accurate flow through a single entity. It was my intention to bring in familiar aspects and add in the historically forgotten complications that modern book culture has failed to take into account. Those well-versed in mythology will be able to pick out elements on their own, but the amount of lore here is wide. Tales of Apollo and Daphne, Pan and Pitip, Fenrir, versipellis, Romanian beliefs of vampires were caused by a werewolf, Wolf of the Cemetery from Haiti, Romulus and Remus, and so on. There are deep seeds that I only give you teasers of the mythology that is mentioned here.

- As for the monsters, you can say thank you to the Medieval Bestiaries. There are so many wild and crazy creatures in these that are no longer touched that I wanted to bring them to life again. Orms, Jidra, and Aitvaras were a few of the frightening things that travelers spoke of and warned each other about in their explorations. I can only imagine what they may have been based on, but there is a great sense of pride I take in including such monsters in my story. Granted, I have not followed their descriptions exactly and have embellished them with my own imagination, but I hope they make my stories more memorable.

In the end, I encourage my thirsty readers to explore what you've read in my *Cedric Series*. Search the names, look deeper into the scenes, places, and events, and discover these in more detail. My goal is to introduce you to the forgotten lores and history while adding my own perspective and imagination into the mix. May this tale make its mark in your heart and open your world to the legacy our ancestors once talked about over the dinner table so long ago!

Happy reading and discovery!

Valerie Willis

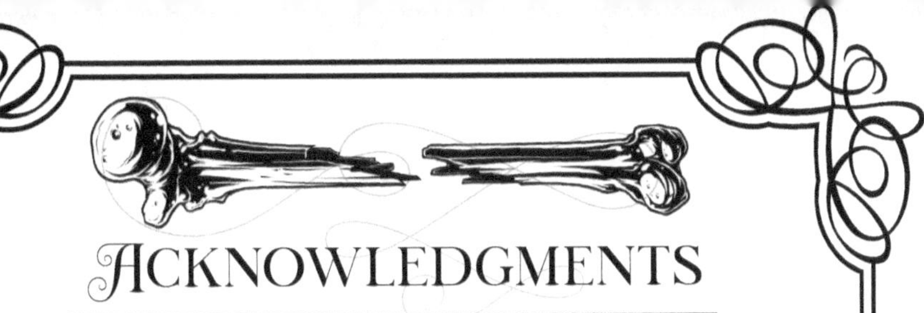

Acknowledgments

There was a very amazing group of people who donated their skills, eyes, and thoughts to make sure this book was at its best potential throughout the process. I started this story on November 1st 2014 to enter it as my National Novel Writing Month piece. By January 15th, with the aid of these super friends, I was able to finish the initial draft and focus on editing with their help.

Here's my BIG THANK YOU to:

Trudy Warman

Denise Mcgaha

Joel Dunckel

Kimberley Adams

Brandy Connelly

Kesa Featherstone

Mina Trujillo

Kim Plasket

Dani-Rey Rogers

Catherine Jones

Jessica Russell

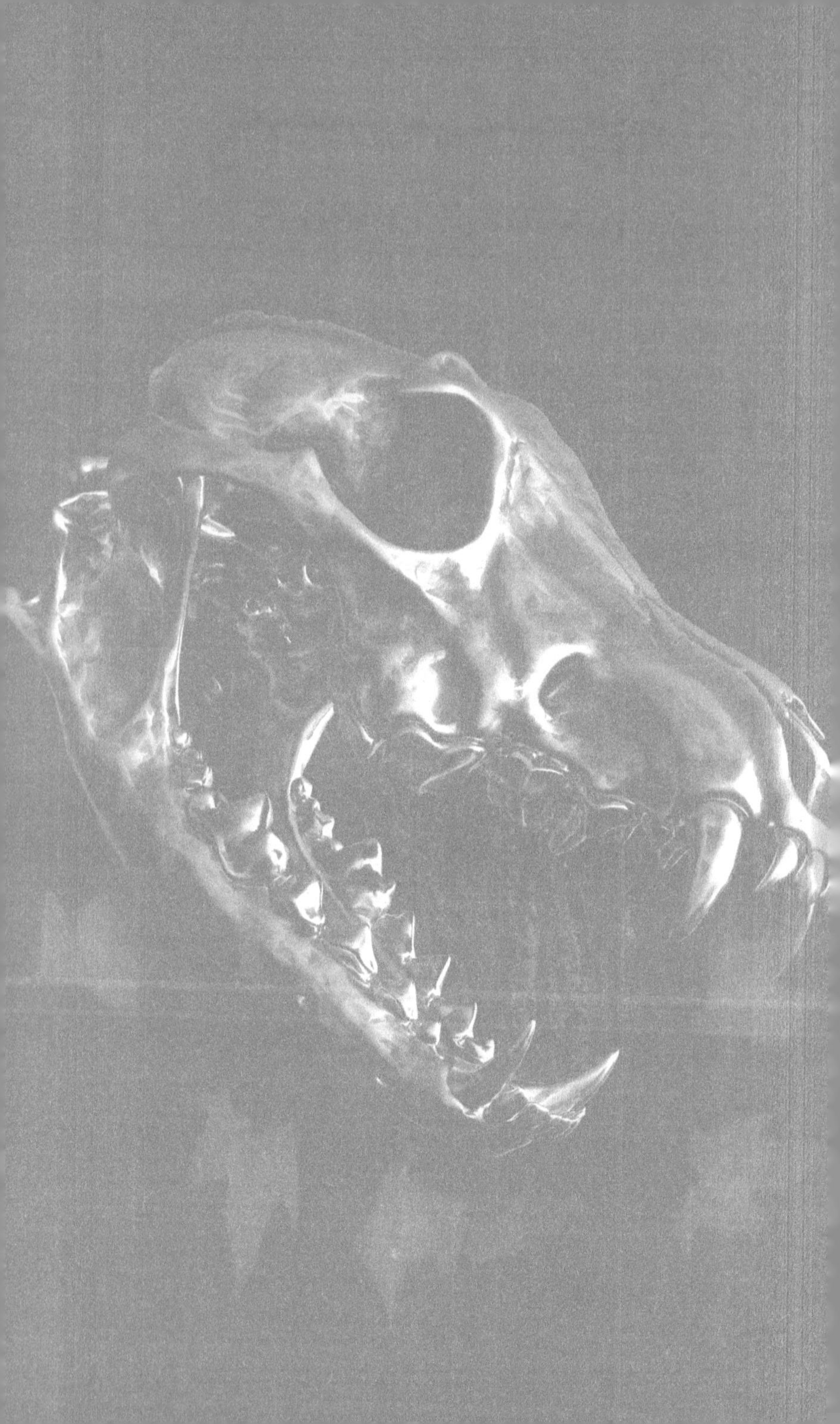

CHAPTER 1

FENRIR

The flies had engorged themselves in the morning light. They bumped into Romasanta's arms and face as he walked up to the blood-soaked field. He covered his nose and mouth; the air tainted with the smell of iron as he looked over what little was left of his bull. Pieces of guts scattered across the mud, but the drag marks led through the broken fence and into the Black Forest. Somewhere in there lay the rest of his bull.

Squatting, he looked over the paw print that lay at his feet. The smallest toe was large enough for his foot to fit inside. This was the work of the demon wolf called Fenrir. The trees, the ground at his feet; all of it was Fenrir's domain, and he tolerated Romasanta and his farm. They lived in the field where no trees grew in hopes that they would be on safer ground. Everything in this land was Fenrir's to take or leave, including Romasanta's life. Waving off another flock of plump flies, he headed back to his hut.

"Was it the bull?" his wife questioned, her brown eyes expressing her concern. "You don't intend to chase after Fenrir this time, do you, Romasanta?"

"No." Grunting, he lugged his travel pack over a shoulder. "That would be suicide."

"What are you doing, then?" She was chasing him out the door as he grabbed his spear. "If you dare cross him, surely he'll take us nex—"

"I just want to see where he dragged the bull. If I can salvage a horn or some leather, perhaps we can get something back." His jaw twitched as a line of sweat crawled down his temple. "I have no plans of staying out overnight, my love."

"Please, don't go." She hugged him tightly, pressing her face hard into his chest. "If the nomads find out you dare leave me alone, they will surely drag me away from this place."

"They will not come close with Fenrir feeding on our cattle." Kissing her on her forehead, he brushed back a lock of her wavy black hair. "Just stay inside the hut until I return."

Standing on her toes, she pressed her lips hard against his, earning his passion in return. It was a bitter sensation as he broke away from the kiss, walking into the Black Forest without glancing back. Her large doe-like eyes watched as he vanished between the thick trees behind the broken fence, still crimson and wet where the blood soaked it.

The drag marks led him into the more dangerous part of the ancient forest. Sunlight speckled the ground where large roots leaped in and out of the earth. Large arches made from these tangled wooden specters reminded demon and man that they were inferior among the trees of the Black Forest. He stayed true to the path that soaked the earth with blood. A raven cawed, startling him as he froze mid-step, his nerves knotting in his stomach.

A horn snagged in a root caught his eye and he worked it free, placing it in the pack at his waist. Perhaps there was a chance to recover some of his lost bull after all. Continuing on, he found himself in a brighter, newer section of the forest. His path stopped on the edge of a crevasse cut into the forest floor. There were no more signs of his bull or Fenrir. Rubbing the sweat from his brow, a glint of red caught his eye. At the bottom of the groove in the earth, something gave off a scarlet glow.

Taking one last look around, assuring himself there were no predators, he started to climb down. Making it to the bottom, he peered upward. The walls of the crevasse were easily four times taller than he, but he was relieved to see no signs of the bull or wolf. Turning around, facing deeper into the unseen parts, he scanned the rocky walls for another sign of the faint glow. The hairs on his arms prickled in excitement as another sheen of colored light called out to him.

An alcove held a glimmering gem about the size of a man's fist. As he approached, its light became brighter, as if encouraging him to free it from the stone. Gripping it tight with both hands, he steadied a foot on the rocks, putting his full weight into pulling it out. Jerking his weight into it, it broke from the rock face, sending him stumbling up against the far wall. As he leaned there, the sunlight hitting his hands, he opened his fist to see what it was that he had claimed for himself.

The gemstone's light dissipated, and within it, a liquid bubbled and swirled. He had heard rumors of bloodstones found in the area, but this was the first time he had encountered one. The powerful vibrations the gem gave off told him this could be something more. It was of the deepest red he had ever witnessed, and it mesmerized him. Heat flowed from it, making the summer temperature feel cool by comparison. Focusing on a sound that tickled his ears, it seemed as if a humming sound was coming from it. A curious sound called his attention deeper into it, almost as if a whisper on the wind.

Growling broke him away from the stone. His gaze stopped at two large golden eyes that glowered down at him. Fenrir had found him. Romasanta shivered as the demon wolf took another step closer, baring his enormous fangs. Staring in awe, one canine was the size of Romasanta's forearm, if not larger. Another step forward allowed him to smell the blood of his bull upon Fenrir's breath as he growled louder. The sound coming from the beast's chest and muzzle shook the air from Romasanta's lungs. He had overstepped his boundaries. Fenrir was enraged. The black wolf had planned to lure him out this far the whole time. Pain pounded against Romasanta's chest, his heart screaming to be set loose as fear washed over him. Fenrir had him; he was to be the next kill. As the monstrous wolf lunged, Romasanta could only raise his arms in defense. The action would do him no good against the demon wolf.

Fangs dug deep into his arms. He screamed from the twisting pain as muscles popped in half, and bones rattled as the impact greeted them. Blinding red light stopped the horrendous bite from breaking his bones. Fenrir's eyes grew wide. The stone pulsed and burned in Romasanta's hand as a red glow engulfed the demon wolf. Both of them were startled as the massive monster swirled in the air like fog. Horrified, Romasanta watched as the stone absorbed the demon into it.

Sliding down to his feet, he dropped the stone. The wounds that still stung in his mind closed before his eyes. He could not stop his body from shaking as a desperate howl echoed from within the stone. Staring down into the bubbling red, Romasanta stared into the fearful eyes of Fenrir. Both knew that neither of them had realized what had happened.

"What in the world is this stone?" He breathed in wonder, hesitant to pick it up. "Fenrir, we may be enemies, but this is a fate no creature should live. I will make a pact to find a means to set you free—if you, in turn, let me live my days out in peace here in your forest."

Another howl rang out, and the eyes of the wolf returned within the stone. The solidarity of the gaze made it clear they had reached an agreement.

Chapter 2

Sister Shaman

The sun had set long before he managed to make it back to the farm. When Romasanta burst through the door, startling his wife, he looked pale from his excursion. Sweat dripped off his bearded chin. He had run the whole way back. The wooden bowl she dropped rattled in their ears as they exchanged bewildered stares. Closing the door, he paused a moment, glaring at his arm where bite marks had ravaged it and magically disappeared. His back to her, he looked at the glowing gemstone in his left hand. Yellow eyes glinted back, and he gasped as her hands touched his back.

"What happened?" He hesitated to turn and face her. "Romasanta, are you hurt?"

"No." Clutching the red stone hard, he faced his wife's worried expression, answering her honestly. "I'm not sure what happened."

Slowly, he opened his hand to show her the stone that lay within his grip. It glowed in response to her stare. She reached out to touch it, but stopped. Movement inside the jewel made it clear this was not a normal gemstone. He tucked it away in his leather pouch, knowing the motion seen within the stone was Fenrir pacing in his prison.

"What sort of magic is in that stone?" Her whisper was barely audible as her eyes looked up into his, reflecting the same fears. "Its magic seems dangerous. Are you sure this is not a cursed stone?"

Gripping her shoulders, he kept calm as he answered. "I will take it to the shaman woman. She must know something about this gem."

Letting go of her, he walked farther into the room as he pulled his soiled shirt off. He couldn't help but avoid her stare. She was full of questions for him, but he still struggled with what had happened between him, Fenrir, and the stone. The pain of the fangs that crushed themselves into his arm still stung at the front of his mind. Even the look in those golden eyes of Fenrir as the stone took him held a heart-stopping terror within Romasanta's mind.

"And what of Fenrir?" she prodded for more answers as she picked up the dropped bowl, scooped him a share of the stew, and set it on the table. "Were there anymore signs of him or where the rest of the bull had gone?"

"Yes, Fenrir had taken the bull." Joining her at the table, he was grateful to take in a deep sniff of the vegetables and meat. "He intended to lure me out to him, after all."

"How do you know that?" She laughed as she turned back to the pot over the fire, scooping herself a bowl of food. "Did he tell you himself?"

"No, but he attacked me." The ladle hit the floor as she looked over at him. "I would not be here if it weren't for that stone."

Sitting down, she could see that Romasanta was not comfortable about being alive as she questioned him. "Then where is Fenrir?"

"Trapped in the stone." His appetite goaded him to take a bite as he continued talking. "That is why I am going to see Sister Shaman tomorrow. Fenrir and I may not be allies, but no man, beast, or demon deserves to be encased for eternity in a cursed stone."

"In all of Arcadia, I have never heard of such a stone." Pausing in thought, Romasanta's wife made a remark that reminded him that she was the daughter of a shaman. "At first glance, it looks like a bloodstone, but they thrive off the dying. Demons and sorcerers of the dark arts use them for various spells and tasks, including healing. But, they trade life from a sacrifice to do so. Of all my knowledge, none have the ability to trap beings within them without recoil or payment."

"Let us prepare for our trip tomorrow." He had finished his meal and stood up. Standing behind his wife as she pondered over the stone, he placed his hands on her tense shoulders. "Please, my love, let us rejoice in me being alive when I should be dead."

Her hand reached up to his, and she nudged it with her cheek. "Oh, Romasanta, what sort of destiny have you brought down on us with this cursed gem?"

A tear slid down her cheek, and his heart lurched against his chest. She may not have been chosen to walk the path of a shaman woman, but he knew she had the gift. Daphne would never tell him if the spirits revealed something to her or if she had dreamed about what was to be next in the unforeseen future. It was unclear if this was something the gifted did by choice or something that had been taught to them. She had made it clear that even if she spoke about it, it would not change what must come to pass.

He leaned over her, kissing the side of her neck. Each touch and suckle of his lips took away more of her tension. As her muscles softened under his touch, he smiled, enjoying the sensation he brought over her. Grabbing her by the hands, he tugged her with him to their bed. Her hands pressed against his chest, insisting he sit on the bed as she kissed him passionately.

Hot tears were falling down her face and he pulled her back. He whispered in a tender tone, "What's wrong?"

The desperation in her face was breathtaking as she collapsed onto him, his arms hugging her tight. "I shouldn't have let you go... I'm so sorry, Romasanta..."

"Daphne, what have the spirits told you?" She curled tighter there on his lap and he could only enclose her in his bulk. "Dammit, just this once, can you not tell your husband?"

She pulled away, looking up at him with her watery eyes. "Let us enjoy our last night together."

Swallowed by his passion and sorrow, he gave her a voracious kiss. She returned with the same appetite for passion. Leaning back, she pulled her dress free as she straddled him. He mustered a smile, and his oversized thumbs rubbed her cheeks free of their tears. Her hand cupped his as her cheek nuzzled into his palm. A wave of pure love hit him, his heart swelling over the compassion they shared for one another. Once more, his arms wrapped around her mocha-colored back. If this was indeed their last night together, then he never wanted to let her go.

Gasps escaped her lips as he suckled at her breast. The grip of her fingers in his hair encouraged him further as they rolled on their bed. Looming over her, he looked down at her smiling face as she squeezed her thighs around his waist. Laughing, he leaned his weight on top of her, enjoying the taste of her lips as they made love. He gathered her in his arms, and her mouth huffed and moaned in his ears. She quivered and he would react with a stronger, more intense movement, hoping to push her to the edge of ecstasy.

"Romasanta!" She breathed. "I love you."

The sun was peeking through the trees as they lay there together. Neither of them had fallen asleep, but the silence had come too soon. The night had been filled with memories of the first time they saw one another, how they stood firm when they decided to be together. Against all the disapproval, they both had abandoned their roles in the inner shaman caste and left to be alone. The retelling of stories had run its course before the sun had risen. But that day would determine how their union would break.

His ribs ached. Whether from her grip or the hours that had passed between them, it didn't matter. Fear had its hold on her and there was nothing he could do to stop what she knew was coming. She laid across his chest, the heat of her breath tickling him. Neither of them wanted to break this moment of affection as he pondered what would happen before the day's end. What sort of things had the spirits shown Daphne that she would want to be in his arms an entire night?

"Come with me." Kissing her forehead, he broke her from her thoughts. "Perhaps there might be something-"

"It ends the same way." Her response was sharp as she broke away, dressing herself. "But I wish to go with you and spend what time is left with you. Just remember Romasanta, what will happen is not your fault, my love."

"My fault?" Frowning, he furrowed his brow as she left the hut. "What horrible fate do we have? Why would I think it's my fault..."

They rode together on the old mare they had, who snorted at having to carry two people. Daphne had remained distant and silent as they traveled down the forest path to the main village. Several times he had tried to start a conversation, but she was far from where she sat. Her grave look and hazed eyes told him that she was preparing for whatever was to happen. He mulled it over; whatever was coming would be happening to her. Perhaps the stone could stop it, or was it the cause of her inevitable peril? Pulling it from the leather pouch, he stared down at it. As if he could feel Romasanta's glare, Fenrir's amber eyes and toothy grin greeted him. How long would he be carrying this cursed stone and its prisoner?

The mare paused and bobbed her head in disapproval. Their pathway was blocked by two warriors from the shaman's village. It was still a short ride away, but this was the normal routine and precautions. They would be stopped and checked a few more times before reaching the huts where everyone gathered. Arcadia was a place full of dangers, human and demonic, with and without magic. Animals were nothing compared to their unnatural variants that had lived decades before any man had stepped foot in the Black Forest.

Today was quiet in comparison to the past trips he had made down this road. No signs of wounded men or tracks of animals across the dirt road were in sight. Even the birds above them seemed to be whispering in lieu of singing. Every thud of the mare's hooves tightened the muscles in Romasanta's back. His wife was gripping his shirt in fistfuls as they rode ever closer to their final destination. There was no mistaking that Daphne's visions would soon come into existence. He prayed that he could change the outcome that had sent her into such a frightened state.

It was a relief to reach the huts without any incidents. The village felt as awkward as the forest, adding to the paranoia growing in his mind. He helped her off the horse, pulling her along hand-in-hand toward the shaman's house. Every emotion was pulling at him. He feared to let her out of sight. Guards gripped him by the arm, stopping him from entering. The glare he shot them made the man flinch, but did nothing to make him let go.

"I am here to see the shaman." Jerking his arm free, he pulled Daphne closer as he declared his purpose. "We are going in to see her on a very urgent matter."

"Only one person is allowed to enter." Snapped the guard, glaring at Daphne.

"She needs to st-" She tugged her hand from Romasanta's and caught his attention.

"It's ok, Romasanta." It was a half-hearted smile, but her voice was stern. "You need to see her. It's very important."

"Will you be ok?" He scanned the village for any signs of danger but found nothing. "Are you sure?"

"Please, it's important that you do this." Kissing him, they spent a moment with their foreheads leaning against one another. "I love you as much as you love me, my husband. Everything will be fine. Just remember, it is not your fault."

"I love you with all my soul, Daphne." Once more he caressed her face with his fingers, sliding a strain of her hair from her face. "It will be short."

Nodding at the guard, he was allowed to enter. Another warrior was waiting just within the door and he followed Romasanta to the center of the vast house, where he kneeled. On a throne of charms, bones, and horns, the shaman woman sat eerily still, as if made of stone. Not a sound came from her as she waved her hand in the traditional welcoming signage.

"Leave us. I wish to speak to him alone." Her voice was powerful and authoritative. "It's been a while, Romasanta."

Romasanta watched as the guard left out the door and the sunlight fell dark as the leather curtain closed. "What makes today so special, Sister?"

"You are a fool, Brother." The shaman stood, showing she was equally as tall as he, pulling off the stag's skull mask. "Where did you find it?"

"In a crevasse deep within the Black Forest." Standing, he began to work the stone out of its pouch. "How did you know I had this?"

"I'm the all-knowing Shamanka Artemis." Smirking, she took the stone from him. "And your sibling. I would think I can tell when my twin brother is hiding something from me."

"Let's see how much you know about the damn thing." Scoffing, he started pacing the floors, anxious to return to Daphne. "I already know it's not a bloodstone."

"True. This, Brother, this is the Eye of Gaea." Pausing, she looked into its glow. "I see you have caught Fenrir using it."

"It was not intentional." Looking over his shoulder, they locked eyes. "I wish to free him. No one deserves that fate."

"You did not put him here?" Furrowing her brow, the muscles in her face grew tense.

"No. If I did, it was not something I wished to do." He subconsciously rubbed his arm where Fenrir had torn into him as he continued his explanation. "I had just found the gem when he attacked. He had my arm, tearing me to shreds when he disappeared into the gem and I was healed miraculously."

"Strange." Fenrir paced within the stone, awaiting the shaman's reply. "Perhaps Gaea can free Fenrir. Brother, I will be giving you this stone in hopes you can return the eye to Gaea. Do not let this fall into anyone else's hands. I dare not hold this stone any longer than needed. Anyone carrying magic in their veins could wield magic with this gem and do ill will to all without recoil. Fear its power, for it may intervene again. As long as you do not wish it to act, you will not feel its recoil. You must never use the stone for fear that Gaea will be angry."

"Where do I start to find where Gaea resides?" Taking the glowing stone from Artemis, he held his breath for an answer.

She sighed. "No one knows."

"Then all I have are fairytales to go on." He glared down at Fenrir within his prison. "It's a shame I have no means of asking you if you happen to know anything."

"They plan on rebelling against me." His sister's hands covered up the stone, demanding he look her in the eyes. "I don't know when, but soon the nomadic Lykaon's will burn this village to the ground. All I ask is that you do not pursue me or them. It will only bring you torment."

"First my wife, and now my sister. It's torture to have no gift to see and hear what you two already know." Turning his back to her, he grumbled on. "All I wanted was a happy marriage and a farm to give my heir. Instead, I am told I will lose the last of my family today and be left with the impossible task of not only freeing Fenrir, but returning the Eye of Gaea to its owner."

Gripping the stone tightly, its glow brightened in his anger. The silence brought no comfort, and he started for the door in frustration. Both of Artemis's hands grabbed the back of his shirt, stopping him. Choking sobs escaped her, a sound he had never heard from her. Not even after the death of their parents and siblings, through all their hardships, had she let herself be seen by anyone shedding one tear. She had been a pillar of amazing strength to him and many others.

Swallowing, he bit his tongue. She pulled at his shirt, whimpering as the tears cut loose from her. At first, the words she struggled to say were hard to understand. Then they managed to escape her lips and his heart ached, bringing a nauseating wave of dread as they lingered there in the air.

"It's not your fault, Romasanta." She shook her head against his spine as his muscles turned to stone. "What is going to happen is not your fault. You are nothing but a man. Don't forget that! You are only a man..."

Closing his eyes, he cursed the world and its spirits. Slowly she let go, pulling her stag's skull mask over her reddened face, returning to her throne. He stood, waiting to see if more tears or words would come. None came to her lips or eyes. Pushing back the sorrow invading his every nerve, he took in a deep breath and left her alone. His chest grew tight as anxiety gripped him. Compared to his wife and sister, he felt blind and naïve to the events drawing near. The day was slipping away, building the weight of his fears on his shoulders.

He continued gripping the stone in his hand as its burden on him became heavier with every step. Throwing back the leather flap, he squinted in the blinding sunlight. Its heat against his face made him frown as his eyes adjusted. The guard returned to the hut behind him as he walked over to the old mare. His gut was tied in knots as he realized Daphne was not there with the horse. Ending his approach, he looked around with caution. The hairs on his arms were standing on end. A realization shook him; there had been no signs of children or the typical village women. In fact, it had been nothing but male warriors the whole ride into the village. Faces he hadn't recognized, but then again he had always distanced himself.

KAPOW!

Heat and light exploded behind him. Stifling back from the explosion, he watched as the shaman's hut was set ablaze. Breaking from his moment of shock, he broke into a run.

Artemis!

"Stop right there!" A large man stepped between him and the fiery wall that claimed the building. "Let the witch burn!"

He blinked, his thoughts scattered in panic. Looking down at the spear pointed at him, he realized it was his own and anger waved through him. "Fine. My wife and I will leave and you can do what you will with the village. We have no quarrel with you."

"That's not what I hear, Romasanta." The man grinned as he nodded for Romasanta to turn around. "We have your wife, but you can leave her here with us. You see, we are running low on woman folk."

Gritting his teeth, Romasanta turned to see one of the large man's men holding Daphne by the arm. Her face was turning red and purple where she had been hit. Something animalistic in him was fueling his fury as he watched the line of blood from her lip drip. Despite the distance, the smell of it was hitting his nose and his muscles ached for him to fight. A strange blend of excitement and rage he had never felt before was rising from within his core.

"She is taken." Turning his attention to the man with his spear, he struggled to keep calm. "What gives you the right to take others against their will?"

"I am the King of Arcadia, Boreas. The king of the Lykaon tribe, who are feared for their abilities to bend magic to their will." Opening his left palm, he set it aflame to make it clear that he had no help from a torch to light the hut on fire. "Rumors say you were the witch's brother."

"Rumors." Romasanta huffed, standing firm as the muscles in his face twitched with contempt. "I will ask one more time; let my wife Daphne go. You can chase the witch to the ends of the world for all I care."

Artemis, you knew he was coming. You're the best magic wielder I know, and you are probably gone by now. Was that even you in the house with me moments ago?

"Perhaps they weren't true." They glared at each other, each carrying their own dark eyes as the man bellowed his desires to Romasanta. "But I will be taking the girl and that glowing bloodstone you hold."

His hand tightened around the heat of the stone. Romasanta glared into Boreas's dark eyes, ignoring all he knew of the Lykaon bloodline. He turned his back on him and marched to Daphne. He had always been a pacifist—another reason why he wanted to abandon his training to be a shaman's protector. As he walked away, regrets of not learning to fight were seeping forward.

"Where are you going?" Boreas roared, angered at being ignored so easily. "How dare you turn your back on me!"

A thudding ripped through the side of his back. His feet failed him and he found himself slumping to his knees. Heat poured across his back where the spear had landed and stuck. Daphne wailed, but his ears could not hear her screams as he looked at her hysterical expression. Confused by the pain that shot through him, he watched as she broke free from her prisoners.

"Romasanta!" Her voice broke through as she collapsed onto him.

"Daphne..." Looking at her, he was helpless as his body grew weak and the blood flowed from him.

Tears were welling up in his eyes as he looked at her paling face. More pain rattled him as she yanked his spear from his back. His scream of agony shocked the faces around them, except Boreas. Standing, both hands covered in flames, he approached. Daphne held the spear to Boreas, ready to defend Romasanta as he fell to the ground.

Dirt struck his cheek as he watched on, his hand still grasping the stone. It shook and pulsed in his hands as Fenrir raged against his prison walls. Romasanta's death was approaching, but he could not go, not with Daphne needing to be protected. He failed once, but he couldn't fail her now. The pain was numbing his senses. Everything was confusing as his ears were failing him. His sight blurred with each stinging throb. Tears rolled down the bridge of his nose, and the stone burned like a hot coal in his hand.

He managed to stand back on his feet. Laying a hand on Daphne's shoulder, he took the lead in their defense against Boreas. He looked over at Daphne; tears were running down her face as she shook her head in dis-approval. Her lips silently repeated, *please, no.* In her eyes was a reflection of himself with Fenrir's glowing amber eyes.

CHAPTER 3

Not Your Fault

"No, please no!" Pleading, she began pounding on his chest. "Don't do this, Romasanta! You don't understand!"

"He will pay for this," Romasanta growled, his lungs burning as he struggled to breathe. "All I wanted was to leave with you."

Sobbing, she hugged his neck begging, pulling at him as she shouted her words. "Romasanta, you can't. This isn't you! Fenrir is taking advantage that you're hurt!"

"Fenrir?" Opening his palm, the toothy grin in red laughed at him.

"Give that stone to me!" Boreas ran at them, seeing Romasanta distracted by the stone glowing in his hand.

Desperate to stop Boreas and Fenrir, Daphne took hold of the spear. "I love you, Romasanta! This was not your fault!"

Daphne slammed the head of the spear into the ground, her primal scream interrupting Boreas's attack. Light poured from where she had struck the ground as a red glow engulfed her. Romasanta fell backward, hitting the ground hard as he watched in horror. Her skin squirmed and bubbled, turning into tree bark. Stretching her arms to the sky, they grew wide before shattering into thousands of limbs and leaves. Daphne looked into his eyes one last time, a smile on her face as she was engulfed by the spell. The love of his life had been taken from him, forever encased in a tree.

Everyone stood in amazement as the laurel tree grew taller and wider than any known before it. Its branches stretched across until it shadowed most of the village. The roots had pushed Boreas and Romasanta far apart as its trunk became a wall between them. Romasanta had rolled all the way back to the mare. The other Lykaon warriors stared at the leaves swaying in the wind above him in bewilderment.

"NO!" Scrambling to his feet, ignoring the pain from his wound, he ran and banged at the tree. "GIVE HER BACK!"

Punching, kicking, and sobbing against the bark of the tree did not ease the aching in his chest. The monstrous plant stood silent, sharing nothing with him. He fell to his knees. His knuckles were torn and bleeding. Panting from his enraged fight with the trunk, all he could do was cry. Sorrow was swallowing him. He could not tell if she became the tree or laid encased within it.

I lost my Daphne...

There was no mistake that this enchantment was connected to the stone. His heart fluttered as he realized he had dropped the gem during his fight with the laurel tree. Crawling and digging at the piles of dirt, he found the cursed possession. Fenrir snorted and avoided eye contact with him. It was unmistakable that the Eye of Gaea had acted on its own accord. He was fuming as he slammed it against the tree in outrage. Shrieking his demands over and over as tears fell from his chin.

"GIVE HER BACK!"

Flames erupted around him; his back burned and sizzled as his shirt fell off in clumps of tiny fires. Boreas had made his way around the massive tower of bark and aimed to acquire the stone. The smell of burning hair and flesh invaded the air. Onlookers were cringing as they covered their noses and mouths in desperation. Romasanta leaned his weight against the tree, gasping as the burning mixed with the pain of the wound in his back. Looking at where the bark had been singed and turned black, he clenched his jaw tight. Turning to face Boreas, he panted heavily, his sense of humanity and peace ripped from him.

"Don't touch her."

Laughing, Boreas readied another flame in his hand. "I will burn that putrid tree down along with you."

He flung the ball of heat at the tree out of spite and Romasanta stepped into its path. Hitting him in the chest, it exploded. Burning snaked across his neck and face. The sizzling of his skin stung in his ears as the fire whooshed about him. The force of the hit had banged his back against the tree, only adding to his ire. Burned flesh stung in his nose and the fire took the wind from his lungs. Romasanta's twisted, mangled look struck fear in Boreas's men as they stumbled backward.

Flames were still working at him as he took a step forward, then another toward his enemy. Glowering at Boreas, the amber wolf's eyes had returned. The stone that had been in his hand vaporized from existence and his strength returned to him tenfold. The pain was a distant memory as rage drowned every part of him, heart and soul. Fur and fangs erupted as Fenrir willed himself into presence through Romasanta. Before the warriors was no longer a man burning alive, but a wolf made of red flames. The snarling and growling from his massive mouth made it known that they had done more than anger a man. They had enraged Fenrir as well.

"I will devour you all." The massive wolf's tail wagged back and forth as he crouched defensively. "The Lykaons will all die by my fangs."

"Fenrir, why are you interfering with this man's death?" Boreas scoffed, sweat forming on his cheek. "You are a god of the Black Forest, you should return home!"

A violent bark silenced Boreas, who flinched in response. The sneer that Fenrir gave him made it definite that he was insulted by his words. Puffing out his massive chest, he towered over the tiny army, declaring his dominance over them. There was no doubt as to why he had been the master of the forest for so long with his muscled body and overall bulk.

"This man had no reason to look for a means to free me." He snorted as he peered down at the unworthy men in front of him. "I will act as his protector so that he may finish the task set before him."

Blinking for a moment, Boreas broke out into laughter. "You've gone soft!"

Growling cut his humor short as Fenrir's lips curled. "You know nothing about compassion for your fellow creature. Not once have you shown respect to me, whom you referred to as a god."

Boreas grunted in response. His hands filled with the fire from his magic blood. With no hesitation, he lunged the flames at Fenrir, no signs of fear on either of their faces. A deafening bark roared from Fenrir, extinguishing the magical flames like delicate candles to the breeze. Boreas's eyes grew wide as he stifled back. The smell of fear coming from his prey excited the demon wolf, and he lunged at Boreas. His fangs tore into the side of Boreas's face before he ran away bleeding. Fenrir's pursuit of the sorcerer failed as Boreas's men braved digging their spears into Fenrir's flesh.

Infuriated, Fenrir devoured and destroyed all Lykaon warriors within his reach. Screams echoed throughout the forest as his fangs made their mark time and time again. Very few escaped the onslaught as night fell over the land. Many men fled with gruesome gashes and broken limbs from his bites. If they weren't eaten, they would surely bleed to death escaping his violence. The moon rose high overhead as Fenrir stood under the laurel tree, panting from the battle. His fur dripped with the blood of those he had ravaged and consumed as well as his own from wounds sustained by the onslaught.

With great pride, he howled long and hard, a warning to any still running for their lives. He would haunt their dreams until the end of days with images of the carnage his claws and fangs had seared into their minds. If they lived to tell their story, they would forever carry the scars to prove what had happened that day in Arcadia. Laying at the base of the tree, he sighed, ready to take his leave. The Eye of Gaea faded back into existence between his paws, and he knew it was time for Romasanta to reclaim his body.

A sickening smell of blood woke Romasanta from his nightmare. Lying on his back, he stared at the leaves waving in the wind above him, confused and exhausted. Like a wave dragging him under, his grief washed over him, drowning his soul. These were Daphne's leaves, and she was gone. Once more he sobbed, not knowing what to do with what fate had handed him. All he had was a stone with a demon wolf inside it, and even then, he could not save the love of his life from her horrible fate. If he had been stronger, or more aware, perhaps this all would not have happened. He should have been waking with the rising sun to mooing cows and her wrapped in his arms.

Sitting up, he was covered in blood, but none of it was his. There were no more burned sloughs of skin, nor a gaping wound on his back. Romasanta was healed. By the looks of the body parts scattered on the ground, Fenrir had feasted on Boreas and his men all night long. Despite the lack of injuries, his body ached and shivered. His muscles were sore, his joints ached, and his skin stung at every touch. This was the repercussion of Fenrir changing him from a man to the form of a demon wolf.

The Eye of Gaea was in his hand, a faint glow coming from it. Perhaps Gaea could undo the damage that had been done. Artemis was gone, so he would have to seek out others who knew how to speak to the spirits or had tales about Gaea. He had to return the gem to her, and perhaps she would reward him by returning Daphne to normal. Even then, she would set Fenrir free, since no one had ever wished to imprison the demon wolf of the Black Forest. Fenrir's place should be out in the world to run free and guard his territory. Sighing, he knew no one deserved the fates they were thrown into in the last two days.

Forcing himself to move, he staggered stiffly to the well at the far end of the village. The soreness in his body started to break away as he neared the well. He pulled water from the well, and poured the cold water over him. He wanted to free himself of the blood of the uncountable number of men killed before seeking out the magic users about Gaea. The village was abandoned. Destruction was all that was left with some of the huts burned and others torn apart by the wild roots of the laurel tree. Looking up at the tree, its size seemed larger than the day before. Was it still growing, aiming to reach wider than the entire village?

Rummaging through the houses, he found clean clothes, equipment, and food for the trip ahead. His stomach turned at the idea of eating, and he swallowed back his nausea. The eerie sensation he felt of being full, even bloated, made his skin crawl as he glanced over at the random digits, limbs, and other body parts. Shuddering, he looked for his mare, but she was long gone. It was unclear if Fenrir had eaten the old horse or if she had gone back to the farm on her own. Regardless, it was for the best that he take a younger horse for the journey he would be immediately embarking on.

His luck was changing. No one had raided the horse stables. Boreas and his men had first focused on Artemis and the women before going for resources. He looked the horses over and chose the heartiest horse there. No one would be returning to this place, in fear of Fenrir eating them or the chance of becoming cursed. After taking his pick of saddles, he set the remaining horses free. There was no telling if any would survive or adapt to the forest about them. Either way, it was a better fate than being trapped in stables with no one to care for them. One horse had hesitated. He was rather hairy for a horse, black with a long, flowing mane. Snorting at Romasanta, it almost seemed as if he were jealous that he had picked a leaner, lighter horse. Romasanta shooed him off, and he thudded off into the forest.

Sitting on top of his chestnut-colored horse, he was at a loss as to which way he should ride. Circling the broken village, he chose the only way none of the warriors had gone. He wanted to leave this nightmare and its participants far behind. He wanted to complete his search for Gaea so he could get his Daphne back. Spurring the horse on, they broke down the less traveled road. Boreas was aiming to conquer and take out other magical bloodlines. If there were no signs of him and his men, then he would be able to find a village he hadn't wiped clean.

The horse protested, frustrated with the tangled weeds and brush that ran across the trail as they rode deeper. Romasanta gritted his teeth as the horse danced under him. He regretted not taking the oversized hairy horse, but then again, there were no saddles big enough for that monstrous equine. Sighing, he gave up on riding and walked the horse through the ever-thicker woods. The horse snorted at him, seeing him having an easier time on the path. His shoulder ached from trying to keep the horse from spooking as he jerked his head, yanking on the reins.

Within its leather pouch, heat was pouring from the stone, but he ignored it. The Eye of Gaea had only brought him grief, and he wanted nothing more to do with it until it was time to hand it back to Gaea herself. It was pulsing and shaking, Fenrir was rattling his cage at Romasanta's waist. He placed a hand over it, trying to keep it still, but it started burning the leather pouch. Huffing, he pulled it out of the pouch. The moment it met his skin, it calmed and amber eyes glared angrily at him. Frowning down at the wolf, he had no idea what the foul beast wanted. He paced within the stone, as if unsure how he could express whatever his message should be. Annoyed, he started to look for a new container to keep the stone hidden from view.

The gem vibrated in his grip and he hissed at the wolf. "Stop it, I wish not to run into Boreas or his men. No one has been down here and there may be a chance a witch or someone like that might know where to search for Gaea."

It stilled. Perhaps he had not thought about the fact that Romasanta was nothing more than a farmer at heart. After walking for hours, fighting the finicky horse, Romasanta managed to find a cleared pathway. Sighing in relief, he sat back on the saddle, encouraging the horse to canter to make up for lost time. The sun was starting to set, and worse, the wind was howling through the woods. A storm was rumbling in the distance, and he had no idea where he was going. His entire life had been spent in that small section of Arcadia, and now he was forced to leave it behind. Sleep was taunting him as he rode on, and found himself dozing off as the horse rocked him. Images of Daphne haunted every small instance of sleep and he would wake with the horrible weight on his chest.

The smell of a fire greeted his nose, and it wasn't long before its glow came into view. Whomever it was, they had set camp against the pathway, a good indication they were welcoming other travelers into their encampment. As he approached, all that greeted him was an old man with a long white beard that dropped down to his navel. It was baffling to see the old man standing there as if he were waiting for Romasanta to arrive. He opened his mouth to greet the old man, but the thudding of the stone interrupted him. Once more, the knotting of his gut told him that his fortune would not improve. Swallowing back his anxiety, he found his voice again.

"I am Romasanta, stranger. May we join you at your fire?" Sliding out of the saddle, his body ached with exhaustion.

"May we?" The old man scratched his bald head and peered behind Romasanta. "But I only see one man?"

"I meant my horse and I." Every muscle in his body tensed as he observed no camp gear, no food, nor any sign of a horse. "We can leave."

"No, you may stay, Romasanta." The man's pale blue eyes stared deeply at him, taking him in as he walked over to warm himself at the fire. "Are you a son of Arcadia?"

Looking at the stranger, he weighed the question with great caution. "I am a man, born in a land we call Arcadia."

The stranger giggled in response, pleased at the care Romasanta had used when answering him. "I am seeking counsel with a witch in a village nearby. You wouldn't happen to know which way I could find it?"

"It is gone." Gazing into the fire, Romasanta could not help but recall his sister's hut on fire. "It was attacked a day ago, and I barely escaped with my own life intact."

The old man paced violently at the news. "And the witch dead?"

Once more, he weighed the strange question. "Her hut was burned to the ground."

Laughter burst out of his white beard. "You are a wise man, Mister Romasanta! I admire you for that."

"Not wise enough." Mumbling, he walked the horse to a tree and hitched him there. "I would be with my wife back home if I had just stayed on the farm instead of going there."

"And your wife's name?" The man quieted, seeing the grave look on his face. "I bet she had a beautiful name."

With a sigh, Romasanta stared up at the full moon. "It was Daphne."

"And your sister's name?" The hungry look in the old man's eyes made Romasanta furrow his brow. "What was her name?"

"I have no sister." The words felt cold leaving his mouth as he lied to the eager stranger. "What is your name, stranger?"

"Merlin. You may want to remember it after this night." A wicked smile crawled across his lips. "For I will be taking that stone from you. Artemis has avoided me again, but I have found her dear brother and ironically, you have what I came here for."

His jaw tense, Romasanta gripped the gem in its pouch. The wind whirled strongly around the man, and it was clear this was the strongest magic wielder in the world.

CHAPTER 4

MERLIN'S CURSE

"This stone is the only means I have to get Daphne back. You cannot have it." He couldn't slow the thudding of his heart.

"I will be taking it." Merlin's eyes brightened into a cerulean blue.

Wind gathered at Merlin's outstretched hands as he gave a devilish smirk. Clapping them together, thunder rang out and a blast of wind slammed into Romasanta. He felt himself bang into the horse, who also fell back into the trees. The sounds and sensations of cracking and breaking did nothing for the agony that took hold of him. Somehow he had managed to keep a firm grip on the stone through the carnage, but it wouldn't be long before he wouldn't be able to hold on. The horse wheezed for a few seconds before it gurgled to a stop. He, too, struggled to breathe as blood filled his lungs. He coughed blood up with every exhale. Fighting to keep his eyes from rolling back, he gasped for what little air he could get. Merlin had taken the stone at some point, but his body was numb with the pain of shattered ribs and more.

"What is this?" Stroking his beard, Merlin stared at Fenrir within the stone with a disgusted face. "You can have this back."

He chanted as he drew invisible marks on the Eye of Gaea, then pulled a glowing red orb from it. Holding it in his hands, he observed it, then frowned down at Romasanta. A smile crept across his face as he rolled the orb in his hand, a thought coming to him. Kneeling over Romasanta, he took no pity in his slow, agonizing death.

"You see, I can't set him loose in fear he will attack. And I would hate to anger Artemis by killing you; she can be quite the bother." His eyes glowed once more as he let out a maniacal laugh. "You can be the rock that holds Fenrir here! Let the magic of Gaea be the chain!"

As Merlin slammed the red orb into his chest, Romasanta screamed, writhing in pain. His body was on fire and searing heat erupted through his veins. Lungs aching, he clawed at his chest, still shrieking. The orb burned a black hole through him until it met its mark. He scratched and dug at his chest, but could not stop it from melting into him. Flailing on the ground, he felt like his soul was being burned out of him. Between his screeches, he desperately attempted to catch his breath.

A new weight had been laid within him, and the fire it brought added to his terror. Merlin left in a flash and a whirl of wind. He rolled onto his hands and knees. Panting, the wizard's spell stung at his chest and in his blood. He had lost the stone. How was he going to find this Merlin again in order to reclaim the Eye of Gaea?

Though he was breathing easier, his mind was panicking, unsure of what the wizard had done to him and Fenrir. Another wave of excruciating pain waved over him. Broken ribs and bones snapped back into place. Grasping at the ground, he could feel his body evolving in a different direction. Staring at his hands, he watched in horror as they turned into monstrous claws. Dread filled him and he stood, feeling large and cumbersome. Smells and sounds far across the forest were overwhelming him and his thoughts. Falling to his knees, he watched fur erupt through his skin, covering his entire body with a thick pelt.

"What am I?" His voice grumbled awkwardly from his wolf's head. "I rather be dead..."

We are neither man nor wolf, Fenrir whispered within his own thoughts. *The wizard has cursed us to share one body.*

"No..." gasped Romasanta. "How will I live like this?"

Laughter came from the demon wolf that shared the same space as Romasanta's own soul. He beat against the ground, infuriated by his life. Several minutes passed before he tired of his useless struggle. Despite his monstrous appearance, he was still capable of crying as he sat there, lost. The last of his hope had been burned from him. His concentration wavered as the intoxicating smell of the horse's blood pulled at his senses.

Saliva dripped from his fangs as the scent met his nose. Another push from the wolf's instincts and he gave into the want for feeding on the carcass behind him. Looking over his shoulder, he gave the dead horse a disgusted glare. Snorting the aroma from his nose, he put his back to it. Romasanta was losing his humanity at an alarming rate. Mental and emotional exhaustion was breaking him apart and the physical instincts wanted control of this newfound body.

A branch rattled near the horse, causing his ears to flick and his blood to rush. Without prompt from him, his body lunged over the horse. Snarling and growling, he came face to face with another wolf and its companion. They lowered their heads, tails between their legs as they backed away from him. Watching them move on, he could no longer fight the urges of Fenrir's animal instincts. Tonight he would tuck away his humanity and allow the wolf his pleasures.

The falling rain was icy and cruel against his naked body. Flinching at each touch, Romasanta finally woke up. He was dirty, bloody, and naked where he lay just outside a cave. Looking around, he was no longer in the same part of the forest. Fenrir had taken him far from there and the village, but left him some place for shelter. He scrambled to his feet, teeth chattering. The chills rattled him as he went into the cave. Slipping on the wet stone and leaves, his knee hit the ground. Bloody drag marks leading into the dark shelter made him pause. The rain was falling harder, but it would not convince him to step any closer to what might be hidden within the shadows of the cave.

I left it there for you, Fenrir grumbled within his chest and ears. *Unlike me, you need these things to survive, so that we can both survive.*

Rubbing at the scar on his chest where Fenrir's soul had burned into him, he pushed back his fears. Standing, he entered the cave with the greatest caution, unsure of what would be there. It took a moment for his eyes to adjust, but he found the dead man that had been left for him. Grimacing, the corpse's face was unrecognizable from where the demon wolf had gnawed at it. Shivering, wet and naked, he began to work the clothes off the dead man. Fenrir had picked someone with the same build as Romasanta, to the point that the details were frightening. As Romasanta stripped the man of all his items, he noticed that the man wore the tattoos of the Lykaon tribe. Fenrir was aiming to fulfill his promise to take them down despite Romasanta's discouragement to keep their distance.

Dressing, he braved the cave entrance once more. The rain hadn't let up, and it was time for the seasons to start their change. Sighing, the only weapon he had was a knife he found among the dead man's belongings. Lykaons were magic users, and they depended on it more so than tools and weaponry. Looking down at his hands, Romasanta felt relieved to be human again. The prior night, he had been resentful about living the rest of his days as a monster and not a man. Perhaps this curse was nothing more than the inconvenience of sharing his body with Fenrir. Time would tell what sort of arrangements and stipulations would be set before them both in how this curse worked.

Braving into the storm, he aimed to walk until he found some signs of people. If the curse would allow him to be a man, then he could still find information on Gaea and his new enemy, Merlin. He had walked for what felt like hours before he came across tracks left behind by Fenrir.

Follow them, demanded Fenrir. A vibration rattled throughout his core as he spoke within Romasanta. *Follow where I came from; you will find them there.*

Regretfully, he did as he was instructed. As he went farther down the path, there were plenty of signs of where men had run for their lives. Random spurts of blood across the brush and pathway told him more than enough about what happened during the night. Half a man laid across the road where the pack of wolves from before paused their feast and stared at Romasanta. He exchanged glares with them for several minutes. The fear he would normally have in that moment was nowhere to be felt. Approaching them, they stepped back from him, making it clear he was the dominant one among them.

Crouching over the head and half torso, he acquired another knife and a wolf-skin hood. Wearing this would at least get him by anyone who may be looking for him. Night was closing in as he saw lights from a large camp. He felt his body grow more excited with the coming night. Each minute that passed was making him feel less human and more animal as his senses grew stronger. Whether Fenrir's pride or need for dominance was interfering with how he held himself, he was unsure. He walked up to the encampment's guards, nodded to them as he held himself tall, and they let him in without question. It seemed that they assumed he was one of them, which meant Boreas had gathered more men into his ranks than he could track. The smell of roasting meat was inebriating, and he couldn't stop himself from pushing his way to it. Taking a large grip of it in his hand, he began to devour it.

"HEY!" Another warrior grabbed him by his shoulder.

Romasanta paused, his shoulder tense under the man's hand as he glared back, his eyes well covered by the hood. "Sorry, I was starving. Been out all night running for my life."

"You survived Fenrir?" Letting go, the Lykaon warrior crouched with a sympathetic look on his face. "Please, it's only your right to eat, my brother in survival. You've earned it."

With that, they did not question him further. Finishing the food he had taken, he walked the camp. He watched the men practicing their control of fire with great interest. Lykaons were all gifted with magic in their blood, but none in the camp seemed to be able to control wind. Whomever Merlin was, he was a special kind of magic wielder. They did have a few females in camp that could manipulate water, but the rest of the girls there had been taken by force. These non-Lykaon women were bruised from the beatings they received for disobeying. Two girls sat by a pail of water, washing their cuts and swollen faces. Their clothes torn, they had endured so much already and continued to live in a hellish enslavement.

His blood rushed at the very thought as he grated his teeth with frustration. He was only one man, and this was a camp full of men capable of beckoning fire from their veins. They paused and stared wide-eyed at him as he glowered in their direction. The one girl gasped, her whisper hitting his keen ears, "He has the eyes of the wolf."

Closing his eyes, he walked away, calming himself. Anger was one emotion that seemed to stir the wolf within him. He would have to master keeping his rage to himself. Continuing his examinations of the camp, there were no skilled blacksmiths among them. In fact, other than the traditional knives and spears, they carried no weapons. They were easy prey for a demon like Fenrir, who would rather be hit by their pitiful fireballs over the cutting of his flesh.

A scream came from a nearby tent and he watched as a woman was dragged out by her hair. Throwing her to the ground, the man spat at her. Picking herself up, she returned the motion and was rewarded with a backhanded slap for her rebellion. The nerves in Romasanta's joints tightened as he struggled to not let his anger show. Blood splattered across the dirt as she fell to the ground. Tears joined the two teeth she spat out, waiting for more punishment.

Why does this excite you so? Fenrir rumbled with curiosity. *Why do you not act?*

"It does not excite me, Fenrir." He hissed, annoyed at how his words rattled and vibrated from within him. "This is anger and frustration you are feeling from me. I cannot act, not yet."

The wolf snorted as they watched on. She was clawing into the ground. A sudden sense of calmness came over her. She willed herself to her feet, her chin held high. The attacker scowled at her; scratches across his cheek made it clear that she was continuing to fight her kidnappers. Lunging at her, he was greeted with a face full of sand. He wailed and cursed at her as he shot a ball of fire at her feet. She grinned. Broken and bloody, she ran from her assailant, seeing her chance.

What a wild creature she is... Chortling, Fenrir was enjoying seeing them struggle with one tiny woman. *Do they not know how to place dominance over their mates?*

Sighing, Romasanta readied himself, seeing that she had dodged a few more warriors and ran full steam in his direction. Reaching out, he caught her midsection with ease and she yelped in surprise. Swallowing her in his arms, he whispered into her ear, "Calm yourself. I am not one of them."

Covering her mouth, he turned to her pursuers. They paused, unsure of what to do with him as he held her with ease. The man with the scratch upon his cheek pushed through the group to them, seething as he huffed at them. A smirk crawled across Romasanta's face as the girl wiggled in his arms. Her attacker was turning red in the face to see him handle her so easily.

"I want her." His smile grew large, baring his teeth as he looked down at the man. "Leave me the wildling. I've earned it after surviving Fenrir."

Glaring at the girl, the man grunted and rubbed his torn cheek. "Fine. Perhaps you like to be bitten in your bed. I prefer a doe, not a wolf."

With that said, they all left him with his prize in arm. He wasn't sure where to go with her. Romasanta hadn't thought that far ahead, and she was starting to struggle in his grip. Looking about, he watched the Lykaons.

It seemed any tent could be his, especially if he wished to use it for making love. He started for the closest empty tent and she started fighting him harder. Her teeth ripped into his arm, but he failed to flinch. There was no way she could understand the amount of pain he had endured over the last several days. All of it had made him numb to something so small as a bite. He lugged her farther on his shoulders, and she panicked as they entered the tent.

I like her Romasanta. Let us take her. She would make a fine mate for a wolf! The excitement and arousal coming from Fenrir felt bitter to Romasanta. *Never have I seen such pride in a human or wolf!*

"No, Fenrir," he grunted, setting her down on the ground. He crouched in front of her. "My name's Romasanta, and I am not with these men. I came to gather information."

Befuddled, she stared at him, frightened. He had not felt pain and had caught her with such speed. Even with him squatting, he towered over her as she blinked up at him. Her speeding heart was thudding in his ears. The smell of her sweat and fear was exhilarating. His breathing had picked up speed as he struggled to contain the animal wants invading him.

Take her, Fenrir rumbled throughout his body. *She is yours. She is showing submission!*

"Fenrir," he growled, turning his back to the girl. "This is not the reason for us being here."

TURN AROUND! he roared, rattling Romasanta's core, angry that he would show submissive behavior to the girl with his body language.

"Are you a madman?" Her voice was soft and angelic as it met his sensitive ears.

Looking over his shoulder, she stared, bewildered by his one sided conversation. "I am a haunted man."

"Are you Romasanta or Fenrir?" Hugging her knees, she looked at him curiously. "You have mentioned both."

"I am both." Fenrir was clawing at him from deep inside, hungry to be set loose. "Stay here. The Lykaons will be meeting their deaths tonight. This is something a young girl should not have to bear witness to—"

"You are only one man." Tilting her head, she showed no more fear toward him. "There are enough men out there to fill a village. How do you plan to kill them all?"

Glaring back at her, his amber eyes glowed in the darkness of the tent as he growled his answer, "I will devour them all."

Leaving her behind, his bowels churned as Fenrir pushed himself forward. He stood at the large pyre, catching the attention of the warriors. Leaning back, he howled long, and it felt electrifying to give into the animalistic sensations. His eyes glowed yellow as he stood tall before all the men who looked on in confusion and terror. They watched as his body exploded into a humanoid wolf, like he had been forced into the night before. Fenrir was taking over and Romasanta did not care. He was tired of fighting the wolf-like wants that had increased with the night. Laughter erupted from his jowls as he looked over the fleeing army.

"Romasanta?" A wet cloth struck his face as the angelic voice woke him from his sleep. "Are you well?"

Rolling to his side, he put his back to where she kneeled next to him. His naked body ached, and he felt bloated. Fenrir had outdone himself last night from the way his head spun. Giggling came from the tent entrance, which brought his attention to his surroundings. A large group of women stared at him, doe-eyed and curious. He furrowed his brow, as some blushed and others chuckled at his uncertainty.

I have earned you a harem! Fenrir announced, excited at the feat. *Never have I gathered so many females so easily!*

Romasanta covered his face, moaning in disapproval. "You foul creature. I do not need a harem or a pack. All I want is to get my Daphne back."

Why would you settle with only one? Fenrir was starting to find human culture fascinating. *Any of these women would mate with you now!*

"It doesn't work that way." Picking himself off the floor, Romasanta gathered the pile of clothes nearby, ignoring the girls. "I pray you did nothing with me last night."

"You rescued us. We wish to follow you, versipellis." She grabbed his arm, demanding he look at her. "You can protect us from the wizards, yes?"

"Versipellis..." Breaking their gaze, he continued dressing. "What does that mean?"

"Skin changer."

30

Huffing, he walked out of the tent to see a slaughter: The tents were shredded and flapping in the wind, heavy with blood. There wasn't a man that was not missing a large portion of his body. Fenrir had enjoyed himself and then took Romasanta's actions beforehand to heart and spared every female within the camp. Taking a step forward, he nearly tripped on a random head. As he watched it roll from his unintentional kick, he recognized the man with the scratch on his cheek. Slumping his shoulders, he looked to the sky, trying to settle the sick sensation he felt. He was overstuffed and his meal had been a cannibalistic one, thanks to the demon within him.

"You brought it to me as a gift." The girl had followed him out and looked at her attacker's head with no remorse. "You gave it to me and then came in to sleep. Do you not remember?"

"Fenrir, you romantic..." Grumbling, Romasanta ignored the women who watched him leave.

CHAPTER 5

KINGS OF ARCADIA

It was hard to say how much ground he had covered over the last ten years. He and Fenrir had a routine down, splitting the time each used his body; a man by day and a wolf by night. The Lykaons were scarce in numbers thanks to Fenrir's relentless hunting. As for clues about Gaea or Merlin, none were found. What little sleep Romasanta managed to acquire was haunted by thousands of faces, bloodied and mangled. How many men had he consumed as Fenrir? The dreadful thought washed over him every day when he woke.

The growing interest Fenrir took in human culture was entertaining to Romasanta. In a strange way, it was keeping him human some place deep inside. Without the demon wolf's questions, he would have given himself to the animal instincts that had grown stronger. Unlike the first year, he could see and smell like a wolf in his human form. His ears could hear a deer a mile away or any who may approach his direction. Romasanta had kept the wolf-skin hood, a nostalgic reminder of what lurked within him. It felt natural, and in some way, acted as a silent warning to the people around him. Many were whispering stories about he and Daphne's fate as well as the story of the versipellis who drove the Lykaons away.

He could not help but wonder how many of these people he had saved as himself, or were spared by Fenrir. Before their joining, Fenrir carried no compassion or sympathy for any man. He would devour men, women, children, and any other living creature without hesitation. After their joining, he made a game of sparing certain individuals. Deep down, he was curious and inspired by the way people reacted to being saved. It was a new variant of dominance that he was starting to accept as natural.

As he walked through a new village, looking about, he hoped that, unlike the other towns, tthis one had a shaman in charge. It seemed

Boreas had succeeded in killing off or gathering those with magic in their blood. Romasanta and Fenrir were still attempting to find a way to smell the difference between those with magic in their blood and those without. If they could manage to hunt and search for such people, it may help them uncover Merlin's tracks.

"The versipellis are attacking the road to the north," murmured a villager to another. "If we cannot get there to trade, we will not be able to survive the winter."

This stopped Romasanta in his tracks as he listened studiously to the conversation.

"They say they pick and choose who they take alive." The fear in the woman's eyes was breathtaking. "No one knows if they are eaten or become one themselves."

What is this? Fenrir roared within him, his chest thudding as he lashed out over what he was hearing. *I haven't been north of here! Who is claiming my territory?!*

"Silence," hissed Romasanta, still wanting to hear more of what these two people had to say. "Listen for a while longer, Fenrir."

"How terrible. Both are horrible fates." The old man rubbed the side of his cheek for a moment. "They say they look like wolves, but walk like men. Rumors believe the Lykaons have turned themselves into monsters."

"What have we done..." breathed Romasanta as his blood ran cold. "There was more to our curse than we feared."

"Whoever they are, man or beast, they leave symbols of claiming lands and villages." The woman huffed as she picked her basket off the ground. "They call themselves the kings of Arcadia, ha!"

"But they've all died off." The old man scratched his scruffy beard as he thought. "Should someone ask the witch for advice? Will she be able to protect us from this?"

"I don't know, Josef. You are nothing more than a shepherd, like the rest of the men here." She gave him a smile of hope. "But perhaps the old witch has a plan to turn us all into undying warriors."

"Excuse me." Romasanta grabbed Josef's shoulder, catching his attention. "I wish to consult with the witch. Where may I find her?"

Josef looked him over, and his eyes grew wide. "I do not know you! Where in the world did you come from?"

Romasanta pointed to a wall of trees to the east and spoke again. "I wish to gain some knowledge of my urgent situation. May I speak with the witch?"

Once more, the old Shepard took in his appearance. "She let you in for a reason. I suppose I will take you to her house."

Romasanta followed close behind the Shepard as they made their way through the bustling village. It was hard to believe it had been ten years since the curse. How many had he touched with fang or claw? So many saved, or worse, a lot had fled in the wake of each assault. This whole time, were they spreading their disease or was something else happening? Did the curse change more than Romasanta and Fenrir? They paused in front of a door, and a smell hit his nose that he hadn't smelled for a long time.

"It can't be." He gasped, taking in the smell once more as the hairs on his arms prickled.

"This is her home." Josef's hat bells rang as he patted Romasanta on the back. "If I didn't know better, I'd say you two were related."

"That's not possible," Romasanta mumbled as Josef walked away. "But that scent, it makes my whole body—"

It's an uncanny sensation, isn't it, Romasanta? Chortling, Fenrir seemed thrilled to share something with him. *This is what it's like to be a wolf. Do you not enjoy the smell of your own kin?*

Romasanta swallowed and pressed his hand against the door, hesitating to knock or enter. Taking in a huge sniff, he sighed in relief and excitement. He leaned his head against the door, weighing his emotions. His heart was heavy at the thoughts of who was about to greet him on the other side. Romasanta questioned if he really wanted to face her in the state he found himself; Neither man nor wolf.

"I already know, Brother." Her whisper shouted into his ears, confirming his suspicions. "Come in. Let us discuss what has happened."

His muscles tensed as he entered, closing the door behind him. She was sitting at the table, a veil over her face, hands clasped over a cup of steaming liquid, with another across the table waiting for him. Skittishly, like a wary dog, he forced himself to approach and sit. Being so close, he could smell that she had not escaped the fire unscathed. His wolf's senses told him that under that veil was a woman scarred for life. He could only wonder if her magic could not heal her or if she had chosen to remain in that broken state. The smell of the tea goaded him to take a sip. He did so as a way to avoid saying anything to her. What would he say? How could he ever explain that he was Romasanta and—

"Fenrir seems to be tamer these days." Artemis knew that her brother was panicking. "You two have made quite the mark on the world already."

Your sister is something else, Farmer, the wolf grumbled through his chest, intrigued by Artemis. *She is strong and I like the sense of respect her words have when they hit my ears.*

Romasanta smiled at Fenrir's words. "Fenrir does as he wishes, so that I may do as I wish."

"That much has been clear." She reached out to touch his hand, but he flinched at the motion. "Please, let me touch you so that I may feel the curse that has been set upon you both."

Reluctantly, he slid his hand back to her. Her hands were as cold as ice, as if she were something dead. Gripping him tight, she convulsed in her chair. Failing to jerk free of her grip, he watched as her eyes glowed in shades of green, red, and blue. The grip was crushing, but he and Fenrir felt nothing of Artemis's struggle. Her mouth opened and glowing steam poured out of her. Tears of blood stained the veil, sending him into a fury of terror. The blood greeted his senses, aiding the growing panic he felt as his heart raced. She still would not let go, and a wicked smile crossed her face. Befuddled, he sat back in the chair he had left in the chaos.

"Merlin, you pester me further, I see." Letting go, she took a bloody tear and allowed it to drip into Romasanta's tea. "Drink it."

"No." His jaw twitched, the blood overwhelming his nose. "I have indulged enough in blood these past ten years. It disgusts me to think about drinking my sister's own."

"Romasanta," Artemis jeered. "I would not ask this of you for sport. This is to aid you in smelling magic in one's bloodline. You will need this ability in the future."

Frowning at the cup, he squinted his eyes as he took the shot of tea. Slamming the cup on the table, his eyes glowed yellow as the tea burned in his chest. Fenrir was excited as his nose seemed to strengthen to a new level, even for him.

"This is not your fault." She sighed, looking into the fire that crackled in the hearth.

"Those words again…" They had soured in Romasanta's mind and they hit him hard as they washed over his ears. "I hate them."

"Boreas and his son Arcas have overstepped their boundaries and will suffer the recoil by your hand. Your quest for the Eye of Gaea will have to wait." Her words stung as she continued. "I need more time to make you the tools which will be needed so that you may recover the stone. Until then, you will be doing the dirty work for nature since you are now one with Fenrir."

She speaks the truth! I am at the mercy of what nature yearns for me to do, Fenrir whispered softly, as if ashamed to admit his true reasons behind the violence. *It is forbidden to use magic against other beings of magic. It does not matter if it were beast or man, but in the end, there is a recoil or curse to be acted on. Often I am sent out to bring death to those who would dare to cross this line.*

"And when will I be allowed to pursue the Eye of Gaea again?" Romasanta bit his cheek, feeling contempt for his sister and her plans involving his life. "Will I need your permission first?"

"I understand you are angry with me, but I promise I will be making the largest sacrifice to help you get Daphne back." Scowling, she demanded silence from him. "You will know when the time has come to reclaim the stone when the tools you need find you. Until then, try to keep your humanity intact and practice patience."

"Tools." He snorted in dismay. "And how does one know your tools from another's?"

"Don't patronize me." The fire roared in reaction to her anger and he realized he had been wrong to say anything at all. "Dear brother, I know that you are suffering, and you will go through more of it before the time comes for the Eye of Gaea to be in your grasp again. The Eye will go by many names before you discover its whereabouts, but I will make sure you serve all the purposes you have been handed so that Gaea will be pleased."

His stomach turned as he soaked in the words she gave him. The instincts turned inside him and his skin crawled with an unsettling chill. "This passing of time, it will be long?"

Her words were barely audible to even his enhanced ears. "Horribly so, and lonely."

It was a struggle to hold his rage and sorrow still. The burning in his chest was strong enough to even make Fenrir quiver within his core. Artemis had pulled him into an unthinkable cursed life that would be torturous. He glared at her as she hugged onto herself and he could smell the salt of her tears as they fell. Whatever her fate was, she would bear the guilt of handling it all on her shoulders.

Getting up, he hugged her from behind, whispering to her. "This is a final goodbye then, dear sister."

She shook as she bit her lip, desperate not to sob as she had done ten years ago. Letting her go, he left. The weight in his gut and shoulders told him this would be the last time he would ever see her. Josef was sitting at the far fence and insisted on exchanging a few words with him.

"Did she have an answer for you?" His sheep ran to the far end of the fenced area as Romasanta approached. "Was she able to help you, stranger?"

"Yes, and no." Grumbling, he stared at the sheep hungrily. "I never like the answers I get."

"It seems to be that way for any who earn her attention." Josef sighed, curious about the man who wore a wolf-skin hood. "This path goes north. There is only trouble in that direction. It isn't safe."

"It is my nature to find trouble, Josef." Romasanta looked at the evening sky; Fenrir would soon be free to roam. "This is a curse I must carry for now."

"Well..." Josef paused and looked at the grief that painted Romasanta's face. "You are always welcomed at Raven's Den. It can be a home away from home."

Looking at the old shepherd, Romasanta smirked. "I will remember that. Thank you."

Saying nothing else, he started down the path. It was comforting that the village was surrounded by such a thick forest. Fenrir was anxious to be set loose. He could smell Lykaons a few miles north. The magical scent of their blood was tantalizing. Romasanta found himself running through the woods, anxious to carry out what he and Fenrir could feel rattling them deep in their souls. It was their duty to take down the kings of Arcadia. Despite night having fallen, Fenrir waited inside Romasanta. Their instincts told them it was far easier to not be detected by these men if they appeared human. The camp was giving off a rank smell of blood, sweat, and wolf. Rubbing at his nose, he and Fenrir tensed, knowing that the rumors they heard before may be true. Crawling ever closer through the brush, he could finally see the camp.

At first, he saw no one in the camp. The silence was eerie and unnatural. Not an insect dared to make a sound within this place. The rattling of chains pulled his attention to a far corner. A girl was desperate, trying to tug her hands free, the skin at her wrist ripping and bleeding. The smell of it excited him, and Fenrir shivered with pleasure.

It's her! The arousal that rattled from his core scared Romasanta as Fenrir spoke. *We found her again!*

Clenching his teeth, Romasanta ignored the wolf's want for the girl. "She has magic in her blood, Fenrir."

I do not care! he roared, angry that he was being denied what he wanted. *She is wild and I wish to tame her as both a man and her alpha. I will take her, Farmer.*

It was hard to keep calm as his anxiety reacted to what the demon wolf was declaring. "You're insane. It would never work."

She was submissive only to us. Fenrir huffed as he rattled deep within Romasanta. *You wouldn't allow her to follow. This time you will not interfere!*

Knots churned in his stomach at the thoughts and sensations from Fenrir that were overriding his own. Movement near the girl stilled their internal fight. Their eyes fell upon a monster, neither wolf nor man. He stood tall, large with gray fur, and the left side of his wolf's head was ravaged horribly, the eye gone.

"Boreas..." whispered Romasanta, the smell confirming his instincts true. "He is alive. You should have bitten him harder, Fenrir."

He will not escape my fangs a second time! They were both feeling angry at seeing that their enemy had survived. *We will take him down together!*

"Girl, do you not want to join the King of Arcadia as my mate?" Boreas's voice was a rumbling growl as he looked down at the girl. "What more could one want than be forever immortalized as the queen of wolves?"

"Go to hell!" She spat at his feet, showing no fear toward the monster before her. "I serve Romasanta!"

"Oh, no..." he groaned from where he hid. "Why would she say something so foolish?"

Fenrir laughed and fluttered with pleasure at the words. *You have made yourself a pack, Farmer! This is what it means to be an alpha!*

Boreas roared angrily at the very mentioning of his name. "Romasanta is dead! You speak of a myth!"

She glowered at Boreas, standing tall with pride as she spoke on. "He lives and he will take you and your men to hell."

A wicked laugh crossed Boreas's canine face as he bared all his teeth. "You will not live to see it then. I will feast on your flesh tonight and take pleasure in doing so."

Fenrir was pushing forward. Gripping at his face, Romasanta could feel himself changing in an instant. He was larger than Boreas in this state. Unlike the gray, aged look of his enemy, he wore the black fur of Fenrir and held the same burning amber-colored eyes. Spurred by the emotions of Fenrir, he broke from where he hid, racing toward the girl and Boreas.

Every muscle was taut, and he shivered with anticipation of the fight that would be coming. He towered over Boreas, who stumbled back, looking terrified. In front of him stood a being with the same amber eyes that still haunted his dreams after ten years. Behind Romasanta, hands gripped the fur of his back as tears fell to the ground. Another wave of excitement swept over him as Fenrir relished in this new sensation of compassion.

"I knew you would come," she breathed. Once more, his ears were blessed by the voice of an angel. "I do not care if my life is given to Fenrir or Romasanta. After tonight, I will owe you both for saving me and I love you both for that."

"We will speak of what to do with you after we deal with Boreas," he grunted, failing to discourage her.

CHAPTER 6

THE FALL OF LYKAONS

"Deal with me?" Laughter came from Boreas as he shook off his fear. "You will have to face me and my army!"

Howling into the night air, steam rolled from Boreas's jowls. Other cursed Lykaons came out of hiding, gathering around them, all growling and fur rising at the powerful intruder who stood in the middle of their camp. He eyed each of them. Many carried scars from where Fenrir's fangs had ripped into them. Sighing, Romasanta thought long and hard about his sister's words about recoils and magic.

"I see you were punished to be neither men nor wolf for your attack on Fenrir." Glowering at Boreas, he spoke with authority. "Instead of learning your lesson, you have continued to defile others who carry magic in their blood. I have come to serve as your punishment."

Snorting at him, Boreas demonstrated that he still had access to his powers over fire. "I will burn you down!"

Anger fueled Boreas as he lunged a great ball of flame at him, but Romasanta did nothing to avoid it. With great pride, he took the hit to his chest. It filled his nose with the stench of burning fur and skin. The other Lykaons backed away, seeing him still standing, not flinching from the hit. The pain was nothing to a man who had been through it all. Boreas growled, infuriated by the pure display of strength and dominance. Insulted, he lunged forward, clawing at Romasanta. He took the first slash across his shoulder, using it to push the girl far out of the way. Catching the next swipe in his grip, he snapped his jaws next to the missing eye. As Boreas retreated, the smell of his terror hung thick. His warriors shifted nervously as the scent of it hit their sensitive noses.

Another round of rage boiled over Boreas and he gathered his nerve again. As he leaped forward, his claws burst into flames. He had combined his magic and his form in a more threatening way. Snorting in annoyance, Romasanta avoided this new danger with ease. Bouncing side to side, Romasanta landed on all fours and ran under another swipe and behind Boreas. Turning to chase Romasanta, he found no one there. Furrowing his brow, Boreas faltered in his focus.

Romasanta rammed his claws into the back of his ribs. Squeezing the muscles and bones, causing a great shrill to escape Boreas as he hit his knees. His back arched as he howled on in agony, flames extinguished, he clawed behind him. Failing to reach his attacker, he attempted to wiggle free. Romasanta gripped and clawed deeper, earning another howl of pain.

He lowered his fanged mouth to Boreas's ears, whispering to him, "Surprise."

As Romasanta released him, Boreas scrambled to make space between them, holding his bleeding sides. He panted and cringed as he used his flamed claws to cauterize his wounds. Blood stopped spilling from him as he wheezed, glowering at Romasanta. It was clear Boreas had not been injured in a fight since his encounter with Fenrir. Unlike these men, he had the advantage in terms of power and experience. Fenrir had taught him how to best use his abilities as a wolf. None of these men know how to translate the nature stirring within them.

It was arousing to be overpowering Boreas. Ten years ago, he had been so weak and unable to protect Daphne from this threat. His clawed finger tips dripped Boreas's blood on the ground, the sound of it exciting. Digging into his back had been payback for the spear that had dug so deeply into him. Looking back, he wished he had known more about how to defend himself, not for his sake, but for Daphne's. Romasanta's tail swished as he smirked. His skills had put hesitation in all who were watching the fight. The girl, who had grown up since their last encounter, stood tall as she grinned. Fenrir was thrilled with Romasanta's ability to control the abilities of the wolf. It was humorous to see how hard the Lykaons tried to stand like men. Not one of them illustrated the want to be on all fours where they felt most comfortable.

Crouching, he awaited Boreas's next move. Puffing his chest out, he watched as Boreas grabbed a sword from another warrior. Romasanta pricked his ears high, frowning. Boreas had given up the animalistic fight sooner than expected. It was down to a competition of fang and sword, since he had proven his magic futile. Boreas roared as he ran at Romasanta, who dodged while on all fours. Another dance of ducking and running under a blind swipe ensued. There was a childish joy as he took advantage of Boreas's blind spot. Boreas was outmatched, but with the missing eye, he had no chance. Under another swing and behind him, Romasanta barked, startling Boreas into another running rage.

Boreas was tiring and foaming at the mouth. Romasanta bounced about, his agility and speed dominating over Boreas's awkward man-like movements. It was a game of chase. Before long, Romasanta tired of it and caught Boreas's wrist. The sword was close to meeting its mark across his head, but that was an intentional tease. Growling grew from Romasanta's chest, and drool dripped from his clenched fangs. Boreas was exhausted. He would have been a better opponent if he had given up trying to remain a proud man of magic.

"You do not know, do you?" They pulled away from each other as Boreas fought out of his grip. "I have the advantage here, Romasanta."

He snorted in response as he watched Boreas and his men with caution. The sword was bright and mirrored, and he was taking too much interest in wielding it. Laying his ears back, Romasanta furrowed his brow as he paced in front of Boreas with his metal toy. The pack that surrounded them grew more excited by this weapon, but all that mattered to Romasanta and Fenrir were their instincts. Deep inside, this metal thing told them nothing. It was another item to cut their flesh. These items only slowed the inevitable want to devour their enemies. After each feast, these gapping wounds simply closed and their body grew ever stronger. Nothing twisted their guts, other than the sensation deep within demanding both their souls to carry out their duty to wipe Lykaons from existence.

Speeding toward Boreas, he took the sword to the gut, smiling as the fear hit Boreas's gray, doggish face. It slid and ripped through him, but the lack of acknowledging his pain rattled Romasanta's enemy. His fangs met Boreas's throat, clamping tightly as he ripped and shook at him. The claws that had once gripped their plaything let go. They dug into their attacker, but did nothing to help Boreas escape his fate. Boreas fell to the ground, blood pouring from his ravaged neck. Romasanta stood over him as he gurgled and his eye rolled into the back of his head.

"FATHER!" Another gray colored Lykaon rushed forward, his ire riding in his eyes. "NO!"

Growling, he ran at Romasanta, who did nothing to dodge the oncoming attack. Ripping the sword out of him, he grunted at the little Lykaon. This sword was supposed to be their greatest defense against Fenrir, and it failed them. He swung wildly, time and time again, and Romasanta humored him with the occasional strike. He and Fenrir were amused by the blind rage only seen in men.

"You are Arcas," rumbled Romasanta, tiring of the slashes and gripping his arm tight to stop the sword. "Son of Boreas?"

"How come you do not feel the swift burn of the silver blade as we do?!" His fur had raised in his fury, and he looked like a crazed dog. "Why do you not feel pain?!"

Romasanta shoved him to the ground, and the sword bounced across the dirt. Romasanta laughed. Looking over the shocked faces of the pack of Lykaons made him roar on louder. Picking up the blade, he sniffed it and hummed in wonder.

"Silver?" The blade had struck him numerous times, but had felt no different from any other blade.

Unlike these men in wolf's clothing, he followed his instincts, and they had given him no reason to fear this. Raising it toward Arcas, the panic and terror struck him. Arcas crawled away on the ground as Romasanta took a step forward, making Romasanta's tail wag. The faces around them were focused so intensely on the blade, it seemed odd. Where ever the blade went, their eyes followed.

How silly... They both entertained it again with another wave of the blade. *Let us test this play thing, Romasanta! Why do they fear something that we do not?*

Without warning, he was on top of Arcas, who yelped. Romasanta pointed the blade at his chest as he lay pinned under Romasanta's mass. All watching eyes were wide with anticipation. Romasanta scoffed in annoyance as his nose was greeted by the smell of piss. Arcas was beyond terrified of this silver blade. A wicked shine came to his amber eyes as he leaned forward to whisper to Arcas.

"You know why silver does not hurt us?" Arcas could only shake his head no. "I am not one of you."

Romasanta slammed the blade through Arcas's chest; it sizzled where it met blood. The smell was putrid as if decaying and rotting the flesh it greeted. Arcas howled and struggled against the blade, but failed. It took only a few seconds for the silver to extinguish his life, like venom to the soul. Fear filled the air as he took up the blade and turned to face the army before him. A few ran off, but the rest readied themselves. They were hoping the thirty or so men that stood solid could down the demon wolf. Fenrir was taking over, yearning for his turn to fight after being kind enough to allow Romasanta to have his revenge. A howl poured out of him, louder and stronger than the one Boreas had made earlier.

Eyes glowed from the dark forest and surrounded the army in a massive wall of fur and teeth. Unlike the Lykaons, these creatures were on all fours, more animal than man, as they growled and barked with excitement under the full moon. Romasanta had failed to realize that the excitement he had felt from Fenrir was not one for sparing lives. He had known about this part of the curse. These last ten years he was building his army, his pack. Part of him wanted to be angry, but without this pack, he would not be able to take out the last of the Lykaons.

Diving forward, silver sword in hand, Fenrir had his fun with the men. They all realized they would not live through the night as the surrounding pack poured over them. Again and again Fenrir would dodge, circle, and surprise them. The wounds from the silver blade burned into their flesh and spoiled their blood. He toyed with them and satisfied curiosities about how the silver worked them over. Many of his own pack fell victim to its sting. Only Romasanta was immune to its bite. He tired of the bloody sport, already full from devouring what he wanted. Now it was the pack's turn to devour what he left for them.

He turned back to the girl. Dropping the sword, he approached her, his fur dripping with blood; his own and his victims'. He towered over her as she stared up at him with green eyes. Breaking her chains with his teeth, he freed her, crouching before her. She honored him with her smile as she clung to his chest. The years had been hard on her, with scars across her skin that made him angry. Her hair was black and wild, her body warm against him; it all made his heart race. Never had Fenrir felt so alive as he did in this simple moment. A woman now stood where ten years earlier an adolescent girl had caught the interest of a demon wolf.

Romasanta could not help but be moved by the compassion coming from Fenrir for this human girl. Her hands rubbed the side of his wolf-like head and he nuzzled in its touch. Opening his big golden eyes, he admired her fragility. Despite that, she had fought hard and with pride. All this time, her thoughts had recalled their first meeting. Even now, he did not know why he had felt a need to bring the head of her attacker to her. He had dropped it at her feet and she had given him her embrace. It had rattled him to have her cling to him. Once more, her skin pressing against him was electrifying.

"What is your name, girl?" Fenrir cooed, relishing in her scent. "Do you even have a name?"

"I am Rhea Silvia." He quivered in excitement at hearing her name for the first time. "And I owe you my life, Fenrir."

"Do you wish to stay with me?" He broke away, standing with his back to her. "Do you know there are two souls that share this cursed body?"

"I know. It is the demon Fenrir and the man Romasanta who are here." She wrapped her arms around him, her hands pressing against the scar in the center of his chest. "It does not matter. Both are worthy of having my love."

"He already has a love," Fenrir grumbled, looking at the night sky. "I wish to help him get that love back, though I do not understand what it is."

"Let me be the one to show you," she whispered, her voice like a bird's song. "You have already shown me compassion, want, protection, anger... let me teach you how to show love."

"It will take time, Rhea. I am not a man. I am a wolf, a demon who only knows how to be an animal at heart." Sighing, he crouched down, pulling her free and looking over his shoulder. "My compassion has been taught to me by Romasanta. I wish for him to teach me how to love so that.."

Fenrir's thoughts and emotions were swirling inside him too fast for him to comprehend what he wanted. Romasanta had sat in silence, feeling the heavy loneliness that welled up in Fenrir with every touch Rhea gave him. Artemis had made it clear it would be a long time before Daphne would be freed. What right did he have to deny someone else a chance to have a love like what he had lost?

"Give me time, Rhea." Nestling his head in her hand again, he sighed. "Please do not let him leave you behind, for my sake."

She kissed the top of his massive wolf's head, and he took pleasure in receiving such a token of affection from her. "I will not leave you."

"Is there anything I can do for you before I sleep?" His wounds ached, and his body demanded rest so that he could heal. "What would make you happy?"

"I am already happy to see you again." Pondering a moment, she seemed to have thought of something. "But when you both wake, we should travel north. There was one among them that did not suffer the same curse. His name is Nyctimus. He was left tortured and tied to a rock."

"In the morning, we will hunt for this Nyctimus and see why the kings of Arcadia feared him so." He lay across the ground at her feet and she simply stroked the fur on his head and neck.

With each touch, he calmed further and further before falling into a restful sleep for the first time since he had been encased in the Eye of Gaea.

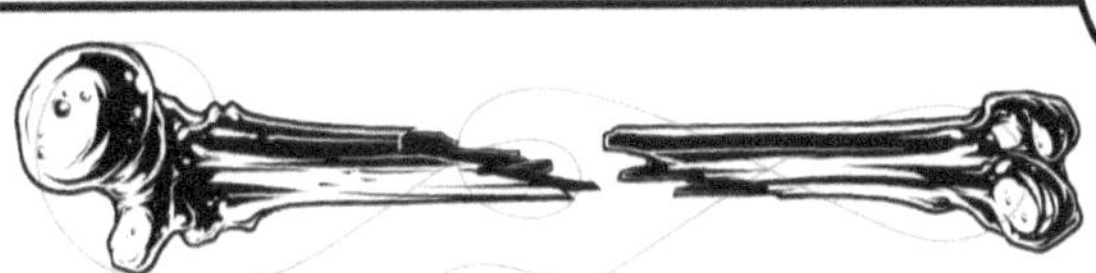

CHAPTER 7

NYCTIMUS

The sun had risen hours earlier by the time Romasanta woke up. His body was sore and the scars of the prior night's fight were still on his skin. The deeper the wounds, the more damage he took and the longer the process was to heal. Sitting up, he stared at Rhea, who waited on the other side of a campfire from him. His stomach grumbled as the smell of cooked rabbit hit his nose. Next to him was a skewered rabbit ready for eating. Without hesitation, he grabbed it, and ate it as if he had been starving to death. By the time he was wiping the mess of meat from his face, she had laid clothes beside him. Her green eyes watched him with caution and care while he disregarded her.

Dressed, he started to rummage through and around the dead heaps of half-man, half-wolf creatures. The sun gleamed off the object of interest, and he eagerly picked it up. He had decided to take Boreas's silver sword for both a prize and an added advantage against any Lykaons left to slay. Looking over his shoulder, he could see Rhea at his heels. Walking through the aftermath had not deterred her from following as Fenrir had begged of her. Rubbing the scar on his chest, Romasanta's feelings were conflicted about the situation. All he wanted was Daphne, and he had no intentions of sharing his affections with another. Deep down, he knew it was something Fenrir had not had the pleasure of experiencing. It was complex and difficult to imagine them being together, but after last night, he knew he would have to endure.

Turning to the north, he took in a deep breath through his nose. Scents flowed into him, his mind picking them out and labeling them in an instant. One was a smell similar to the Lykaons. He eyed Rhea, and they started in that direction. Somewhere in the distance, they would find the Lykaon named Nyctimus. The air told Romasanta he was still alive, but nothing more.

Sweat ran down his back as the sun beat down on him. Romasanta was thankful for both the silence of Rhea and Fenrir. They understood what they were asking of him and he would need time to deal with his own feelings. Closing his eyes, flashes of Daphne's smiling face haunted him. The memory was so lively in his thoughts as the sun beat down on his face. He could almost hear her laughter, feel her fingers grasping his arm—Jerking from Rhea's touch, he struggled to soothe his anger. She froze, her fingers outstretched to his arm where he had been seeing Daphne's hand. His glare was wild and dangerous as he looked down at her. The blood in his body boiled and churned, an uncanny surge of anxiety throttling him.

"What are you doing?" he roared at her, failing to calm the thudding of his heart against his chest. "I do not want to be touched."

Furrowing her brow, she frowned at him before speaking. "She had a very pretty smile."

Befuddled by the words, he questioned what he thought she was implying. "You could see my memories?"

"And feel." A tear welled up and fell down her cheek as she recalled his sorrow. "It is part of the gift I was given."

"The gifted are cursed." Huffing, he marched on, wanting to increase his distance from her. "You can never replace her, Rhea."

"I do not want to replace her. She is yours." He had upset her and her voice stung at his back. "I am Fenrir's, not yours."

Stopping, he looked over at her as Fenrir rattled in his chest. His excitement and arousal overflowed into Romasanta. The burning sensation of Fenrir's yellow eyes reflected in hers and Romasanta knew he could never drive the two of them apart. Indeed, this woman was wild at heart. She wanted to be with Fenrir, and somehow, she had earned his want in return. Fear crept into Romasanta. Rhea had an uncanny, unpredictable ability to sense his memories along with the emotions they brought on. This was why she could sense the two of them as separate beings.

Was it this gift that helped her see through Fenrir and grasp his heart so easily? Regardless, he would have to be clever and alert. At every turn, it was undeniable she would be attempting to use her abilities against him. If she was going to be the lover to Fenrir, it meant finding a means of also being his lover. The thoughts soured on his tongue and the muscles in his face twitched. Turning away from her, he continued toward the scent that was so near now.

The ground had grown rockier as they came upon the edge of the forest and the beginning of a mountain. There, chained to a great boulder, a man huddled naked beside it. His body was branded and marked, the scars deep and permanent. Romasanta examined the symbols on the man's bare skin. He bore the signs of a Lykaon, a priest, and a blood relative to Boreas. As Romasanta squatted before the chained man, the man did not raise his head or show signs of acknowledging their presence. Unlike the other Lykaons, he was not half-man, half-wolf but he held a bloodline carrying a similar magic. The scent of the magic seemed strange, lacking the robust signs of ever being used.

"Can you not burn the chains from your hands?" Rubbing his nose, he waited as the man sighed. "Are you not the son of Arcas, grandson of King Boreas? One of the magic-wielding Lykaons?"

"I am a priest. We are not tamers of fire." Looking up through his sweat and blood-soaked hair, he glared one rebellious hazel eye at Romasanta. "And I would hardly consider myself the son of Arcas, seeing that my father has left me here by order of my grandfather Boreas."

"Why have you not turned skin like the rest?" Eyeing the tracks on the ground, he saw a mixture of human and wolf-like prints. "Are these not your tracks?"

"You are no ordinary woodsman." He stood, his arms wrapped in the chains coming into view as he staggered to keep his balance. "If you free me, I am yours. I will serve you for the rest of my life."

"So be it." It took several swings of the sword before a link of the chain broke.

The leash unraveled from its prisoner, and he rubbed the rips they had left on his skin. He was not the height of Romasanta, but he was broad and heavily muscled. For a priest, he was built more like a brute. He arched, stretching himself out, and bellowed long and loud. It reverberated off the mountains as he huffed, relieving himself of his frustrations. Turning his hazel eyes to Romasanta, he kneeled before him, eager to express his gratitude. Looking over Nyctimus, he and Fenrir weighed their thoughts on this Lykaon offspring. His magic was dormant, whether he knew this or not was not a concern. What intrigued them was the fact he was like them; a man by day, a wolf by night. This was the first time he had witnessed the scent of it. It was yet to be seen in this priest.

Lykaons carried magic in their souls and when touched by their curse, whether by fang or claw, they fell into a permanent state of doglike men. As for those Fenrir had spared, despite wounding them, they would turn into monstrous wolves at the peak of the full moon. Then again, it was uncertain if this was the beginning of a slower process, which they had not seen its cycle finished. Time would be needed to see what stain they had left by letting this go unchecked. The man before him seemed capable of turning if he willed for it to come. Whether magic was an element, was hard to say. Romasanta and Fenrir had much to learn about their own curse and how it worked on others. It spared no one who came to harm by tooth and nail. The way it reacted differently to each man and woman was puzzling.

"I ask one favor of you." Nyctimus's hazel eyes stared into Romasanta's own as he spoke his wish to his new master. "Like you, I wish to wipe the Lykaons from this earth. Please, let me be the tool for that purpose."

"And how do you intend to do this?" Lifting an eyebrow at the naked man in front of him, Romasanta's words were stern. "How do you aim to undo what your father and his father have worked so greedily to create?"

"I intend to take the throne, and in doing so, break down the very system my kin have wrongfully created." There was a hint of the wolven pride shining in Nyctimus's eyes, and Fenrir stirred in response. "But I cannot start this great task without your aid, my liege."

"What would you have me do?" Fenrir was holding dominance over Nyctimus while Romasanta questioned the man's words. "How would I be able to aid you in taking your own throne, essentially?"

"I first must defeat Aitvaras, the black dragon that guards the royal house." It was a desperate plea as he continued, "He was Boreas's pet. No one knows where the foul beast came from, but he will not allow anyone to enter the royal house where the throne sits. All I do know, is when Boreas was home, he was nowhere to be seen. During this time, when the dragon was missing, Boreas's treasure room grew while the neighboring lords lost their riches to what was believed to be the 'Curse of Boreas.'"

Aitvaras is back from hell! rumbled Fenrir, shaking Romasanta from within. *Romasanta, you are a clever man! I do not have my true form to match the size and power of Aitvaras, but I have seen your words and wisdom. This dragon keeps a secret that I have not found.*

Scratching at his chin, Romasanta rolled over the details. "Never when Boreas was home?"

"Yes." Nyctimus shifted nervously, fearing he would be refused. "The dragon is the size of the royal tower, but vanishes without warning when Boreas returns, without fail, every time."

A smirk crawled across his face as the question hit him. "Then what is only seen while Boreas is home?"

Nyctimus furrowed his brow; memories being recalled could be seen in his eyes as he searched the air. "I am not sure..."

Rhea was pulling clothes from a pack she had been carrying. She had tired of the naked man before Romasanta and night was falling. Throwing them between the men, she made it known it was time to set camp. Grumbling curses under his breath, Romasanta went for a walk in the woods. The aura and glare he gave them sent the message well to not follow him. Fenrir and he were still mulling over the request and its obstacle, Aitvaras. Confident he had wandered far enough away, he flopped to the ground.

Closing his eyes, he let the images from Fenrir's memories come to him, seeing Aitvaras for himself. He was massive, with scales thicker than any armor made by men, and eyes red like ruby jewels. The body of this dragon was long, his wings shadowing the sky. He whipped his tail out at Fenrir as the memory played out. Fire rolled from his thin snout, searing and melting anything it touched. Romasanta fell forward, his shoulder feeling the hit Fenrir took and remembered with such great detail. His flames were something he would have to avoid at all costs as the stinging bore deep into his flesh.

The memory continued, sweat sliding down his face. Fenrir had battled this great dragon in the past and it had nearly killed him. Bones were shattered, flesh ripped or melted from him before he had found his chance. Fangs crushed the scales that had troubled him. Dragon's blood danced on his tongue and its smell whirled in his nose. Clenching harder, he had shaken and strangled the dragon to his death for attempting to steal from Fenrir's territory. It was an exhausting feat, gaining a memory from Fenrir as his own. He questioned how many times he may have accidentally done this to the wolf. So often had he found himself walking in the still forest thinking of moments he had with Daphne. If it worked both ways, perhaps this could be where Fenrir was learning to feel as a man. These memories of love and happiness of someone else could have driven his want for Rhea.

Wiping the sweat from his face, he picked himself off the ground. "I am not going to fight a dragon, Fenrir. You barely escaped with your life last time against Aitvaras."

I already know this, Farmer. Fenrir grumbled, waving his frustration to Romasanta. *That's why this battle will be yours. You are clever. Merlin would have attacked sooner if you had not answered him so cautiously that night we were made as one.*

"I should have gone home that day." The thought of Merlin and his powers made his scar ache. "But as you know, Fenrir, I am just a farmer."

He snorted and pressed on, *You are a fool to think that anymore. Boreas died by your hand, not my fangs! If you think like the alpha you truly are, Boreas's territory, and all within it, is yours! When you killed him, you became him!*

Fenrir's internal barking raged on, but Romasanta dwelled on the words spoken to him. "I know what to do..."

Excitement filled him as he rushed back to Nyctimus and Rhea. They stared at him, bewildered by his eagerness to rush upon them. A wicked grin crawled across his face as he stood with pride. No one knew who stood before them: Fenrir or Romasanta?

"Have you found an answer to my question?" Romasanta looked Nyctimus in the eyes, and he saw he had found it. "And the dragon who serves Boreas?"

"Yes, vanishing on Boreas's return every time."

Nyctimus looked worried as he responded to the questions. "And I am still pondering your riddle. What plan do you have?"

"I will become Boreas." Romasanta carried an animalistic shine to his dark eyes. "I plan to return to the Lykaon camp and recover what little is left of him so I can fool Aitvaras. Like the wolf, dragons often depend more on scent than eyesight. They tend to be blinded by the day's light, so we shall take advantage of all these things to fool the beast."

"But how do you gain Boreas's scent?" Rhea was huddled by a fire, confused as to how this plan could work. "During the day, someone is sure to notice you drenched in blood."

He laughed in response, disregarding her concern. "When was the last time Boreas came to the tower?"

"Before the curse, ten years or longer."

"Perfect." Fenrir's heart was racing as much as Romasanta's as the plan unfolded. "I will approach as a man, but this can only work if I can recover enough of Boreas's corpse to acquire his scent."

"I will accompany you." As suspected, Nyctimus shifted into a humanoid wolf, much like Fenrir. "With both our noses, we should be able to find what we need."

"Rhea, stay here." His eyes glowed yellow as he turned to her. "We will be back, but a larger fire will be needed when we return. Make it as hot as possible."

Without a fuss, she started to build up the fire. Nodding to one another, the two versipellis ran into the forest; one black and one brown with the scars of the Lykaons on his shoulder. It took a third of the time to retrace their travels of the day. The camp reeked of decay from the day's heat, sour and putrid. A pack of wolves had paused from their scavenging and backed away at their presence. Both Nyctimus and Romasanta were having a difficult time picking Boreas out of all the flesh scattered across the ground. Sneezing his nose clear, Romasanta caught a hint of what they had come for. The body had been dragged away from the campsite and into the forest. Sniffing about the trail, they looked at one another as they gathered information about the new smell.

"What on earth is that scent?" Nyctimus still had his hazel eyes, looking awkward in his wolven head as he rumbled, "I do not recognize it."

Looking over the drag marks, no signs of prints had been left behind. They continued following it, sniffing and gathering more information. What seemed to be an eagle's feather was smashed into the mud. Picking it up, Romasanta breathed it in, taking every clue it may hold into his large nose. His fur ruffled in response and he looked about furiously.

"Ravenna." Growling, Fenrir had taken hold as he looked at the trees. "It is the one that calls itself Ravenna. A harlot for corpse-eating and stealing..."

"Is that Fenrir I hear?" A woman's voice called from behind a large tree. "What brings you into my territory so suddenly, wolf? It's been a while since we've crossed paths."

"You've taken something I want." He motioned for Nyctimus to hide. "May I bargain with you? I am not here to claim your land, Ravenna."

"Is that so?" There was a long moment of silence before the woman spoke again. "A bargain you say?"

Wings fluttered, and from around the tree, she came. She had the head and torso of a voluptuous woman, her arms were replaced with magnificent eagle wings, and from the waist down, she had the body of a snake. From her forehead, a horn curved upward, like that of an antelope. She glided over to meet Fenrir. Grinning, she revealed the thin needle-like teeth that her elegant lips kept secret. The blue in her eyes was entrancing as her long, dark hair fell about her elegant face.

"Why, this is an interesting change in appearance." She hissed her greeting as she settled on the ground in front of him. "What do I have that you would want? I have nothing, you silly demon."

"You have a meal behind the tree. A man named Boreas. I need to recover what's left of him for my own wants." Grunting, he could see Nyctimus was working his way to it. "What do you want from me so that I may have it?"

Chortling, she stretched her wings wide, moving herself closer to him. It was hard for him not to snarl or look disgusted by her. She had never been a monster to trust, and she had the reputation of being a scavenger of evil men's corpses. It was natural for her to be here, where so many carrying corrupted hearts had been slain. Slithering around him, he did not flinch as he knew Nyctimus was grabbing the body. She was marveling over this newer Fenrir, excited to see he had taken on a more humanistic form.

She leaned against him, whispering into his ears as her bare breast rubbed against him. "I would love to make love to you now that you can take the form of a man."

He said nothing as his muscles grew taut.

Slithering around his waist, she leaned into the other ear, rubbing herself against him. "As a wolf, I never cared to take interest, but even in this form, you intrigue me, Fenrir. How many women have you dominated since your curse? Did their lustful screams satisfy your desires?"

Closing his eyes, he huffed at her, his ears flattening.

"Since when does the great Fenrir run out of words to bark at me with?" The venomous grin on her face teased him further. "If you want the body so badly, this should be a simple task, no?"

Fenrir's ears pricked forward as a distant howl echoed through the trees. Nyctimus had claimed Boreas's body and was already halfway back to camp with it. Smirking, he bared his fangs at her. With a great flap of her wings, she let him go, backing away in fear of an attack. His amber eyes glimmered in the night air and her smile faded. Wagging his tail, she realized he had wasted her time.

"My friend needs me. Go find another demon to play with you." Scoffing, he took off in the direction of his camp, where Rhea awaited him.

CHAPTER 8

AITVARAS

There wasn't much left of Boreas as the mangled heap lay next to the roaring campfire. His eye, internal organs, and even his fingers had been some of the first things devoured by the beasts of the forest. His face was ravaged, something Ravenna had done. In the past, Fenrir had encountered her and learned much about her nature. She was a monster who wished to be human. Her monstrous appetite for decaying flesh reminded her she would never achieve this, and it fueled her anger. She destroyed their faces first, so that they could not watch her feed upon their insides. The lore Romasanta knew of her spoke of her coming for the bodies of adulterers and men with evil hearts. Out of all the bodies lying in the pile, she had picked out the one who had lived a life devoted to such values. This was nature's way of ensuring they would not be buried in peace.

Fenrir and Romasanta shuddered as they stood over the broken body. It was giving off a foul smell, and Nyctimus refused to be near the heap any longer. Shifting back into a man, Romasanta disregarded the need for clothes. Instead, he grabbed a knife and pot, and went to work on the carcass before him. Digging his fingers deep, he removed the skin and pulled slabs of fat from Boreas's misconstrued body.

What are you doing, Farmer? Fenrir's curiosity was vibrating through him as he filled the pot with fat. *Do you aim to consume Boreas? If so, this is not the best part...*

Romasanta shook his head, engulfed with his labor as he poured salt into the pot and set it on hot coals. "I am making tallow, for soap."

Fenrir snorted, *This is no time to bathe, Farmer.*

Chuckling, Romasanta explained what he intended on doing with the tallow, "My dear Fenrir, you humor me at times. This soap, I will not be adding flowers to, it serves a different purpose. Instead, I will be adding Boreas's hair and slithers of skin so when I bathe with it, I will be scented the same as he. Did you not tell me Aitvaras has poor eyesight in the day?"

Excitement rattled in his core. *This is the clever man I have come to envy!*

"You do me too much honor to envy me. I am nothing but a farmer, Fenrir." With the greatest care, he cut thin, small slithers of Boreas's skin and fur, adding them to the boiling pot of fat. "I am doing this to avoid being burned alive. If it overwhelms our nose, it will fool him for sure."

Nyctimus crawled closer to Rhea, whispering to her in hopes Romasanta could not hear. "Who in the gods is he talking to?"

"Fenrir." She beamed, enjoying the interaction between man and beast. "They were cursed to share Romasanta's body."

"How do you know which one you are talking to?" Furrowing his brow, his hazel eyes seemed big against his brown wolven head. "Is there a secret to recognizing the man from the wolf?"

Sighing, Rhea watched as Romasanta hovered over the boiling pot. He was dipping out large chunks of meat that broke away from the melting fat.

She turned back to Nyctimus with a reply, "You are always talking to both."

Looking over his shoulder, Nyctimus gave a sorrowful gaze to the cursed naked man at the fire. "And I thought my curse was difficult. I am simply a man who turns into a wolf, but he is two beings..."

Satisfied he had only fat in the pot, Romasanta let it continue to simmer without his aid. Gripping the putrid corpse, he dragged it with him. Nyctimus was awed at the ease with which he shifted from human to wolf. The entire process was painful as muscles stretched and bones shattered to make room. Anyone who was near them could hear the snapping and popping of the forceful metamorphosis that took place at incredible speed. Romasanta left them at the fire as he carried the body farther away. He zig-zagged while ripping it to pieces, hoping it would prevent Ravenna from finding them before daybreak. They knew she feared the light because it made her monstrous features obvious. In darkness, she was capable of tricking many men who fell victim to her sexual exploits.

By the time he returned, Rhea and Nyctimus had fallen asleep. He removed the pot from the fire, setting it to the side to cool. Soon the tallow would rise, hardening, and then he could lather himself in it. Letting the fire dwindle to a pile of hot coals, he stared at Rhea. He could not help but wonder if she would tame Fenrir, or if she, herself, would grow wilder. She had spirit, much like Daphne, but this was not a matter of whether he could love her. This was the question of Fenrir being able to love a girl. Could the demon really understand she was fragile, despite how tall she stood against the greatest of enemies?

Shivers trickled across his skin as a breeze brushed over him. It wasn't due to the chill it brought, but the scent it had carried over. Rhea's aroma graced his nose and his chest ached. Within his soul, two forces clashed every time he caught her smell in the wind. The fragrance was soft; it made him think of the red and white dianthus that grew in the forest from time to time. Regardless of the joy it brought to take it in, it was causing chaos within him. Burning pain seared as his tidal wave of anxiety bashed into the mountain of Fenrir's compassion. These emotions were equally matched, and unless they found a way to tame these elements, it would destroy their symbiotic relationship.

The sun was peering through the trees. Over the last hours, the tallow had risen and stiffened on the top of the pot. Cutting it free, he headed to where his ears told him water was running. Splashing his face, he rejoiced in a moment of cleanliness. He was exhausted because he had too much weighing on his mind to sleep. Another round of brisk water across his skin washed away his grogginess. He sat in the stream; it barely came up to his navel. Glowering at the hunk of soap in his hand, he could only feel annoyed. His time with Fenrir had made him callous to what should have made his stomach turn. Scrubbing his skin vigorously, it foamed and lathered across him. Unlike the soap he used to make for Daphne with roses and lavender, this reeked of Boreas.

Rhea's hand touched his back. He had sensed her coming through the trees, but had ignored it. Obediently, she picked up another piece of the rancid soap and began to lather his back. Closing his eyes, he allowed himself to relish in her affectionate strokes. Fenrir's heart soared, a burning excitement welling up within them both. His muscles tensed as she flowed across the divots of his back. Fingertips stopped over the scar where the silver sword had ripped through him. Dancing over the outline, she leaned in, her lips kissing it. The soap ended the loving touch, and she continued to cover him. She washed his hair with it, circling him, paying no heed to the glare he gave her. Seeing all had been taken care of, he stood.

Rhea wrapped her arms around him, her fingers grasping at his back. Her face was buried in his chest, and Fenrir was aroused. Nuzzling him harder, her hands slid down, waving over his waist, and he gripped her arms. Cringing, she looked up to see his yellow eyes gleaming down on her. She gasped as he kissed her, pulling her back into him as his arms grabbed her.

Her lips broke free, and a tear ran down her smiling face as she whispered to him, "I am so sorry you must endure our love, Romasanta. But thank you..."

Sighing, she turned away, heading back to camp. Her gift had let her feel both of their emotions, and it had been overwhelming for her. If anyone understood the internal struggle between them, Rhea could.

Romasanta looked to the sky, dropping the soap into the stream. "Daphne, please do not shun me for all the things I must do."

The walk to the tower was a silent one. Following behind Nyctimus, they took on the roles of Boreas and his prize, Rhea. She had explained she was the daughter of a ruler in a far-off village. It was the reason she had been kept, and hunted by Boreas after her first escape. Luck was on their side as they neared the clearing, with the sun high and bright above them.

"That is him. Aitvaras." Nyctimus nodded to a large black heap of shiny scales. "He stays here day and night until Boreas returns."

"Before I go, do you know what appears only when Boreas is home?" Romasanta grunted, pleading as he asked again. "There is always a catch when gaining such a pet."

"No." Nyctimus looked ashamed for not being able to answer such a simple question. "But if I see it, I will tell you."

Snorting, Romasanta lowered the wolf-skin hood. They looked at one another, taking deep breaths to ready themselves for the encounter. He had shared what Fenrir had learned from his battles with Aitvaras in the past. The second the dragon realized he was not Boreas, they were to flee and he would serve as the wall to slow him down. Wrapping chains about

Rhea's arms, he felt Fenrir shift into an emotion of guilt. The imagery of the chains lying across the rips that had not healed yet had shaken something deep within the wolf. Romasanta gazed into Rhea's green eyes, hoping this would calm him. His concern was honorable, but there were more important matters. Focus would be needed as they attempted to trick Aitvaras.

They broke out of the trees, tall and proud in their stance. Aitvaras stirred, glowering their way, but did not seem alarmed. His large reptilian nostrils sniffed the air a few times, his tongue flickering at the air toward them. He rose on his hind legs, stretching his wings wide. Romasanta swallowed his fears at seeing the creature so close, so massive. Fenrir had kept them from hesitating, though Nyctimus had stumbled over his own feet. Glaring at the door of the tower, Romasanta chose to disregard the massive beast. The ground shook as it walked closer, the sounds of it sniffing filled the air. It was true. The red beady eyes could not see who stood before them. He had given away he was relying on his nose to tell that this was not a foe.

"Boreas! You've returned!" Aitvaras hissed, excited to see his long-lost master. "Is this the prize you have gone after when you left so many years ago?"

Romasanta froze, unsure of what to do. Boreas had conversed with the dragon and they had failed to take that into account.

Speak, Farmer! growled Fenrir as he shook in his chest. *Aitvaras is stupid and blind! Ten years is too long for him to recall Boreas's looks or voice!*

Groaning, Romasanta replied, "She is the reason I took so long, Aitvaras."

Chuckling, steam rolled between his teeth and out of his nose. "She smells like a fighter indeed! She will make for fine breeding stock."

Rhea scowled and jerked at the chains.

Huffing, he entertained the conversation further, "Let me get this wild thing inside. I wish to tame her after I've recovered from my battles."

"Yessss..." Shifting, the black dragon made the way clear for them. "Your scent shows many battles. Perhaps you should take time to wash your enemies' decay from it. Boreas, your stench even insults my nose."

Nyctimus and Romasanta burst into laughter as they walked through the tower's front gate. The soap had done far better than they could ever hope for it to do.

I wish I could kill him again. He must've made a pact with Beelzebub to return. Boreas would have traded his soul to gain such a stupid creature like Aitvaras. Pacing within Romasanta, Fenrir was annoyed by the situation. *If I get out, I will surely take him down.*

"Servants will arrive soon." Nyctimus led them to the throne room as he explained, "You must sit here, proud with Rhea at your feet. It's what he would've done and has done so many times before."

"Breeding stock." Rhea's words were sour as she shot a warning glance at Romasanta. "I am not your cow."

Fenrir chortled as Romasanta gave her a smirk. "And this all started when I lost my bull."

Nyctimus had earned their trust as servants entered the tower to continue their duties for Boreas. The sun was starting to set and Aitvaras had vanished. Strangely, as Romasanta whispered with Nyctimus, both could smell the dragon still there. Romasanta did not hear the dragon, nor feel the shaking of the ground like when they first arrived. Instead, they had the wafts of the sulfur and sour smell that always came with being a reptile.

A black cat was pacing and rubbing Romasanta's leg as he continued to accept offerings from the villagers paying for Boreas's protection. Fenrir was raging, eager to have him kick or torment the feline. Ignoring him, he continued to play the part, occasionally jerking Rhea's chains. In turn, she would frown or even spit at him. Each time, he'd laugh and scoff at her, both of them enjoying the game it had created.

"The cat." His affectionate gaze with Rhea had been broken by Nyctimus's excited whisper. "Boreas's black cat is only here when the dragon is gone."

Looking down at the cat, its red eyes glimmered in the light of the torches. Picking the feline up, it purred and snuggled into his lap to sleep. Inhaling deep and long, it was there, the scent of a dragon. Sulfur and bitter, here in Romasanta's lap was Aitvaras in the form of a black cat. He indulged in the thought and smell, a wicked grin snaking across his face. Fenrir took hold. Shifting into the versipellis, his enormous wolf's jaws scooped up the unsuspecting cat. With great pleasure, he gnawed and shook it. Still grinning, he swallowed the ravaged beast whole as the servants ran shrieking. Howling, he beamed with excitement, the dragon's blood running down his bottom jaw and chest. Joy and laughter erupted from him as he relished the flavor on his tongue and cheek.

"Fenrir." Nyctimus's voice was soft as he looked on at the humanoid wolf before him. "This is when Fenrir is in charge."

Fenrir paused, his ears flicking before his amber eyes looked down upon Nyctimus. Furrowing his brow, Fenrir understood he was acting feral in comparison to before. His heart raced as he gazed over at Rhea. Despite the blood speckling her face, her green eyes looked up at him in wonder. Crouching down, he relieved her of the chains that had upset him to see across her scarred skin. Her hands rubbed his cheek, and he sighed, his victory no longer what he wanted. Watching them, Nyctimus was starting to understand why Romasanta carried such a heavy heart. Pondering on the situation, he, too, saw the turbulent issues haunting the idea of Rhea and Fenrir's love.

"Aitvaras is gone, thank you." Fenrir broke away from Rhea, standing to tower over Nyctimus who bowed his head as he continued, "Please rest as long as you need. Gather and restock, take horses; anything here is yours."

The silence Fenrir kept was eerie, but he turned back to Rhea. Grabbing her hand, he pulled her away, wanting nothing more to do with humans and dragons. They raced out of the tower and faded into the woods. She struggled not to stumble and his heart swelled with each misstep. Picking her up, he raced into the darkness with haste. It wasn't long before they came upon a cave. Gently, he sat her down on her feet and she simply whirled around to grasp onto him. Her cheek was soft against the scar on his chest, adding to the burning he felt there. A mixture of anger, excitement, and resentment boiled and mingled as he and Romasanta struggled to untangle themselves. His tail wagged as she nuzzled harder against him.

"Do you even know who you are right now?" Rhea's voice mumbled against him, as if speaking to his heart. "Do you know which feelings are yours and his?"

"No." His voice almost failed him as he answered, "We are twisted."

Breaking away from him, her back faced him as she continued her riddles. "Is this what you want?"

With care, she slid her dress off. His amber eyes watched as she exposed her broad shoulders, her back strong as her hips appeared before him. It was as if he was watching a flower unfurl for the first time. Her dress let go of the top of her thighs, resting in a pool at her feet. Drinking in her body, he saw her for how fragile she was and how he could break her without a disciplined touch. A shiver crossed her skin, and he rushed to her. His warmth wrapped around her from behind, his claw cautious where they met her delicate skin. She leaned into him, fueling the arousal he was struggling with. No longer could he tell if he was Romasanta or Fenrir, but the boiling feelings failed to mingle together peacefully.

Eager to know more of her, his tongue raced across her shoulder and neck. Savoring her flavor, he felt intoxicated by her aroma. Fenrir nuzzled his canine head into her neck as his claws explored the soft curves of her flesh. Never had he felt so excited to touch something, someone. She was a feral beast, and she had allowed him to take whatever he desired from her.

Turning in his arms, she hugged him, whispering to him. "Do you know who you are?"

Again he replied, "No. We are twisted."

The question resonated within him and he could not tell who Romasanta or Fenrir were anymore. Shifting into Romasanta's human body added to the confusion settling in his core. Neither could pull themselves out of the other as their souls fought with their emotions.

"What have you done to us…" Bewildered, he stared into her green eyes. "I do not know which emotion belongs to me… or who *I* should be."

Romasanta and Rhea's hearts thudded loudly as they stood naked in the night air. Rhea was just as aroused as he was, but the one feeling coming from both Romasanta and Fenrir was fear. It was the terror of knowing what was to come of this union. Grabbing his jaw, she kissed him, their passion and hunger for one another encouraging them to go farther.

Releasing her kiss, she answered, "I have shown you that you are meant to be one. For tonight, be both and the same. I love you, Fenrir and Romasanta. You both need to know you are loved."

A thrilling sensation flowed through him as he pulled her to the ground. Their skin rubbing against each other was both new and familiar to him. Rhea groped at him as she pushed herself on top of him. She would not be tamed tonight. Her heart had been set on taming them;

the man and the wolf. Goading him on, she rocked in his grasp, moaning as they took one another in the darkness of the forest. Wanting to taste her, he suckled at her neck, her salty sweat fueling the pleasure he took in their unification.

"I love you, Rhea." His voice was deep, his eyes gleaming in amber as they rolled on the cave floor. "You are mine, and I am yours."

"Yes, I am yours." She arched her back as she screamed in ecstasy.

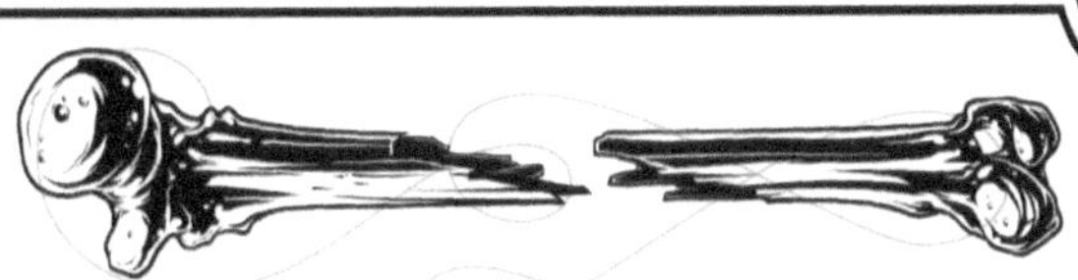

CHAPTER 9

SEVERED

It was hard to say how many years had passed by them; fifty, seventy, maybe even a hundred. The curse extended their life. At least there was something good it did for the mortal man. The older versipellis did die of natural causes eventually, and Rhea even suffered from the curse. All it took was the slightest cut for someone to fall under it. This was a burdensome fact Romasanta and Fenrir had found frustrating. Unlike he and Nyctimus, or even the Lykaons, Rhea was more wolf than human, like the others. Three nights surrounding the peak of the full moon, her ability to stay human would fail. It had taken years for her to be able to speak when she turned, but never did she get angry with them for her curse. They had both failed to acknowledge the risk and found themselves tangled as they watched her belly grow.

Rhea was with child.

Excited and frightened, they didn't think it was possible. They had lain with her so many times over the decades and assumed the curse had rendered them sterile. Romasanta's feelings often won, a terror he felt with the risk they had placed on Rhea. He and Daphne had tried for a child but were never blessed with one.

This had to be Fenrir's child.

It was strange to see how her pregnant state carried into her versipellis form. Fenrir's guilt grew more with each passing day. The once proud and mountainous demon wolf now sat next to Romasanta's own soul, as if he were a fellow man. Watching her sleep, curled on the cave floor, they were drowning in their worry. This was no place for her to have a child. Leaving her, he ran through the forest, wanting to resolve his concerns. Nyctimus was waiting for him on the cliff's side. Below them, a river twisted across the valley and the torches from a village flickered in the darkness. Romasanta crouched, looming over the scenery. He felt the burning sensation throbbing through his scar. The pain often came when he and Fenrir's feelings contradicted one another.

"Are you sure this is what you want?" Nyctimus's voice was soft and sincere. "Does she know what you plan to do?"

A heavy sigh escaped Romasanta's lips as he closed his eyes, hoping they could dam back the tears welling up in them. "Yes, this needs to happen. My list of enemies is growing with each passing year. Gaea wills us to do her work, and in turn, the world despises us. We both know this is no place for any woman to have a child…"

A howl rang out from the forest, and the nerves in Romasanta's body unraveled as he breathed whom it had come from. "Rhea!"

Both men ran at great speed in the direction of her call for help. Shifting from man to versipellis, their noses searched for an answer. Cursing himself, he and Fenrir could not still the panic in their hearts. He had been so cautious, ensuring that no one to find her or see him leave. A scent reached him. He was so close to where he had left her. The smell was a mixture of bird, snake, and human. Another hint reached him as he pushed himself to run faster.

"It's Ravenna!" Eyeing Nyctimus, he nodded.

In their silent exchange, Nyctimus knew his plan would be the same as the last time. He would distract Ravenna while Nyctimus waited for his chance to take Rhea far away. Reaching the cave, Ravenna's serpent lower half was coiled tightly around Rhea. The monster's eyes glared at Romasanta as he stood huffing, desperate to catch his breath. Unlike before, Ravenna looked gaunt and the wild look in her eyes spoke of insanity. The years had been rough on her or she had pursued him to a point of going mad with desire.

"I see." She scowled at him. "This one is yours. The rumors were true about Fenrir and his pet harlot."

Growling rolled from his muzzle as his yellow eyes flashed his rage. "Let her go, Ravenna."

"Not so easily." Hissing, she flared her needlelike teeth. "Before I release her, I want to make a trade. You owe me a trade, Fenrir!"

"Fine." He snorted, knowing she was sour about him stealing Boreas's body so long ago. "What would you trade for her life?"

Rhea struggled in Ravenna's grip. Her strength had left her weeks ago as she pushed closer to the end of her pregnancy. His child would be born soon, and it burned at his chest. If he failed to appease Ravenna long enough, Nyctimus would not be able to take Rhea to safety. Sighing, he awaited Ravenna's answer as she pulled Rhea, demanding she stay still.

"To trade places with her." Puffing her bare chest out, she smiled down at him, her wings wide. "You will bed with me until I tire of you."

"Done." Snarling, he gazed into Rhea's eyes. "I'll trade. Now let her go."

"Not yet." She jeered, her great wings dragging her and Rhea to him. "I want her to watch. See you with me, like I've watched so many others."

His lip curled as she drew closer. "Ravenna, you've lost your mind. Let her go."

"I will squeeze her to death if you don't comply." The darkness in her eyes reflected the irrationality in her mind.

Looking away from Rhea, he allowed himself to turn human. He felt ashamed, standing naked and powerless in front of the monster named Ravenna. This was a time he felt at his lowest, just like the day Daphne had sacrificed herself to save his life. The muscles in his body tensed, his left shoulder twitching in response to the boiling regret. Reluctantly, he stared down at Rhea with his amber eyes shining in the cold night. The green in her eyes wavered as tears fell. Her compassion was the only piece of humanity she had maintained. Alone, he would have gone wild; a feral, rabid beast would have stalked the forest here. Taking in a deep breath, he reassured himself Nyctimus was still lying in wait, his scent thick behind the trees. Rhea nodded, a sign of acceptance and knowing her help was within reach.

His gaze shifted, staring at her swollen belly being squeezed tighter. Desperately, he reached out, grabbing Ravenna and pressing his lips to hers. Her grip loosened, encouraging him to continue his angry lust. Romasanta kissed and suckled her neck and shoulder as Ravenna moaned. Folding her wings, she pressed her weight against him. Using the moment, he allowed himself to fall back, to have her in his arms, as he worked his way to her breast like a ravenous babe.

"Fenrir!" Exhaling in pleasure, Ravenna released Rhea as Fenrir's tongue graced her nipple.

Romasanta felt her tail twisting around his waist and legs. A flash of hazel eyes let him know Nyctimus had succeeded in his task. Satisfied they had gone far enough away, he worked his kissing back to Ravenna's neck. Her skin was cold and clammy, unlike the warmth and gentle folds of his dear Rhea. Another groan of exhilaration escaped Ravenna's lips.

"Do you enjoy this?" The words were angry as he whispered them into her ear. "Is this what you have longed for?"

"Yes, yes!" Wings lay around them. She had let all of her defenses go. "I want to feel more of you!"

"As you desire, Ravenna." A wicked fanged grin crawled across his face. "I shall give you more of me."

Claws gripped into her wings, crushing the bones with ease. Shrieking, she attempted to slither away, releasing his legs. Pouncing on her, he took pleasure in ripping into her delicate, feathered appendages. The wailing escaping her spurred his rage and excitement. Emerging before her was the versipellis. Drool dripped from his fanged mouth as he growled and roared over her. Horror filled her at the realization of what her wrong-doing had led to; she had unleashed something horrible and animalistic in him.

"No one threatens me in my territory!" he barked. Foaming drool slapped across her terrified face. "You are mine and you will feel death by my fangs!"

Gasping was all she managed before his teeth clenched over her neck. Pain erupted through her. She gurgled as a popping sensation set her free. Like a wild animal, he tore and shook at her flesh. Ripping and dragging her apart. All his frustrations, ire, and humanity were leaving him with each mouthful he devoured. No longer did he want to face the troubles of what it meant to be a man. Fenrir and Romasanta together wanted to return to what it meant to be free and wild; to simply be the wolf. They bellowed out to the night sky, steam churning as it escaped from his bloodied mouth.

Rhea would be taken to the village in the safety of the valley. Nyctimus, who had dissolved the Lykaon bloodline as promised, had the task of watching over her and the child. As they grew old, he would never age. Romasanta could feel in his gut he had become immortal.

He watched all the decades float by him while Rhea aged. She may have grown older slower than a normal human, but he had not changed since the day Merlin's evil magic had melded his soul to Fenrir's. His memories of Artemis and Daphne were dulling, growing stale in his mind. No longer did he get the waves of anxiety at the thought of his lost love. All he could cling to was serving his purpose and hunting for the stone taken from him. Until that day came, he would remain the wolf. Artemis would send him the tools he would need to achieve his goals.

With each hunt Gaea instilled in their nature, with each creature they devoured on command, their enemies grew in numbers. It was no longer about keeping his humanity, but doing what was necessary to survive. He had lost his grip on the cursed ones, and they spread their disease farther than he had reached. They would become disposable to him. No longer did Fenrir wish to have a pack. Their souls tangled, twisted together; they yearned for solitude. Traveling far from the village Rhea would call home, he lost himself to the hunt.

The years floated by, and he did not care to fret over it as he had done before. He rarely allowed himself to become human. It served as a means of trickery for his prey. With the overabundance of feral packs of versipellis, he was often mistaken as the same thing. Demons were becoming more abundant as the times grew darker around him. Watching from the shadows, he learned all he could of this world of predator and prey. No matter who, or what, he faced, he would maintain himself as the top predator. A whistle rang out over the forest; someplace close by someone was calling their trained pack of versipellis back to them.

"Mutt, why do you not come when your master bids it so?" A man's voice interrupted Romasanta's thoughts as he crouched, eating a deer. "Does your stomach yell louder than my voice?"

Flicking his ears, he peered over his shoulders at the mysterious man, who smelled of dead flesh and cold blood. This was a new creature he had encountered recently. They called themselves the strigoi, or as the humans referred to them, vampires. Snorting, he went back to his meal, his teeth gnashing at bones and he suckled the marrow from them.

"I command you, heel!" The strigoi glowered at him as Romasanta once more disregarded him. "Stop eating! Damn you, the sun will rise!"

Licking the blood from his muzzle, Romasanta looked up at the night sky. Thinking over the strigoi, he speculated they were a perversion of his curse. The mutation of the curse had brought the dead back, which fed on the living to continue their immortality. Merlin's magic reached far and wide through Romasanta, turning and distorting nature itself. Romasanta sniffed the air; it was the first time a first descendant of this new demon had ever approached him. There in the creature's scent was a small hint of the Lykaon's bloodline. Another inhale told him more; his nose was stronger after years of devoting himself to being an animal and not a man. Lykaons with second- or third-generation versipellis curse was what the aroma told him. This man was ill while cursed as a versipellis and after dying, he returned as a strigoi.

Weak against sunlight, they kept to the shadows of the night. An interesting thing he had noticed was how the strigoi could command the cursed ones. It was assumed the cursed ones were more human than wolf and the magic connected them just enough to control the versipellis. Regardless, he was alpha to the pack and if it came down to it, his will would become theirs. Anything he asked of them, they did so without hesitation and with great pleasure to serve their master, the father of werewolves.

"I will only command you one more time." The vampire sneered at him. "Heel."

Grunting, Romasanta laid his ears flat on his head. Crawling on all fours, he growled at the vampire, who stood unmoved. Pausing in front of the pale dead thing, he stood, gigantic in comparison, both in height and bulk. The vampire swallowed, realizing he had mistaken the demon before him as a normal werewolf. The strigoi whistled, his eyes wide, as he looked up at Romasanta. Half a dozen werewolves came panting to the vampire's side. Barking and snarling at Romasanta as they made a wall of protection around their master.

His ears high, Romasanta snorted at the way this strigoi used these humans. They may treat them like dogs, but he would never forget these were once people. It seemed the more feral the werewolf, the more wolf they became, never changing back to human again. Sadly, all of these had lost their ability to be human. The yellow glow of his gaze brought them to silence, and they whimpered. Their master had lost his dominance over them with just one glare from Romasanta.

"Devour your so-called master." The vampire's eyes grew wide as fangs snatched him up at Romasanta's command. "And when you are done with him. Devour one another so none will remain. Consider this a blessing to end your curse."

The bickering and snarling went on for some time as he finished feasting on the deer. There was no sympathy or guilt for what he had asked them to do. They were tearing each other apart, wild and fierce. Each was happy and eager to do what they had been asked to do by Romasanta. A heavy sigh escaped his chest as he checked to see if all were dead. One wheezed, his chest ravaged as his broken ribs dug deep into his lungs. Without hesitation, he gripped the fellow werewolf's neck. It was effortless as he ripped out his throat to finish off the last life remaining. At least these versipellis had been spared from continuing life as feral dogs serving a lowly demon.

Screams cried out in the distance and the smell of men, blood, and fire told him something foul was in motion. His instincts stirred, pushing for him to see what chaos ravaged the nearby Sabine village. These were people who had survived Boreas's exploits, and he had grown fond of them. Without a doubt, they were the same people Rhea had once lived among before he pulled her into his curse. Shaking off the memory of her green eyes, he raced through the forest with haste. Flames whipped high in the air as the smoke stung his nose. Men were injured and dying along the path where horse tracks and scents of metal and leather were left behind. Ignoring the villagers who squealed and sobbed at his demonic appearance, he chased after the aroma of horses. His curiosity was peaked by the scent of Sabine females with bronze-covered men. By the time he had caught sight of the backside of the horses, the sun had risen higher than the forest trees.

Sitting in the dark shade, he panted in the heat of the day. They had slowed their gait as they drew near city walls. Groaning, he wished to go no farther, but the burning in his chest insisted he investigate further. At first, he was reluctant to shift into a man. The shuddering and rattling in his chest let him and Fenrir know they were being called upon to do their work inside the city walls. Who or what they would be pitched against did not matter. He was Alpha.

CHAPTER 10

HOUSE OF ROMULUS

The people of the city moved away from him as he walked the streets with authority. Whispers tickled at his ears as they called him the wolf-man, and he smirked each time he heard it. Adorning his wolf-skin hood, he took his time learning the layout of this strange world of paths trapped within walls. Sniffing and searching, he caught a hint of the stolen Sabine women from the village. They took them down the main path leading to where the leaders of this city resided. It annoyed him being around so many people in such a little piece of land.

The sight of the children and their mothers made his skin crawl. Rubbing the burning in his chest, he pushed back the guilt and regret. In order to protect Rhea, he had to give up his humanity. He became an animal, the lone wolf, so he would never have to face coming home to a slaughter. Ravenna had been the piercing point to the sharp-edged sword of enemies he had faced since then.

Something small bounced off his leg.

Pausing, he stared down at a small girl who looked at him in wonder. He could see himself in her big brown eyes. Losing himself in the reflection, he no longer looked like the man he once was. Dirty and rough, he had grown taller somehow and the muscles covering him were twice as thick as he had recalled. The farmer from the past had been taken over by the warrior. Tears danced in those tiny eyes as her mother scooped her up. Fear wafted from them both, earning a grunt from him as he continued his march toward the scent of interest. The street was growing more vacant as he trailed onward. It wasn't long before he was greeted by guards, leather- and bronze-clad men with spears and shields.

"Who are you?" bellowed the larger man, who smelled of wine and sweat. "You can't just march into the king's house like you own it."

They laughed but soon fell silent as Romasanta's dark eyes glared at them. "I wish to talk to your king. It is concerning the Sabine women he's taken into his house."

The guards gritted their teeth. "He does what he will with them. If you intend to free them, we will kill you right here."

"Is that so?" Romasanta snorted, a smirk sliding across his face over the empty threat. "I see you will not allow me to go farther. Just tell your king that I will see him before I leave this place."

Before they could register what he meant, he had walked away. Night was nearing and then he would have the advantage over the men who filled the city. As he wandered the streets, he noticed a queer thing about the population here. It was in the air, here inside these walls lived very few females, though the ones he had seen on the streets were healthy and fruitful with children. This must be the reason they were seeking the Sabine's females. It was the same principle between wolf packs, but it made him unsteady over the fact they would not compete for the women's affection.

"Dammit!" A keg of wine slammed the ground nearby and rolled in his direction. "Wa-watch out!"

A well-placed foot stopped it with ease as Romasanta furrowed his brow at the man. "Is this yours?"

"Y-yes." Rubbing sweat from his forehead, the man looked up at him. "Thank you! You saved my skin. I need to load this in my wagon."

Without further prompt from the man, Romasanta lugged the barrel up into his arms and placed it in the wagon with ease. "This wagon?"

The small man's mouth gaped, and it took him a moment to gather his thoughts. "Yes! Are you looking for work? I could use a helper today to deliver these to the king's house."

Giving him a toothy grin, Romasanta shook the man's hand. "I am new in the city and have no money. It would be my honor to serve the king in such a way."

"Thank the gods for sending such a strong lad to help me!" Waving him over, he revealed the three other large caskets of wine needing to be loaded. "After you get these on the wagon, we'll head over and join the feast! They just brought us more women and we are celebrating tonight."

"So there is a lack of females here?" Eyeing the man over his shoulder, he lifted another barrel. "I thought it seemed odd for so few women to be in the market."

"Our great city will die if we do not find women to help us thrive. What good is such a grand place if we have no sons to give it to?" He had a grave look as he spoke of the city's problem. "So Romulus and Remus have promised to bring us women, and by the gods, they have!"

Romasanta remained silent as he loaded the last wine barrel. The man was excited to be heading to the king's house with a helper who could lift such weight. By the time the wagon met the front entrance, the guards had switched shifts. They were eager to see the load of wine, and without further questions, waved them inside. He unloaded the barrels, finishing the work as promised. This gave him time to observe the people there in the house of the king. The celebration was at its peak and many were drunk from feasting all day. He seemed invisible to the men here, but the Sabine women saw him. Their eyes were big as he stalked through the trees of flesh that swayed in their drunken state. Childhood stories had told them about the versipellis, the werewolf haunting the forest they called home. Their whispers to one another were words of confusion as to why such a wild beast would be there within those walls.

They had been washed, and given clothes, food, gold, and anything else they desired. None wore chains on their wrist, but guards surrounded them. Men were allowed to greet them, perhaps as a way to encourage them to meet and marry the men of this great city. There was one woman who came and went from the group. Upon the anxious shifts of the group, she had rushed back over. It was clear she had been in the city far longer than the group she mothered.

"What is the matter?" Concerned, she saw they had become nervous about something. "Who has disturbed you?"

One girl whispered her fear, her eyes never breaking from his dark gaze. "The father of versipellis is here."

Her breath caught in her throat, her turn slow and elegant as she dared herself to look where the group watched. Romasanta had weaved through the crowd and bowed at her feet. He had watched servants approach her in this manner in the time he had been there in the house and saw it as a non-threatening motion. With the wolf skin across his back, it looked as if a wolf had come to bow to her in servitude. Silence remained as hearts raced and fear filled the air about him. Looking up, more gasps rang out as his dark eyes turned golden.

"I have come to assist the women who were taken from the forest." Deep, stern words flowed from him and they looked at one another, surprised. "Your fears as to who I am are not mistaken. Bowing before you is the father of werewolves."

The woman regained her commanding aura as she spoke to him. "And what if they do not wish to return to their villages in the forest?"

"Then they can stay," he scoffed, frustrated to be bending his instincts in such a way. "But the spirits have sent me here for a reason."

"Remus." Her voice was barely audible as she whispered to the wolf at her feet. "Romulus can be a good man, but Remus, he is cruel and takes pleasure in terrible things. This brother prefers pillaging the women, but I can persuade Romulus to make a peaceful truce. Remus will be the death of us all."

With that, he left them, fading into the crowd and no longer visible to any of the women who had watched him so intensely. It was alarming to see even those who stood guard had taken their fill of wine. No one had enough focus to distinguish whether he was dressed in celebration or an intruder. Tiring of dodging the falling and stumbling men about him, he settled for a dark corner where two men were raised higher than those around them. The woman from before approached the one man, who sat in his chair with a stern look and a golden goblet in his hand. She whispered something to him and he smirked. The other man sat on the ground, groping two women as he sang loud, slurring the lyrics as his wine sloshed out of his cup. One of the girls was just as intoxicated as he was, but the other girl was upset. She had been with the new group; Romasanta could smell the village on her still, and she pushed the man's hands off her. Romulus disregarded his brother's squandering as he continued to whisper with the lady of his house.

The night was starting to end, birds were singing of the sun's next coming outside. Romasanta was running low on patience. Crouched in a dark corner, the house had emptied and the lady had left Romulus with a smile. Remus took the sober girl in his arms, fondling her like one would scrub a stain from a cloth. Like any cornered animal, she bit him and started to flee. Gripping her arm, he backhanded her face, and she fell. Blood dripped onto the floor. Each tap against the marble floors drummed loudly in Romasanta's ears. The smell of her blood invaded his nose, his teeth ground, and his muscles became taut. Remus stumbled toward where she cried. He lifted his foot, aiming to continue her unjust punishment.

Devour him, Fenrir's voice rattled, resonating with the same ire boiling in Romasanta. *He will pay!*

Romasanta's speed did not register to the drunk he now grasped by the throat. Lifting Remus high as he stood guard over the girl at his feet, Romasanta snarled. A goblet was rolling to a pause as Remus kicked his feet, desperate to breathe. Romulus had a dagger at Romasanta's throat, digging hard enough for him to feel the warm line of blood crawling down his neck. His amber eyes glowered at Romulus. The girls had squealed and fled. They stood in their stalemate for several minutes before one of them broke the silence.

"He will die here." Romasanta's words were cold. "Nothing good will come of him if he lives. This is why the spirits have willed me to be here."

"Who are you?" Swallowing, Romulus questioned the fearless man at the end of his blade. "He is my twin brother. Do you not know who we are?"

"None of that matters." Remus's movements were slowing as he gagged in his hand. "You cannot stop m—"

Romulus shifted, his weight ready to slit Romasanta's throat. Dropping Remus, Romasanta gripped Romulus's wrist. The dagger dropped; its clattering on the floor echoed throughout the building. They glowered at one another, frozen in this state, while Remus wheezed and coughed.

"Let go of me." A smirk came to Romasanta's face to see someone so daring to speak in such a tone to him. "Did the Sabine send you?"

Romasanta let go of Romulus; neither would break the locked gaze on one another. "No. I came on my own. No one commands me, but Gaea's will."

"Gaea?" Romulus blinked, pondering a moment before he spoke again. "She is nothing but a fairytale."

Romasanta frowned and deep inside him, he remembered the glow of the Eye of Gaea. "I wish it had been a story."

RAAAAAAGH!

Remus roared, charging toward Romasanta with Romulus's dagger in hand. The blade ripped through muscles, grinding between ribs. Confused by the lack of reaction, Remus looked up at Romasanta's monstrous wolf's head. No longer was his opponent a large man, but the father of werewolves had revealed his true form. Remus was still gripping the dagger, his shock paralyzing him. Romasanta growled down at Remus, drool raining down on him. Claws snatched the hair on his head, lifting him free of the floor. Too terrified to scream, Remus looked into the rage-filled golden eyes of the wolf in front of him. Romulus had stammered backward, befuddled at the speed of the mutation which had taken place before him.

Romasanta was swift as his great jaws wrapped around Remus's throat and ripped it from him. Blood filled his senses, and he dropped Remus, backing away as the information flooded him. Tangling together, both Fenrir and Romasanta fell to their knees as horror and panic filled them. Staring at the mangled body of Remus, tears fell from his wolven eyes.

How did we not see it? Fenrir whispered as they struggled to keep themselves from tangling deep in Romasanta's soul. *What manner of task has Gaea given me to do such a thing?*

"REMUS!" Romulus crawled to his brother's bleeding body, tears running down his face. "What have you done?! You drunken fool!"

Claws clacked on the marble floor as Nyctimus raced toward the massacre. "No! I was too late!"

"Why didn't I smell it?" Romasanta looked at Nyctimus, who panted from his excursion. "Not one inkling that, that he was mine."

Nyctimus joined them as he fell to the floor, exhausted. "The spirits taunt you the most, Romasanta. My own distraction is surely part of it all..."

"Ro-Romasanta?" Romulus looked over at the two wolf-like monsters before him. "My mother, she spoke of you often before she was captured and killed."

Romasanta leaned forward, no longer able to sit up as he took all his humanity back in. Romulus's words burned at him, *...mother... captured and killed.* Fenrir now knew the pain which ravaged Romasanta so long ago when he lost Daphne. Punching the floor, he roared and sobbed. He had left Rhea to a horrible fate, and worse, he had not learned he had fathered *twin* boys. Nyctimus had sensed something was not right, but could not stop the inevitable. This had been the will of Gaea and her so-called justified nature.

"How much more will I need to sacrifice?" Romasanta screamed to the spirits, his sorrow drowning him all over again as he howled on. "Now you have me taking the lives of those I hold close! Does this humor you, spirits? How long will you make me live before I will be allowed my peace?"

Nyctimus shifted back to his human form as he watched the painful task of Romasanta becoming a man at heart again.

"Uncle?" Romulus was filled with sorrow and confusion; his father's bloodline unfolding before him. "So it was true. Rhea was a she-wolf..."

Nyctimus answered in a silent glare before looking back at Romasanta. "And your father, a cursed man."

Clawing at his own head, he shook all over. The scar on his chest felt like it was melting into him again as he allowed himself to remember. Artemis had not sent the tools he needed, and he had outlived generations of men. Daphne was nothing more than a tree, still. Worse, he had absorbed, no, given himself to his animal side. He had done this so deeply, he had failed to hunt for information about Merlin or Gaea. And then, Remus...

"I've failed her. All these wasted years..." Changing back to a man, Romasanta fell to his side, the dagger still deep in his ribs. "And I can't die. I can't age. There is no peace for me. I only have my impossible tasks..."

"I am sorry, Romasanta." It was comforting to hear Nyctimus's voice. "What good am I to you if I have failed you so much? I, too, thirst for death, my friend. Perhaps this was our flaw?"

Walking over, Nyctimus pulled the blade from Romasanta's side. He handed it to Romulus, his hazel eyes sad and affectionate. "There is much for you to talk about. I will miss Remus, but his mess will come back to bite you and your city."

Romasanta spent several weeks with Romulus, retelling how he met Rhea and their life together. As a parting gift, he bestowed Boreas's silver sword to him. It was a reminder of the past and background Romulus had recovered through Romasanta. After much discussion, Romasanta shared his concerns about the feral versipellis who ravaged the land. Romulus proposed he and his army train to take out werewolves and demons. With the current increase of the non-human population, it seemed appropriate for Romulus to bear this weight while growing his great city with survivors.

If Artemis had failed to make him tools, then Romasanta would provide his own. After Romulus made peace with the Sabine, he would begin training future generations in the art of slaying the versipellis, strigoi, and other demons. It would be Romasanta and Nyctimus's task to bring back information on the monsters they had slain. With this insight and experience, the mortal man could gain the advantage against beasts and demons. The head of the Romulus house would carry Boreas's silver sword in honor of Romulus and his bloodline of the wolf, Fenrir. Confident his remaining son could protect himself, it was time Romasanta started his search for the stone, Merlin, and Gaea.

Romasanta and Nyctimus split ways, each searching and seeking information and clues. Romasanta's attempts with shamans and witches had failed. His new aim was the creatures, monsters, even gods, dwelling in the world. Ravenna seemed tame compared to some of the demons he discovered. He adapted to the challenges, taking in all the information he could. Fenrir's want to be alpha did not recede, and gave him the advantage of seeing the caste system of demons. He was climbing the tiers of this caste with alarming speed thanks to its dependencies on power and age. Many names were given to him as he went about hunting these other monsters. *Ancient One* was growing in popularity, but he ignored it. Titles meant nothing in the changing tide of time.

Years, decades, even centuries were passing him by and he watched as man changed. No longer was the land scattered with villages, but great cities with stone walls were taking over. Within these fortresses were powerful men who commanded many other men and women. It was as if the land were scattered with large packs of wolves. Like the wolf, territories were crossing paths which led to violent wars. Many of the fields no longer bore the beauty of flowers, but held the final outcome of the territory wars of men. It was more common to come to a clearing and find piles of the dead and dying. It was a breeding ground for the worst demons and gods, the ones who took pride in pestilence.

A peculiar scent caught him as he raced through the remnants of a battlefield. Foul, it mixed many scents into one; dog, crow, human, lizard. Romasanta found the scent confusing, but it piqued his curiosity and he aimed in its direction. It was a creature he had not faced before and could, perhaps, provide him with information. Leaping over a pile of rotting corpses, he found the owner of this new scent. The body of a woman, the head of a dog, the feet of a crow, and the tail of a dragon greeted his eyes. This was not a demon. Here sat the Queen of Pestilence, an ancient god from a forgotten time. She enjoyed wallowing in filth, disease, and worse, stealing newborns from mothers who were dying from childbirth.

"A demi-goddess?" He crouched before her as she stared down at him as he addressed her. "May I know your name, goddess?"

Looking over the intruder, her muzzle curling into a smile, pleased by the greeting. "I am the demi-goddess Lamashtu."

Romasanta observed what she held in her hands; it was a suckling baby in her arms. "A child?"

"Oh?" As if it had escaped her mind, she looked at her arms holding the baby suckling at her breast. "This? I stole him from the possessed sorceress. Beelzebub is an annoyance, and he wanted this child so badly. I took it for myself just to cross him."

Over the decaying bodies and the demi-goddess, he could not smell anything strange about the baby. "Do you plan on raising it as your own?"

Laughter erupted from her. "No."

"Then what do you plan on doing with it?" Furrowing his brow, he was unsure of what he would do with the answer. "Will you eat it?"

"No." Sighing, she pulled the baby from her breast, lying it on the ground in the hands of a decaying corpse. "It's quite boring to me now. You can eat it."

She stood and walked aimlessly away. Her mannerisms were odd, as if she were sleepwalking in a dreamland. A demi-goddess of her caliber was left out of the pyramid of power he was included in. There was no way to kill whatever she was, nor was there any understanding of what provoked her to do anything. Snorting, he looked back to the crying babe. Hints of red hair graced its head and the desperation of its naked state in the bony rotten hand pulled at him. Sniffing at the air, searching for the closest man or woman, he caught a scent that made him smile. It was an exciting smell and his hair prickled and his blood rushed.

"You are fortunate." Relieved, he found a more suitable cloth to wrap the baby in and placed him in a more visible spot. "My kin is coming this way. He has suffered much and is the last of my son's grandchildren's lineage. Perhaps you can renew the task of being my demon slayer."

Leaving the baby behind, he spooked the old knight's horse in its direction. By the time he calmed his mare, he could hear the crying baby. Turning his horse, the old knight marveled at the corpse that held the tiny red-haired baby. Without hesitation, the knight took the baby into his arms, shushing it. In an instant, he set the horse for home to the House of Romulus. Satisfied with this, Romasanta turned his focus back to the next trade town, where rumors awaited him.

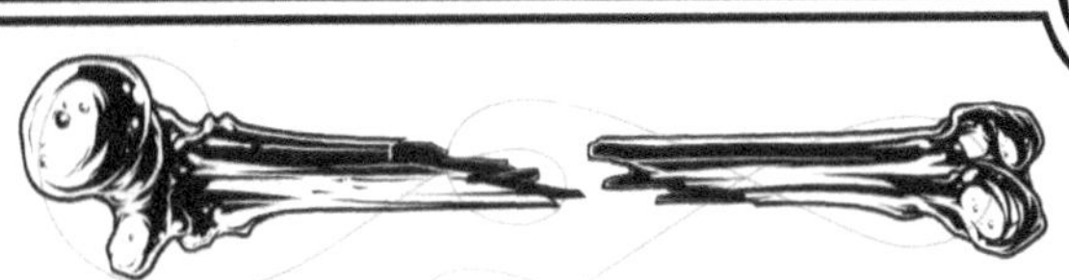

CHAPTER 11

THE TEASE

The world of man was evolving ever faster as the decades rolled past Romasanta. There had been leaps and bounds in science and medical treatment; even religion and politics had advanced. Yet, war was a constant in human life, along with the waves of pestilence brought on by man and demon alike. Within the cities, a new order had risen that blended science and magic together. These men called themselves alchemists and were joining his hunt for the stone. He was still unsure about the decision to spread the rumors of the *philosopher's stone,* but he needed more eyes and ears.

Despite their efforts, he and Nyctimus had little information about Gaea or Merlin. It was a desperate move, but taking the stone from a man would be far easier. Changing the name was his way of tracking where the information might be coming from. He was in a vast city, which one, he could not say; they were all the same to him. Each place he visited was cultured in different languages, customs, and looks. At its core, it was a place full of men in his mind.

Rumors had come to him that someone here in this city knew something about the stone. The frustrating thing about these alchemists was their habit of going by the name of Hermes. Every one of them was part of a secret order that developed sometime after the third century. As time poured into the tenth and eleventh centuries, they had a member in every major city. Romasanta grabbed a young boy, handed him coins, and pled with him in the back alley.

"Is there a man here who goes by Hermes?" The boy shifted as he looked at the coins in his hand. "A man who makes smoke and fire from nothing? Practices the most horrible smelling magic?"

Furrowing his brow, the boy nodded. "Yes! He lives in the smaller tower near the lord's own!"

"Thank you!" Dropping more coins in the boy's hand, Romasanta shooed him off.

He had learned the hard way to not smell for an alchemist. They tampered with mixing and heating the most destructive scents he had ever experienced. It made him long for the smell of Aitvaras's sulfur. Snaking through the streets, he spotted the tower with its owner at the door, key in hand. Smirking, he rushed across the busy street and pushed himself onto the old man. The alchemist found himself swiftly put into his own home; the door slamming behind the stranger who had helped him there.

"Who in God's name!" The old alchemist spun about and was greeted by Romasanta's towering build. "You!"

"I see my reputation is becoming common knowledge for the members of the Golden Dawn." Grinning, he awaited the Alchemist's reply.

"Romasanta, you are sly and we would give anything to gain the elixir of life from you." The alchemist snorted, waving Romasanta in, and offering him a chair as the alchemist dug a book out from under a stack of notes. "I see you caught wind of my rumor?"

"Yes, but I wish you all held your own names." Grunting, Romasanta sat down, wanting to hear what the old man had found for him. "Tell me, Hermes, what leads have you gained in this new city?"

"Lillith," he breathed, sliding the book over to him. "She has been seen here many times. The queen of succubi might know something of use to you, since her kind has been here since the beginning of mankind. Even the Bible whispers her name."

"Succubi?" Leaning onto his knees, he recalled all that he had devoured and fought. "I don't think I know what this creature is..."

"They are clever creatures. It says in this book that the queen succubus and her counterpart, King Incubus Boto, have held the top of the demon hierarchy since they came into existence. Unlike other demons, these feed off pleasure and desires of the flesh." Pointing at a paragraph, he explained, "They do not eat or drink. Simply, aroused men or women, and perhaps other beings, give off the energy they need. Strangely, it seems to me they are not known as killers, but I do not know any more than what is written here. It claims both are immortal and undying demons."

"May I have this book?" Standing, Romasanta stretched his muscles, ready to run free of the city and its walls. "Or does this have an owner?"

"Take it!" Hermes was shoving the book in his hands and eagerly shoving him toward the door. "Be gone and do not come back until you have a clue for me involving the philosopher's stone!"

The door slammed behind him as he returned to the bustling street. He smirked as he headed out of the city with a clue to chase after. At night, most of these places closed massive gates; a means of protecting them from the evil growing in numbers in the forest around them. Placing the book in a satchel, he picked up his pace to leave the range of human eyes. Traveling as the versipellis, or werewolf, had proven the most efficient means for him. Never had a horse kept up to the speeds he had found himself enjoying.

It was a growing hobby, collecting tomes and books on demons and tales. They were proving their weight in gold. The House of Romulus had built a massive library for him to keep them all in, and it proved a valuable resource for his kin. First, he would take this one there for safekeeping, seeing as it was a rare find. The current Lord Romulus had done a fine job making his home and village a training hub for battling demons and monsters. The demon-hunting rangers were favored, their leader a mysterious ebony-skinned woman they simply called Lady Ranger Ann. Seeing her brought back fond memories of Artemis before she was given the task of a head shaman. The way she had mastered the bow resonated with the level of skill his sister held, besting any man who challenged her.

A howling rang out, and he knew Nyctimus was near. It was rare for them to cross paths. It gave him great joy to be in the company of his friend, who also found himself unpleasantly immortal. Neither of them understood why the curse had worked so differently with Nyctimus over everyone else. They assumed it was due to the Lykaon magic in his blood. He had carried a dormant variant that had protected him in a strange way. It hadn't turned him like the others, but it changed him. He would have died after the beating Arcas and Boreas had given him. Even then, being left in the state he was in would have been the death of a normal man.

Conceivably, his near-death experience triggered a secret within the dormant magic. It would be natural for there to be an offensive and defensive version. The dormant defensive bloodline must be an extremely rare occurrence, since they were either born with or without it. In all the centuries, they had not come across another who had the magic pulsing through them, yet lacked the ability to use it. The magic in Nyctimus worked as a shielding mechanism. It required just the right interference of physical and offensive magic for it to blossom in a unique form. Nyctimus still could not decide if his bloodline was a blessing or a curse.

"Nyctimus!" he bellowed as they hugged each other. "It's been too long, my friend!"

"Aye!" He chuckled, both of them with wagging tails. "Let us sit and enjoy the setting sun together. I have some news!"

"It seems we both have information." Romasanta's muzzle curved awkwardly into a grin, flashing his fangs. "What have you discovered?"

"There is talk that a sorceress carries a red gemstone." His tone was stern as he spoke. "She uses it to conduct powerful magic using the dark arts against magical beings with no recoil."

The hair on Romasanta's neck and back raised in hearing this. "The Eye of Gaea has resurfaced."

Swallowing, Nyctimus continued, "They also say she is protected by the head demon."

"And who is at the top of this pyramid?" Memories of the stone made him rub at his scar as he absorbed the information Nyctimus had brought to him. "Who is the alpha in this demonic hierarchy we find ourselves in?"

"King Incubus Boto," whispered Nyctimus. His tail started to wag and his hazel eyes sparkled with a sense of pride. "It seems that you're also on this top tier."

"Is that so? As Fenrir or Romasanta?" His ears laid flat on his head, furrowing his brow as he weighed himself against his inner demon. "I don't understand how I have been included on a list I know little about."

"The top is Boto, then it is Lillith, and after that, it is the one they call the Ancient One." Pointing at Romasanta, Nyctimus chuckled. "The Ancient One has been here for a long time, influencing the will of man and striking fear in their hearts in the form of a black wolf. They whisper he is the father of werewolves. Is that not you, Romasanta?"

Snorting, he pushed Nyctimus's hand down. "Yes, that's me. I thought they would stop calling me that, but instead, it has become branded in the hearts of demons. How annoying..."

"Have you encountered an incubus or succubus, Master Romasanta?" Lying back, Nyctimus watched as the lavender sky gave way to a dark blue color. "I did once. She was part succubus, but there was something peculiar about how her power worked. They suffer much like we do; raw and animalistic. Most of their actions are instinctual..."

Romasanta watched the sorrow in his eyes as he recalled this girl. "I cannot say I have or haven't faced one."

"They can make you feel the most amazing pleasure. Even replace pain with the most breathtaking desire and arousal." Sighing, Nyctimus closed his eyes, shuddering as he recalled a distant memory. "They say once you have lain with one that it can spoil a man's soul. I have to admit, it's true. Never have I achieved the ecstasy I experienced with her."

"And what happened to this halfling?" Romasanta recalled the scripture, becoming curious about exactly how undying those beasts were. "Did she die?"

"Yes." Eyeing Romasanta, Nyctimus looked broken. "I had caught wind that you were headed to Rome where Romulus and Remus were, so I was not with her. They say a great winged beast came down from the sky and slaughtered her. It was a fate she had told me would eventually come, if Boto would discover her whereabouts."

"I see... we both had our hearts ripped from us that year... Why does Boto hunt his own kind so harshly?" Romasanta's interest was gaining about these strange new demons. "This seems excessive."

"She says only they can kill one another." Sitting up, Nyctimus gazed off into the trees now covered in the night sky. "Never did I figure out why, but from our experiences, I can only assume it's something in the blood."

"Let us break ways." Romasanta helped Nyctimus to his feet. "I must get this tome back to Williamsburg."

Once more, they embraced in a hug and silently went their separate ways. Romasanta's thoughts were doing their best to piece together his existing knowledge with this new information. The crescent moon rose high over the forest as he raced through the trees. His muscles were happy to stretch and burn as he twisted through the forest. When Hermes had pointed to the page, Romasanta had caught a glimpse of a line that stated how to summon a succubus. When he got back to the library, he would have enough time to read what stipulations were needed to summon such a powerful demon more carefully on. It seemed natural for men to be greedy enough to want to call forth a master of lust to give them their desires for the flesh. How could anything possibly increase the sensation of arousal?

"How does one summon Lillith..." Mumbling under his breath, it felt strange he had never encountered her, but he humored the idea of a sex demon, "Where would I find this queen succubus? The whore house? I haven't lain with anyone since I left Rhea... I want Lillith to come to me and—"

Crraaaasssssshhhh!

Something smashed through the trees above him. He leaped back as great bat-like wings blocked the way he was aiming to go. Growling, he readied for battle as he crouched on all fours. The demon standing before him was tall, and a tail swished about behind it. There was a long pause before the wings folded and the curled ram's horns on its head could be seen on its silhouette, one broken. Chainmail clattered as it bent down, picking something off the ground.

"It finally broke all the way." Scoffing, she dropped the object again, her red eyes peering in his direction. "Is this some sort of joke? I thought someone powerful called my name? Perhaps Boto fucked me too hard last time..."

Romasanta observed her hourglass-shaped gray body, the demonic feet much like a gargoyle's, and claws to match as she scowled at him. She had placed a hand on her hip as she glowered at him, waiting on a response from him.

"Werewolf, did you whisper my name?" Sighing, she sat on a nearby boulder. "Do you even know who I am? Who you whispered your want for?"

"Lillith." He mused as he stood on two feet; taking in her scent sent shivers of arousal across him. "The queen of succubi."

"And who are you?" She started to relieve herself of her chainmail top and skirt, which had done very little to cover her breasts and body. "Your whisper tells me you are high on the hierarchy, which means you are of the greatest interest to me as well. What is your name, dog?"

"I am Rom—" Stopping, he realized this was the time to accept the name he had been given. "I am called the Ancient One."

The name brought an animalistic grin across her face. "So you wish to lay with me, Ancient One?"

"No." A wave of arousal waved over him from her words and he knew this was the outskirts of the type of power she possessed. "I hear Boto protects a sorceress that has a gem I am in need of. Is this true?"

Lillith stared at him, and he watched as she left her pedestal of rock and walked ever closer to him. "And if it is true, what do you want to do with it? This gem?"

"Take back what was stolen from me centuries ago." The thudding of his heart fueled the raw desire she enticed within him, her naked body prodding the raw feelings now drowning him. "That stone belongs in my hands."

Leaning her red lips close to his wolf's ear, she whispered, "And what do I get for revealing Boto's secret?"

Her claws slid over his jawline, sending his sexual desire into a frenzy. "I don't want to do that."

"Was that not the purpose of calling me here?" She lifted an eyebrow, her hand resting on his chest, continuing to excite him as the contact tingled. "It's been a very long time since you've enjoyed another—"

Shoving her hand off only added fuel to the fire as he fought the exhilaration this gave her. "I said no. It was an accident that I called you here. All I want is information on how to kill Boto."

"Angry and aroused." Biting her lip, she tilted her head as her curiosity in him grew. "And bound to a tree."

His hair ruffled. "What did you say?"

"Succubi are very sensitive to these bondings. We gain much pleasure from our own, but it's a shame you are taken. I have a nasty habit of collecting and disposing of mine for that peak sensation it brings when the bond breaks upon their deaths. It's much like cutting oneself because it brings unfathomable pleasure." She reached out to touch him again, and he allowed her fingers to touch the scar on his chest. "Exactly how does someone bind himself to both a wolf and a tree, I wonder?"

"It's why I need that stone. She's not a tree... and his name is Fenrir." The intoxication he felt from the stimulating touch of her skin on his flesh was breathtaking. "Do you entice everyone like this?"

"Only the ones I want." Cutting off the waves, she walked back to the boulder, grabbing the chainmail from it. "Call me when you decide to end this ridiculous, centuries-long quest for abstinence. When that happens, I'll tell you what you want; Boto, Morrighan, her precious jewel..."

The disconnection from her waves of arousal had hit him like a winter's breeze. "I thought you lost interest when you couldn't bond with me?"

Her tail stopped its playful swing, and her wings flinched before she looked over her shoulder. "Normally I would. In your case, I am making an exception."

"Then why the interest in a cursed man, an imprisoned wolf, and their bond to a tree?" He dared himself to come closer, enjoying the sound of her chainmail as it slid back where it had started. "Why tease me so much?"

"Do you even know what a succubus is, dog?" The cold tone of her voice hinted she was avoiding the truth behind her own desire involving him. "Unlike you, eating things does not improve my power. Think of me like the bitch who never comes out of heat."

"No." He looked down at her with his golden eyes, pitying her as he took in the amount of claw marks scarred into her skin. "Those scars. Who are they from?"

Furrowing her brow, she hissed, "What would you care?"

Smirking at her, he shifted back to his human form, finding her no threat. "See, it's not nice to pry in another's affairs."

She scowled at him; he had managed to sour her mood. "Call on me when you decide you're ready to bed with a real demon of the flesh, Ancient One."

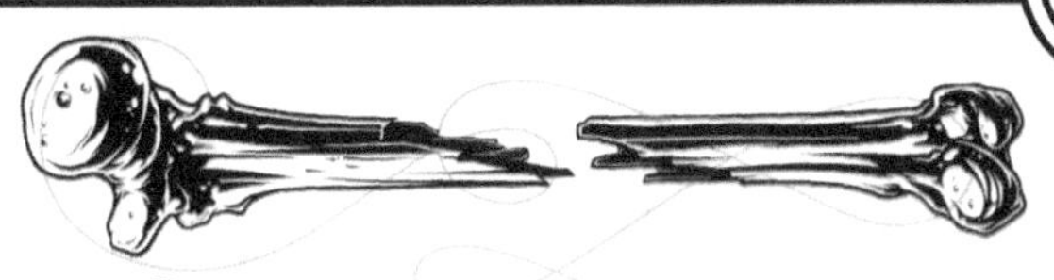

CHAPTER 12

A HOUSE BROKEN

Romasanta had discovered interacting with the world in the form of a traveling merchant these last years was excellent for gaining information and contacts. People readily freed their tongues when you had something they wanted, or even better, money. Supplies and items were easy to come by with wars raging at every corner of the known world. Lords argued over land and territory, while diplomats and priests threatened one another in terms of who should hold supreme rule over men. Regardless, those below the political tier, where debates caused wars, were continuing their lives tending to farms, raising families, and dying from the long list of diseases that dug ever deeper into the masses.

Leprosy, the Black Death, smallpox, dysentery, and gonorrhea were on the rising edge of the pestilence encouraged by demons, such as Lamashtu. Romasanta and Nyctimus seemed immune to these diseases or even to poor health. It was hard to be thankful for their curse, but it was fascinating to see how beasts and demons had the ability to accept the most rancid things into their bodies for the sheer pleasure of spreading them farther without the risk of suffering from them. As for the demon Lillith, he had not seen or heard from her since their peculiar meeting in the forest years ago. Occasionally, he would experience an electrifying sensation on his chest where she had touched him, and it led to a struggle with desire.

Shuddering, he downed the last of his meal. His expedition for information required slower travel and more interactions with people. In doing so, he would stumble upon those with the werewolf's curse and their noses let them know who he was. A lot learned the hard way to keep their distance from him; whether they were scarred horribly or died, it did not concern Romasanta. If he had the chance, he would wipe out the cursed ones completely and return order between men and the wild creatures of the dark.

The brothel was busy as the lady of the house struggled to rotate what girls she had between the high-paying customers. Not far from there, a battle had taken its course, and these men were celebrating their survival. Lords who fought over land were the worst in terms of who they chose to go to war for them. Often farmers with nothing more than hay-filled sacks for chest plates and pitchforks were thrown on a field against each other. If they managed to survive, they were paid well. Not that the money ever made it home from a slaughter like that, instead it landed here in the brothel.

A scent greeted his nose and he started looking about for its owner. Some place among these drunks and whores was a goddess. Laughter erupted at a table as a mysterious patron slammed their emptied mug on it. A bronze and silver mask resembling a bird with horns covered the upper half of her face, and dark hair fell wildly from the back of it. Her bare arms were muscular and her large chest had been firmly wrapped and bandaged to flatten it as far as her breast would allow. A long white skirt covered from her hips to the floor with raven's feathers flowing out of the bottom and through several rips. Another waft of her scent came to him, and there was no mistaking she was the goddess.

He ordered another round of mead and took a mug to her. Pushing through the singing troops swaying in front of her, he thumped the mug down, catching her attention. She glared at him. Her eyes could barely be seen in the shadow of her helmet. Two dark pools glittered while scars invaded her plump lips and tan chin with purple and pink tones. She grinned, her teeth a startling white, and guzzled it down. Standing, she was taller than most men in the room, but she was just shy of eye level with him and this earned him a laugh and a slap on the back.

"Where's your room? I like you! Let's go!" The strength she used to turn him about surprised him as she wrapped an arm around his waist and led him up the stairs of the brothel. "Who are you, and why have you sought me out in that crowd?"

"Romasanta." She displayed no signs of slurring, despite having fin-ished a casket of mead by herself. "I sensed a goddess in this place and

I wanted to seek your council on some matters that I have been put in charge of."

"I see." She pulled him into a room. They found themselves alone, the door slamming as she locked it behind her. "Romasanta, was it? You are not a warrior I am familiar with."

"No, I am not one to wage war. I try to keep my battles to what is only necessary or asked of me." The goddess was leaning against the door and his shoulders tensed at the thought she had caged him here in the room with her. "May I know your name, Goddess? And why you've rushed me off into a private room?"

"I am the Battle Goddess Badbh." Gracefully, she closed the gap between them, but he found himself shifting back a step, his eyes glowing gold in reaction. "That's what I was looking for! You're the father of werewolves?"

"Yes." Swallowing, he felt ashamed she had done something so tactfully sly. "I see you know how to make someone falter and reveal themselves."

"They don't call me the battle goddess because I'm strong, Romasanta." Laughing, she gave him hard playful pats on the shoulder, breaking the tension. "What matters did you want to discuss?"

"A red stone and its owner." Furrowing his brow, he noticed how she had tensed. "I see you know what I am talking about."

"Yes." Sighing, she removed her mask and shook her wild hair free. "The owner is my sister, Morrighan, and the stone is the Amulet of Avalon, or so said the wizard who gave it to her."

"Wizard?" The pressure in his chest boiled up old memories; this was the first clue he had gotten regarding Merlin. "The old man, Merlin."

"Ah, you've met this so-called Merlin?" Raising an eyebrow, she motioned for him to sit on the dilapidated bed. "I wish for the man to be dead for what he's done to my sister."

Rubbing his scar, he encouraged her to continue. "He's done more wrong than you could ever imagine. What did he do to her?"

"He failed to explain he was giving her a stone holding Beelzebub within it." The anger in her voice was sharp as her cheek muscle twitched. "My sister is now possessed, and the stone allows him to do magic unchecked by Gaea's law. It was Gaea who gave us the ground we walk on, the breath of life that we breathe, and blessed many with her essence in the form of magic. Her love for all beings is the reason she forbids them from harming one another. Doing so would recoil, cursing them tenfold or even lead to death. But that gem, I don't know what it is, but she is creating chimeras from demons in hopes of making the perfect being. I can only assume for the sole purpose of creating a more worthy body for Beelzebub."

Romasanta took in the information. It seemed Merlin was trying to avoid recoil himself. "Any idea how to defeat Boto?"

Scoffing, she shook her head. "If I did, I'd wage my own war to gain access to her castle. We may be sisters, but Morrighan and Nemaine both loathe me. I am the physical sorceress, where they are into black arts and venoms. Boto bonded himself to Morrighan a long time ago, and I never understood why. I can only guess for more power, but he commands her army of chimeras."

"All I know is he seeks out his offspring and kills them off at an alarming rate." Leaning on his knees, he stared down at the worn-down wooden floor. "Lillith might be my only source of how to take him down."

"Lillith is a very dangerous temptress. If you thought I was sly, she is far better at the mind games. Boto may be more powerful than her, but she is smart." Placing her mask back on, Badbh stood again. "Sorry I cannot aid you further. If you figure it out, I can only ask that you take pity on Morrighan. She dwells in the black arts, but Beelzebub fuels the perversions of magic that have taken place in that castle for centuries now."

"That will not be for me to decide." Thoughts of his encounter with Lillith years earlier brought back the pleasurable tingling where she had touched his chest. "As for Lillith, I am not ready to face her again."

"Who is it that you serve, Ancient One?" Offering a hand, she pulled him to his feet as if an old friend. "You did say you had been put in charge of recovering the stone, but by who?"

His mouth opened, but the eerie silence of the brothel called away their attention. Glaring at one another, they were both ready for what might be happening downstairs. Badbh cracked the door, but Romasanta grabbed her arm and motioned for her to be quiet. Having sensitive ears, he could hear the brothel below and it had not emptied. The scent of sweat hit his nose. A fear-soaked man had interrupted their celebration downstairs and the sounds of a wet rag being drawn came to him. No blood painted the air, but something terrible had happened.

"A man smelling of fear has come in and everyone is waiting." She smirked at him. "There is nothing else here besides us."

"Are you sure you don't want to become a warrior?" They left the security of the room and headed for the man who had sobered the crowd around him. "I could use someone like you on the battlefield."

Smirking at her, he turned his attention to the pale man who wheezed to catch his breath. Everyone had grave looks as they waited to hear what had startled him. He had raced into the brothel like a madman, but Romasanta recognized his face as a fellow traveling merchant. Rushing over, it took several tries to get his vacant stare to focus on him.

"John, what on earth happened? Were you attacked by a pack of werewolves?" Looking him over, there were no signs of a fight or wounds. "What spooked you?"

"Wi-Wil-Williamsburg." Stuttering, he struggled to keep the panic from shaking him. "It's gone. Just a bloody burni—"

Romasanta ran for the door, his heart racing. Rushing through the trade town, he did not slow for a horse as he took the nearest entrance to the forest. No longer within earshot of humans, he shifted into the versipellis and speed took hold. Burning in his chest bubbled up long-suppressed sorrow. Faces and the feelings attached to them were ripping through him as he tore through brush and trees. His path was set for the place where he had left the last of his humanity. Where his kin had lived and he had enjoyed their company off and on through the last few decades. *Williamsburg.*

The last of the Romulus bloodline had lived in Williamsburg. Now only one man of his blood remained with the adoptive son he had left for him on a battlefield years ago. Iron and wood burned at his nostrils as he drew near the destruction. Breaking into the edge of town, he stumbled to a stop. Shock took hold as he looked at the torn village, its ground stained black from the amount of spilled blood. Sniffing the air proved painful, mentally and physically, as it all blended and singed his senses. This event had happened months ago, yet houses were still smoldering and the scent of blood was overpowering. The land would be forever scarred, possibly cursed by this event. Not one life had made it out of town. Romasanta circled the outskirts of Williamsburg, hoping to catch any signs of someone left intact from this hellish event.

Despite no signs of anyone coming or going, someone had taken the time and effort to bury the bodies. A massive field for farming was engulfed by dirt mounds and poorly constructed wooden headstones. If the last Romulus had truly passed, he wished to see the body in order to understand who or what had demolished a town of skilled demon hunters. These men and women had perfected their art of killing the inhuman and had learned a lot of it through Romasanta and Nyctimus. It was something they had done with Romulus himself and filled the library in secret as a means to support them. No one had known he was still aiding their progress.

It took digging into several graves before finding the one holding Lord Romulus, the distant descendant of Romasanta's son. As he dug up the corpses, he salvaged what he could so as not to waste what remained. Someone had put them to rest with rings, swords, and other valuables still on them or dropped into their graves for them. They would not need them in the afterlife. Each time he uncovered one, the head had been chopped off, their bodies were belly down as if they had kneeled before their graves. Faces were distorted, fanged even as if they had fallen under a curse far worse than the one he had set loose. Williamsburg fell to something unseen and new.

Digging as the werewolf was efficient and quick. He had been caught in the past doing this work when in need of merchandise to sell. Rumors of a new monster had spread; *Loup Garou du Cimetiere,* Werewolf of the Cemetery. Lord Romulus had been buried with the silver sword of Boreas. This was a sentimental notion, and it meant someone was still there, alive. Stabbing the sword into the ground above, he climbed out of the deep grave. He fumbled at first, his thoughts taking it all in and piecing it all together. Was this an enemy of theirs? Or an enemy of his? Did someone figure out the connection?

RRRRRAAAAAAAAAGGGHH!

In a flawless motion, Romasanta gripped the blade and spun around. The point of the sword glided into the center of the attacker's abdomen. Green eyes gazed up at him in shock as they stumbled backward. Recognizing the red-haired young man as the adoptive son, he pulled the sword back, confused by the scents coming from him. Somehow, he had changed, and the scent was unrecognizable. The blood in his veins tingled with magic stitching, the curse of the strigoi and something else bit at his nose.

"Cedric..." Furrowing his brow, he watched as Cedric stood tall, blinded by rage and tears. "Did you do this?"

"How dare you dig up their bodies and take my father's sword!" His wound ignored, Cedric ran full steam at the werewolf in front of him. "Give it back!"

Romasanta dodged him, his ears flattened on his wolven head as he watched him fumble face-first into the dirt. "It's mine. I came to claim it."

"You can't! It's his!" Cedric picked himself up off the ground, and Romasanta's eyes fell upon Cedric's abdomen, healing at an alarming rate.

Bewildered, he mumbled his fear of what he brought upon the House of Romulus, "A demonic chimera..."

Cedric tackled him to the ground. Fangs were creeping forward as Cedric's green eyes glowered down at him. He swung to punch Romasanta, but found his wrists had been grasped in his blind rage. Kicking Cedric off of him, Romasanta got to his feet and picked up Boreas's sword. Silver had proven the most efficient way to tell evil-hearted beings from those with good wills. He, Nyctimus, Rhea, and very few cursed ones had proven this true multiple times. A strong heart with good intentions would not feel the searing pain of a silver blade.

Another angry bellow came from Cedric as he charged after the grave robber in front of him. Romasanta smirked as he rammed the blade into Cedric. Again, the surprised ignorant green eyes looked on, but this time Romasanta gave the blade a twist. Romasanta sliced deeper and waited for the signs. He lacked the smell, the sounds, and reactions of one's blood being purified by the touch of silver. Cedric was something different, or at least had been spared from this one weakness.

Romasanta pushed the sword harder, and Cedric stumbled backward from the pain it held. Shoving with great force, Romasanta launched him into Lord Romulus's open grave. Falling to a heap, Cedric did not stir with the silver sword still lodged in him. Romasanta squatted at the top of the deep hole, taking in the odd smell of Cedric's blood. He had been so sure he was human the day he found him in Lamashtu's arms. Then again, the battlefield and demi-goddess's scents may have masked what was there. Magic was blended into his blood, but not in a way he would find in a magic wielder's bloodline. This was a curse forcing Cedric to be this thing he had become, much like Romasanta. The difference between them was without it, Cedric would stop existing.

Another noseful told him this magic was not his own, but forced into him by the Eye of Gaea. It carried the same tone his own blood carried since Fenrir had been burned into his soul. Staring down into the grave, he pitied the creature lying there. Part of him wanted to kill him, but he saw himself in those green eyes; angry and young again. They even reminded him of Rhea's own pride and strength. Shaking it off, he took what jewelry he had found in the graves. Cedric was unconscious. His bleeding had stopped, but the ragged wound was failing to heal with the sword still placed in his abdomen. With a heavy sigh, Romasanta leaned down and reclaimed his heirloom.

Snorting, he gave Cedric one last look, the flesh healing where the blade had been moments before. This child had destroyed the last of what he held dear, but he had also taken his crime to heart by burying them all. Alone, it had taken Cedric weeks to see every person buried. Whatever happened, it would not be happening ever again. Deep down, Romasanta could only wonder what he would do with this thing lying in his kin's grave. Cedric would wake and he would be furious with Romasanta. Grunting, Romasanta smiled at the thought. When the boy grew stronger, he would seek him out. Perhaps then, he might share his secrets with Cedric if he could prove himself worthy.

It took Romasanta two days to backtrack to the brothel. He was eager to bathe; he wanted to free himself of the blackened soil. Picking up the bag full of jewelry, he headed for the church. He knew what Lord Romulus would want to be done regarding Cedric. Shoving the doors open, he ignored the curious eyes of the other patrons who were visiting. The priest was startled by Romasanta's intrusion as he marched toward him with a look of determination. He poured the jewels into the nearby pew, and the priest's eyes grew wide.

"I don't understand?" Baffled, he looked to Romasanta, wary of what deal was about to be asked. "What in heaven's name do you want?"

"A priest to visit Williamsburg to save a lost soul." Looking down, Romasanta picked up a blue gemstone that smelled of Cedric. "I'll keep this one, but someone needs to bring that town to rest."

"I will not risk my life to visit such a cursed place." The priest was shoving the jewelry away, terror filling him. "It's a suicide mission to go there."

"I will go." They both peered at the doors of the church where the gentle voice had come. "I will go appease the spirits there. They have already requested me to do this task."

"A cynocephali?" breathed Romasanta, who had only seen a few in all the centuries he dwelled in the forest. "Are you willing to help the lost soul that is there?"

"Yes. That is why I am going." His dog head on a human body looked odd compared to the blend a werewolf held. "My name is Wylleam, a son of the head shaman in my village."

"Wylleam, thank you." Romasanta started for the door, but Wylleam raised his hand to make him pause. "What is it?"

"She says to remind you that it's not your fault, Romasanta." Wylleam furrowed his brow, unsure if the tension in Romasanta was from sorrow or anger. "To remember, you're nothing but a man."

Scoffing, his dark eyes flashed the ire of amber at Wylleam. "Ask her where my tools are..."

As he stomped out the church doors, a great wind blew and slammed them in response. Wylleam and the priest stared at one another in wonder.

"I'm glad I'm a priest," mumbled the petrified man.

Groaning, Wylleam's one ear drooped. "I wish I was a priest. Spirits are such troublemakers."

CHAPTER 13

LUSTFUL SINS

Cerdanya had proven to be a trade city rich with information from across a wider scope of land, much farther than Romasanta had ever cared to travel. It was surprising that the original culture here had not faded during the time his son Romulus's people took it over. Not far from Cerdanya, was a large colony they called the City of Lepers. Those who had fallen ill with the disease were banished from their homes, towns, and cities. Being immune to the pestilence he had encountered, Romasanta found refuge within the refuge for the dying. For the last several years, he had been the main source of trade between the lepers and the rest of the world.

Bells hung from every neck of the leprosy infected. The bells chimed in unison, the tone Death sang through them mesmerizing those who looked upon the lepers, cutting deep into every soul. This had been a very effective means of preventing the disease from spreading, but it also condemned those infected to a slow death. They had managed to become successful potato farmers and put them to good use, developing a unique liquor with them. This strong drink was as clear as water, and strong in taste. The old Romanians called it *vodka*. Not only did the spirit intoxicate the drinker, but it also made an effective disinfectant for wounds. They produced massive amounts, which Romasanta took to Cerdanya's merchants, who paid him very well in trades and money. Most of the goods he returned with were what they lacked in medical supplies or everyday needs. Without him, the colony would have been a rotting field piled with the dead and the dying. The disease left no stone unturned as it destroyed young and old, man and woman, adult and child.

Odd reports were pouring in as travelers were encountering new beasts coming from some place to the north. These were not the chimeras from Morrighan's castle, but enchanted things that were hunting for something or someone. Rank and salty, they left scents that Romasanta would catch on occasion. Whatever they were after, it laid some place east, maybe even southeast from where he called home. After the destruction of Williamsburg, he had traveled west, never intending to return. He kept his distance from the Black Forest where Daphne rested and left the south alone with its sour memories of killing Remus.

As for Cedric, seventy years had passed and he couldn't care less about what had happened to him. Whether the shaman had managed to pull him out of the drowning of sorrow was unknown. Romasanta had been there. He knew the look in those green eyes, turning toward the darkness in his heart. That was a costly mistake for anyone, man or demon. Last time he allowed himself to fall into the cold black realm of his own soul, he blindly killed Remus. If he had allowed Rhea and Nyctimus to pull him free, it would have ended differently. The guilt made his chest ache as he entered a hut with a crate of medical supplies.

Inside, a little girl lay drenched in sweat as her fever burned through her entire body. No one knew what her name was or where she had come from. She was found on the road to the City of Lepers, horribly ill, and sadly, most likely dumped there by her own family. Rolling up his sleeves, he set to work. It was rare they ever recovered from a state so severe. He started soaking her wounds with vodka. The single reaction was the occasional furrowing of her brow and a trembling bottom lip. A heavily bandaged woman attempted to provide her with water, but she began choking, gurgling as she struggled to breathe. Romasanta lugged her over one arm as he patted her on the back, hoping they hadn't drowned her. He had watched so many of them die there, on the roads, or even burned alive in the cities.

Living there among the suffering, he had reminded himself that he was only a man. With all the power and immortality he had, he could not help the innocent who were in pain and tortured by the plagues of the world. Wheezing, she had managed to clear the fluid from her lungs. A sigh escaped Romasanta as he laid her on her side and handed the disinfecting supplies to the woman. Standing, he looked over her frail frame. Dark wild hair cascaded past her shoulder, pink lips folded out like a rose petal, and something about her scent hinted she had come from a bloodline of magic. Her clothes were torn, weathered and thin, and they failed to keep the skin under them from harm. Handing over the last bundle of supplies, he gave her fresh clothes for the girl.

He left, walking through the grim activities of the colony. Every hour, they checked the unmoving citizens. Most had passed since they were last checked. As they were being carried off to be burned, even more sick were joining them, having nowhere else to go. Like Romasanta, many of them had been stripped of their humanity and treated worse than the most vile demon. What concerned him the most was how a majority of those dying held hints of magic in their veins. At this rate, the world would be cleansed of all magic users.

"MANUEL!" One of the farmers hobbled toward him, his face pale. "A demon has fallen to the ground by the edge of the colony!"

"Clear everyone out. I will take care of it." He ground his teeth, his muscles tensing at the thought that someone would seek him out there. "What did it look like?"

"Gray skinned, but injured horribly." The diseased farmer struggled to keep pace as he tried to recall the creature. "Massive wings, a wicked thing with the features of a woman. It had horns like a ram and long white hair, a she-devil for sure!"

That's all he needed to know as the arousing tingle rippled over his chest. Blood filled the air, but the scent was not what he had expected. It had a sweet, inebriating aroma that pulled at him. The instinctual side of it reminded him of the yearning he felt when hungry and a fresh kill would greet his nose. The succubus's power was indeed an animalistic one. As he rounded the next line of buildings, there she stood, blood flowing from her stomach where she held her clawed hand. He halted his approach. The sight of her brought on a breathtaking wave of sexual provocation. The sweat on her gray body glittered in the sunlight as she grinned, her red eyes glowering at him as she panted. Staring at her in awe, Romasanta was confused as to why she had dared to come into his territory in such a weakened state. There were slashes across her neck, a puncture hole in her shoulder that oozed as a metal arrowhead remained within her flesh, and the worst of it was a hole in her stomach. Her hand did nothing to cover the injury, and he could see hints of light glistening through the waterfall of blood.

"Heh, I brought you a gift, dog." A wicked smile came across her face as she dropped part of an intestine at her feet. "It's not Boto, but it's one of his offspring. You will need him to defeat that asshole."

Dropping to her knees, she moaned as if enthralled by an unforeseen passion.

"Why?" Romasanta watched her. She was smiling and enjoying the waves of pain as if they were a lover's touch. "What do you—"

Her arousal was washing over him, beckoning him to come closer as she huffed her answer. "I am tired of Boto. He's been king incubus for too long."

"To risk your life and seek me out?" The excitement took hold, and he rushed to her, the touch of their skin electrifying.

Blood splashed with each step, its warmth lapping up against his ankles as he carried her into the closest building. She began to kiss and suckle at his neck, giggling. Erotic waves spurred him to follow her lead as he laid her across the bed. Cupping her jaw in his hands, they kissed and chased one another's tongues. The blood held within her mouth broke her corporeal hold on him. Stumbling back to the doorway, his fears of what she could do swept over him. The flavor there had not been the sweet intoxication that had lured him.

"Cedric." The mixture of magically stitched bloodlines danced on his tongue. "Boto's offspring is Cedric."

The glimmer of her eyes added to the smirk on her face. "You know this boy? I apologize, I did indeed bite him."

She licked her lips, sending shivers across him. "I still don't understand why you are coming to me if he is the one that needs to take down Boto."

Another arousing wave hit him. She was far from being in a weakened state. For years he had avoided Lillith, knowing if he dared to come close, she would simply take him for her own pleasures. They stared at one another, her tail snaking patiently to and fro. This was a game to her, but his instincts told him there was a far deeper thing she was masking. Swallowing, he could feel himself sweating from the excitement pouring out of her; all of it focused on him.

"Cedric isn't strong enough. It may take you helping him to get close to Boto." As if no longer bleeding, she stood, dropped her chainmail top and skirt, and took steps toward him. "I hate having to resupply a brood every couple of centuries. And worse, with someone who takes too much fascination in torturing those he lays with; it does not resonate with what we were meant to do."

His back slapped against the closed door, something he regretted doing. "Can't you resupply your brood with someone else?"

"The seeds must be tainted with someone who has a strong mix of incubine blood." Her fingers landed on the spot she had cursed so long ago, ecstasy waving into him. "Boto has killed them all. This one he missed."

Sighing with pleasure, he couldn't resist nuzzling and kissing her neck, whispering, "But why are you here with me and not Cedric?"

The sliding of her hand thrilled him as she cut the buttons on his shirt one by one with her claws. "You called me first."

Much to his own surprise, he laughed at the answer. "I suppose I did."

"It's ok, I waited until I could bring something to trade." Nibbling at his earlobe, she started undoing his pants. "The sex is what I wanted."

As his pants slid to the floor, he grabbed her tight into his arms, his lips brushing against her ear. "Have you really been looking for the answer since the night we met?"

Pulling back, something wavered in those red eyes. "I'll keep your secret, if you keep mine."

His heart raced at her response, and he pushed her back to the bed. Ravenous, they groped at one another, taking in the exhilarating touches. Pushing her farther on the bed, he paused a moment, fascinated at how much the wound on her abdomen had healed. A fanged grin called his attention to her again. There were no signs of the scratches on her neck. The arrow and its wound were gone, and a scar was left across her stomach from the mortal wounds. He kissed the scar, licking the sweat from her. Then he worked his way back up and over her breast to her neck.

"How do you heal so fast?" His lips tickled at her ear as she moaned while he pushed between her thighs, her tail quivering as it wrapped around his waist. "I can't heal so efficiently from a wound that wide. You make me jealous."

Grinding herself against him, she cooed. "I answered this the first night we met, mutt. I do not eat or rest..."

Claws dug deep into his back as she arched her own, humming as she waved her orgasmic sensations at him. Goading him on, he knew what she was doing; guiding him to what she wanted from him. Nails ripped down his thick muscled back, adding to the pleasure, before she pushed him off. Her wounds vanished, and sweat dripped from her chin as she pushed him to the bed, trading places. Drowning in her intoxicating aura and amazing scent, he let her have her way. Straddling him, her wings spread wide as she leaned down to kiss him. Fangs nipped at his shoulder and neck, her playful giggling making him smile.

"Thank you." Her voice was full of compassion, which excited him. "I wanted something more during this heat and you have given me the strength I needed. Thank you."

Romasanta's eyes flashed gold as his arms held her down. Suckling at her chest, he realized the queen of Succubi simply wanted a moment of empathy. Both of them were forced into roles that were necessary but painful to abide. She had to lay the seeds of lust while he devoured those who broke Gaea's laws. In the throes of passion, they understood each other's plight, despair, and needs. Reaching the top of the demon hierarchy had happened by mistake. Neither of them were interested in competing for the ultimate seat of this pyramid pushed upon them.

Romasanta found himself staring at the ceiling of the tiny shack with Lillith curled next to him, asleep. Grunting, he shifted under her, trying to relieve himself of the broken horn digging into him. It was a strange thought: the queen succubus he had run from for over a hundred years just wanted to feel human for a night. Perhaps Artemis had given him this hint, this answer when she had said, *you are only a man.*

"What happens after this?" he grumbled, unsure if Lillith was awake to hear him. "Do we keep one another company behind closed doors, so we can feel human for just a few minutes in these never-ending bodies?"

"I had a mortal life with one man before I was cast out." A lonesome sigh escaped her as she spoke. "My taste for lust corrupted me. Now, I cannot undo what lustful sins I performed in the early days of man. Boto and I made a pact, but he broke it when he bound himself to Morrighan to gain power. After that, he wiped out any chances for a successor and thinks of me as a plaything who comes around every couple of centuries. His only wish is to remain on the top of this devil's game."

Taking in a deep breath, Romasanta let his thoughts wander. "We do what nature asks us to do."

"Don't you tire of it?" Shrinking into a ball, her voice sounded weak for the first time. "Does the wolf ever tire of being a wolf?"

The muscles across his body tightened, and the silence was the answer she had been looking for.

"May I visit you later, Romasanta?" Leaving his side, she picked her clothes off the floor. "Or do I need to bring you a new gift?"

"What happens if Cedric takes down Boto?" Sitting up, he leaned on his knees, staring at her muscular back that held her massive wings with ease. "Does that mean he becomes the new king incubus?"

Lillith paused as she placed her top on. She refused to look over her shoulder at the amber eyes burning at her back. "He will be the new king and be responsible for carrying out the duties required by nature."

Scowling at her, he prodded further. "Which means he will need to make his own brood?"

"Yes." Dressed, she leaned against the door, wanting to answer his questions. "And after that, it will be the population that will control my heat. Boto wipes them out quickly, and thus I spend a hundred years resisting the instinct to return to make the new generation. If Cedric allows them to flourish, it will become a rare necessity unless he finds himself a more suitable queen."

Finally, her red eyes peered over her shoulders at him, waiting to hear his words.

"He is my adoptive grandson." He rubbed the side of his jaw, and they both started to laugh.

"What a horrible fate you find yourself tangled in, my wolf." Smiling, she left under the night sky.

Morning came quickly, though he had not slept. Thoughts and everlasting waves from Lillith were still taking their course through him. He had found a companion in the hellish world, someone who he did not need to worry over. As for Cedric, the smell of his decaying flesh had been marked to memory. It was the smell of someone he had not decided was good or evil. The scent he held was shared with Boto, but as for the other half of his bloodline, it was a deeper perversion of the strigoi's curse. A curse started by Romasanta so long ago. It was something rare and deadly, a variant he had never seen. Whether it was active or dormant, it was not in his power to decipher.

Cedric was a vengeful creature, with stories rolling in of his thirst to find Romasanta and take down Morrighan for his creation. It was still a mystery as to how he had discovered his creator on his own, but Romasanta was relieved he knew. Mulling it over, he decided he would wait for the abomination carrying his son's name with pride. Cedric would seek him out before following his suicide mission to face Boto and Morrighan in her castle.

Grunting, he whispered, "Is this my tool, Artemis? Or was this the one I made?"

Retracing his steps, he returned to the hut where the small girl was suffering. With a heavy sigh, he pushed the door open to find the bed empty. Rubbing his neck, staring at where she had slept, he knew her fate had followed that of so many others before her. Closing the door, he paused. Her scent was faint, but lively. It reminded him of his sister's smell, and he remembered the peculiar excitement it had brought him when smelling someone related to him. Perhaps it was why he took an unusual interest in her when they brought her in. Somehow this girl had managed to regain an older blood within her veins and it made him feel nostalgic.

"She ran off." The woman who had assisted him broke his thoughts. "Woke up as if by a miracle, thanked me, and ran off."

"Really?" Furrowing his brow, it seemed strange to him someone should break from their disease so easily. "Are you sure?"

"I am positive, Manuel. The girl's eyes were gripping and strange." Leaning on her crutch, she wobbled closer. "One brown, one green. Said she had to find her father, and with that, shot out the door faster than a deer. No one saw which way she went. I'm sorry."

Mustering a smile, he rubbed his chin. "Perhaps we gave her the care and rest she desperately needed to finish the journey. What do you think, Miss Ivette?"

"I'll be praying for her." The woman smiled as he headed for his wagon to head for Cerdanya.

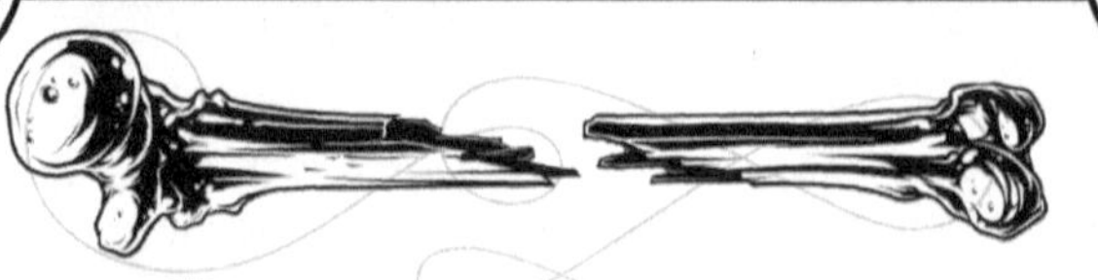

CHAPTER 14

ARTEMIS'S TOOL

The city had been cleared again to burn out the plague. Those too sick to evacuate found themselves burned alive where they lay as the fires worked over the streets and buildings. The people of the city were desperate to wipe the Black Death and other diseases out of where they lived and tended to business. It was considered a bonus if a couple of the elderly and homeless were made into ashes with the sick and dying. The aroma of burned flesh was becoming a callous smell to the masses. What should have made people's stomachs sour was perceived as the smell of security.

He had managed to get there in time to send a group of lepers to the colony. Sitting on his wagon, he stared at the blackened stone and bricks where they had been, and where the city guards had started the cleansing fires. It was sometimes fascinating to see how cruel humans were to one another, but then again, he already knew. Many times had he been the victim of this cruelty in the last days of his mortality. The sins Boreas had performed in his last days were unforgivable. Romasanta rubbed the back of his neck; he was struggling against his own heart to keep the past alive somewhere inside him.

He felt lonely. Fenrir no longer spoke; he had gone silent after slaughtering Remus. Romasanta assumed the demon wolf had fallen into horrible guilt and sorrow. It was also understandable he wished to never be the instigator to take action, since it was his words that pushed the attack. Over the centuries, Romasanta had replayed the day over in his head, and in the end, Remus was doomed. The Sabine had attacked, Romulus had been spared thanks to the women who stood up between the two armies and pushed for peace. If Remus had been alive, he would have brought death to his brother at that moment. After speaking with Romulus, it had been clear Remus had no interest in peace.

Worse, since the fall of Williamsburg, the area was starting to be plagued with the cursed ones. The versipellis were running rampant once more. The strigoi controlled armies of werewolves and used them as fodder against each other, or whoever opposed them. It wouldn't be long before he and Nyctimus would need to consider a plan of action to annihilate them. No longer were the two of them naïve about what they were and how the inner details worked. There would be no more outbreaks after they cleared them all out. The pack would die.

Romasanta sighed. Then his nose caught a tickle in the air, breaking him from his pondering. Looking down the alleyway, he took in another waft and chills ran across him. Standing, he walked in the direction of the familiar, yet strange, scent. Another sniff made his chest ache. He reached the end of the alleyway; he had left his merchandise out for any customers to look over. There, a woman squatted, dressed as a lady ranger from Williamsburg. The muscles in his back tightened as he watched her try on the blue-gemmed ring he had taken from a grave so long ago. It was the ring Cedric had buried with a woman of his same age...

"That one is cursed, they say." Dropping the ring, she stared up at him with brown eyes so much like his sister's. "I'll sell it for half the price it's worth. I have had no luck with selling that one."

"Excuse me. Are you Blanco?" It impressed him that she had weaseled his merchant name from the Kerretes, but she carried the scent of Artemis's blood. "I am looking for enchanted blades."

"I am Blanco, and that's a tall order you are asking for." Another aroma mixed with it, making him snort as he scratched his beard, his curiosity peaking. "But for you, Lady Ranger, I think I can oblige. I keep such wares in my wagon, you will have to follow me into the alley to the recently burned out courtyard. It no longer bears signs of the plague, but many do not mess with me there. It has been a long while since I've seen a demon-hunting ranger in this area, but it was common to have them ask for such items."

"Do you have very many blades?" Artemis had sent her tools, but the other smell blending so smoothly in her blood concerned him as he rolled up his merchandise. "I want to buy a blade for my lord."

"I have several enchanted and cursed blades. So, Lady Ranger, who is your lord?" He already knew the answer, but he needed to hear what his fears speculated, as she followed him back to his wagon. "I do not see rangers or ladies here in Cerdanya very much. I have traveled far and wide and it is pleasant to see people not from my homeland here."

"I am Lady to the Lord Romulus." There was a mixture of pride and reserve in her voice as she confirmed what he had sensed in her fragrance. "Have you heard of him?"

"Lord Cedric du Romulus. The demonic knight from Williamsburg." He grunted. He could smell him from where they were and Cedric was panicking. "*Si*, I've heard of him. Met him once before, in fact."

"Really?" They had made it to the burned opening, and he motioned for her to wait as he put away his things. "Hopefully it was on good terms."

"No, unfortunately, it was during a disaster a while back." Laying out some enchanted and cursed blades, he returned to his wagon, hoping the lack of appearance would give Cedric enough pause to talk first. "I'll be back in a moment, Lady Romulus."

As he sat there, taking in all the scents and sounds, he marveled over what he had observed. This girl was Artemis's reincarnate, but at some point, her bloodline mixed with Cedric's. Oddly, this was not the bloodline of magical turmoil. Once more, the odd shift was present with the essence of the Eye of Gaea calm inside it. Perhaps Artemis's magic was the key to controlling the magic the stone held. With Merlin so hungry for its power, it was understandable why his sister had wished to keep it separate from herself. She already knew she was the supreme compatible magic wielder for it. There was no way she would give the evil wizard a chance to get both things he sought.

The question left on his mind was his tool, Cedric. How did he find the girl and did he even realize what she truly was? What did he do to her in the time she has been his lady to not only shift her bloodline, but calm his own? The sound of angry footsteps and the smell of sweat were approaching. The answers he sought first did not need words. Lillith had told him much about the art of bonding during the year they had spent together. It seemed like Cedric's hunger for power may have led him down that path. Romasanta smirked, knowing the queen succubus had her ways of pushing for things to happen. There was a great chance she had pushed him to bond with the girl in fear of becoming her plaything or to aid his ability to beat Boto.

"ANGELINE!" Cedric roared as he entered the small courtyard, stumbling to a stop as he looked down at her. "Angeline..."

"Cedric?" Romasanta could hear the confusion in her voice, and the scent of fear coming from her to see Cedric in a state of panic. "What's wrong?"

"Where is he?" Cedric growled, knowing who had led her away. "Where is Romasanta?"

"Here." Romasanta left the wagon, the gold shining in his eyes as he looked over an older, stronger Cedric. "I could smell that she was yours. Seeing that you were able to find me, I assume that's why you have come so far. You were looking for me specifically."

"Roma ... santa?" Scrambling to her feet, Angeline rushed behind her protector. "Cedric, I—"

"Just stay back. This is between him and me." Cedric's glower was intense as his green eyes dug into Romasanta. His mind was filled with centuries of rage for the *Loup Garou du Cimetiere*. "It's been a very long time, Romasanta, since we last saw each other in Williamsburg."

"Maybe for you, but I must admit, you have grown since your days of pouting like a little girl." Romasanta took off his vest, shirt, and shoes; it was time to see what sort of power and blood the new man before him held. "I can't believe you would willingly let your pet wander about in my territory without a more watchful eye. I could have picked her ribs clean with my teeth in the time I have spent with her. If it were not for the stench of your blood mixed with hers, of course, I would have indulged in doing so. No offense, Lady Ranger. However, it is shocking to see you bound to a magic user. I was hoping your hatred of their kind would keep you from searching for me, but here we all are."

"She can take care of herself." Romasanta's jaw muscle twitched to hear him say something so ignorant; Cedric may be older, but he was none the wiser. "I owe you payment for what you did in Williamsburg! How dare you come to my town, dig up the graves, rob their dead bodies, and then dare to kill me with my own father's sword!"

"Well now, aren't we sour about that ordeal? I have learned there is no shame in gathering supplies from the dead, but you were so lost sulking in your own filth that I did not think it mattered that much. Survival takes precedence, and the dead are no longer actively surviving, last I checked.

As for the sword, it was on the top of the pile when I reached for a blade, nothing personal. Just reacting to an attacker. I was in the middle of digging when you came at me from behind." Shifting into his versipellis form, he watched the terror in Angeline's eyes; his form superior to the werewolves she had encountered prior. "Let's see if we learned any new tricks in the last seventy-eight years."

"I've learned plenty." Fascination washed over Romasanta as he watched Cedric shift into a more incubine appearance; ram-like horns and claws reflected the kind Lillith held. "You took something very important from me. Between that and the stunt you just pulled, you've earned a permanent spot on my shit list."

"Do you realize who or what you are challenging, pup?" Now his nose could sense so much more; moroi, a rare offspring of the strigoi. This had happened once, but the curse evolved into something new when everything aligned just right. Vladimir, a first-generation strigoi, had found him and calmed the blood in Cedric's veins, but it went beyond anything he had encountered before. "Does your moroi side tell you what the strigoi know about me? I am interested in knowing if that blood knowledge applies to something like you. I can smell Vladimir's touch on you, and trust me, he wouldn't dare to walk into my territory."

Cedric made it known this was a match for testing their brute force as he tossed his sword to Angeline. Despite the unknown element, Romasanta would win this fight easily. Engulfed by so much, Cedric's focus and understanding of his own abilities were far from being under his control, let alone understanding. Vladimir's scent was still fresh, which meant this new calm had been far too recent for challenging someone like Romasanta. As a breeze trickled over them, there was a hint of dread in Cedric which made Romasanta smile. The boy knew he might not survive a fight with the father of werewolves.

Cedric launched himself at Romasanta. The full-on frontal attack was pointless against someone as seasoned in fighting. Grabbing Cedric by the arm, Romasanta grinned at leading him around and back to where he started. His hope was to convey that an attack like that gives the enemy control of your movements. He gave Cedric a hard shove on the release, sending him barreling into a wall next to the startled Angeline. His golden eyes had not followed his opponent, but watched for reactions from her.

As Cedric hit the wall, she faltered in her steps, falling to the ground. Sweat poured from her, confirming what he had feared. Cedric had bonded with Artemis's tool. He would have to either work with Cedric or take the girl by force.

Romasanta flicked an ear as he heard Cedric fumble over the crumbling wall. Panting and bleeding, Cedric's green eyes flashed wildly as his hair shifted to black. The smell of the shift in his blood was exciting as his moroi bloodline let the incubus within him take hold. It was uncanny. The aroma evolved from iron to sweet, so much like the blood of Lillith. Muscles tense, Romasanta's left shoulder twitched, prompting him to roll it with the joint cracking in response. This time Cedric ran lower to the ground, attempting a more evasive frontal attack.

Stepping back, he could read what Cedric thought was going to happen. With a toothy grin, Romasanta played along with a swipe of his claw. Dodging it, as predicted, Cedric evaded behind him. The claws grazing his back were only a distraction working against him as he took another step backward. The explosion of fear as Cedric's back slapped against the wall was thrilling. Excitement filled Romasanta as he lunged forward with his massive jaws, eager to see what he would do in a cornered state. Looming over Cedric, he grinned and hummed, hoping to prompt a reaction.

Cedric's answer was stronger than he had hoped. Kicking off the wall, he made good use of the ram horns on his head as he slammed Romasanta back several feet. After gaining enough distance to take a better assessment of his environment, Cedric came back at him. Claws locked, the strength so close to matching his own, Romasanta could feel his heart thudding and racing in his chest. He felt alive again from the thrill of the fight, but it was time to teach Cedric his lesson in the flaws of magic. Being bonded had its advantages, but the disadvantage had severe consequences.

Digging his free hand into Cedric's shoulder, he spun him to face Angeline. Her horrified brown eyes had been watching with intensity, but they needed to understand the limitations of who and what they had become. Confident the confusion had hit its climax, he rammed his head into the back of Cedric's left elbow. The force had been brutal as the snapping of bone and muscles echoed in the courtyard. Screams escaped them both. Dropping to the ground, Cedric could not still the panic and fear of watching Angeline sob and hold her arm in the same spot. Both in pain, Cedric failed to control the magical bond between them. Romasanta's lesson written across their faces, Cedric shook himself free of the werewolf.

Romasanta sat, waiting, smoking a pipe as he pondered what to do with them. It took several minutes before Cedric was able to catch hold and control things. Her shrills had shifted from pain to pleasure. Releasing puffs of smoke from his mouth, he stared at the pale, sweaty victims on the ground with pity.

"Lady Ranger." He stared into her brown eyes, hating how much she reminded him of Artemis. "You should have listened to your lord and stayed out of the fight. His arm and your pain were an unwanted result because you thought you could assist by aiming your arrow at me. I have no patience for such tricks, and I am far too old to play with him after such a lack of respect on your part. Nonetheless, I respect your courage, and against some other opponent, I hope you do not hesitate to use that tactic."

"How did you do it?" Cedric's hair was completely black, the scent of moroi gone from his blood as he relied on the incubine bloodline. After seeing Lillith in her state, he was making the stronger choice as the bone protruded out of his arm. "What did you do to undo my control of our bond? How did you stop it from working?"

"Nothing," Romasanta grunted. He was still unsure what to do with them. "A moment of confusion can be one of the most deadly weapons in a battle. Not only is that moment a break in thoughts and movements, but it is capable of interrupting abilities. You can thank me later for this essential life lesson. Remember it well; it may save your life one day."

"I see." Cedric pushed the bone inside him again with a strange look of pleasure shivering across him. Allowing the sensation to ease, Cedric continued, "I should have never come. What do you plan to do with me, since I have clearly trespassed?"

"Nothing." Pulling on his shirt, Romasanta decided he would keep them together. Putting too much distance between them may do more harm than good. "I merely wanted to show you your place. It seems no one has taken the time to do you this favor. You are welcome, pup. I admit it's been a while since I have had someone land a mark, so you get some merit for that accomplishment."

"You are setting me free?" Cedric was right to question his motives. This was not a normal circumstance, and neither of the children before him would understand it all. "What makes you think I will willingly go?"

"That." Romasanta nodded in Angeline's direction. He could not tell if Artemis's tool broke his, or his tool broke Artemis's. "That is why you will leave Cerdanya and give up this futile attempt at revenge. You came here over false pretenses, anyhow. Young, you failed to see the world does not revolve around you, Cedric."

With a heavy sigh, Cedric looked back at Romasanta with a sincere glare. "You're right."

"*Si*, I am always right, my friend." Patting Cedric's back, he started to lead them out of the courtyard. "Come on, you look too pitiful in front of your lady. Perhaps I will cut you some slack for still being new to this world over the rest of the monsters, like myself."

After they healed, Romasanta would make it clear that if Cedric could not defeat Boto, then Angeline would be his for the taking. Cedric did not need to know why, nor did Romasanta completely understand what Artemis had done. With Angeline's life on the line, Cedric should have enough willpower to follow through. After their fight, Cedric was ready to set his vengeance off to the side and enjoy a life with this girl. This was something Romasanta could not let happen just yet. He needed the Amulet of Avalon, the Eye of Gaea, so he could finish the task he had started thousands of years ago. It didn't mean he had forgotten how to be human and compassionate.

"Ah, here you go. I believe this is what you were pissed about." He grabbed the ring, which told him at one time Cedric had dreamed of giving it to the love of his life. "I see you two are missing these."

"But this is—" His green eyes were wide as he stared at the pair of rings in his hand, one with a blue gem between two pearls. "You never sold them?"

"I tried, but fate must have decided that you would earn these back. Today was your lucky day, since out of the lot, your lady ranger picked your rings out." Angeline was in shock, unaware of the moment passing between the two of them. "My, you may want to get yourselves taken care of. I will let the Cerdanya Inn know you will be staying as my personal guests. Heal up and we will have a drink with one another for fun."

With that, Romasanta headed to the inn to make arrangements. He had settled up with his adoptive grandson, but Cedric still had so much to learn about life and pain. It wasn't the question of physical hurt, but the type of agony that came with loss and sorrow. The death of one's soul and the excruciating burn of reviving it, reliving it, time and time again. This was a lesson Cedric needed to achieve the final goals set before him. Perhaps Romasanta had failed to see his curse was not a tangible one, but one of the soul and heart. There was nothing more he could do to save Cedric from the plights of his life and those yet to come. All he could do was watch from afar and keep him out of the darker places of the animalistic tendencies they both suffered from; lust and hunger.

"Nyctimus." Sitting at the inn's bar, his hazel-eyed friend smiled warmly. "My grandson and his wife will be here shortly. See to it that they are treated well."

"Like I would ever do any different," scoffed Nyctimus as he poured a glass of vodka. "What dread weighs on your shoulders now, my friend?"

"Artemis's tool is Cedric's wife."

Nyctimus dropped the carafe. He opened his mouth to ask, but Cedric and Angeline came through the door. The question would have to wait until later. After Nyctimus provided them with a room, Cedric returned downstairs to have drinks with Romasanta. They talked for some time about their plans for the coming week. It pained Romasanta to have to put so much on Cedric's shoulders. If what Lillith had told him was true, he was the only creature alive who had a chance to do the impossible: kill Boto. He and Nyctimus could take care of the chimeran army lying between Cedric and his targets. It was obvious the youth was unaware of the most important element; Morrighan's amulet. There was no obligation to inform him this was the true reason for the assistance and the push for him to take the role of king incubus. In the end, Romasanta would carry the guilt of using them as pawns, much like his sister Artemis had done with him.

"If I can pull together an army..." Cedric was still adjusting to the vodka Romasanta had given him, but the tension in his muscles was starting to relax. "But I will need to find a lot more of your mutts to be able to get enough to have a slight chance of breaching the frontlines and castle gates."

"I assumed you would take advantage of that trait." Romasanta scratched his beard. It was a relief to hear that Cedric had enough common sense to know he would need a legion. "Don't think this is to help you, but it's just convenient timing. There are a few things I have wanted to do, and this seems like a good time to invest my time for a change."

"You mean to tell me you have plans and wants?" A grin snaked across Cedric's face, turning the mood into a meeting of old friends. "I am curious to hear what these things are."

"Well, I can get you your army within the week." The casual atmosphere was shattered as he spoke to Cedric, making him realize how close and quick this would be on them. "Being the father of werewolves, my call takes priority over their vampiric masters. A lot of strigoi these days have been collecting my offshoots like weeds and then encouraging their growth via breeding or ravaging towns. I am responsible for letting the curse boil over so much. I will call them to arms and lead the war effort on your behalf in hopes of annihilating the cursed ones and the chimera abominations from the earth."

"Is that all? You only wish to wipe out chimeras, your cursed underlings, and make a clean slate again?" Nyctimus gave the distraught Cedric another mead as he stared into Romasanta's dark unmoving eyes; fear and concern visible on his face. "Is there anything else?"

"Yes." Feeling the words stick in his throat, Romasanta downed the carafe of vodka, freeing the concrete task he would be placing on Cedric alone. "You must kill Boto."

"I hope to kill him and Morrighan." Cedric scoffed as he took a large gulp of mead as if needing to find a moment to reassure himself of his own goals. "It is the reason I am going to war."

"You did not hear me, pup. You *must kill* Boto." Flashing golden eyes, he watched them reflect in Cedric's green irises, burning their message deep. "That creature has crossed me one time too many, and if you dare to spare his life, I will devour your Lady Ranger. I have grown tired of Boto as the king incubus. It is long overdue for a new king to take his place."

"How do you suppose I assure his death then?" Cedric's jaw twitched as he asked the question. "I have had no luck finding information on how to ensure I kill him."

"You are his offspring. That is all that is required in their caste for one to kill another. To be the strongest incubus, you simply have to hold some blood in your veins of being one and the ability to defeat the current king." It was taxing to have to answer so many questions. Then again, Romasanta had once been that way. "You are too wet behind the ears. Perhaps I am putting too much faith into you."

"Then I should be fine. Boto will not live, if that's what it takes to keep your filthy teeth out of Angeline's ribs." Romasanta found himself smiling at Cedric's response. "This is a deal that stands for the rest of her lifetime, yes? That you and your mutts are to never to harm her as long as I hold up my end of the bargain."

"*Si,* it holds true." The irony in the words was astonishing.

Unknown to Cedric, Romasanta would never harm the girl, who, without question, was Artemis's tool. What concerned him was that despite the magic being there in her blood, it was dormant. If things take a bad turn, the defensive magic would do something wicked and haunting. If his instincts were correct, Cedric had provided her with his own blood, which put the defensive spell into full swing. Much like Romasanta's blood and curse invading Nyctimus, it simply needed a moment, one life-threatening instance, to trigger what it intended to do. Odds were she would become immortal, like them, but what she would turn into was a mystery. Incubus, strigoi which carried a mutation of his own curse, and the strongest magic in the world, Atemis's gift.

After sitting there in silence, having no more words for Cedric or Nyctimus, who had listened to the conversation with great interest, he headed upstairs. A scent rolled to him, sweet and arousing, and it was waiting in his room. Grabbing the door, he paused. A sigh escaped him, but did nothing to relieve the tension he felt. His chest ached from guilt and worry, and he went inside to greet his lustful lover. Lillith sat on the bed, naked and waiting patiently for him. He kneeled before her and the bed, resting his head in her lap, wanting empathy. Her claws stroked through his hair and her voice sounded like heaven as it whispered to him.

"Does Cedric know that only he can kill Boto?" It was strange to see her not smiling as she kissed his cheek. "I'm sorry his fate had to come to this."

Romasanta stared up into her red eyes. They were watery as she cupped his jaw in her hand. "Can it be that the wicked she-devil feels for other creatures?"

"Stop it." Shoving him from her lap, she turned away, lying on her belly with her head in her arms. "Don't be so harsh, wolf."

"I'm sorry. I won't tease you so much." Freeing himself of his shirt and pants, he towered over her. His eyes enjoyed the flowing curves of her body as they snaked across the bed before him. "How come Cedric doesn't sense you here?"

"I have my ways." His hands glided up her legs and thighs, her tail wrapping behind him, pushing him closer. "Whatever happened to your sense of fear to lay with me?"

"I know your secret." Kissing her lower back, he worked his way to her shoulders, tender and soft. His lips tickled at her ears as he whispered, "Your sense of humanity never left you, Lillith. The strength you carry to do what nature has burdened you with makes me envious of you. At the very least, I am honored to be your *concubinus.*"

She laughed as his beard prickled at her neck. "My, that is a term I have not heard since ancient Rome's start. I suppose it is the truth between us. You are at my mercy, yet there is no further option either of us can take from here."

His arms dove under her, his massive hands finding the breast they sought to grope. Pushing his thigh between her legs, he coaxed her onto her knees. Reaching back, she gripped the hair on the top of his head as he suckled and bit at her shoulder. Tonight was a rare moment where she had let her wings vanish; her gray skin was now tan under her straight, white hair. Releasing his grip on one side, his hand slid across her abdomen, exploring farther until he found the valley he had aimed to play in. A moan escaped her, her hand gripping his where it still groped at her breast. He pushed his weight on her while she was on all fours, continuing to tease her.

"Does this position arouse you, wolf?" Wiggling her hips against his waist, she enticed him further. "So much play tonight, what fun…"

Breaking from his actions, he grabbed the nape of her neck, putting her into a deeper submissive pose. They were starting to sweat from the heat of their arousal. Lillith's toxic smile had returned as she allowed him to hold her there, the weight of him on her, goading her want for his desires of the flesh. There was a glow from his golden eyes, his teeth more fanged as he allowed her to cajole his animalistic hungers to the surface.

The heat of his breath washed over her shoulder as he spoke. "Is this not what you told me you wanted?"

Exhaling, he took her and her back arched as she shuddered under him. Gripping at her hips, full and wide, he powered over her as she moaned and panted. Waves of pleasure shot through him as she enjoyed each connection they made. Hard and wild, they tore at one another as they rolled in the bed. The weight, stress, and tension of his guilt left him as she took the lead, nibbling at his neck. His heart thudded and his lungs were hungry for air as she kissed down his chest and stomach. As Lillith set to work, his eyes rolled back, his hand gripping onto her succubine horn. How far would he allow her to spoil his soul?

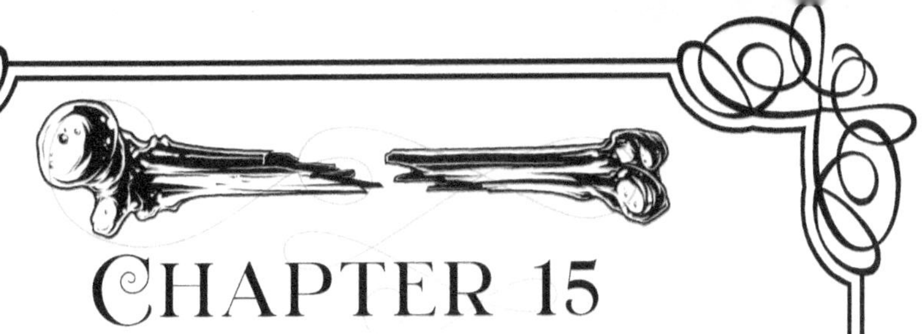

CHAPTER 15

ANNIHILATION

Morrighan's castle was on the horizon as Romasanta stood with Cedric to discuss the battle. The shaman had appeared, and it was clear Cedric had developed a strong friendship with Wylleam, as Romasanta had with Nyctimus. The cynocephali had grown old, with gray hairs speckling his muzzle. Even his silky mane of hair seemed to show streaks of silver. They all turned, watching Angeline leave. Satisfied with her distance, Wylleam spoke.

"The spirits are in quite the uproar over this." The shaman shot a look to Romasanta, and he knew it was Artemis who he was referring to. "I cannot sleep for their cries are so loud. Despite this, they understand the intentions and give you both their blessings to clean up the messes that have been made. One voice discourages this event, and that is the ancestor of Angeline. You both must watch her whereabouts in this battle; something may go wrong according to that one. That spirit knows too much about the things to come. I do not enjoy listening to either the old witch's ramblings or her anger."

"Tell her to show herself if she's got an issue with my ongoings. She chose me against my will for her descendant to bind with. It cannot be undone because what I do displeases the old hag." The words made Romasanta's muscles twitch and the look he flashed the shaman made it known Cedric's words startled him. "Should we follow one of the packs that will be providing an attack from the sidelines?"

"No. Morrighan and Boto will be focused on your location above all else. I will provide a distraction in the heat of battle east of the gates here. No one will be expecting me to join this fight. This should draw both their attention long enough for my elite pack members to open a line for Barushka to lead you swiftly through the gates. Reserve your strength; let the dogs do the fighting. If you are to succeed, you need all your energy

121

for Boto." Sniffing the air, he reassured himself of his plan. He needed to stay closer than he originally had planned. If Artemis feared something would go amiss, it would. "It seems the last pack just arrived within the territory. We will rest here tonight and ready ourselves for war tomorrow."

"Right, we will follow your lead, Romasanta." Cedric gave the map to Romasanta, whose amber eyes burned as a reminder of their agreement involving Angeline. "Now, if you don't mind, I would like to catch up with my friend, Wylleam."

"Understood." Shaking Wylleam's hand once, Romasanta whispered low enough for only their canine ears to catch. *Meet me afterward, Shaman.*

A flick of Wylleam's ear let him know he heard and agreed.

"I regret meeting you under such circumstances. Take care, Shaman." Romasanta left to wait for the two friends to catch up on current events.

It took what seemed like hours before Wylleam came back into the woods. They walked far from prying ears before stopping to discuss the otherworldly matters not known to Cedric and Angeline. There was so much more riding on this attack than those two could ever imagine. Long before their births and creations, someone had been setting the chess pieces in place. Details laid out, including their union, Romasanta's involvement, and so much more, were still unknown. How much longer would he watch Artemis's and Gaea's plans unfold before he would possess the gem in his hands again?

Rubbing the never-fading scar on his chest, Romasanta could not decide whether it was his guilt or his fear burning inside his core. Instincts drove him more than reason these days and it was a frightening realization. If Gaea's will was for him to take Cedric or Angeline out, he would be helpless to resist. It was a cruel consciousness of what his curse truly meant. Artemis's scent had excited him. Those carrying the bloodline of Romulus gave him a sense of excitement when their scent hit his nose. None of this had happened with Remus on the day he was sent to kill him.

A heavy sigh came from Romasanta as he started first. "Did I hear the boy correctly? That Artemis pushed for their union?" Staring into Wylleam's calm, doggish eyes, he hoped his tongue would answer him directly and not in riddles. "That she intended for them to meet and be bonded?"

"Yes, it's true." The ears on his doggish head flattened as he furrowed his brow. "But that's not what has her against this attack."

"What has Artemis so concerned?" A cold breeze blew over him, her scent on it as it chilled his skin. "I am not going to address you directly, Sister. You are not of the living and you've done me wrong one too many times over the centuries."

"Angeline has cursed Cedric." Romasanta's stomach twisted in knots. He knew the cost of cursing another magical being was death, often the punishment delivered by his own hands and fangs. "This is why Artemis is upset and fears that Gaea's law may take this as an opportunity to teach the two of them a lesson."

"Do you speak with Gaea now, Artemis?" Things were connecting quickly in his mind and there was a frightening awareness that rocked his soul. "Was my curse part of your plan, per Gaea's request, this whole time? How much more did you plan? How far does this burden go?"

Another wind bellowed in the trees around them, its scream much like a woman's from a faraway place.

Wylleam's voice called Romasanta's attention back. "Gaea will need her eye returned, and the warrior chosen for that task was you. Clever and strong, only you would be capable of doing such a laborious mission. You were able to tame the demon wolf, a task deemed impossible."

"Fenrir was part of the plan, too." His jaw ached as he clenched his teeth in anger. "And what about Daphne? Was she part of this plan? That day when she became a laurel tree, was that all written in the book of fate by you and Gaea long before I came to see you?"

A gasp escaped Wylleam as his legs weakened and brought him to the ground, breathless as he spoke. "Yes. All of it, even now. Much more is to happen before you can start your search for Gaea herself. Artemis is wary of tomorrow's events. She fears for you, your humanity, her brother's compassion failing him when he needs it the most. All she repeats to me is, *It's not your fault, Romasanta... you're only a man.*"

Dropping to his knees, Romasanta stared bewildered at the shaman, taking it all in. "If I am the warrior, then what purpose does bonding Cedric with your tool serve? Nothing good can come of this."

"She will not answer." Wylleam was short-winded as he pitied the tortured man before him. "I know nothing beyond this point, or I would risk my own life to reveal it. You have been wronged so many times by the powers of the spirits and gods. Perhaps in my afterlife, I can aid you in the future, but as of now, I am at their mercy as well."

"Can she answer me one thing?" Romasanta pressed, ignoring Wylleam's physical exhaustion from communicating between the dead and living. "Where is Merlin?"

"She does not know because he distorts time to hide himself." Staggering to his feet, Wylleam leaned on his shaman's stick, sorrow in his eyes. "She can only tell you that he is one of the sons of Gaea. That is the secret he keeps, and that is who he truly is. A child of ill-will, punished and now rebelling."

The forest fell into an unnatural silence around them. The wind had ceased and nothing moved, fear echoing off of every leaf and blade of grass. This was all Artemis could do before being called back to the other side; Gaea had cut her time short. Romasanta knew who had pulled his sister away. He could feel it there, like he had felt so many urges to carry out his mindless tasks. The skin across his back tingled and crawled with anger. He had been nothing more than Mother Nature's puppet. It had been strange how Artemis stayed with the cynocephali. Then again, Cedric was the part of her plan she needed to keep an active hand on to make it happen. Knowing she feared what might happen during this battle added to the anxiety destroying Romasanta.

Wylleam left him alone, his gruesome task finished. Romasanta was a destroyed man on the ground, taking in all the shattered pieces he had been given. Worse, his sister confirmed what he feared the most. More time would need to pass, perhaps double what he had already lived through. Nyctimus appeared, kneeling next to his dejected friend. Romasanta wondered if Nyctimus had been Artemis's doing as well. Was he an experiment that gave her the courage to manipulate the living further on to recreate his unique scenario as a fail-safe? Time would be the judge of what she had done, and in the end, he would be tossed into its turbulent waters. Artemis may be carrying the worst of the guilt, but it was his hands and body that felt the pain. Romasanta was the one who bore the sting of the distortion put into play in the world by her will.

There were so many questions about her connections with Gaea and his own links with the slumbering goddess that no one knew anything about. All he knew was the wizard was one of her sons. There was plenty of time to seek out the stories, the history needed to unravel some of this secret. Romulus's people had gathered much information about Gaea and the titans. There was a chance the clue he needed was among these beliefs and lore.

"Are you alright, Romasanta?" Nyctimus furrowed his brow, his hazel eyes bringing calm with them. "Did you get the answers you were looking for?"

"I'm still not sure." Rolling onto his back, Romasanta stared up at the branches, greeting the first breeze since the agonizing stillness. "You ever get the feeling your life isn't your own, Nyctimus?"

There was silence as Nyctimus sat on the ground beside Romasanta; Nyctimus's answer was a heavy sigh.

"Me too." Images of Daphne floated in his mind and tears crawled down his temples. "I should have stayed home. None of this would have happened if I had stayed, given up on chasing that wolf with my bull."

Chortling, Nyctimus shook his head in dismay. "Is that what started this?"

A smile forced its way across Romasanta's face as he answered, "Yes. I was so pissed, I was going to get back anything I could from my bull."

"A farmer chasing a demon wolf over a dead bull?" Lifting an eyebrow, he looked down at Romasanta. "What a fool you are at times, Romasanta."

"I know." He giggled, covering his face with one hand as he thought about it. "All I got was the horn, and I don't remember what I did with it. I think I dropped it on the ground on the way home."

The laughter grew louder and harder as the thought rolled in their minds. It had all started so simply and stupidly. A fit of merriment had been overdue. The burning in their lungs reminded them that in the end, they were foolish men at heart. They were cursed, immortal now, but at the very core of their being, they were human. Both had loved and lost many through the passage of time. Neither had regretted choosing love over solitude. What remorse they carried was from when they had acted too quickly in anger and sorrow. Each time they fell to these emotions, they found their wounds ripped wider. Scars, physical and mental, were the reminders of mistakes made in these passing occurrences.

"I'm sorry to tell you, but we have a lot more to endure after today." Sitting up, Romasanta leaned on his knees, staring at his hands. "Even then, my friend, I cannot promise you freedom from this curse."

Strong pats slapped his back. "This curse was given to me by my bloodline, Romasanta. I do not respond to your bellows like the cursed ones. Your guilt for me is misplaced."

"True." Rubbing the side of his jaw, Romasanta pondered, "I fear what will become of the girl."

"Why is that? She is merely a human." Tension crawled across both of them. "Or is there something I am not aware of, Romasanta?"

"Like you, she has a dormant bloodline. This one is of a powerful magic rooting back to my sister's gift." Exchanging severe looks, they felt the shared concern. "Being bonded to Cedric, in contact with his cursed blood, there's a chance it could happen again."

"Don't you mean it will happen again?" Taking in a deep breath, Nyctimus continued, "But this isn't the animalistic one we have with the wolf. The curse he has goes deeper, much older than—"

"It's both. The strigoi developed a rare mutation within its ranks, a moroi. He also carries the demon blood of an incubus, which yes, is older than us." Rubbing the back of his neck, the tension would not leave him. "He used to have the magic from the Eye of Gaea stitching it all in place, but that's not the case anymore. It has faded, or left him, and now, the smell, it has changed."

"How does one change their blood?" Sweat trickled down Nyctimus's cheek as they sat there. "What is he?"

Staring over at his friend, Romasanta's yellow eyes glimmered. "He is something new and old. Perhaps this is how demi-gods were created in the past, but those bloodlines have been soothed by Artemis's magic. They are melding into one peacefully. Slowly, but without a doubt, the strings that were once needed have been dissolved, and he is becoming something unknown. Abomination undermines what Cedric has become."

"Don't you mean what *they* are becoming?" interjected Nyctimus, a shudder rolling across him.

"I pray I will not be the one asked to annihilate them. I don't know if I am strong enough to take down something of that caliber..." Romasanta jerked to his feet, walking away from the conversation which had turned sour.

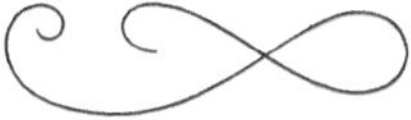

Romasanta found himself filled with a strange sense of pride as he stood in the mass of werewolves. The ground shook from their movements, and the air vibrated from the excited yelps and growls. This was Romasanta's pack. He was Alpha, but he would soon be the lone wolf. After this battle between werewolves and chimera, he and Nyctimus would wipe out the last of the versipellis in the world.

Romasanta looked at Cedric and Angeline. Snorting, he recognized the shag foal as the cumbersome horse from his distant past. Eyeing Romasanta, Barushka puffed out his chest and shook his head. Romasanta chortled over the stubborn thing. It felt good to see this horse had taken the path of adaptation, and like him, had found himself immortalized. *What a strange cursed world we live in.* Barushka was the only one there who had known him as simply a man, and unknown to his riders, had lived just as long as Romasanta himself.

He watched as Angeline's wide brown eyes took in everything around her. The sea of fur around them made her shift in the saddle, nervous and frightened, before her eyes stopped on the field below them. The hot sun blared down on the majestic scene, the multicolored flowers danced in the breeze, oblivious of the waiting armies. Today, their springtime celebration would end as they were trampled to death. Blood would pour upon them, drowning and smothering those that managed to avoid being flattened. If all went as planned, only three men and a girl would walk away out of the thousands who aimed to go to war that day. Their success would end with walking on the heaps of corpses of cursed abominations, both tainted and influenced by the misuse of the Eye of Gaea. None of these hellish beasts should be there.

Romasanta approached them, nodding to Cedric as he whistled for Nyctimus. It was the only means of attention that didn't excite the pack, which responded to the slightest variant of his howls. The old familiar golden brown versipellis shone brightly against the drab of the gray and black versipellis engulfing them. It would be his task to stay close to Cedric and Angeline, be there to watch their backs, to make sure nothing would go wrong. Nyctimus bowed at Romasanta's feet, and they shared the silence of knowing today would not go as they planned. They would aim to meet the goals they had laid before themselves, including the girl's protection. Both prayed Artemis's choice of Cedric had been correct and they would not be needed to shield anything that may happen inside the castle.

"This one will lead the group that will break a line to the gates for Barushka." Shooting a glance at Nyctimus, he responded with a wag of his tail. "Are you both ready?"

"As ready as one can be for war." Angeline smelled of fear as she tightened her hold on Cedric's waist. He shifted in the saddle in response as he nodded to Romasanta. "On your command."

"Excellent." As he shifted into werewolf form, his skin crawled with excitement and a grin snaked across his lips. "Remember our bargain well, pup."

Bellowing into the air, it felt good to release a solid, loud, and long howl. The pack shuddered, barking and howling in response to their master, their father of the curse plaguing them. It brought a strange asphyxiation that hit them, as if they were breathless or losing more of their humanity. His interactions brought an uncanny sensation of pleasure to serve Romasanta without question. This reflected the interactions he had felt with Lillith and the powers of a succubus. Regardless, the placid lake of fur now flowed forward in turbulent tumbles, gaining speed as they aimed for the field and castle before them.

The heliodromos floating above the field would take out a large portion of the pack before the mutts figured out how to snatch them. Those vulture-like creatures looked frightening to the unskilled eye, with features of a lion and dragon mingled in their being. All he saw were overgrown vultures needing to be put in their place. As he ran the forest line, far from the heat of the battle, he watched the fountain of blood shred across his pack. Barushka did not flinch as he aimed to follow the brown werewolf in front of them, who cut a clear path for them. Romasanta could have advised the pack from a distance on taking down the heliodromos, but he had aimed to kill the sea of cursed ones off in the end. It did not matter whether it meant several would die before hitting the castle gates, Nyctimus had his task and Romasanta needed to do his.

Breaking from the woods, he had made it to the eastern gate. Howling long and hard, he let Nyctimus know he had arrived and would follow through with his job as a decoy. A toothy grin stretched across his muzzle as he took in a deep breath. With great speed and force, he rammed a shoulder into the wooden gate. It shattered, the excitement of destruction goading him on to devour all opposing him. The aura of the battle shifted its focus to the power that made their skin crawl. The Ancient One, the father of werewolves, had freed his animalistic supremacy for the first time in hundreds of years.

Vines wrapped around Romasanta's ankles, knocking him to the ground. Swiping his claws with precision, he cut himself free. Screeching rang out as he leaped back to observe what had attacked him. A jidra had emerged from the ground, something rarely seen this far north. Shaking off the surprise, he felt relieved his nose had not failed him since the ground could mask many things. The jidra were curious beasts, spending most of their time under the ground, only leaving to feed. It unfolded its red-as-blood protective petals, revealing the yellow tear-shaped center with its slit full of sharp teeth. These teeth were interesting since they were the tips of the ribs, which helped give the jidra its shape. They also made it impossible to escape if eaten. Romasanta was not shocked that Morrighan possessed one, since their bones were famous for their magical healing properties.

Another round of vines flowed out to him. Swiping and dodging, he stifled to the side only to feel the grip of vines on his ankles once more. Looking down, it had pushed these out of the ground under him. It had planned ahead, something he did not realize it was capable of doing. Reaching down was another mistake as vines wrapped around him, tying his arms to his sides. His jaw smacked the ground as he fell forward. He was being dragged closer to the drooling bud of the jidra. Growling, he clenched his teeth as he glowered at the fleshy tongue behind the teeth vibrating in excitement. Straining against the vine, he could not break free. They tightened with each movement he made, adding to Romasanta's frustration.

He eyed the vines. They would not be following him within the toothy prison of the jidra's mouth. A wicked grin crossed his face as it lifted him off the ground. The slimy, sticky tongue stretched out like a frog's, gripping him tight, and securing its prey. The tongue wrapped him in its heat, filling his nose with its rotten stench, and he felt the vines fall away. In an instant, he was sucked into the gap. Teeth raked and ripped his shoulders and legs as the jidra pulled him into the mouthy cage. He felt it quiver as his blood dripped and ran against the inner walls of the bud. The tongue had let him go, lying across the exit, protecting what it had eaten and aiming to keep him until he rotted to a slush.

He pushed against the walls; the ribs were impressively strong. Romasanta had made a mistake in thinking he would be able to free himself once inside. The air within the bud was dissipating fast as more saliva poured around him. Snorting, he snarled in annoyance as the jidra's drool stung at his cuts, thinning the blood and encouraging him to bleed out. It was a very complex beast for a plant. The bud tightened around him, earning more growls from him as he fought for space. It rocked and shuddered, shrieking as it battled something from outside. Romasanta dug his claws into the tongue, hoping to coax it from the toothy exit. He was growing lightheaded, dizzy from the lack of oxygen as he shredded the tongue. His fangs dug in, ripping and shaking the tongue free as his fury grew. Once more, the jidra rocked as something slammed into it from where it held its mouth closed.

Desperate, he slammed his claws between the teeth. It took several attempts before he managed to get between the bony razors with two of his fingers. Suddenly, the creature rocked back, lifting off the ground before slamming down on its side with him still inside. His claws slipped from their wedge, earning an angry roar from him. Light blinded him as its mouth voluntarily opened and it wiggled as it withered away from him. Pulling himself free, he looked over at a blood-soaked Nyctimus panting from his efforts. He had sent the beast rocking before getting his grasp under the bud, ripping it free of its root. The jidra could not survive if it was ever severed from its connection to the ground. Both sighed, exchanging grins.

"How did you know?" Romasanta shook his fur free of the jidra's foul-smelling drool. "I was struggling to do anything against the beast."

"Didn't you learn anything from the rangers at Williamsburg?" scoffed Nyctimus, who flopped down to rest as the war went on around them. "Wasn't it the Lady Ranger Ann who was hired to collect jidra bones all the time? You were there when I asked her how she did it, alone. *'One arrow to the root,'* is all she ever said to me."

"Glad my family managed to learn more than me." Grunting, Romasanta looked to where the battle was spilling into the castle's broken doors. "Shall we finish killing these unfortunate creatures?"

"Yes, let us finish the gruesome task of cleansing the earth of the cursed beasts." Taking Romasanta's paw in his own, Nyctimus used the leverage to pull himself back to his feet. "I'll take the group close to the castle doors, where Cedric is battling the king incubus. I can keep them from going any farther."

"I will clean up what is left in the fields." With that, they raced apart on all fours.

The field had been ravaged. Blood-filled mud was all that remained where the flowers had once celebrated the full swing of spring. Amazingly, his pack had proved themselves stronger, but at a great cost. Most were injured horribly. Dying, they continued to attempt to ravage and devour the chimera they had happily taken down in the name of their master. It was a horrid task to put them out of their misery as a cold wind began to howl over the massacre, painting the ground red. Horse hooves thudded from behind Romasanta and the wind screamed with the scent of Artemis. His fur ruffled as he willed himself to look.

The grave look on Cedric's face told him something worse than death had happened to the girl. Barushka raced away, the boy's task already set in his mind. The scent of Cedric's blood wafted to him on Artemis's wind, telling him he had done what was asked of him. After killing the last of the group in front of him, Romasanta raced for the castle. Bellowing, he howled for Nyctimus to meet him. They stood before the smashed doors, their claws clacking on the black marble floors as they approached where the Battle Goddess Badbh stood next to her slumbering sister Morrighan.

"Did my battle blessing aid your pack, Romasanta?" Her smile was simple, but encouraging to see. "It was a glorious battle of matched sides today."

"It was what we—" The scent engulfing his nose turned knots in his stomach.

Everyone watched as he sniffed and followed the smell which had cut his conversation short. His yellow eyes were wide, his breathing racing, as fear rattled his core. Grabbing his head, he roared as the scent made itself known. It was unmistakable. This smell, the airy fragrance of magic and salt, mortality and godliness.

"Merlin," he growled. "Merlin was here."

"Yes." Badbh sighed as she frowned. "He took the girl with the ancient bloodline with him. His ambition is to use her to gain immortality."

"No," gasped Romasanta, looking at Morrighan's dress where the amulet had once been. "And the stone?"

"He took that as well." He fell to the floor, fading into a man as he punched the marble until his knuckles bled. "I will kill that wizard for this! Sister, you fool! Why would you fuck with nature in such a way?!"

No one knew what to say to calm the raging man who continued punching the ground. The pity they all had for Romasanta was crushing as they watched the naked, broken man carry on with obscenities and angry screams.

"Fenrir! You bastard! Where have you gone?!" Tears fell from his eyes, his face red, veins in his temple and neck bulged from the lament of his tantrum. "Why did you leave me alone, please, don't be silent! Not even this wills you to speak! I... I can't tell who I am anymore without your voice!"

Nyctimus whimpered, realizing something he had missed during the last few decades. There were no more moments of Fenrir pulling forward. It had suddenly stopped around the time Romasanta had started living with the lepers. Fear waved over Nyctimus as his thoughts raced for answers. If Fenrir had vanished, then why would the curse remain?

Rolling to his side, Romasanta shook as he covered his face, sobbing. "Daphne, if only I had you, just maybe, for an instant, I could be the man I started as... but how could I ever face you again as the monster I've become?"

Badbh and Nyctimus looked at one another, neither of them realizing how deep their friend's inner torment had gone. Merlin's scent had ripped open old scars and ravaged him all at once. There was no consoling someone lost, drowning in so much persecution, tracing back to one or more people in his past life.

"I'll take him." Lillith's voice startled everyone from their gazes on the man who wept on the floor unflinchingly. "Finish the annihilation of the chimera and werewolves. Romasanta will be my issue."

"Wait!" growled Nyctimus, who bravely put himself between his friend and the queen succubus. "How do I know I can trust you? What do you plan on doing to him?"

"Don't you mean to ask what I plan on doing *for him?*" Lillith raised an eyebrow, her wicked smile sending shudders across the brown werewolf before her. "You must be Nyctimus. I have heard of your friendship with this cursed man."

Once more, he and Badbh looked at one another and the battle goddess intervened. "It seems you and Romasanta have developed a friendship, Lillith?"

"Perhaps." Coyly, she shrugged, her tail whipping about, playful and unnerving. "He is losing his humanity, his faith, and hope as we dawdle here. I can salvage what is left."

"How?" Badbh was proving the calmest in the room as her curiosity grew. "I know the succubi and incubi have many secrets about their abilities, but can you really do that?"

"For him, yes." The smile faded from Lillith's red lips. "When he returns, I will ask you all to keep an eye on him. If we do not tame him, he will annihilate this world with the rage and sorrow that is eating him alive."

CHAPTER 16

ISOLATION

As the next few centuries rolled by, Romasanta kept to the isolation Lillith had provided him. There in her temple, there was no fear of coming into contact with humans or other demons. His mind was riddled with self-conflicts and waves of despair swallowed him. Drowning in sorrow, his soul would fall into a dark place so deep he would become numb to his surroundings. Often, he would pull out of the abyss and wake in a different area of the temple. As he looked out across the mountainous snow-covered landscape, he struggled to decipher who or what he was anymore.

No longer did Fenrir talk to him...

No longer was he the farmer...

No longer did he want to face Daphne...

He had become a monster since the days of his mortality. Leaning a shoulder on the stony archway, he watched the sun sink deeper into the horizon. The solitude in this place was remarkable, as the changing seasons did very little to alter the environment: forever a cold, wet forest with its rivers and rocky slopes. The sky held no clouds today, but the sun seemed to never warm the air, something he preferred. His body yearned to be as cold as he felt at his core.

Sometimes he lurked as the werewolf, other times he was the lost man, naked and shivering. Neither form felt more comforting than the other. Changing skins no longer brought him the pain it had in the past, and that had added to his frustration. The ripping and breaking had reminded him that the wolf and the man were not the same. Without its sharp sting, he could not tell which form was truly him. He could only conclude both forms had been accepted as part of him, permanently. Each time the thought rolled into his mind, his stomach twisted into horrible knots.

Somehow, at some point, Fenrir had left the complex equation. He questioned often whether his soul devoured the demon wolf's or they had lived in one body so long they had lost the ability to stay separate. He feared the answer to this terrifying realization. Sinking to the cold, stone ground, he looked on as the colors of the sky shifted from gold to lavender to the blackening blue of night. A wind blew in, the scent making him shudder, and his stomach soured as it carried its information to him. One tear pushed its way down his cheek and he swallowed, covering his face in his hands. It was exhausting being able to decipher so much about the world around him by one simple sniff. Even more so, the sounds reaching his ears had become burdensome. Between these two senses, he could tell where animals dwelled, if Lillith had returned or slept in her chamber. It seemed that with each passing century, his senses grew eerily stronger whether he was actively using them or neglecting their existence altogether.

Pulling his face away from his palms, he propped his head on the archway, watching a blue full moon climb over the forest. His wolven eyes made every tiny movement shout and shine in the bleakness. A buck leaped through the trees and away from the temple. Not far behind him was a pack of wolves who found themselves pausing, staring up at the mysterious eyes watching them hunt. One seemed to have met his gaze and howled a long, mournful bellow in response. It was a means of respect for the powerful, godlike wolf residing in the temple above them.

Closing his eyes, he swallowed his emotions as they began to swirl violently in his mind. There were only naïve people—humans, his thoughts corrected—who did not recognize the monster he had become. Nature knew him well, and worse, he was placed horribly high on the demonic pyramid of power. With King Incubus Boto dead, the contenders left for the top tier were: him, Queen Succubus Lillith, and Lord Cedric du Romulus. Between them, it was understood that the Ancient One—the name given to him by an unknown source—was the supreme master. Boto held the spot by extinguishing his underlings, and without thinking his actions through, Romasanta had done the same. The lack of care or need for an army, or even minions, was a terrifying level of power that very few achieved.

He was something evil, feared.

"A blue moon is rare." Lillith had kept her distance during his stay, but that night, she ventured closer. Perhaps she was yearning for his affection like he had given her before his fall into desolation. "This happens after certain events across the earth align with the right amount of ash and dust between us and the moon's light. Does it please you to see it, my wolf?"

Romasanta opened his eyes, breaking away from his morbid thoughts. His golden glare shifted upward at the blue moon rising high in the sky.

"I've been looking for information for you." She sighed as she walked closer, his chest still holding the tingle from the very first time she touched his skin. "They say the gypsies to the west of here might hold answers for you, but much evil is at work in that place."

Her hands slid over his cold bare shoulders as she nuzzled the back of his neck, her breath warm as it washed over his skin.

"A strigoi there has lost his soul and now massacres everything living." Lillith's thighs rested on either side of his torso as she squatted behind him, waving her arousal into him with her power, her want for him making his body heat up involuntarily. "Their gifts can see curses with such clarity that they can reveal how one could break from it."

"Is that so?" His voice rattled awkwardly in his chest, Lillith's excitement flooding him as he willfully allowed himself to speak after so many years of silence. "Can they truly do this?"

"Yes," she breathed as she began kissing his neck and shoulder. Intoxicating sensations vibrated into him from her touch, stirring his body in anticipation of the pleasures she was promising. "I have confirmed they are capable of this feat."

The muscles under his skin tensed as her fingers slid over the scar on his chest. "Then I will leave. Seek out a means to break this curse. I cannot be with Daphne if I allow this rancid anathema to live on inside of me."

Lillith stopped her playful advances, resting her cheek on his shoulder as she stared at his stern look, his eyes glowing gold. "And if it can't be broken?"

Breaking his gaze at the moon, he glowered over at her. The twitching of his jaw muscles and the feral look in his eyes told her more than she wanted. With a frown, she pulled away from him, standing as she held herself, her back to him. There was a long moment of taciturnity as the cold wind from the archway howled in their ears, as if spirits screaming disapproval of his thoughts. Lillith shivered and he could smell the deep aroma of true fear on her scent for the first time since he had met her.

"If you choose to go feral, I will be obligated to stop you." Her voice was authoritative despite her emotional state. "I'm sorry I cannot help you hold on to your compassion for the living, your humanity, as you all love to call it."

"Was that the reason why you brought me here?" The words he spoke seemed lifeless and stung any who could receive them. "You aimed to protect the world from my wrath?"

"No..." A whisper graced his ears, and the wet smell of salty tears made his heart thud against his chest for the first time in decades. "I wanted to save a man. A man who once had no fear to love those that came into his life despite his immortality."

Eyes wide, he stared at her in awe. Picking himself off the ground, he walked to her, his hand reaching out to her as another tear slid down his cheek. Shifting, she gave him a mournful look over her shoulder, tears flowing down her face, streaking her gray skin. The red lips so many had come to loathe trembled. Biting her bottom lip, she failed to still it with her fangs. He turned her, taking her jaw into his hand as he stared into those watery red irises. His golden eyes reflected like the sun over the two swirling roses in her eyes. There was no mistake, there in their isolation, she was revealing her true self; a caring, compassionate creature, the world had wrongly shunned into a dark corner.

The blood in his veins rushed through him as his heart thumped ever quicker. Pressing his lips to hers, he started to feel alive again. Hungrily, he grabbed her into his arms, ignoring the cold of her chainmail vest and skirt as it slapped against his skin. As they kissed, they stumbled back against the coarse stonewall, pinning Lillith under him. Sucking at her neck, he yanked away her top, sending it clanking away from them. The fragrance of her was exhilarating, a sweet smell of roses from a forgotten time. She gripped the hair on the back of his head as he moved to her breast, his hands working off her skirt. A wave of arousal erupted from her as the chainmail slid off her hips and thighs.

It delighted him to feel the divot at the center of her back as she arched. His fingers followed it down, his palm greeted by her hip as another wave of pleasure shot through him from her arousing aura, enticing him to continue. The soft gray curve of her buttocks was smooth in his hand before it met her thigh, pulling her up on his hip. He shoved her harder against the rocky wall, lifting her with ease, pressing his hip against her. An excited inhale filled his ears, breaking him from his suckling as he grinned, fanged and wild. Panting, she looked down at him, heat waving off of one another, into each other. The warmth of his breath washed over her chest, sending an excited shiver across her skin as she shuddered in his grasp.

Once more, he pressed her between his bulk and the wall. The bristly hairs of his chin tickled her shoulder as he nibbled at her ear. Claws dug into his back as she moaned from each press of his pelvis. Lillith arched her back, her horns scraping across the wall, her breasts pushing into his chest as she whimpered. His lips pulled away from her ear, and he paused, his weight crushing her against the wall.

"How long have you been holding this heat?" A smile snaked across his lips as he nuzzled her neck. "You're in heat, like the first time we laid together."

A sigh left her, leaning into him, her lips tickling his ear as she whispered, "I never laid with Boto... you quelled my heat, my wolf."

Resting his forehead on her shoulder, he huffed as he took this into consideration. "And your brood?"

"No brood has been laid." Wrapping her arms around his neck, she kissed his neck before answering his concern. "That takes an incubus."

Romasanta pulled away, freeing her from the wall. His muscles tensed as he walked back to the archway. "But you are obligated to make a brood..."

"Yes." Leaning against the wall, she stared up at the cobwebs drooping down from the ceiling of the rotting temple she called home. "Do you know what this place is?"

"A place of isolation," Romasanta grunted, the freezing wind stealing her warmth from his chest. "A safe haven for keeping me."

Lillith laughed. "No. This is the place I am to house my brood before releasing them into the world."

Breaking from his sour thoughts, he turned to stare at her. Lillith stood frowning, hugging herself, unwilling to look into his amber eyes as she leaned against the stone walls. Her gray skin, naked, was beautiful against the ugliness of the crumbling surroundings of a derelict temple. The scene tugged at him, his compassion returning to him as his heart waved in empathy. Marching back to her, he pinned her, his hands gripping the crumbling stone of the walls on either side of her. He glowered down at her, and her jaw tensed as she refused to look at his golden stare. Leaning in, his breath trickled over her ear and neck.

"I was brought here to save your humanity, not mine." There was almost a frustrated growl in his voice as he spoke. "Am I just the pet dog you use to get what you want? The plaything that you keep close to quench your thirst for—"

"No." Lillith shoved him in the chest, but he refused to budge as she stared angrily into his eyes. "You act like a child, Romasanta. Sorry if you weren't the center p—"

His lips interrupted her words, but he pulled away once he felt her tension release. She sighed as his voice softened. "Please, you need to do what nature has set before you, or I will be sent to end it permanently."

Turning away, he started to leave, but she grabbed his arm, pulling him back. "Stop."

Heaving a sigh, his amber eyes looked back to her, out of focus as his past haunted his thoughts. "You should understand what I mean."

"I do." Furrowing her brow, she tugged for him to come closer. "But I need your help. I, I can't find *him*."

"Cedric?" The frown on his face deepened, bewildered by the idea. "I thought you could seek out any incubus you wanted?"

"I can." Fussing at him, she hugged him as she spoke into his chest, memories of Rhea waving over him. "But the moroi, the magic... perhaps both have shielded him from me. He was in a monastery where I could not enter, but he left. I failed to notice. Even in my heat, he no longer reacts to my aura at its peak, as he has done in the past."

Pulling her off, he turned back to the archway. The wind was constant as it flowed over his skin. He closed his eyes, clenching his teeth as his left shoulder twitched under the tension. Chills ran across his skin as he readied his nerves, the freezing wind the least of his concerns. Long and slow, he inhaled through his nose. The hairs at the nape of his neck raised as he took in all the scents. The muscles in his abdomen tightened, a shudder rattling his shoulders as he found a hint of what he was looking for: the scent of blood, skin, and hair that had been burned into memory. Even with his isolation, his senses had become those of a legend, a god.

Swallowing his remorse, he opened his eyes and was greeted by the stars. "He is traveling toward the strigoi."

"Are you sure?" Her fingers made his back flinch at their touch. "What on earth could he want with the strigoi?"

"Trust me." Gritting his teeth, he shook off the scents, eager to put the godly ability back in the dark corners of his mind. "He is headed for the strigoi. There is no doubt about the scents that I found. Regardless, I will make certain that he fulfills his duty as the king of incubi."

"I'm sorry." Hands slid around him from behind as her horns dug into his back. "I didn't mean you any wrong. Please believe that. I would... I would die for you to just feel you by my side. Daphne may hold the core of your heart and soul, but your compassion fills a void in me that I had given up on centuries ago."

The scent of wet salt invaded his sense of smell as the warm drips hit the skin of his back. "Does it really take this much isolation to feel human again?"

Swallowing, she rubbed her cheek in the valley between his shoulder blades. "It's the only place safe enough for monsters like us to show we still yearn to be human..."

A wave of heat flowed from her and she pulled away. His ears followed her steps through the broken temple of solitude. She had returned to her chamber, her heat still pulling at him, goading him to follow. Looking to the stars, he allowed himself the guilty pleasure of howling. The rattle in his lungs and burning of his throat excited him as he bellowed long and hard. Panting from the feat, he could not hold back the smirk as the pack from earlier howled their respects to their wolf god in the temple.

With one last look through the rotting temple, he shifted to the werewolf. He would make haste to intervene with Cedric and the soulless strigoi, Vladimir. What had ravaged the vampire so much to turn so feral was not his concern. He was the keeper of nature. If Cedric failed to do this one task, Romasanta would be provoked into something terrible and against his will. This time he was aware, and he would correct this path. After dealing with the matter, he would turn to hunt the gypsies.

The curse would be broken by any means necessary.

CHAPTER 17

HORRIBLE TRUTHS

A blizzard was rolling in, the snow thick under his claws as he ran through the dense mountain forest. It had slowed him down, making his travels cumbersome these past few days. Shaking his fur free of snow, he pushed closer to the scent of interest. Cedric was not far from his reach, but the knots in his stomach added to the anxiety continuing to build. Nearing the last few miles, the information he detected from the temple was correct: the strigoi was Cedric's grandfather, Vladimir.

As the wind gusted over him, he could smell the massive number of decaying bodies. Snorting the scent out, he neared the tree line to peer down at the valley. It was a gruesome sight. Corpses impaled on tall stakes rocked in the blizzard's wind like morbid flowers dancing in a white meadow's breeze. There was no compassion for the living or dead here. His ears flattened on his head as he furrowed his brow, his golden glare taking in the rotting faces of soldiers, farmers, women, and children. Romasanta snarled as thoughts and emotions reacted to the thousands of wrongful deaths from a mutation of his curse. He marched for the castle. If Cedric failed to take out his grandfather, Romasanta would end the senseless slaughter at all costs.

He may have freed the world of werewolves, but he had not given any thought to the vampires. Their curse did not spread so easily, since they required an exchange of blood. Even then, the participant had a high chance of dying, unlike the versipellis who turned any who met their fangs. Unlike their werewolf predecessors, the strigoi were communal and aimed to resolve feral vampires themselves to keep their coexistence with humans a peaceful one. Over the centuries, an ever-increasing secrecy of their presence and involvement in human society had taken hold. With each passing decade, the vampire became more of a fairy tale than a tangible reality.

Cedric's appearance there may have been the result of being sent to take Vladimir down by the strigoi council. It was a strange version of affection they expressed, with immediate family members putting down those who could no longer bear their immortality. Insanity had brought most of them to an end, very little of the original mutated cursed ones remained. Family was also summoned due to abilities this curse brought out from the watered-down bloodlines of the gifted ones, like Artemis. Those who were closer in relation to the target had a higher chance of being immune to, or aware of, their abilities. A family member would have a better chance of taking down a raging demon whose actions were no longer consistent or logical. The feral cursed had a nasty habit of being highly self-destructive while destroying their surroundings, gluttons for massacring anything living.

Another shudder rattled through him, ice flicking from him as he worked his way to the cliffside leading to the castle entrance. The night had added to the freezing temperatures, but it would keep humans from bearing witness to the violent tasks needing to be done here. A gust of wind slammed his wolven head, making him squint as he took in scents from it. The heavy-bodied horse from before would be close by, but the scent was barely visible with the amount of blood in the air. Copper and sour warmth came on the wind from the castle as he pushed against the blizzard. The strength of the blood-soaked gust had washed out all of the decay-smelling wasteland surrounding him.

It was hard to say who had won the battle, Cedric or Vladimir. He was late in arriving and both of them had spilled insane amounts of blood. A faint glow was just ahead of him, the blizzard thickening as it grayed the world around. The air was growing warm as he neared the raging fire on the cliffside. When it moved, he paused, his ears raising high. The ball of fire shifted a few paces toward him. His eyes were wide as his fur raised across his neck and shoulders. Neighing erupted from it and he saw the bobbing of a horse's head; relief waved over him.

Romasanta came closer, enjoying the warm fire covering the shag foal's body. It pranced nervously, neighing at him, working around him to shove him toward the castle. If only he had chosen this horse so long ago, perhaps he would have prevented his meeting with Merlin. There was no mistaking the bulky equine was concerned for his rider and was demanding he go check. Snarling in annoyance, he shook off the wet snow and continued up the pathway. The ledge there was just wide enough for his bulk. It would have been easier to traverse as a man, but he had no desire to experience the blizzard in the nude.

Reaching the castle, it looked fitting for the devil himself. Bodies embellished the broken stonewalls as he followed Cedric's scent. Impaled, piled, and neglected, the bodies covered the entryway as a warning of the monster who took refuge there. Romasanta sniffed about the hall, traveling ever deeper. The castle's tapestries were ragged and cobwebs were thick on the walls, screaming of the neglect taking place. Cedric's blood filled the air, while Vladimir's scent was stale. That was a good sign. The pup had managed to win, but was wounded, bleeding out. Another smell mixed in, one of ashes. Not the kind from a fireplace or hearth, no signs of scorched fabric or stone; it was the stomach-turning aroma of ashes made from flesh.

Peering through the door brought him to the location of the peculiar smell and he found Cedric. Romasanta's amber eyes glowed into the darkness of the room. The only sign of Vladimir was a pile of ashes lying across the floor in a pool of Vladimir's blood. This was the curse extinguishing itself from existence upon a vampire's death. His stare fell on the slumped figure in a throne-like chair on the far wall. Cedric was no longer conscious, his breath barely tickling at Romasanta's ears. The wounds at his neck were flowing, pulsing his blood free as it painted his chest. He had been like this for hours, possibly all night.

There was no time. He needed to resupply Cedric with blood, but it couldn't come from him. Fear swelled up in him as he rushed back to the castle's exit. Cedric gained power from feeding, but Romasanta dared not let anyone take on the curse from its original source. Nothing good had ever come from that side of his wolf's bane. Light had started to fill the sky as morning pushed back the blizzard. Reluctantly, he braved the concentrated smell as he had done for Lillith. Closing his eyes, he soaked everything in, his ear flicking at the sound of a crow.

"Badbh." Without hesitation, he leaped to a run.

Scrambling across the cliff, he nearly fell. Barushka startled as he sped past and headed for the valley where so many battles had laid waste to the landscape. The sun was rising, and he had no idea how much time remained. His thoughts spun in a panic, questions of Gaea's law and what would happen if he failed to salvage the situation. Would he still have to kill Lillith if she had no mate? Was there an unknown circumstance where he would become the new mate? An adaptation determined by the unspoken caste system they all knew existed for the demonic monsters lurking in the shadows. If a horse could turn immortal and wield flames by his will, why wouldn't he be picked to carry out the duty of replacing Cedric?

Swallowing, he begged his terror to stop as he pressed forward. Leaping over broken barricades, he was joyous to see the battle goddess. Badbh was standing on the hilltop, looking over the dreadful remains of the last battle. She was fussing with her ravens when he yelped to gain her attention. Turning, she saw him racing through the bodies and debris. She smiled at seeing such an odd thing.

"Are we that happy to see me again?" Waving the ravens off, she crossed her arms. "Is this your way of wanting to join me?"

"No." Catching his breath, he shook off the anxiety of his thoughts. "Cedric is dying in the castle. He defeated Vladimir, but he's bled out far too much and passed out before healing..."

"Let's not waste time." Badb grabbed his shoulder, and they were swallowed in a swirl of raven's feathers.

The feathers tickled his nose, and he sneezed as they blackened the world around them. His eyes widened as they began to fall, drifting away on the wind. The motion had been swift, smooth, and flawless, like an agile warrior. They now stood in the darkness of the room where he had left Cedric. He backed away, moving himself to the doorway as she marched over to the unmoving body. The dim morning light sparkled in the lines falling from Cedric's wounds. Badbh's fingers touched his skin. Jerking away from the startling cold it held, she shot a glance back at the wolf at the door.

Huffing, she bellowed, "Well, you are up here after all!"

Her voice brought some movement to his pale body, his eyes cracking open as his chapped lips whispered. "Angeline?"

"Oh, no! Wrong girl, lover boy." Chuckling, Badbh's magic was impressive as she summoned cloths for his wounds. As she worked to clean his lacerations, Romasanta recalled fond memories of the woman from the Leper's Colony tending to the ill girl. "Looks like I missed a hell of a battle!"

"What are you doing?" Cedric hissed, giving a baffled stare at his unhealed wounds. "Who are you?"

"For crying out loud, it's me, Badbh!" Puffing, she scrubbed harder, annoyed at how unaware he had allowed himself to become. "We found you out here bleeding to death! Who the hell did you get into a fight with?"

"Vladimir." He was blinking a lot, his eyes desperate for blood flow so he could see clearly again. "I was sent to end his tyranny by the strigoi and..."

"Ah, I keep forgetting the strigoi like to clean up after themselves." Badb finished his neck, the bleeding stopped, and she moved on to Cedric's shoulders where muscles were torn through to the bone. "Shame I missed this one, though. I was in the area after I had gotten word of some nasty battles. I was hoping to participate and give those Turks a boost of morale. It tends to keep the wars motivated for my entertainment."

"Wait." Cedric pushed Badbh away, sitting up, startled, fear wafting from him. "What did you mean by, *'We found you?'*"

Romasanta's golden glare met Cedric's green glower. He watched as Cedric shifted to his chest and back again, reassuring himself it was who he had suspected. Romasanta's shoulders tensed at the fact he was very aware of the mark Merlin had melted into him. More so, he was relieved to see Cedric awake from the little Badbh had done. Romasanta was able to allow himself to relax again. Looking over what other wounds Cedric had, Romasanta's eyes paused at Cedric's left hand. A smile crawled across his canine face to see his ring finger was still missing. He knew he was capable of regenerating it, much like himself, but to be so stubborn to deny himself a digit humored Romasanta. Deep down, he felt the same devotion to Daphne. But the things they would both have to do to get their soulmates back might destroy who they once were.

"Romasanta found you, and then called on me." Sighing, she stood and looked back at Romasanta for a second. "How he even knew I was in the area, I have no idea."

"How did you find me?" Cedric leaned forward, but hissed as his body screamed its disapproval. The uncanny sound of him breaking free of the chair's cloth made Badbh wince. It was unclear if the sound was from dried or frozen blood that had glued him to the throne. "What are you doing out here?"

"You spilled so much blood that the smell was making me sick." Grunting, Romasanta wasn't ready to reveal he had indeed come for Cedric. "And like you, I am searching for information on the matters that concern my situation. My research led me here, but instead, I found you, pup. It seems we were meant to cross paths again."

Cedric glared at them, sighing as he took in their faces. Reaching up, he felt the devastation Vladimir's claws had left on his neck. Paling, he covered his face, tension growing as he took in his situation. Romasanta knew what was rolling through Cedric's mind. He was dreading having to feed on someone other than Angeline. Since the day Merlin took her, no other blood had graced his tongue for the means of pleasure or healing. A sigh escaped Cedric, and Romasanta shot Badbh a knowing stare as he left the two of them alone. He needed to signal Lillith he had found Cedric. Afterward, he would seek out the gypsies who could reveal more about the curse he carried.

The sun was high, the sky clear as he took a deep breath in and howled long and hard. Before the last of the steam rolling from his snout stopped, his chest tingled where her touch had left its mark. He decided she was keeping a close eye on him, but for what purpose, it was hard to say. At least this mark was pleasing and did not leave a scarred reminder of a terrible memory. Every time he felt its prickly, warming sensation, he was reminded he wasn't alone. His sigh ended in a huge puff of steam as he looked back at the castle.

His nose twitched as the scent of Badbh's blood floated to him. The deed had been done, Cedric was healed and nothing negative had happened to the battle goddess. At most, the sweat mingling in the air told him the incubus in Cedric made the experience pleasurable. Grunting, he wondered if the fang marks tingled for his victims as Lillith's first touch does for him. A gust of wind shifted, bringing him a fragrances from the nearby forest. There, on the wind, he caught a hint of what he was also here for: gypsies.

146

Looking about his clawed feet, he found what acceptable clothing he could from the dead. He shivered a moment, paused, then sniffed once more. The fiery horse was still down the cliff a ways. The idea of changing near a warm fire was much more pleasant than attempting to do it in this dead, frozen palace. Scrambling down the hill, the horse danced, eager to hear what had become of Cedric. He was no longer aflame; his black, hairy coat was shiny and his mane and tail were long and wavy. Barushka snorted, and Romasanta grinned, petting him on his nose to calm him.

"He's alive. I made sure he would make it through. Now I need your help, old friend." Barushka bobbed his head in agreement, but he paused. Cedric had caught up to him, something Romasanta hadn't expected.

"What sort of deal do you want out of me this time?" Cedric greeted Barushka, his forehead leaning affectionately on the horse's as he patted his bulky neck. "I know that look, and we both know you do not save others unless there is something in it for you. What will you ask of me now?"

"Well, let's just get to business." Frustrated that Cedric had recovered so quickly, Romasanta huffed, steam rolling out of his nostrils like a dragon's breath. "I believe we are chasing the same foe."

Pausing, Cedric's green eyes were sharp as they glared at him. "And what has Merlin done to you?"

"You are looking at it." Snarling, he was trying to gauge how much to reveal to the man in front of him. "Merlin is the one who did this to me ages ago. I am immortal and tortured to live as a disease upon humankind for his enjoyment."

"Then, are we to work together to get both our hands on the bastard wizard?" A grin snaked across Cedric's lips as he cracked the stiffness from his healed neck, with no signs of his injuries on his skin. "Is that the deal? Free exchange of information between the two of us?"

"That is essentially the deal." It was not doing him any good to keep Cedric out of the equation. He held his massive paw out. A truce between them would benefit them both in order to take down Merlin. "I want the killing blow when we find him."

"I just want Angeline safe." Cedric's grip was firm as they shook in agreement. "But what makes you think I can locate someone that an old dog like you has failed to do so?"

"Let's just say I have a gut feeling that you already have a plan and just need time." His golden glare locked Cedric's eyes in them.

"What else are you not telling me, old man?" The smile fell from Cedric's face, their hands still gripped, neither willing to release in fear they would leave before they had asked their questions. "You were here looking for me. I see it in your eyes."

"Yes." The glare they exchanged was fierce, each standing their ground. "Have you forgotten your duties as King Incubus?"

The muscles in Cedric's face tightened and his jaw twitched before he spoke. "Unfortunately, no. I have not forgotten the task I must carry out with Lillith."

"Gaea's law will not allow it to be delayed any further." It was best to be blunt since there were fewer questions about his involvement that would be asked. "Lillith will be coming here shortly to see this done."

Romasanta could smell a wave of fear wash over him as Cedric growled, "I suppose I should sit and wait for her."

"She's not what you think she is." Romasanta's heart ached, knowing that no one but him had seen the compassion she truly hid inside. "If it makes you feel better, you should have enough time to think about how you can use this to your advantage."

Cedric grunted, spitting to the ground, seeing no good in being forced to make a brood with the Queen Succubus. "We'll see."

"May I borrow your horse?" Their grips released; each had their task ahead of them. "I will be going to the gypsy camp for information. Once I finish, I'll return him to you. Besides, I have business with Lillith."

Cedric shot a look to Barushka, who pawed the ground, nodding that he was fine with this. "Fine."

Romasanta hummed to himself as Cedric marched back to the castle. There was no mistaking Cedric's fears about Lillith. The two of them ravaged each other in a ferocious battle so long ago. Sighing, he looked at the sky, knowing Lillith was uneasy about the deed needing to be done. Knowing her, she would find a way to seduce and appeal to him without it feeling forced. Shuddering, he hated the fact he was having to push them to make a brood. The fear of Gaea's will calling him into action to take either of them down was something Romasanta wished to avoid.

His eyes fell back to his claws, where the tattered clothes awaited him. "Dear Barushka, may I ask for a fire?"

The horse exploded into flames. Swallowing, Romasanta shifted back into a human, the cold slapping his skin like a wall of ice. Desperate, he fumbled to get the clothes on and layer what he managed to carry. Heat waved off the shag foal, a saving grace in his naked form out in the wintry weather. Nodding he had finished, Barushka quelled his flames and allowed the old acquaintance to climb into his saddle. Adjusting himself, Romasanta smiled, patting the base of Barushka's neck and shoulder.

"If only we had this saddle back at home, hmm?" Barushka nodded and neighed as he cantered back to the woods. "I guess we've both come a long way since those times."

It wasn't long before Romasanta and the horse came upon the circle of wagons. A large fire in the center had provided heat for the gypsies during the blizzard. They paused in their work, glowering at the ragged man on the large horse. Sliding off, he returned their glare with his amber stare and a few gasped in response. Whispers bounced in his ears in a language he had never heard before. A small boy was sent to a wagon and, after several minutes, he rushed back out. Without fear, he ran to Romasanta, taking him by his hand and leading him to the wagon. As if this had broken all suspicions of who he was, they went back to their activities as if time had temporarily frozen them.

The boy stopped outside the wagon's cloth door, motioning he enter alone. Paranoid, he sniffed the air and the scent greeting him made his eyes grow wide. Romasanta looked down at the child, who ran away giggling to see a man act like a dog. It was a scent he had not smelled for centuries, but his heart raced. That girl had been human. Or had he not seen something back in the days when he hid himself among dying men? Her scent had reminded him of home. He should have taken more interest in who she could have been. But in those times, he had failed to notice the things in front of him. Gathering his nerve, he entered with a huff, his muscles taut. A tall woman stood with her back to him, her black wavy hair cascading down her back.

"Just wait a moment, Romasanta." Her voice sounded like a flute, soothing to his ears. "I do owe you for nursing me back to health so long ago."

The thud of his heart made his chest twinge as nerves tightened in his joints. "You can't be..."

Looking over her shoulder, a brown eye looked him over before turning away. "It's difficult to explain. Like you, my life is complicated and I must be patient before the time comes when I am needed."

"Who are you?" he whispered, entranced by his own curiosity. "What are you?"

Coyly, she looked over her other shoulder, and a green eye gleamed at him. "Call me Cleo. And I am simply a gypsy for now. Later, I might choose another role."

"Don't dodge the question, Cleo." She turned, crossing her arms with a smirk as his tone deepened. "What are you?"

"An abomination." Walking over to him, she kissed his forehead as she whispered, "Do you really want to know the answer to your question? I think you already know what I am about to say."

"I am tired of guessing all the time." He furrowed his brow as she stepped back, her two colored eyes locking with his golden ones. "I need to know exactly what happened..."

"Your fears are correct." Her forehead creased as she rubbed his cheek. "Fenrir is gone."

"I don—"

Pressing her thumb against his lips, she continued, "Your curse is gone as well, and has been gone since Fenrir chose you as his heir and faded into the spirit world."

Tears wavered in his eyes as he took it in.

"Romasanta, you are a man who has been given a rare gift from an unlikely source." Mustering a sincere smile, her thumb released his lips to rub a tear from his cheek. "I know this is what you feared most, but please, I promise. Fenrir has left you a wonderful gift in hopes it will help you get Daph—"

Romasanta gripped her wrist, and yanking her hand from his face, he snarled, fangs showing. "Do not dare speak her name to me, abomination."

Failing to jerk her arm from his hand, she snorted, her jaw twitching as she glowered at him. "She's there in the black forest waiting on you."

"Do I look like I don't know that!" Throwing her hand to her, he roared as anger drowned him. "I can never go to her like this! THIS ISN'T WHAT SHE LOVED!"

Rubbing her wrist, she scoffed at him. "That's not for you to decide! She is capable of seeing through it. How many times have you visited her since the day you left? Tell me that, you coward!"

"WHO ARE YOU?" Romasanta pounced on her and she lay on her back, his hands holding her arms against the wooden floor as the wagon rocked from the motion. His weight crushed down on top of her as he asked, "Who told you about this?"

Laughing, her green eye sparkled as she whispered, "Gaea."

Scrambling away, he covered his face. Thoughts and emotions tangled and spiraled out of control. His body reacted to his mind as it shattered into a million pieces that it was locked in a form between man and wolf. He was a broken being. Her fingers grazed his shoulder, and he jerked like a petrified animal. His ears no longer heard the words she was trying to tell him. Instead, they were deafened by his terror and the sound of his heart thudding. Another touch and he bolted out the door, rushing past Barushka. All Romasanta wanted was the comfort of the cold forest. There, in his solitude, he howled and screamed in rage and sorrow for all to hear.

He would be forever lost, his humanity taken from him. One curse removed while another gained in its place. Why did the demon wolf Fenrir favor him so deeply to allow him to keep this monstrous form permanently? There was no breaking an inheritance given from a dying soul to the living. The spirits had given him a gift, one like his sister and his wife had been forced with, but so much more painful. No cure, no hope, no longer a man. How could Daphne ever forgive him and ever accept a monster where her husband once stood?

This girl with the gypsies was Gaea's abomination who knew every detail of his self-inflictions. Cleo had simply told Romasanta what he had been told instinctually. Clawing at his head, he had turned to his werewolf form in his tantrum. No longer did he care to be the justicar for Gaea. From that day forward, he would abandon his compassion and all would learn to fear what lurks in the shadows of the forest once more. The centuries to come would be fueled by his rebellion against Gaea, Lillith, and all of them. If he was a demon, he would play the part and spill blood every chance he saw.

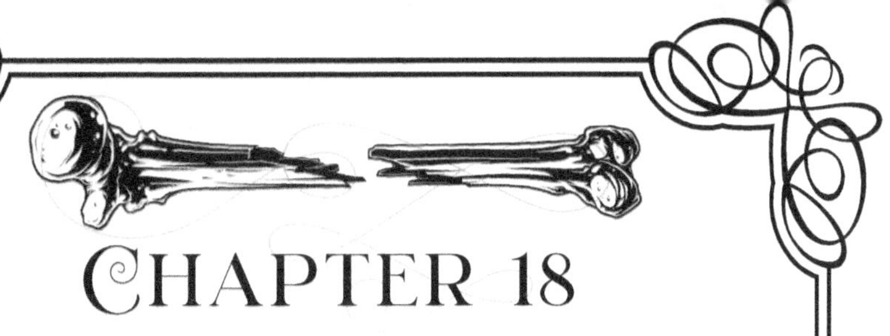

CHAPTER 18

THE TALLOW MAN

"On this sixth day of April 1853, the court finds Manuel Blanco Romasanta guilty of thirteen known deaths in which he consumed human flesh, rendered their fat for soap, and attempted to resale their belongings." The judge's voice bounced off the silent courtroom walls as everyone shifted, staring at the scruffy man in chains before them. "Do you have any more you wish to say, Romasanta?"

The deep brown of his eyes locked with the judge's as he reminded them with eerie calm, "I told you, I am cursed as a wolf. They were attacked and eaten because I was hungry. Be thankful that I did not let any part of them go to was—"

A woman's wailing broke his speech short as other spectators shouted their disapproval. They were outraged he felt this was a justified reason for the actions he took. Looking over his shoulder, his dark eyes silenced the crowd, and their faces paled. This act of submission excited him, but he swallowed it down; this wasn't the time to show such pride. He had grown tired of running loose and devouring the living. This wearisomeness had led to his standing here in this ridiculous session of justice. These people were naïve to think they were containing him in these pitiful iron bands at his wrists and ankles. If he wanted to, if he desired to do so, he could slaughter them all and walk away unscathed.

Sighing, he humored the guard, who led him to his tiny prison. It was dark and damp; he welcomed the cold stone walls that would hide him from the sun. This was a more fitting place for him to lose himself to his sour thoughts. The world was evolving and the days of running amuck in the forest had increasingly become an annoyance. Human populations bounced beyond the times of the Romans. No longer was there a rash of random villages, but townships and cities were there to stay for future generations.

Sitting, he leaned against the damp stone, a smile crawling across his face. The guard shuddered, slamming the thick oak and iron door closed. Then came the rattling of keys locking the latch. His nerves unwound with the acceptance he took at being jailed. They were indulging in false securities if they thought the door and lock would hold him there. It was only Romasanta's desire to rest and hide away that allowed them to lead him about on the weak chain leash. He took in the musky, damp smell of the cell. It was a place of decay and rot, physically and mentally. Here he found what he wanted: solitude.

Lillith had pleaded with him numerous times for him to return to the enchanted temple in the wintry mountains, but he had no desire to keep his heart open. He closed it, encouraging it to freeze over, and allowed the last tiny piece of his humanity to fall away from his soul. Gaea's whispers went silent and if any of the demons he encountered had been sent from her, they failed to end his reign of terror. Each earned their turn in his fangs and were destroyed by his claws. He was indeed the top demon in this world.

As for the girl Cleo, he never saw her again. He had his fun ravaging the gypsy camps as a message to her and her creator Gaea to stay out of his life. The darkening vengeance even gave him the desire to chase down Lillith's halflings, a form of shouting, "Keep away!" Every time his chest tingled, he immediately sought out the closest succubus; whether a water-downed version or full-blooded, he did not care. Their powers did nothing to him. He saw through the temptations and knew they only had power when he also desired what they promised. Unfortunately, he had not sought them out to fill his thirst for pleasures of the flesh. He had come for the feast.

Grunting, he rubbed the tingling at his chest. Lillith was no fool, but neither was he. Deep down, they both desired the comfort they brought each other, but he had grown tired of the rollercoaster his fate had become. Too many times had he climbed to the top of the mountainous obstacles thrown at him to only fall back to the lake of fire waiting at the bottom. Even living a dull life of squandering and doing as he pleased during the past four centuries had failed to quell the emotional torrents boiling up within him. It felt desperate to be seeking out solitude in prison, but he hadn't found it on the road or even in the forest. Perhaps, deep down, he felt he needed to pay for the crimes he had committed in the last few years. Crimes that were so unspeakable, he earned the title of the Tallow Man.

The succubus halflings were seen as humans in today's world. Something about the succubi traits carried aphrodisiac properties into anything produced by their bodies. From personal experience, he knew the saliva alone could induce breathtaking arousal wherever it touched. Fat from a succubus descendant, especially when rendered into soap, worked better than the finest perfume to attract lovers. Women had flocked to his wagon, and he always sold out of any soaps he had made. His exploits all ended when he became lazy, and didn't pay attention to the people in town when selling his victims' clothes. A relative recognized a dress they had made for one of the women and reported him.

The guards had approached him, nervous and terrified, since he easily towered over them in height and bulk. When he confessed to his crimes and held his wrist out, they had become baffled. Everyone in town had thrown rocks and spit on him, but he did not flinch or care. He wanted to see what this justice system had in store for him. At the very least, he would rejoice in solitude. Exhaustion was the single sensation he felt when required to interact with another creature. Life had grown into a nuisance and having no end in sight, he could only settle for imprisonment.

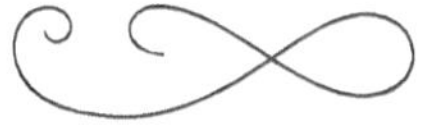

The sour musk of a rat greeted his nose, making him snort. He cracked one eye open, an amber glow peering out into the bleakness of the lightless stone box. A tiny nose and whiskers were poking out of the crack in the wall across from him. His lips curled into a wicked grin, fangs baring as he watched it waddle out into the open. It had become too complacent with its living space. The rat no longer made the piss-soaked trails across the walls or verified routes of safety like it should. Stupidly, it ventured closer to him, its instincts muddled by false security built up from human prisoners. Some may have fed him to be so fat, but there was a hint of rotting flesh smell coming from the pudgy rodent. He had indulged on the dead numerous times.

He pierced his fingertip with his thumbnail so it would bleed, and he grinned further. The rat paused, its nose bobbing high in the air to decipher where the smell floated to him from. Soon the tickling of whiskers greeted his waiting fingertips. Teeth nibbled at the bleeding fingertip, and Romasanta still did not flinch. Gripping the greasy creature in his hands, it shrieked and squealed. It gnashed its teeth desperately to escape, and it broke his skin. Golden eyes glowered down at it struggling in his crushing grip. He could feel the popping and snapping of its fragile bones under his fingers. The sensation was exciting, reminding him of the countless ribs he had broken between his canine teeth.

The motion was gruesome and swift as he grasped its bony skull in his teeth, ripping it free of the convulsing body in his hands. It rolled on his tongue as he peered back at the tiny square of light where horrified eyes peered through the iron bars. Spitting the skull from his mouth, it smacked the bars, sending the guard scrambling backward. Laughter rolled from Romasanta's chest as he tossed the rat's body against the door with a sickening thud. The guard had yelped, but it was the smell of urine that made Romasanta giggle. At least one man here knew they kept a monster as a prisoner.

Leaning his head back against the stony wall, he closed his eyes, his laughter dying down. Here he could sleep, paying no heed to the time or the passing days. His death penalty was humorous. He would deal with that when the time came. The idea of it was nice, but did not rattle him with fear like it did so many in this rancid place. If they were capable of ending his wretched life, he would have entered the justice system long ago. A heavy sigh left his lips, and remorse started to boil up from his core. Again, he wrestled with his conscience. Haunting thoughts and memories wanted their turn in his mind, but he denied them. He did not want to be reminded of Artemis, Daphne, Rhea, Lillith, or even Nyctimus and Cedric.

Swallowing the remorse down, his anger burned all of it back into the darkness where he kept his soul. Remorse had only caused him pain in the past. He had given up his search for the stone, for Merlin, for answers to anything he had once wanted at any cost. The more his questions were answered, the more hopeless his situation felt. Answers brought no comfort, and they complicated everything, wrecking his mind and heart. His soul had tangled itself so much it had suffocated under the weight of his emotions. All that remained was the monster he accepted himself to be until the end of days.

Another wave rolled up from the abyss. Daphne's face and voice called out to him in his sleep. Fear and heartache made him sweat as he woke from his restless sleep. Two rats were engorging themselves on his food at the door. It was hard to say how long he had let himself sleep, but he did not hunger for food, not anymore. Those days had long passed after the time he had spent with Rhea. Rubbing his face, he tried to wipe his eyes free of their faces, but without the sunlight, it was impossible. Still shackled at the wrists and ankles, he stumbled to his feet and staggered to his tiny window, where a storm blew icy rain into the cell. It was nighttime, with lightning flashing on occasion.

A tingling at his chest added to his ire, and he banged his head into the stone wall. Why could he not forget? Another teeth-shattering slam between his skull and the rock sent his ears ringing. Tears fell from his eyes as warm blood dripped down the bridge of his nose, splattering the floor at his feet. Another wave of emotions swallowed him. His ears were ringing, but he still heard the words he dreaded most, '*I love you, Romasanta! This was not your fault!*' He bashed his head into the wall again and stumbled back, his vision failing him. All he felt was the thud of his body hitting the damp floor.

"How long has he been doing this?" His body failed to move, his eyes unwilling to open. "I asked you a very important question. How long has he been beating his head into the wall like this?"

"Mo-months." The guard's words fumbled over themselves. "The man is insane. He sleeps forever and wakes in fits and—"

"Yes, we all know this man is insane, sir. But to allow this level of self-mutilation is deplorable!" This other voice was familiar to his ears, but the chemical smell in the air muddled his nose. "These wounds are horrendous. How much longer will the judge be? I wish to take this man to the hospital for treatment."

"I am here. Now what in God's na—" A gasp came from the new man. "Good God! Who did this to him?"

"N-no one, sir." Stuttering, the guard stumbled away from Romasanta, his feet scuffing the ground. "He did this to himself."

"And who are you?" roared the judge in alarm. "What is going on here?"

"I am Dr. Lykaon. Can we strike a deal?" This man had guts; his voice was more authoritative than the judge's. "I will relieve your men of this prisoner, seeing that they fear him to the point of not being able to care for him properly. You can choose to tell the public that he committed suicide or to tell them he was sent to my hospital for attempting suicide."

"Sir, we tried to tell you the loon was beating his head in almost a year ago..." The voice of his other guard had entered the conversation. "I say we let the doctor do whatever he wants with the man. No one will know who he is. His face is shattered."

"Y-yes!" agreed the frightened guard. "I haven't seen a fucking n-nose on him in m-m-months!"

There was a long pause. Romasanta tried to move, but his mouth and nose were greeted with a rag full of the chemical smell, muddling his wherewithal.

"Get him the hell away from here," groaned the judge, his footsteps moving away. "He's dead if anyone asks."

The tingling on Romasanta's chest brought dreams he wished would let him forget. Growling and thrashing in his sleep, he wanted to wake, but his body pushed him back into the dream world. The voices of Daphne and Artemis constantly reminding him, *"You are a man. It's not your fault,"* echoed in his mind, and his heart pounded in his chest. He was rotting in prison to try to forget this, not to be forced to remember it. Roaring, howling, he slashed out, angry at being this way. No longer did he want to be a man. He was a monster, and all related to his human side needed to go away!

His blood boiled in his veins, his body heating up with the rage fueling him. Fighting to wake from his nightmares and his memories, he ran full steam on all fours. His ribs stung as something slammed into them and he rolled across the dusty stone floor. He shook his wolven head, his eyes opened, his amber stare frantic to take in his surroundings. He caught a glimpse of light through a tiny square and ran for it. Putting his weight and force into the wall, his shoulder did nothing to rattle the stone of this place free.

Panting, he searched his new prison. At some point, he had allowed himself to turn into the werewolf, but Lillith's mark tingled at his chest. Her sorcery had a deeper reach than he feared as it blinded his senses. More memories rattled his core. These contained days at the farm and the times he enjoyed Rhea as himself or watched Fenrir with her. Growling, foam dripped from his jowls. Shaking his head, his sight wavered, and he saw the wooden door.

Once more, he dashed for the escape. Again, the burning thud against his ribs sent him rolling across the hard floor. Unlike the damp prison, this place was dry and plumes of dust rolled up with each movement, smells masked by its fragrance. Wherever he found himself, it had stored hops for beer, and the spice burned in his nostrils. He wheezed; his ribs were cracked from the unknown attack. Grasping his side, he slumped to the ground. This was a battle he could not win.

"Are you there, Lillith?" he grumbled. He would have to face the reality of who was behind this entrapment. "Was this your doing?"

"I am here, my wolf." The heavenly sound of her voice greeted his ears again after over three thousand years. "But this was not my plan."

He flopped onto his back, his ribs taking their time to heal. "Who outsmarted me then?"

"Me." It was the voice of Dr. Lykaon from before. "Or have you forgotten about me so easily, Romasanta?"

Sitting up, his ears pricked high, he faced two glowing hazel eyes in the far corner of the room. "Nyctimus... Nyctimus Lykaon, I should have known..."

Silence engulfed them as his golden eyes glowered at the hazel-eyed wolf in the corner. "Sorry to force this on you, Romasanta, but I was instructed to do so by someone who has information for your ears only."

"I'm not interested," he growled, picking himself off the ground and shaking the dust from his fur. "I no longer desire to search for answers."

"Merlin is one of Gaea's sons," barked Nyctimus, catching Romasanta's attention. "But for the rest of the information, you will have to go to her."

"That gypsy cunt can rot in hell." Snorting, Romasanta started for the door. "Nothing is worth dealing with her again."

The door swung open, and Lillith stood firm as she blocked the exit. "You have to go to her because she hasn't been able to move locations since she risked her life for you."

He staggered to a stop as he looked into her red glare, wide-eyed. "No, I can't. You don't understand, I can't go to that place..."

"You've been avoiding her all these centuries, you have to go see her." Nyctimus's ears flattened as he furrowed his brow. "She asked us to help you, told us to remind you that you're only a man. None of this is your—"

"STOP!" Clawing at his own ears, he shook his head, clenching his teeth. "Not another word!"

Tingling burned at his chest and he shot a feral look toward Lillith's grim face as she warned, "Romasanta. Don't make me drag out everything you hold in your heart."

"You can't..." he breathed as he slumped to the floor, still pulling at his head. "I'm a monster. She can't see me like this."

"Leave us," she hissed, shooting a glare at Nyctimus.

Nyctimus looked at his broken friend, whimpering as she slammed the door behind him.

"I have been patient with you, my wolf," she huffed as she marched over to him, looming over him. "But it seems you are the one who failed to see what it is I am capable of doing to someone."

"Lillith, please don't do it." His large canine eyes watered, the gold weak in them as he pleaded with her. "I don't want to remember. This whole time I tried so hard to forget—"

"The heart of a man will never forget his love for others, for his life, and for faith in the world." Taking his bottom jaw in her hand, she stared down his muzzle into his eyes. "That's why you can never forget them, Romasanta. You were never a monster, but always a man at heart and soul. That is why you have caught my love. As someone who once wished for a man to love her as his wife."

160

"Daphne could never forgive me. I have been unfaithful." Tears rolled down his cheeks as he shifted back to a man. "Rhea, you, and the lives I have..."

Breaking from her grasp, he lunged to the side, puking as faces of his crimes flooded him. So many he had maliciously slaughtered without reason or cause. Before he fell into his sour ways, he could rest easy that it had been Gaea's will to take them down. What excuse did he have now?

"Romasanta, do you understand why I am drawn to you and marked you on our very first time meeting you?" Her voice was softer, her back to him as she hugged her arms. "There is something you have that I steal..."

Wiping his mouth, he glowered over at her. "Steal?"

"Yes." Her shoulders rose and fell with a heavy sigh. "There are very few who hold the love and devotion you have for your wife. It is that essence of love that is the rarest for me to find, let alone get the chance to feed on multiple times."

"So I'm just a meal for you." Scowling, he felt hurt and angry, sickened by the idea that every time they had lain together she was feeding off his love for Daphne. "Is this why—"

"No, that's your own doing." Hissing, she shot an angry glare over her shoulder. "Not even I can weaken memories and compassion for another. You're responsible for that foul action and neglect. It's just the purest form that empowers a succubus into godlike status. I marked you as mine so that none could pull that from you."

He paled as it became clear why the halflings never could use their power on him. "I have been so naïve..."

"Beyond measure." She headed for the door, pausing as she frowned down at him. "You have no choice. We are taking you to her in the Black Forest."

Hot tears fell across his naked skin as he stared up at Lillith. "Will you come with me? You and Nyctimus? I—I can't do it alone..."

"We will be with you." Her face softened, and a smile came to her lips. "I am coming because I know the love you have for her. Nyctimus is a good friend, and you need to learn to accept him in your life, you dumb mutt."

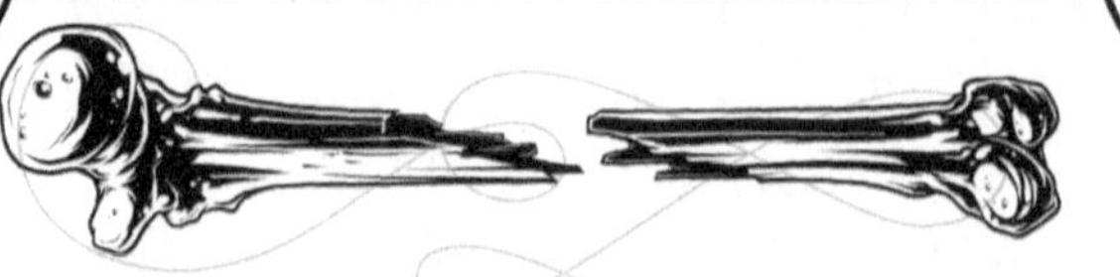

CHAPTER 19

THE RETURN

The creaking of the door broke him from his nightmares. Curled in a naked ball, his body ached from the extensive healing he had endured. His face and skull were no longer fractured. His ribs were strong and unbroken. All of it made his body feel weak and sore. The smell of raw meat greeted his nose and his stomach rumbled in response. Rolling over, he saw Nyctimus smiling, a plate of steak in his hands. Furrowing his brow, Romasanta stared at the raw meat. The burden of what he was weighing became heavier on his heart. He was an animal, devouring raw flesh was nauseatingly satisfying to him. It was far more exciting if he had the chance to stalk it, chase it to the ground, and lick the bones clean as a reward afterward.

"You have to be starving." Nyctimus frowned as he threw a sheet on the floor next to Romasanta. "Cover up and come with me. At least you can still eat at a table like a man, can't you?"

A flash of gold hit his eyes as he glowered at Nyctimus's smirk. Reluctantly, he grabbed the sheet and pulled himself up on his feet. The smell of the meat made his mouth water as he fumbled to secure the sheet around his waist. Swallowing constantly, desperate not to drool like a starving dog, he followed Nyctimus out of his cell. His nose crumpled as the smell of kerosene lanterns invaded the cellar hall and they climbed the stairs. It was a struggle to break his gaze on the food, his animal instincts overwhelming him as the need to eat—to survive— pulled at every fiber within him.

He rubbed his chest, the scar greeting his palm, and he gave a heavy sigh. He feared that the day Merlin burned it into him was the day that he had become what he was. Even when Fenrir was active, terror rolled in his soul, wary of the demon side he was succumbing to in order to achieve his goals. With that knowledge came the horror of facing

Daphne, knowing he would not be able to hide the curse. The wolf's bane haunted him. She had sacrificed her life to save him, entrapped as a laurel tree, and he had abandoned her. The muscles in his chest tightened as his sorrow, his shame, drowned him. How could he forsake the one person he loved most in this world? Thousands of years had passed, and he had no reason not to return to her.

Gripping the wall, his knees were giving up on him. He sank to the floor, a hand over his face as tears soaked his cheeks. Daphne's face had stayed so clear in his mind after all the rage, all the feral actions and thoughts, even after he had lost his mind and humanity. Even now, she was saving his life. That last day with her, she had tried so hard to beat it in his head that whatever happened, it was ok. No blame or anger toward him, but she had known what would become of him. Still, even with that, he failed her. Reckless, he squandered the chances, and countless times he had given up all hope of recovering the stone, finding Merlin, and more importantly, rescuing her from her eternal prison. How would he justify any of it? There was no way to justify even half of the things he had done.

A warm hand gripped his arm, tugging him back to his feet as it coaxed him to go a little farther down the hallway. Nyctimus helped him into a room, making him sit at a small table as he opened a curtain. Wincing, the sunlight stung Romasanta's eyes, making him realize he had lost track of the last time he had even looked at the sun. Blinking a few times, he saw the windows here had bars on them, but the white-painted walls were refreshing in comparison to the stone walls of his prison cell. He observed the tiny room: he had a table and chair, a bed in the corner, and lastly, a dresser for clothes. Simple and efficient for a temporary stay. It was clean, with no signs of the rot, filth, and rats he had spent years living in, accepting it at a level of normal.

His eyes returned to the bright red, wet meat on the plate in front of him, his stomach tensing, fighting the hunger. Again, he swallowed, trying to keep up with the copious amounts of saliva forming in his mouth. He felt if he ate the flesh offered to him, he would be accepting what he was, a wolf in a man's body. His hand moved for the fork, but he jerked it back to his lap. The sore and weak sensation in his body would be gone if he ate, but that was the only form of pain he experienced. His muscles tightened in his chest, his breathing short and rapid as anxiety started to take its hold of him.

"Romasanta." Nyctimus's voice broke his stare on the raw food. "You've always been an anxious person, but if we are going to take you to her, you'll need to eat. At least this is reasonable, versus what you have been doing..."

Creasing his forehead, he looked down at the plate. His hands shook as they took hold of the fork and knife. He sliced a small chunk; the smell was intoxicating. His stomach rumbled, goading him on to eat it. Shoulders heavy, he closed his eyes as he caved to his instincts, the flavor on his tongue pleasurable. It took every muscle to slow himself as he took down the slabs. On the last bite, he dropped the silverware, unable to keep himself from licking the plate clean. Slamming the plate down, he realized how much he had truly lost himself. Before, he would have never had a hard time pushing back the wolf-like behavior. Losing his humanity, his self-awareness, had made him no different from a feral dog.

Panting, his heart raced as he panicked over the difficulty he was having to be human. His body shook as his nerves unraveled, every muscle taut as the tears of terror fell from his eyes. Suffocating under his regret, he flinched as Nyctimus's hand touched his bare back. A gentle smile came across his hazel-eyed friend's face and Romasanta realized he had made so many mistakes. This whole time he had been stubborn, dealing with his curse alone, yet there was a man, also cursed, who had been trying to be a great friend to him.

"I'm so sorry, Nyctimus." It took Romasanta a few tries before he found the words. "I've been so blind, and failed to see the friendship you have always offered me. How can you smile down on something so vile..."

"Because we both know you are a fool, Romasanta." Nyctimus raised an eyebrow as he gave him a baffled look. "Never did you intend to set your curse loose upon the earth. Nor could a farmer realize that chasing after his bull could lead him to a life full of torture. Like me, deep down, we are only men. That is the reason we break so easily. Even I have had my times of being the animal, but it is how we repent, correct our wrongdoings, that counts the most."

Romasanta mustered a half-hearted smile. "Yes, deep down, I am only a man. A man terrified of the things I am capable of doing and a cowardly husband whose heart breaks at the very idea of seeing his beloved still spellbound as a laurel tree."

Patting Romasanta's back, Nyctimus gripped his shoulder tight. "She is lucky to have a man who loves her so deeply."

Romasanta shook his head in disagreement, his face souring as he furrowed his brow at Nyctimus. "No. I don't deserve her. I have given up on her so many times, loved others, and worse, could not bring myself to face her. Looking back, it sickens me to know I had the ability to fall so far down that the devil himself smiled at me for the evil I have done."

Sighing, Nyctimus dug deeper into Romasanta's regrets. "But, if the devil ever approached you during all that, I know the man inside you would have ended his misguided temper."

Covering his face, Romasanta digested the idea. "Perhaps you are right. Often I am blind to the severity of what I am doing until it's too late."

"Exactly." Walking to the door, Nyctimus paused. He saw that Romasanta had stopped shaking, his nerves calming. "What do you plan on doing to repent?"

"Make amends starting with Daphne." Staring into Nyctimus's hazel eyes, his deep brown eyes made his resolve concrete. "I am ready to return to the Black Forest."

Nyctimus huffed; pride could be felt coming from Nyctimus upon hearing those words. "First, let's clean you up. This is, after all, a very special occasion."

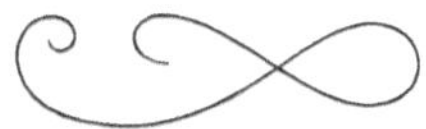

The fresh breeze filled Romasanta's lungs as he squinted up into the bright skies, a few birds flying over. He was waiting for Nyctimus to join him and the horses. The Arabian fidgeted under him, displeased with the sort of creature his rider's smell revealed him to be. Romasanta clicked and hushed; the horse settled again as he adjusted his grip on the other two mares. Footsteps were rounding the nearby wall. Nyctimus and Lillith were both accompanying him on this trip. Catching Lillith's red eyes, he frowned at her, unsure as to why she had agreed to come along. Regret rolled in his thoughts for asking her to help him face Daphne.

Unlike the centuries prior, Lillith took on a more human appearance. Still, she had a curvy, voluptuous build, with a broad chest and wide hips, and her pale skin accentuated her trademark red lips. Her hair was long, straight, and white as it fell heavily on her back in its clasps. Romasanta watched as they mounted their horses and shifted in the saddles. The smell of roses hit his nose and his shoulders shuddered at its nostalgic scent. Lillith's fragrance brought back waves of lustful memories, making his skin crawl. A sparkle in her eye caught his stare, a grin growing on her lips. She felt the wave of arousal from him, and like always, teased him with the tingling of his chest.

Grunting, he attempted to rub it out as he addressed her, "Is it necessary for you to be here, Lillith?"

"I am here for someone other than you, Romasanta." Her smile faded as she whirled the horse about. "Shall I lead us there, or do one of you have a key for entry?"

"No, I have never been able to find it since I left before the days of Rome." Nyctimus led his horse to follow Lillith as he spoke. "I understand that entire region is hidden, under some spell of protection, right?"

"Yes. Only those who are requested or strong enough can enter that barrier." Lillith shot a glance over her shoulders. "I will take you there. Follow me, this wa—"

"You're going the wrong way." Romasanta's muscles tightened as he rolled his left shoulder. "I can take us there. Stop toying with me, Lillith."

Swinging his horse in the opposite direction, he broke into a canter. Nyctimus blinked at the two of them as Lillith snickered, following Romasanta's lead without another word. As the woods thickened around them, he would slow the horse, taking in deep breaths. Scents unfolded before him and he would jerk the horse right or left. It was as if he was asking the woods permission to open up unseen trails between trees. They had left any known road or trail hours ago as the sun started to set. His horse snorted on occasion, demanding a break, but a squeeze from his legs told it to keep going.

"How many days will it take?" Nyctimus broke the silence as the night sky took hold. "We should camp soon? Let the horses rest?"

"We're almost there..." Romasanta's words drifted as he stopped his horse, sniffing about. "The horses can't go any farther. The entrance is here."

"So much faster for the guardian to find the door." Yawning, she slid off her horse but saw the tight-lipped glare Nyctimus made to Romasanta's backside. "Romasanta, did you not tell him?"

Leaning a shoulder against a tree, Romasanta had let go of the horse's reins as it ran away. Sliding to the ground, he squatted there, his head low, shoulders slumped. The glare Nyctimus gave him burned at him, his heart swelling as he worked through his own thoughts, feelings, and memories. At the sound of the other two horses fleeing, he gave a lonesome look to his friend. Shame and regret drowned him as he watched the anger seep into the man he took as the calmest creature on earth.

"Fenrir locked it away after we left." Romasanta's voice came out in a whisper as his throat tightened. "He said if I was to keep her safe, it would be best that he lock the doors to the enchanted forest until I could break the spell."

"I lost my home, thinking it was gone forever," Nyctimus growled, the tension in his body growing. "How long have you been able to control the gate without Fenrir, Romasanta? HOW LONG!"

Romasanta covered his face as he fell to the ground. "Since we accidentally killed Remus. Fenrir went silent and... and I was too far in my denial to accept I was all that remained..." The weight of the silence was heavy as he sobbed. "It was not aimed to hurt you, Nyctimus."

He flinched as a hand gripped his shoulder tight. Nyctimus's voice was deep and low. "I understand, but you should have told me..."

Romasanta peered up at him. There no longer was anger on Nyctimus's face, but concern as Romasanta pleaded, "It's still there. Your home is intact as if time hasn't touched it. The people left the Black Forest slowly, but now it's a sanctuary for the magical animals and beings. Someone inside controls the gate. It's not just me."

"Someone?" scoffed Lillith. "Don't you mean Daphne's will?"

Swallowing, Romasanta looked back to the forest. "I suppose it would be her. There is no way for me to know unless I entered, and I refused to return until today."

Shifting into his werewolf form, he shuddered as new trees started to appear between two old oaks. "That's the door. I cannot become human on the other side, not like you, Nyctimus. The bond as guardian pulls Fenrir's powers to the surface, and that is why it terrifies me to see her.

The ability for me to become my human self is not allowed because this place forbids it."

Opening his mouth, Nyctimus paused. There were no words Romasanta wanted to hear, nor could he find any that would be worthy to say to a broken man. Deep down, Romasanta had always known the stipulations the Black Forest held for him. Returning here came at a cost to himself, the inability to be the man that she remembered as her husband. It was something he did not dare speak out loud, in fear of making it a reality. Avoiding contact with the Black Forest added to the amount of denial and effort he put into eluding the factors feeding his fears.

Stepping between the trees, new smells hit both men, making them shiver and hum. It was a mix of nostalgia and new, the magic heavy in the scents welcoming them back to their homeland. That was where it all started, there on that soil, under the watch of those trees. A gentle breeze floated past, and his nose twitched as an ear flicked. Shuddering, he could smell the flowers of the laurel tree. Its aroma was floral, with a hint of Daphne's scent intertwined in its fragrance. His chest tightened, his heart thudding in his ears as it drowned out anything Nyctimus or Lillith were asking of him.

Staring ahead, there in the speckled sunlight, he could see the trunk of the tree he had beaten his knuckles raw against. He crawled cautiously in that direction, his tail between his legs. A few steps, a pause to swallow down his panic, a few more steps. It was a struggle to make himself venture closer to the enchanted tree that had taken over this part of the forest. Roots dove out and back into the ground in grand archways embellished with flowers and bright green moss. The village had vanished, its ruins reclaimed by nature centuries ago. Standing tall, he gazed into the grooves of the bark on the tree. His clawed hand shook as he pressed his palm against it for the first time since he had ridden away from the village, abandoning it. Much to his surprise, it was warm with life. Tears swelled in his large, wolven eyes. Clenching them shut, dropping to his knees, he rested his forehead on it. His teardrops fell heavily across his thighs and ground, his ears flattening. Pushing his head harder into the trunk of the tree, he gritted his fangs as choking sobs escaped him.

"I am so sorry, my love..." The ache in his chest tightened as he resisted the urge to slam his head into the tree. "The weight of the sins I have committed in all these centuries crushes my soul. So many times I have performed such evil deeds without reason, other than the pure intent to kill and devour. I cannot and I will not ask for forgiveness, but please know that I love you even now."

Warm hands surrounded him. Pulling his head away, he looked up at the lipless wooden face of Daphne. Sap ran down her cheeks from her lifeless wooden eyes. The fragrance of her sent shivers throughout his body. His golden eyes, in awe, took in every detail. Her hair flowed out of the trunk in wavy vines as they attached to her head, while only her navel to her face could lean out from the tree. A wave of hope washed over him, goading him to hug her, and take her in his arms at last. He shook as he sobbed, his face against the hard wood of her bosom. Again, the warm hands glided over his canine head.

"It's not your fault." His soul pushed against his chest upon hearing her voice, his sensitive ears picking it out of the mixture of rattling leaves and running water. "Romasanta, I am glad you are finally here, my love."

"Daphne, I…" The words were lost as emotions drowned him.

"I understand your fears." Hot sap thumped on top of his head as she hugged him tighter. "For a long time, I hid inside the tree, fearing what you would think of me. I should have rushed out and shown you I was there when you beat against the tree. We are both at fault for the sorrows we've caused one another."

"But I have been a monster, both in form and presence." A sigh rattled as his crying continued. "The things I have done. So many lives lost by my hands… I'm no longer the man you loved…"

Shushing and calming him, she nuzzled her cheek into the fur of his wolven head. "You are only a man, my husband. I accepted that before our curses were set upon us."

"I don't know what to do anymore," he confessed, letting his tears and guilt fall away. "I have no leads for the stone, no leads for Merlin, and I—"

"I have a lead on Merlin." Breaking their embrace, she rubbed his doggish cheek, the fur wet from his tears. "He is the son of Gaea and has changed his name in order to hide from enemies."

"What is his name?" his brow furrowed as he pleaded. "Please tell me you have more information."

"His name is Kronos, the youngest son of Gaea. He led a revolt against Gaea and her husband, in which she only survived. In fear that his mother would stop his rise to the throne, Kronos devoured his enemies one by one, including his own children. Failing to subdue Gaea, he managed to capture one of her eyes, sending her into a deep sleep. What he did not realize was that she had managed to curse him. Kronos is trapped within a mortal body as punishment for his disregard for the lives of others. Though she sleeps, she still has power through her dreams. She aids any she feels may hold the key to defeating Kronos, or Merlin if you wish to call him by that name."

"When I find him, I will be the one devouring him." Growling rattled his teeth as his anger grew. "He deserves death for everything he's done."

"Do not kill him." Her hands gripped his shoulders tightly. "He may not realize this, but killing him will allow him to escape the mortal body he is attempting to preserve. Let Gaea's law take him; her magic might be able to contain him. Freeing Kronos from his mortal body will unleash his full range of powers."

"I understand." He snorted, giving her a mournful stare. "But I do not know where he took her eye..."

"He has the ability to manipulate time. You will have to be clever to find the dimension, much like this place, where he hides." More sap ran down her cheeks as she continued. "The spirits are saying you have a long time before that gateway is to be known. My dearest Romasanta, you must endure more centuries before any progress will be made. My love, I beg you, please be patient. Don't wait until then to come back to the Black Forest. I am alone here..."

A hand scruffed the back of his neck, ripping him from her arms. Lillith was between them as he fell to the ground. A crimson-red smile snaked across her face as she peered over her shoulder. Wide-eyed, he saw his golden eyes reflected in Lillith's one red iris. Roaring back onto his feet, he ran on all fours as his eyes caught a glimpse of her clawed hand digging into Daphne's chest. Leaping up at her, she caught him midair, her red eyes glowing, wild and excited. Claws dug into his chest where it tingled from her first touch. Struggling to pull her claws out, he felt burning erupting through him. The sensation was painful and pleasurable as he gasped, overwhelmed. A moan escaped Daphne and he dug at Lillith's hand as it pulled at his flesh.

"Stop it," she hissed at him, letting him drop to the ground. "I've done nothing foul."

Panting as the sensation waved inside him, he peered up at Daphne, a faint glow fading into her chest. Baffled, he fumbled at himself, unsure whether Lillith's magic had healed his wound or his body. His lip curled as he snarled over at Lillith, who was licking his blood from her fingers. Seeing the angry glare, she sighed. Lillith took a step closer to him. A wave of arousal hit him, causing the burning sensation to swell. Huffing, he leaned forward, the sexual excitement suffocating him with the new strength it held. Daphne gasped, her wooden eyes wide as she released a moan of pleasure. Laughter rolled out of Lillith, who watched with great pride at the exchange of sexual excitement between husband and wife.

"See, now you can share your fun with her." She walked over to him. Her touch on his shoulder sent another breathtaking shock of arousal to him. "Enjoy that."

As Lillith's fingers left his shoulder, he gazed up at Daphne, who gasped in response. His stomach tensed and twisted, his feelings and thoughts racing through him. Being a monster was complicated, but this new curse Lillith laid on his shoulders was terrifying. Tears of sap flowed from Daphne's wooden eyes as she looked over at Lillith.

"I have not felt this human since the day I slammed the spear into the ground." Her voice shook as it hit his ears. "Why have you done this?"

Lillith scanned Romasanta, her fingers tapping her lips a moment before she answered. "Until your curse is broken Daphne, I want Romasanta for myself."

Silence took hold as Romasanta and Daphne stared into each other's eyes. Neither of them wanted to give an answer. His soul rattled in his core, both ecstatic that she felt human from his pleasure, but terrified to be at Lillith's mercy. Accepting the bargain would be adulterous but a means of rekindling Daphne's sense of self, salvaging her humanity along with his own. Lillith's touch tingled at his chest and Daphne touched her own chest where Lillith's fingers had dug so deeply. Any form of pleasure he experienced would be reflected in her. A reminder he was alive, even happy for an instance, and sharing it in the physical sense.

Closing his eyes and bowing his head, he whispered, "It is your choice, my love. I will do whatever you see as best for the both of us, Daphne."

It was quiet, but he dared not open his eyes. Deep down, he didn't want Lillith or Daphne to see the fear waving inside him. The very idea of this new connection scared him. More so, why would Lillith be forcing this on him at a time like this? Every muscle in his body tensed with each passing second as he waited for Daphne to answer Lillith's proposition. His left shoulder twitched as he creased his forehead.

"Will it harm him?" Daphne's voice was stern, but still, he did not open his eyes as his ears flicked. "What is the secondary effect of this?"

Scoffing, Lillith replied in a cool tone, "The only thing that will be harmed will be his pride for having to lay with me instead of you."

"And when my curse is broken, we will both be free of this?" He was glad he had laid this in Daphne's hands. He would have failed to ask these questions. "And it is only pleasure being passed on?"

"Yes." Lillith sighed in frustration. "I hate that everyone assumes I only do other's ill will."

"Then so be it. Romasanta and I will agree to your bargain." He opened his eyes, swallowing his concerns back as Daphne continued, "With this, I can feel human for a moment and my soul yearns for it."

"I understand." Glaring at Lillith, Romasanta sneered at her toothy grin. "With your blessing, I will allow this."

"Excellent, then I will let you continue your reunion." They watched as Lillith left view, the tension in his muscles fading.

"Are you sure?" he groaned as he came closer to Daphne.

"Should I not trust her?" Daphne embraced him in her arms again, each enjoying the comfort of the other's warmth. "Has she given you a reason not to trust her?"

"No..." he whispered as he nuzzled in her arms. "Honestly, she has not done me any wrong."

"Then let us enjoy the fact your pleasure is also my pleasure." Her wooden chin and cheek rubbed against the top of his head. "It is a chance for me to learn to feel human again during the centuries we know are still coming. I wish for you to be a man and she can provide a need that satisfies us as one. If only I could be in your arms again, my husband."

Another tear fell down his cheek as he whispered, "It scares me to know what I am capable of..."

"I'm so sorry you've had to endure this all alone..." She let go of him, pushing his chin up so he would look her in the eyes. "Can you find it in your heart to forgive me for not being by your side?"

"You tried so hard to tell me..." His clawed hand cupped her wooden cheek, his thumb failing to rub it free of its falling sap. "I should have stayed home with you. How could I leave you behind, risk running into Fenrir, and dying? I'm so sorry, Daphne."

"Please come and talk with me. Tell me what you've seen and experienced through your own eyes." Closing her eyes, she sighed. "My voice will always be here, eager to tell you how much I love and miss you. I will not hide myself from you, and I hope you will no longer hide from me. I love you, Romasanta. You're my soulmate."

"I just want to be able to kiss your lips with my own again..." A tear fell from Romasanta's eye as he gave a mournful stare at where lips should have been on Daphne's wooden face. "To feel your skin against mine, like our last night together. I miss coming home to you..."

Her brow furrowed as more sap slid from her wooden eyes. "Forgive me, I am growing tired... this wooden body has its limits. Fenrir's spell pulls from all the life here and I am the foundation for its creation. I think the old wolf knew I was here and gave me access to it on purpose, but it has its downfalls. Please, don't go just yet. I might have to recede into the tree, but I am here and can still talk to you, my love."

He held on to her hand as long as he could before it was pulled back into the tree. As promised, her face remained in the bark of the tree with sap sliding down her flattened cheeks. Taking his thumbs, he wiped them away, kissing her forehead the best he could with the awkwardness of his muzzle. The sun had set at some point during their embrace, but he sat leaning his back on the trunk of the laurel tree. They whispered to one another about the things they had seen and recalled the times from before their curses. It was as if they were continuing from that last night together so long ago.

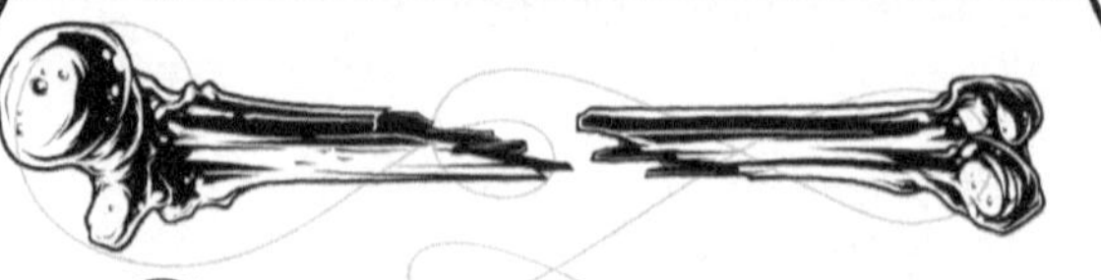

CHAPTER 20

THE PLAN

It pained him to leave Daphne after spending only a week at her side, but he had renewed his drive to search for Merlin and Gaea. Lillith and Nyctimus had left them in peace, heading to the castle once owned by Boreas Lykaon, Nyctimus's grandfather. Romasanta raced toward the castle as the air shook with thunder and lightning flashed across the sky. The occasional gust of wind rocked the trees and branches overhead while he raced through the forest. Making it to the clearing, the storm seemed calm. The rain fell in heavy drops, icy as they pelted his wolven face.

Closing his eyes, he tilted back his head, letting the rain wash away centuries of mistakes and anger. He felt reborn, his rage caused by guilt no longer weighed on his shoulders. No more resentment ravaged his soul, blinding him to the things deep inside his core. Thunder rumbled and rattled in his chest, as if to applaud him on his efforts at his newfound acceptance. He was neither the wolf nor the man; he was Romasanta, the father of werewolves and Ancient One to all born after him.

Shaking off the water gathering in his fur, he headed for the castle. The rain thickened as the storm rumbled on. It was hard to say if the sun was still out with the darkness the storm brought. Once more, he shook his fur free of the rain before entering the heavy oak doors. It was warm inside the main hall. Much to his surprise, it was busy with movement. Women were doing various chores; dusting, mopping, and moving objects and furniture. One of these paused in her task, a smile growing on her face as he gave her a befuddled look.

"You are Romasanta." Her voice was soft, a pleasant mezzo-soprano. "They are waiting for you in the war room. Please, follow me."

"Who are all of you?" A few girls paused from their dusting to giggle in his direction. "Where did you all come from?"

"Master Nyctimus has taken many of us into his care over the years." She walked with grace as he followed close behind her, noticing the abnormal beauty they all carried. "We are succubus halflings. Many of us were working in brothels before he found us."

Palming his head, Romasanta chortled. "Of course, Nyctimus would seek you all out. What a facetious old man he can be..."

The girl pushed open two grand oak doors, revealing a war room where everyone fell silent. Nodding his thanks, he entered as the doors boomed closed behind him. Groaning, he took in the occupants of the room: Lillith, Nyctimus, and, to his surprise, Cedric. Nyctimus grinned at him as they all stood in respect, motioning to an empty chair reserved for him. Sitting in the chair was awkward as he huffed at trying to find a comfortable spot to put his tail. He was starting to miss the ability to switch back to his human self.

"Now that Romasanta is here, we can discuss our plan of action for Merlin." Nyctimus sat down, leaning over the table as he eyed everyone. "Where shall we start?"

"Let's start with the fact that Merlin is indeed a son of Gaea by the name of Kronus." Cedric's distant gaze refocused to meet Romasanta's golden glare as he spoke. "But I must warn you, Cedric. We cannot kill him for fear that he may escape the mortality curse his mother has placed on him."

Cedric gritted his teeth as he slammed a hand on the table. "I want his damn head for the torture he puts her through!"

"We understand that he's trying to extract the girl's magic, but I promise you, he won't get it." Nyctimus's voice hit everyone's soul as he spoke, a grave expression on his face. "She carries a rare variant of defensive magic, much like I had. I assure you, she cannot die. On the same note, we must be wary of Merlin, or whoever he is, since he has outsmarted Romasanta and Cedric."

"We need to locate where he is hiding away. From there, we might be able to create a plan." Concerned about possible rash actions, Romasanta demanded eye contact from Cedric. "Do any of us have any clues as to where he may be residing?"

The cold, stern looks on everyone's faces were heart-dropping. Each looked off to distant memories, digging, hoping to find some missed morsel of information. His ears flattened as he recalled that sour moment he met the old wizard. The scent of Merlin filled his nose, and the look of his eyes as they glowed with the forbidden magic he had obtained filled his memory. What manner of creature was Kronus? A demonic soul in an aging human body? Being able to master and sustain such control over a curse was frightening. Kronus managed to slow a human body's aging process to near immortal status.

"Coinn Iotair," Cedric mumbled as he pondered. "They were in Raven's Den, but I didn't pay attention back then..."

"Raven's Den?" Romasanta's ear pricked forward. "Why were you in Raven's Den?"

"Angeline grew up there... and hellhounds were seeking out the magic in her blood, according to the old witch." Cedric noticed the queer look on Romasanta's face as one of his ears flicked at the word "*witch*." "What importance is Raven's Den to you?"

"Aren't Coinn Iotair from the United Kingdom?" questioned Nyctimus, trying to keep the focus on Merlin and not Romasanta's private affairs. "They had to be Merlin's, yes?"

"They definitely came from the English channel." Digging into his memories, Cedric covered his mouth as he recalled the salty, enchanted flavor he had devoured that night. "And the magic was unlike anything I have encountered before or since Merlin. It had to be his, but where is there a place to hide in England or any part of that region?"

"A dimensionally protected island, perhaps?" added Lillith as she began pacing the floor. "My brooding temple and the Black Forest can hide within a mainland. An island would be easier to maintain and protect from intrusion. Was there not an island called Avalon?"

"Yes!" Leaning back in his chair, Nyctimus's hazel eyes sparkled. "That would make perfect sense. Look at Napoleon's Devil Island; no prisoner can escape, nor could someone approach unnoticed. Why not use some place similar to hide from one's enemies, magical or human? I assume an island would be easier to ward and protect."

"Absolutely," scoffed Lillith. "So much so. Someone who goes around intentionally burning every demon and magical being like he does would indeed need to be able to do multiple types and layers of wards, depending on the island. Additional physical location defenses, like a rocky shore, would aid the protection. Avalon was once a place where men were invited and returned empowered. It would seem Merlin is taking in and encouraging humans to take over while wiping out his competition. Never has someone with magic connections or non-human blood set foot on Avalon, that I know of. Maybe those King Arthur tales do speak about the same Merlin we've been seeking."

"It seems we have our location." Romasanta nodded approvingly at Cedric. "And mainly thanks to you, Cedric."

"How does one get to Avalon?" There was a dangerous glimmer in Cedric's sharp, green eyes as he peered over at them. "There has to be a key of sorts..."

A raven squawked from the small window high above them as lightning flashed behind it. Leaping off its perch, it grew large, before bursting into a swirling explosion of feathers. Romasanta's tail attempted to wag, but slammed against the chair's back, earning a grunt from him. As the tornado of feathers whirled to the ground, three figures emerged. Badbh, Morrighan, and Nemaine bowed before the table of demons. As his eyes met Badbh's, within her trademark bronze and silver raven mask, he earned a smile from her scarred lips.

Together they were known as the Witch-Daughters of Calatin long before Romasanta's existence. He knew the legends well, of the cow herder Cuchulainn defeating the evil sorcerer Calatin and all his sons and nephews. During the last battle between those legendary figures, Calatin's witch-daughters, each bearing a blackened left eye, were sent as a distraction. Unlike the stories, they were not killed, and neither did they bear the cursed eye of their father's ill-will. They had repented, devoted themselves each to a practice of magic, and earned goddess status.

Badbh had earned the title of Battle Goddess. She was the embodiment of war and having her choose your side in battle was assured victory, no matter what odds stacked against you and your army. The Crusades were a time of fun and bloody gore for her, and beyond that, her touch could be seen in some of history's most memorable battles. Wherever it seemed implausible, where numbers or harsh conditions should have fell the men who won, a raven would be among them, cawing its battle cry, soaring over the war, and blessing the best warriors with a sacred feather that floated to the ground at their wary feet.

Nemaine was the Venom Goddess. She had sewn her imagery into the history of man in more unique ways. She had been coined many names, earning many myths, including as Medusa and as the creator of the legendary visha, a poison the nagas in India used against their enemies without remorse. Anywhere that the lore mentioned poisoning, venom, or snakes and spiders; make no mistake that Nemaine had a hand in it. Often her work was labeled pestilence, but it was blurred with Lamashtu's rancid work of spreading disease. Nemaine preferred the art of poison and the skill and technique needed to perfect it. A single target would suffice for all she cared. As for appearance, she looked like a Greek goddess in both attire and behavior. Markings much like the rattlesnake or viper tattooed in deep green, warned those of her touch.

As for Morrighan, she had spent her time free of Beelzebub seeking Merlin. If any of them had been able to get close to discovering anything about Merlin, it would be her. She knew more about the magical arts than any other person still alive. Her goddess status was a reflection of becoming the modern mother of all things magic, a protector or keeper of what was left in the world. Over the years, she had made the biggest impact on mankind, a force that pushed back and drowned Merlin's influence. She was worshipped and at one point considered Morrighan the Fair. Brushing her black, silken, waterfall of hair behind her, her maroon eyes looked at them with excitement. She had learned the magical arts of her father, Calatin, keeping the family heirloom spells and abilities alive, as well as spanning to the darkest corners of magic. Her black leather dress was still adorned with bloodstones she had collected so long ago, when the earth still poured magic from her soil.

"Good evening, my dear demons." Morrighan smiled as she stood tall before them. "My sisters and I would like to join this battle against Merlin. We can assist and advise in several ways, seeing that we have been blessed by Gaea and gained immortality."

"You all owe me, do you not?" Cedric raised an eyebrow at them, earning a scowl from Nemaine. "And wasn't it Merlin who set you up to be possessed by Beelzebub, Morrighan?"

"Yes." The smile had faded as she spoke with authority. "It was he who set me up and opened the door against my will for Beelzebub to possess me. I am under the impression that the two of them are working together, but for what goal I do not know. Your speculation of his work to encourage the growth of man while annihilating everything else is correct. He intends to eventually be the only magical force left so that he may rule over man as he sees fit. Until then, he will empower lesser beings to do his dirty work."

"Which explains the Coinn Iotair and the tales of Arthur," huffed Cedric. "He seems to have more important matters involving hiding and torture to attend to..."

Romasanta glowered at Cedric, silencing him. "What do you three know of Avalon?"

They looked between the three of them before Morrighan replied, "Like you, we believe he resides on this island. Back in the time of our father, this was where powerful magic wielders were sent to train in their art. It used to be accessible by several bloodlines, but Merlin managed to close its door even to us. We once walked its rocky shores, but we cannot tell you what its current condition is, nor give an adequate floor plan. The castle shifts constantly to its inhabitant's needs."

Silence fell upon the room as everyone digested the information. Their thoughts broke at the sound of Cedric's excited voice. "Bloodline?" A wicked smile snaked across his face. "Lillith and I have taken the steps to help us discover his bloodline, though I need a second nose to keep up with the expansion of my ever-expanding bloodline."

Furrowing his brow, Romasanta dug for more answers. "What are you implying?"

"Initially, I had decided to create the brood of succubi and incubi in hopes of sensing when Merlin came out of hiding. It would be like having eyes at every corner of the earth, but it's becoming more complicated as my bloodline begins to water down." His eyes were sharp as he continued in his deep tone, "They lose their connection completely with me and Lillith after so many generations. I can tell if they are of my blood by scent, but their abilities fade and they become nothing more than attractive humans. If we need blood relatives of Merlin to get to the island, there may be a chance he will fall to the desires of the flesh. It's simply natural to do so for any creature in a world full of sins and desires."

"That would work. Avalon simply requires a blood relative to willingly, of free will and want, to give the drop of blood to open the portal to the island. It was how they added new bloodlines so that they could add themselves to the ancient book that keeps records of the family lines." Pausing a moment, Morrighan's own words rattled her, sending chills across her skin. "Having access to that book is why Merlin was able to wipe out all the magical bloodlines. My father would allow us access to the island, but our names were never added to the book. Only our brothers and nephews were ever blessed to attend and learn the arts on Avalon. This is something I failed to take into account."

"Well, that is why you three are the last true witches of the new world." The saddened look on Nyctimus's face reflected how everyone else was feeling. "If we had realized it sooner, maybe we could have saved—"

"There would have been nothing we could have done," interrupted Badbh, crossing her arms. "Not without a union like this created first."

"She's right," Lillith added, her voice almost a whisper. "Even I could not hope to slow his work. Perhaps he was the reason behind the madness that Boto succumbed to, starting my torture so long ago. Kronus was before my time, which puts his magic, knowledge, and experience beyond us, even as a group."

"Then why does he need Angeline?" Cedric's jaw twitched as he glowered at every person in the room. "Why was Angeline an exception, brought to the island, left alive and tortured?"

All eyes turned to Romasanta.

Cedric's confusion wracked his face as Romasanta answered in a mournful voice, "Because her bloodline is the rarest, even believed to be the oldest. She is the human descendant of Artemis, an ancient witch who held the strongest bond to Gaea herself."

A wind howled and screamed through the room. Artemis was there in spirit as she blew her icy wind across them all. Cedric had risen to his feet, recognizing the presence from Raven's Den. His words were sour as they rolled off his tongue. "The old hag's name is Artemis..."

Romasanta's chair screeched as he started for the door. Looking over his shoulder, he commanded, "Cedric, come with me. We have much to discuss in private. We are not needed for the plans being made here."

Obediently, Cedric marched behind him and they left the warmth of the castle. The storm had eased, but the cold rain still fell sporadically on them as they headed for the forest. Without question or pause, Cedric followed Romasanta ever farther. Eyeing over his shoulder, Romasanta saw the glowing green of the catlike pupils that trusted him instinctually. It was pleasant to see that the boy had learned to trust his gut. It would never lead him astray as long as he held fast to his sense of self, his compassion, and his humanity.

They stopped at the edge of a pond, its surface in constant movement from the rain breaking its still waters. Cedric was quiet, waiting with breathtaking patience for Romasanta to gather his thoughts. His nose twitched as the salty smell of sweat greeted his nose. Glancing over at Cedric, he once more saw the out-of-focus stare in his eyes as the perfume of pain wafted from him. Romasanta's wolven ears flattened as he furrowed his brow.

"I am sorry. Perhaps this was all my fault." Cedric grunted at Romasanta's words, his eyes still staring off at the unseen torture happening so far away. "I should have kept her close—"

"Old man, there was nothing we could have changed the day we stormed Morrighan's castle." Cedric was growing tenser as he prepared himself for the increasing torture he would be taking on for Angeline's sake. "We have a plan, a team even. As hard as it may be, I can swallow back my fears and sit and wait for our opportunity to present itself. Now, could you please tell me why we had to walk this far away from prying ears?"

"I'm going to tell you something that no one alive knows. Only your friend Wylleam managed to unravel this." A heavy sigh escaped his muzzle as he stared at the broken lake surface. "Angeline is of my blood, her magic, the heritage given to her by my twin sister Artemis."

Cedric's focus came back to him as he stared at Romasanta wide-eyed. "How did I not notice?"

"The demon wolf that I inherited my abilities from has changed my body completely. My blood is more like that of a wolf than a man." He snorted, checking himself once again that the smell was as he explained.

"The similarities are so far faded between us that your nose would not have noticed at the time we met. Maybe now you could, but not when it would have aided you most. Then again, neither of our lives has been in our own control for quite some time..."

"What do mean by that?" Cedric snarled as he started to grow irritated. "How much are you keeping from me?"

Romasanta's golden eyes turned to meet the angry green glare, sorrow across his wolven face. "I think Gaea has been pulling our strings for a long time, Cedric. If you want to know, that name you carry with pride, Romulus, gives me great joy."

Confusion settled on Cedric as he scoffed, "Joy?"

"It was my son's name and heritage. Romulus founded Rome and gave humanity order in a time of chaos. With my help, and my watchful eye, all the generations that followed were taught to be aware of the non-human threats of the world. I even found you, and gave you to the man you called father, the last of my descendants."

"You what?" Cedric's hand gripped Romasanta's throat, but Romasanta did not flinch. "Why did you dig up his grave? Who does that to their family?!"

"I was reclaiming the silver sword of Boreas that I had given to him. With no one to carry it, I took it back." A snarl rolled on his muzzle as Cedric retracted his grip. "Was it not my right to take that sword back, assuming that even the adoptive son had died in that massacre?"

Silence took hold of Cedric as he clenched his fists at his sides, his jaw twitching.

"The last time I saw my sister was at Raven's Den. When I left, she cast a spell so that I could never return." Romasanta's voice faltered, and he swallowed down his emotions. "It was too dangerous for me to be there with her because of Merlin's curse."

He demanded Cedric to look as he pointed to his chest. "Is that where it came from? Merlin?"

"He used the Eye of Gaea to force me to share my body with a demon wolf. After that, I realized, too late, that all who met my claws and survived would become werewolves, the versipellis. It grew further, and mutated as I left it unchecked." He pointed a claw at Cedric's chest as he burned his sour lessons into him. "It was then that the third generation of my curse

182

created vampires, giving birth to Vladimir and many others. Why do you think they were the only ones besides myself to command the werewolves? Because at its core, it's the same curse."

Rubbing at his missing left finger, Cedric took in all the secrets. "What is your connection with the Black Forest?"

"It was my home, and the forest was guarded by the demon wolf, Fenrir." His chest ached as he laid all his secrets down. "And the tree nymph, she has a name, boy. Daphne. She is my wife, also cursed."

The words sucked the wind from Cedric as he covered his face with his hands. "So you know the loneliness I feel..."

"Tenfold."

"But without the comfort of the bond..." A tear fell from Cedric's chin as he shook his head. "I am so sorry. It is I who should feel for you..."

"Speak none of this to a soul," growled Romasanta, his golden eyes glowing in the stormy night. "I tell you this because she is of my sister's blood and you carry my name with my curse in your veins. You are the only one who deserves to know the truth of my connections with what haunts both your lives."

Romasanta turned to walk away, but a firm grip caught his shoulder. "Wait, Romasanta."

"I have nothing else to say," he huffed. Looking over his shoulder, he could see the desperation on Cedric's face. "What's the matter?"

"I will need your help to find which of my offspring contains Merlin's bloodline." Confident Romasanta was staying, he let go. "You and I are the only ones who know Merlin's scent. I am already struggling to keep up with the brood as it spreads and waters down. Are you up for this task?"

Sighing, a toothy smile crossed Romasanta's face. "Yes, this I can do, and do well. Let us wait for the time we can start the next step. May the next few centuries be kinder to both our souls."

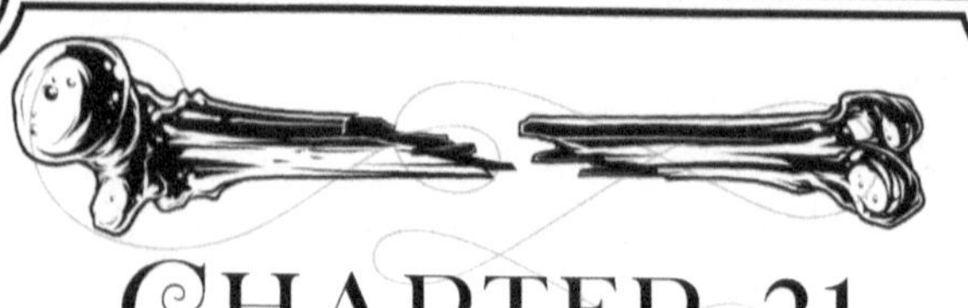

CHAPTER 21

PRESENT DAY

The brick wall against his back was warm as the sun beat down on his scruffy face. Coins clanked into the cup at Romasanta's feet, making him crack one eye open. It was a busy day, but Fridays were the most lively in the city. Work and leisure rushes would mix and crowd the streets long after the sunset. Romasanta was posing as a bum in order to sit in high-traffic areas hunting for scents. Cedric's and Lillith's brood had grown wide and far in the last two hundred years. The halflings were watered-down to the point they no longer held any powers, but were still effective for seeking out Merlin's bloodline.

The hairs on his arm stood on end as he caught the aroma of Cedric's bloodline. It was weak, but it was the scent tangled within it that excited him. His eyes opened wide as he sorted through the crowded streets with his golden eyes. Unable to pick out who was carrying the smell, he pulled himself to his feet. As he left his place on bum alley, he handed the coin-filled cup to the homeless teen next to him. She had taken comfort in sitting next to him since he showed up.

"Take this." Clearing his throat, he glanced at her. "Go to the shelter and push yourself for a better life. I will not be returning and thus will no longer aid you as a protector, girl."

Startled by the amber in his eyes, she nodded and ran off in the direction of the shelter. The fragrance of Merlin and Cedric washed over his nose again, his heart racing as it pulsed in his chest. Snaking through the crowds was growing more difficult as he entered the club and bar section of town. Frustrated, he had lost the fresh trail, but fortune smiled on him. He had managed to track an older trail of scents, a path this person walked often. Following it, he was hoping to gather clues as to where to find this individual. He paused; the path led him to a bar called *Rusty's*.

The bells above the door announced his arrival, and he grunted in response. Two girls at the counter paused, looking him over. He took in a deep breath, his nose filtering the information as he eyed them. They were vampires. In fact, every person who left a scent in this place was a halfling at the very least. It was rare to find places catering primarily to the non-human crowd, but in a city, it seemed more likely to happen. Scratching the side of his jaw, he pondered whether to sit and wait or to follow the scent trail back in the other direction.

"Either you buy a drink or you leave," hissed the dominant blonde, fear escaping her as a bead of sweat formed on her temple. "We do not cater to bums."

Snorting, he approached the bar top, and they both stifled back, feeling the weight of his aura. "Give me the best vodka you have and a rocks glass."

"I don't think you can afford this." The redhead lifted an eyebrow as she pulled a gold label bottle from the shelf. "You'll have to pay up before I crack this open, old man."

"You two need to learn some manners. I'm pretty sure the elders taught you to watch your tongue around those who sit on the top of the food chain." Both of them flinched as a flash of gold crossed his dark brown eyes. "Here's two hundred for your forty-dollar bottle of vodka."

Snatching the bottle from her, he reached over and helped himself to a rocks glass. He found a booth in the back, which was dark and isolated, where he poured himself a drink. The girls whispered, fear still resonating from them as they realized the current patron was something they had never seen in person before. A smirk crawled across his face as they speculated about who or what he might be, pausing often to look in his direction in wonder. One started to share a story about the *Ancient One* and he grunted as he finished the glass and poured another. A male voice entered from the back door and it made his ears and nose twitch. This was the carrier of the scent he was searching for.

"Tony!" The redhead hugged him as they fussed over the male bartender. "You're here! I can leave now!"

"So soon, Becca?" He laughed, breaking from her arms to put a change of clothes under the cash register. "Anything the boss wants done tonight? Last Friday I had to flush the tap lines before leaving... ugh."

Peering over his shoulder, Romasanta watched as the blonde vampire behind Tony pushed a glass off the shelf, smiling. "Oops." It shattered across the tile, making Romasanta cringe at the loudness of it. "Watch out, Tony... I bumped into the shelf again. Didn't know it was sitting there, dear."

"I swear this happens every other day." Tony, exasperated, rubbed the back of his neck before squatting down to start picking up the larger pieces. "If it's not you, it's one of the other girls."

"Coming through!" The redhead, Becca, pushed on his back in such a sly move he cut his hand. "Oh no! Tony! Are you hurt?! I was just trying to get to my purse, love."

Romasanta snorted, the fresh blood making it clear there was no doubt he was both Merlin and Cedric's blood relative.

"Ouch." Standing, Tony grasped his hand. "Just when I thought I was being careful enough..."

"Aww, let me see." The blonde vampire kissed it, a ploy to get a small taste. "Did that help?"

"It never helps," Tony moaned as he began searching behind the bar top. "Where did the first aid kit go?"

"Maybe the boss used it?" Becca and the blonde were toying with him, using their fingers to pick up and lick the droplets of his blood behind Tony's back. "Maybe in his office?"

"It's locked." Tony rested his head against the boss's door. "I have no good luck..."

Romasanta clanked his rocks glass on the bar top, startling all three. "Here's your glass back, Becca."

The two vampires looked at one another, fear welling up in them. Tony started to wrap his hand with a rag, wandering off to the bathroom. Becca searched for the courage to get close to Romasanta. She knew he wanted her to come close, but what he intended to do was a frightening unknown. Shakily, she reached out for the rocks glass and he slid it back. She leaned closer and his lips tickled at her ear, making her freeze.

"You touch the boy again, and I'll be eating your guts for breakfast." The growl made her jerk back, sending her stumbling into the blonde. "That's for you and the rest of the trash working here. Any harm comes to him on your watch, and you'll find out who and what I am."

They nodded as his golden eyes seared his warning well.

"Here's a thank you for your hospitality." He tossed a crumbled hundred-dollar bill on the table and left.

Weaving through the crowded streets, he went unnoticed. Like the lepers so long ago, the homeless were invisible to the masses. It wasn't long before he made it to the area full of luxury high-rise apartments and approached one with a keycard in hand. Sliding it, the door buzzed, signaling it was unlocked so he could enter. Everyone was either home or out entertaining themselves at that point, which made the lobby empty. On the elevator, he slid the card again, prompting the doors to close, and it started its ascension toward the top. The elevator opened to an apartment that took up the entire floor. Kicking off the weathered boots, he wandered deeper into the apartment. The living room was a large open room with an uninterrupted view of the city beyond.

Pulling off the unkempt trench coat, he tossed it on the red couch as he stared out at the lights of the city. Sighing, he continued down a hallway, pulling off his shirt and unbuckling his pants. His muscles ached with excitement, but there was no place to run in the city like he did on his visits to the Black Forest. Entering the bathroom, he started a hot shower, pausing to stare at the rustic man in the mirror. Dropping his pants to the floor, he entered the glass enclosure, drowning his head in the steaming waterfall. Rubbing his face free of the oil and dirt from the street, he turned, the heat beating the muscles in his shoulders.

"Must you always invite yourself in?" Scoffing, Lillith leaned on the bathroom door frame. "In fact, why must you undress one article of clothing per room?"

A smile crawled across his face, his eyes closed as he enjoyed the hot water beating on his tense back. "I have to give you something to do while I shower."

She threw the coat and shirt on the bathroom floor with his pants. "And are we going to share why we feel so strangely excited?"

"I found one." Turning the shower off, he leaned against the tiles, his yellow eyes glaring at her. "Merlin and Cedric's bloodlines in one person. It worked."

Her eyes grew wide. "And he's here in the city?"

"Yes." Romasanta smirked. His cheeks were red and his eyes sparkled with excitement. "He's here."

Rushing out of the shower, he gripped her by the shoulders and kissed her.

She squirmed out of his hold. "And you're drunk! I see we were celebrating early. I'll send word to Cedric. Then, it's up to him how we should do this. Unlike you, he has far more patience."

He walked back down the hall and into the kitchen on the opposite wall. Popping open another vodka bottle, he took a swig from it. Laughter burst out of him, relieved at being able to uncover the key to Avalon after so long. There was still much more to speculate, but it was something his soul was starving to have: the joy of progress. Standing tall, he puffed out his chest and raised the bottle to Lillith as she entered. Taking a deep breath, he took a long guzzle of it, allowing himself this small victory.

"You are a funny man, Romasanta." Smiling, she looked him over, brushing her white hair back behind her. "Even after giving birth to the porn industry, there is still no man that looks so comfortable being naked as you do."

His eyes glowed amber as he gave her a toothy grin. "Since the day I was born, nothing could shame me for being comfortable in my own skin."

Slamming the bottle down on the counter, he walked up to her, nose to nose. Staring into her rose-colored irises, his hand slid over her cheek and she leaned into it. The tingling at his chest added to his delight, knowing that Daphne would feel human tonight as he rejoiced in being a step closer to freeing her from the laurel tree. Pressing his lips onto Lillith's sent shivers across his skin. He was pushing her back into the living room as his fingers fumbled with her blouse. If he could not run the forest, then he would spend the energy on Lillith.

"Since when did you start wearing such tricky clothes?" He laughed as he started to nuzzle at her ear, still struggling with the buttons. "How annoying..."

"Just rip it," she huffed as she kicked off her heels, still stumbling backward. "Since when did you take caution with my things?"

Popping the buttons free of their stitching, he pulled her blouse open. His hands crawling across her back, they broke the clasp of the bra keeping him from his prize. Desperate to keep up with his savagery, she shuffled off the tattered blouse, it and the bra hitting the floor. A yelp escaped her lips as her calves locked on the couch and she fell back, still wearing her black pleated skirt. She watched him grin as his hands slid between her thighs and disappeared under the folds of the skirt. Lifting an eyebrow at him, she let his fingers meet their destination and he furrowed his brow playfully.

"I think you forgot to do something this morning." Smirking, he made her moan as he played. "Either that or you lost your panties at some point today."

A wave of arousal escaped Lillith. As it washed over him, it hit the spot on his chest, intensifying the thrilling sensation rattling his core. The spell Lillith had pushed on him and Daphne was more unique than he could have ever conceived it to be. It wasn't his arousal Daphne felt; she would feel the pleasure he gave Lillith. This meant that to Daphne, every time he lay with the queen succubus, it felt as if he was lying with her. The connection wasn't a direct one between Romasanta and Daphne, but they were linked through Lillith like pieces of chain made of pleasure and emotion.

It had given him something back from his life before the stone. Every touch he gave Lillith was like touching Daphne, whether it was the rubbing of her cheek, the glide of his hand on her thigh, or the sensation of his lips at her ear. The spell made Lillith a medium for husband and wife to make love once more as a man and a woman. It was still a mystery as to what the interaction gave the queen succubus, but it gave him a reason to feel alive again.

Her back arched and she hummed in delight, waves flowing from her goaded him to continue the foreplay. Satisfied with her panting, he started kissing her navel, working his way between her breasts. He suckled at her neck and she giggled as his unshaven chin tickled her shoulder. Her fingers tangled in his hair, clawing at the back of his head when he groped her other breast as she wiggled under him. Pushing his knee between her thighs, he let her know he was not done toying with her. Moving off her shoulder, his lips teased her nipple as his hand freed the other breast, enjoying the ripples of her ribs. He licked and sucked as his hand continued its journey over her robust hip, sliding down and around her smooth skin, further arousing him.

"Stop teasing." She flustered, failing to pull his head back. "Must you wait until I've drowned us bo—"

The words failed as he sucked harder; another push of his knee made her shiver and moan. Releasing her nipple, he looked up at her flushed face as she panted. Sweat was forming on her skin, sparkling like the city lights with its sweet and salty scent. Sitting up, she pushed him back, her lips aggressive against his as her tongue coaxed his to come out and play. He found himself sitting on the couch as she straddled his thigh. Breaking from his lips, she suckled on his earlobe and began whispering.

"It's no fun if only one of us gets teased." Her fingers glided over his chest, and a breathtaking wave of pleasure shot through him as they slid over her mark. "Let me return the favor, my wolf."

The tips of her fangs tickled at his skin as she kissed his neck and shoulder. Her warm fingers slithered across his ribs, slipping across his lower abs, and beyond. His heart thudded hard and quickly in his chest as he began to pant from her toying with him. Catching his breath, he pulled her back up as she sat on his knee with nothing but a skirt around her hips.

"You're not playing fair," he fussed, shoving her off him so he could stand. "In fact, you're cheating again."

"But doesn't it feel good?" Hugging him from behind, she kissed his back as her hands snaked across his abdomen and chest. "What's wrong with me using my abilities?"

"It's not the same," he groaned, staring out over the city with its twinkling lights of white, red, and green. "And you know I'm right."

Pausing her play, she pulled away with her back to him as she looked back at the couch. "I see I've ruined the mood. I'm sorry, I thought you wanted something more intense, but I should know by now you prefer it all-natural. Enjoy your vodka, wolf, since I never get anything out of you after spoil—"

Grasping the back of her neck, he pushed her down to the couch. Skillfully, he spread her legs with his knee as she gripped the couch, bent over before him. She tried to stand back up, and he shoved her harder as his other hand gripped her hip with a firm, authoritative motion. He pushed his hip hard and firm against her; she was beyond ready. Lillith gasped and Romasanta began his dominant rhythm as she wiggled to break free. Horns were crawling from her head as her tail snaked into existence from under her skirt. Releasing his hold on her neck, he took a more powerful hold of her hips as she panted ever harder, moaning with each stroke.

She looked over her shoulder, her face flush again with both anger and pleasure. "I hate not being the dominant one in bed. Sorry, I cheated." He laughed, pushing her harder into the couch and his hands dove around her, gripping her breast, making her scream in pleasure. "You taught me a long time ago that you cannot resist an alpha male."

Pulling away from her, they gazed at one another, panting as sweat dripped from their chins. She sat on the couch, freed of his hold and no longer in the forced bent-over position. Provocatively, she spread her legs with the skirt hiding what she enticed him with. Catching his breath, he smirked at her, drunk on the waves of pleasure and arousal still erupting from her. Twisting, she laid across the length of the couch, propping one leg over on the back as she started caressing her own breast. The wave of desire hit him in the chest again, pushing him to take action.

The heat of her body added to his excitement as he pushed against her. Once more, her back arched as she moaned with each stroke he made. Hugging her in his arms, the weight of him on her thrilling as his exhilaration started to peak. She moaned and squealed with delight. Her thighs tightened around him, the motion sending him over the edge, and he began to moan. His lips tickled her ears as warm tears slapped against her neck and shoulder.

"I love you so much, Daphne." His eyes were clenched closed as he rode out the last of his climax, still hugging Lillith. "Another step closer... so close..."

Sighing, Lillith nuzzled his neck, hugging him back. "Such a broken, love-drunk man you are, Romasanta."

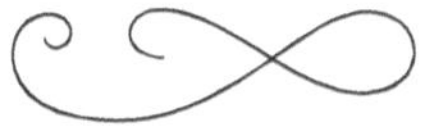

The next several months were spent watching Cedric decide what to do with Tony. The Thursday he arrived in town, he insisted on seeing the boy first. Much to Cedric's frustration, it was only the girls working that night. Romasanta had stayed at his booth in the back corner, but he enjoyed watching the game of cat and mouse Cedric played with the vampires.

They knew who Cedric was: the head of the Vampiric Order, Lord Cedric. Over the last two hundred years, he had overtaken many of the demonic power heads in order to amass the resources he might need to face Merlin. Regardless, Romasanta had told Cedric of how the vampires had been toying with Tony before he ended the games.

Romasanta watched as Cedric purposefully cut his own lip with his fang. His green eyes glowered at the girls, who visibly froze as his scent hit them and they grew pale. The scent was close to the blood they had been taking such joy in stealing from the male bartender. The meeting of their eyes with his made it clear that the monster at the back booth had informed Cedric that they had been taunting Tony.

"Master Cedric, we did not know..." The blonde silenced as he stood up, his lip healed. "We didn't know he was of your blood, sire."

"Now you do." Sneering down at them, Cedric's voice was deep and stern as he spoke. "See to it that he works here alone every Thursday night so that I may watch over him more easily."

"Y-Yes," the redhead stuttered, looking at the blonde before adding, "but I'm not sure we can convince Himeros to allow him to work alone."

"Tony is part incubus. There is no need for him to have eye candy working with him," Cedric growled. He looked at Romasanta, who watched with glowing eyes of gold, amused by the scene. "As vampires, Himeros will have to believe you, since you've been getting your kicks off the orgasmic flavor of Tony's, my, blood."

Swallowing, the blonde nodded. "You are right. It will be done, Lord Cedric."

Cedric and Romasanta left in silence. Romasanta envied the sense of patience and cleverness Cedric had strengthened over the centuries. For three months they came to the bar, and Romasanta watched as Cedric sat at the bar top observing Tony, weighing his options. One fateful night Romasanta heard Cedric address the boy for the first time. Tony was nervous and excited to talk with Cedric; the fear wafted from him, but it did not stop him from pursuing the interaction he had been denied every Thursday for months. Cedric indulged in retelling his meeting with Angeline and the journey that brought them together. Romasanta sat, listening with Tony as the next few weeks passed. Each chapter of the story unfolded and reminded Romasanta of his own experiences. Both had been victims of being pawns on a grander scale. It seemed recently they managed to break free of the chains that had led them about during those dark times.

Sipping his vodka, Romasanta could not help but feel pride for the feats and obstacles his adoptive descendant had managed to overcome. It still didn't ease his guilt about what was still happening to Angeline. Worse, what condition she would come back to Cedric in was a mystery. Part of him prayed silently to the spirits she would pull through with very little trauma, thanks to the bond they held. From what he was hearing, the bond was much like the new one Lillith had bridged between him and Daphne. Slouching over his drink, his mind pondered over his own connection. Was it possible that Lillith bonded to both him and Daphne? Is that what really happened? Had she gained power by sharing her soul with two unnatural beings? Rubbing the side of his jaw, he sighed as he rolled it in his mind. Was it possible to bond with more than one being?

Looking over at the bar top, Cedric was paying his tab and over-tipping Tony again. Soon the midnight group would roll in, a sorry bunch of halflings mixed with everything under the sun. Regardless, he had been appointed the guard dog for Tony until a decision was made about what Cedric wanted to do with him. At closing, he kept to the shadows, following Tony through the subway and to his home in the bad part of the city. Romasanta's duty required he stand watch as a homeless man sitting in the bar or on the street.

CHAPTER 22

THE WARNING

Romasanta broke from his thoughts as Tony sat a bottle of vodka on the table along with a rocks glass. They exchanged a silent, observant stare before the bartender broke away.

He was of average height and there was nothing extraordinary about Tony at first glance. Like most men in their twenties, he had a faux-hawk of dark brown hair that complimented his green eyes, much like the color of Cedric's own. There were other signs of their blood relation; the strong jawline, the shape of their eyes, and even the way they stood when feeling tense. These were the echoes of descendants seen in physical form, like he had seen in the Romulus bloodline until it had been killed off. All the boy lacked was the muscling Cedric carried in his shoulders and back. Again, this was something Cedric had gained from battles and chances were Tony would never be able to achieve his full bulk in today's world. Romasanta grunted to himself; the odds were he wouldn't live through anything he and Cedric had ever faced in their never-ending lifetimes.

If it hadn't been for the vampires cutting Tony's hand, Romasanta may have concluded he was nothing more than a halfling wafting Cedric's scent with uncanny strength. There were no hints of dormant magic in his blood, but there was that scent of Merlin lightly stitched into the iron. It was faint enough to tease Romasanta's nose until the rich wet smell of Tony's open wound filled his nostrils.

Glancing over his shoulder, he saw Cedric smirk and nod. It seemed he was planning to try something soon, but how far he would go with Tony was hard to say. It wouldn't necessarily be that night, but they were prepping for the attack. The ritual demanded the person opening the portal to Avalon be related to Merlin by blood and be willing, with no signs of spells on the individual. That was where Lillith would come into play, if needed. The moment Tony showed any signs of refusal, the queen succubus would do what she does best so no harm would befall the boy. In the end, no one knew what to expect once they managed to open the door to Avalon.

Popping open the bottle of vodka, Romasanta filled the rocks glass as he listened to the conversation continuing at the bar top. Cedric had warmed up to his estranged kin as he took a deeper interest in the story being shared between them. There was no mistaking the talk with Tony was filling a gap that Wylleam left empty after he passed away. It was sad when the cynocephali shaman died. He had moved into the Black Forest with Nyctimus, living under the refuge of Daphne's protection. When he beckoned for Cedric to be at his side, Romasanta had been asked to bring him.

"So what does a guy do over so many centuries?" Tony's voice withered in Romasanta's ears as he spoke to Cedric. "I'm sorry. I didn't mean to upset you."

"No, you are right. What does a man or demon do with so much time?" Cedric's glass clunked on the bar top, his tone deepened with sorrow as he continued. "I wish I could say I was very productive, but there were centuries of sulking or dedicating myself to research and further knowledge. There were battles fought, and many friends and family lost in that time. Not to mention the pain I felt and knew she was going through..."

Cedric's voice failed him. The memories were so sour and painful they drowned his words before they could escape. It was a feeling Romasanta knew all too well, something the two of them had in common. The loss and pain they had faced was far more than any man or demon could ever take in and while maintaining sanity. Each had struggled to keep their minds intact, but had failed many times. Recently, the silent glares he and Cedric exchanged spoke volumes of the emotional and mental anguish they endured with every breath and beat of their aching hearts.

In 1927, it had been hard to swallow. He had sought Cedric out to go say goodbye to the only friend he had ever known. Romasanta had found companionship in Nyctimus, and even in Badbh and Lillith. Cedric was different. Losing Angeline had sent him into a long, deep silence. As for losing the shaman, it was his last cornerstone being ripped out. There was no sense of friendship between Romasanta and the demonic knight. He had been nothing more than the tool Artemis had promised him so long ago.

Cedric asked why Wylleam had summoned him. Romasanta said nothing. It wasn't his place to prep Cedric for something so inevitable. As Romasanta stared into his green eyes, Cedric knew why Romasanta had been sent. Only he could open the entryway to the Black Forest without the need to be in Europe. The need to save time was enough of a sign of what was waiting for him. The Americas had been a way to break away from the reminders of the past for them all, a fresh start in some ways. The one place that reserved the nostalgia they sought from time to time was the Black Forest, a sanctuary for the *Ancient Ones.*

As they arrived at Wylleam's cottage, Romasanta had intended to leave, but Cedric grabbed his shoulder. "Wait."

Glowering at Cedric's hand for a minute, he finally looked up at the concerned green eyes. "What is it, pup?"

"I'm no fool. I know he is near passing, but," Cedric paused, heaving a sigh, "do you not want to come in? Perhaps your sister is near?"

As Romasanta fought the idea, his chest ached before he, too, sighed. "Fine. I will come in as well."

The room was dark and charms rattled violently as they passed them. Wylleam was lying in his bed; his chest rose and fell in heavy, strained heaps. His once tan and brown fur had grayed, his eyes sunken in his old age. This was the last cynocephali: the shaman who lived tenfold to see that the path was set right for his friend. As his eyes opened, his pupils were white and cloudy, revealing he had gone blind at some point. Cedric kneeled at Wylleam's side and awaited what the old dog wanted from his longtime friend.

"I am sorry I can no longer see you through the rest of your journey on this plane, my old friend." Wylleam's raspy voice shook and his muzzle contorted into a smile. "But you've surprised me with your inner strength."

A smirk came across Cedric's face as he huffed. "It's only thanks to what you taught me, Wyll. Otherwise, I would still be sulking on the graves I dug even now."

"Aye, that is true. No priest would go there, you know?" The smile faded and Wylleam took a deep breath before continuing his confessional. "I suppose it is time I tell you that the witch woman sent me to you. Her spirit haunted me until I had no choice but to seek out her brother, Romasanta."

Romasanta tensed at the whispering of his name, his yellow eyes staring at the dying shaman.

"I understand there is much in motion in the realm of spirits when it comes to both Romasanta and me." Shooting a quick glance over his shoulder, Cedric's eyes showed no sense of surprise. "Romasanta has told me more than enough for me to be able to conclude what may be going on."

Wylleam's nose twitched, struggling to smell. "Ah, I see he is indeed here with you."

Keeping his distance, Romasanta took in a deep breath as he whispered in his wolven tone, "Thank you for everything, Shaman."

"I'm afraid it is far from over for you both." A tear welled up in his blind eyes, rolling over the fur of his cheek. "Please know that *we* are all doing what we can to aid you on the other plane. There are words of warning for you both regarding a necessary obstacle in the future."

Wylleam started coughing, wheezing as he struggled to catch his breath.

"I do not want to hear anything from my sister," snorted Romasanta, turning away from the struggle for death. "Artemis's words have never changed my fate for the better in the past, so I don't expect them to help me now."

Wylleam gripped Cedric's shirt tightly, rolling to face Romasanta's direction as he rasped, "This is a message from Fenrir."

Romasanta's ears flicked, his golden eyes wide as he faced the determination Wylleam had in relaying the message. "He warns that when you face the queen and king of Olympus, they will not let either of you pass."

"Who are they?" Cedric aided Wylleam as he pushed his weight on him, holding the frail cynocephali in his bed. "What are you talking about?"

"Fenrir says Romasanta will know." He wheezed again as he struggled to find the breath, the strength to speak. "They will not let Romulus or Romasanta pass to the Oracle due to the death of their son, Aitvaras."

A gasp escaped Wylleam as he slumped forward, heaping onto Cedric where he kneeled. The message had taken all the energy his body had left. Cedric bit the inside of his cheek, gingerly laying Wylleam back in bed, his thumbs gentle as they closed the old canine's eyes. Romasanta had tensed, frozen as he digested Fenrir's warning. The demon wolf and cynocephali had found a way to get a message through, more than they should have.

"Who is Aitvaras?" Standing, Cedric's green eyes burned into Romasanta as anger stirred in his voice. "Exactly why is this a threat to the both of us?"

"Patience, I am still trying to figure out all that was in that message." Growling, his amber eyes quelled Cedric's temper. "Fenrir and Wylleam are both very clever. They gave me a lot in that last moment, more than you realize. I just need a few minutes to digest it all."

Crossing his arms, Cedric pondered on the words. "Wouldn't the king and queen of Olympus be Zeus and Hera?"

"No. Fenrir knows I am desperate for answers and mentioned Aitvaras the Black Dragon." His eyes grew wide as all of it hit him. "It will take much research before I am sure of my assumptions. All I can say is that we will be facing dragons at some point."

A bell broke his memory as the blizzard howled and screamed outside of the bar. "Ugh, it's a shitty time for a blizzard." Badbh had walked in, fighting with snow flurries as her fingers tangled in her curls. "Couldn't you have rescheduled this, Cedric?"

"Weather is weather. You've been around long enough to not be bothered by it." Cedric rose to his feet, a custom from long ago when warriors saw the battle goddess enter a brothel or tavern. "Where's your sisters?"

"No worries, they are on their way, but it seems it may be a few weeks." Pouting, she sat down at the bar top next to Cedric. "Gimme some Jonnie! Make it a double neat, no, a triple. Why the hell not?"

"You two know each other?" Tony poured the triple shot of Jonnie Walker with a bewildered look on his face as he watched the casualness between Cedric and Badbh. "From your story, Cedric?"

A coy smile crossed Cedric's face as he pulled his hood down. "Yes, that's correct. Tony, meet Badbh. Badbh, this is Tony, that bartender I was telling you about."

"Badbh?" It was odd to him that the names from the story had faces and he questioned his thoughts out loud. "The battle goddess?"

"AH! That's one way to warm your ass up!" Now Romasanta was smirking from his booth as Badbh's voice bellowed through the building like trumpets. "When was the last time you and I sat down for a drink like this?"

"Not long enough if you ask me." Sighing, Cedric looked over his shoulder, catching the smirk on Romasanta's face. "Anyhow, I was about to tell Tony about what happened to Vladimir."

"Oh?" Badbh's voice went soft as she recalled that day herself and humored the idea. "I haven't heard this story either. Do not let me stop you. I've been wondering about what happened myself."

"Yes, please tell me what happened to your ... grandfather, was it?" Obediently, Tony poured Badbh another round and turned his interest back to Cedric. "I thought he was a vampire. Don't they live forever?"

Romasanta zoned out as the tale continued. He knew it, and Badbh, she just liked hearing stories of great battles, even if she was there for the end result. If the battle goddess was joining them there in the bar, it meant Cedric had called the sisters. It was time to discuss the finer details of the plans for their assault on Avalon. There was a mountain of pressure on his shoulders on what to do with the Eye of Gaea. Guzzling back the full rocks glass, he clunked it on the table, refilling it immediately. He was the only one who knew the true identity of the Amulet of Avalon. Even though it had many names, in the end, it was still *The Eye of Gaea.*

As he continued his reconnaissance on Tony, Romasanta weighed everything involved with revealing more about himself to the others. Lillith knew more than she let on about everything, but he still could not find complete comfort in confiding his inner workings to her. She was one who acted before revealing anything she intended to do. He could not afford something happening without him being involved in the details of the action being taken.

A raven came hopping up to his feet, and he smiled. It was Badbh was messaging that it was time for the final meeting. How things went in Avalon would determine what he would do regarding his plans. Even now, he was still taking the lone-wolf attitude toward returning the Eye of Gaea. The more he mulled it over, the more he knew there was no way for him to go any farther alone. Rubbing his scar, he recalled Fenrir's message, and it even suggested that Cedric would be there for that future battle.

By the time he had made it back to Lillith's apartment, the sun had set. Once more he found himself the late arrival as everyone stared in his direction. Silently, he took his seat and waited for one of them to commence the meeting. At this stage, the main goal was to rescue Cedric's wife, Angeline, so it was not his place to plan anything. He mused over the team: A wolf, a succubus, an abomination, and three witch-daughters turned goddesses. If they could not challenge Merlin and his power, then the world would have to be left to its fate.

"I am confident Tony will willingly give us his blood," Cedric started, taking the lead. "This will resolve concerns about any entrapment spells tied into the gateway summoning. It is Rusty, or Himeros, that may crawl out of his hole to interfere."

"I'll take care of any outside distractions, then." Lillith lit a cigarette, blowing the smoke from her lips. "I enjoy being the wildcard."

"Let me remind you all, we cannot kill Merlin for fear of releasing Kronus from Gaea's curse." All eyes turned to Romasanta as his voice hit hard in their ears. "He may not realize it, but his mother wanted to teach him a lesson in mortality, not kill him."

"We've been mulling it over since the last meeting in the Black Forest." Badbh leaned on the table, her voice stern, demanding attention. "My sister Nemaine is skilled in the art of venom. Anything poisonous or toxic over the centuries, she's had a hand in it. She has developed a venom that should prove painful enough to make him fear he's dying. It is also resistant to magical cures, so we pray if we can sneak one bite in that it will weaken him enough to do as we hope."

"Yes, Nemaine is fond of slow painful deaths," groaned Cedric as he rubbed his arm that still held the scars from Nemaine's cobra's bite. "It will definitely give us an opening at the very least, even if he breaks free of it."

"What's wrong, little brother?" Nemaine's vibrant green eyes sparkled as she watched him rub the scars. "Does it still hurt?"

"Stop pestering the boy," Romasanta cut in, annoyed she would dare antagonize anyone at the meeting. "We still need to resolve the matter of what will be done with the Amulet."

"It will need to be cleansed." Morrighan's face was rigid as she spoke. "I do not wish to keep it, but I do intend to undo what vile spells he may have placed on that unholy gem. After that, someone who has no magic in their veins should be its protector. After my own encounter and usage of the stone, it is not for a magic-wielder to possess."

All eyes shifted to Romasanta and Lillith, who sat next to each other. Furrowing their brows, the two questioned which one would be taking the stone.

Choking on her cigarette, Lillith's face flushed. "Good Lord, not me. I already have a shit list long enough to last me a lifetime. And I'm not in the mood to reveal any of it to you all."

"I will take it." Romasanta's heart thudded hard against his chest as he caught the wink from Lillith. "If anyone should hold the stone, it should be one of the top three. Cedric cannot due to his ties with magical bloodlines. I am second in power. I will take it after you have undone his damage, Morrighan."

"Does anyone disagree with this arrangement?" Morrighan made eye contact with all the other members, reassuring no discrepancies were apparent. "As soon as I am confident the stone is restored to its natural state, it will be placed in your hands from my own. I dare not let even my own sisters deliver it, seeing how unpredictable it can be."

"I sure in the hell don't want the thing.," huffed Cedric. "Is there anything else we can do to aid in recovering Avalon as a resource? Even, maybe turn the tables and block Merlin from his sanctuary?"

"We've given this thought as well." Morrighan nodded to Nemaine, and she laid pages across the table as Morrighan continued, "We've been trying to figure out where these were taken. These are pages from the book on Avalon, which allows certain bloodlines access to the island. A fail-safe was enchanted into these, and lucky for us, I have all my father's books. These pages had appeared in one of them, which means setting these upon the book in the Avalon library should restore our right to be there. If we can manage this, we can land a sneak attack on Merlin and start the process of revoking his right to be there as well. We have signed our names. There will not be any special stipulations for us to move freely within Avalon's walls."

"I will be able to find the library faster than anyone else here." Romasanta grabbed the pages, folding them and tucking them into his coat pocket. "There is no way for any of us to know the floor plan of the castle. Instead, I can match the scent on the pages to the source. Once I have laid them on the book, I will race back to the fight. Surprise and confusion should disrupt any solid defense or offense he might have against us."

"Agreed." Badbh crossed her arms, standing tall. "If anyone is capable of this task, it's the wolf."

"Fine." Cedric closed his eyes, his brow furrowing as he thought it all over. "Our first priority is to locate Merlin while Romasanta restores the book pages. Once the fight starts and we're all there, we will either shift to one of us rescuing Angeline or finishing subduing Merlin somehow. We can only pray that the element of surprise teamed with his ever-growing fear of death will aid us in facing him."

Satisfied with the meeting, Romasanta stood. "Seeing that we are all on the same page with our plans, I will be taking off. I wish to visit Daphne before next Thursday's death wish. Badbh will watch the boy until then. A raven is less creepy than the oversized homeless man."

Cedric held back a laugh. "Please do visit her. There's nothing really important left to discuss. There are too many unknown factors that can happen Thursday."

"Let us at least bring your Angel home." Romasanta's voice was almost a whisper as he marched out of the apartment, his heart aching at the idea of the torture the poor girl had been under since the battle of chimera and werewolves.

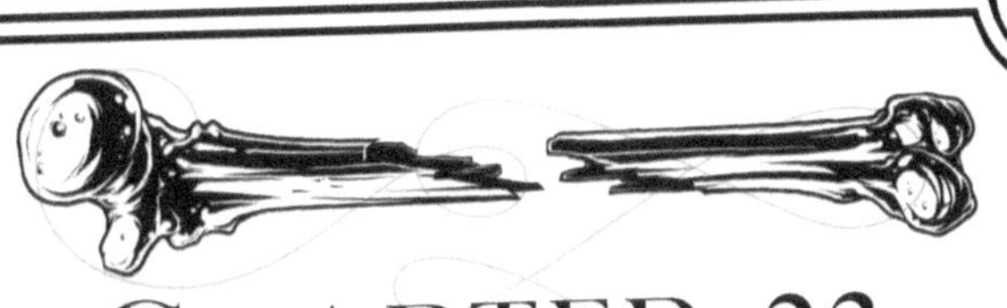

CHAPTER 23

AVALON

His visit with Daphne had been short, and he kept the details of what would be happening minimal. They were both aware that getting the Eye of Gaea back was just the start of a longer journey that had no end in sight. Some place on the earth was a doorway to the spiritual plane of Gaea, but the details about its location were vague. In desperation, Romasanta was trying to keep the weight on his shoulders limited to one task at a time. For now, until the stone sat in his palms once more, the location of Gaea would have to wait.

Part of him hoped that somewhere in the Avalon library would be an ancient book to solidify the clues Fenrir had left him. Some of the books hinted at a mountain but as to where or what was waiting for him, there was missing information or the details were too inconsistent to know which was closer to the truth. The passing of information through generations had failed to keep details, let alone keep fact from fiction. In the end, most of the modern world would never believe vampires came from werewolves, or there were monsters like Ravenna that devoured evil men.

Tony's voice caught his ears as Romasanta sat at his booth, waiting for everyone to show up. "Whoa, so Merlin is the one that cursed Romasanta? Man, this wizard really likes to piss people off."

"He's a clever one." Scoffing, Badbh glanced over to the booth, where he ignored her. "But I was wondering what the deal was and why you two became buddy-buddy."

"By the way, would you like something to drink with Badbh and me, Romasanta?" Cedric brought the attention to him, seeing he had ignored Badbh's reaction.

"No, thank you." Annoyed, Romasanta's eyes flashed gold before he turned back to the white haze in the window near his booth. "Badbh is far too much for me these days."

"What is going on?" Fear wafted from Tony. It was a sudden reaction as the reality of his situation started to pull at him. "These are the people from your fairy tale. This is insane, I must be dreaming. Is this some sort of prank?"

"We have much to discuss with you, Tony." Another wave of fear poured from him as Cedric spoke. "But just wait a moment longer; we have more on their way. When they get here, I will explain what is going on. Please, do not be startled, no harm will come to you."

"Harm?" Bottles rattled and shook as Tony backed into the bar shelves and his voice heightened. "Are you crazy?"

"What a mess!" Morrighan and Nemaine pushed through the door as the blizzard roared outside. "You were never good at being diplomatic, Cedric."

"It has nothing to do with my lack of diplomacy." Cedric snarled, almost pouting as they joined him and Badbh at the bar. "I blame your sister."

"Stop knocking your knees together, boy, and pour me another round of Jonnie." The trumpeting Badbh broke the tension as she crossed her arms. "Or just hand me the bottle."

Glaring over his shoulder, Romasanta watched as the witch-daughters giggled at Tony. Tony's nerves were rattling through him as he handed Badbh the Jonnie Walker bottle, his hand trembling. Cedric watched Tony with great care, his stare calling the boy's attention. With each physical character from the story walking into the bar, he grew more terrified. For months, he had listened to a story he thought was for pure kicks. Seeing the faces of the names from Cedric's story gripped his instincts, choking out his assumptions about what defined reality.

A bottle wobbled behind Tony. Romasanta watched as it rolled away from his elbow and exploded against the tile floor. The bar went silent, Tony's fear sucking the life from him as he stood at the center of the non-human stares. Tony's eyes bounced from one creature to the next until they hit the golden eyes in the dark corner of the bar. His body froze as he lost himself to the glowing wolf's eyes. Romasanta smirked, his fangs no longer hidden under his lips as terror exploded from the bartender.

The office door banged against the bar top as a red-faced obese man glowered over the commotion. Grunting, he scratched at his navel. Romasanta may have been far away, but he found himself rubbing his sensitive nose free of the pestilence flowing from the bar owner. As Cedric had already made them aware, this was not a human, but a Greek godling by the name of Himeros. It was clear that this godling was not aware of who sat in his bar, the way he shoved himself past Tony. He leaned over the bar top, staring down Cedric as the witch-daughters smirked. Salty sweat started to form on his forehead as he began to realize Cedric wasn't just another vampire pestering his worker.

With a deep rattling voice, Himeros engaged the troublemaker before him. "What's with all the ruckus?!"

"I have no clue what you are talking about." Cedric refused to be intimidated as his green eyes cut into Himeros. "I invited some friends over, that's all."

"I know who you are, and you are going to cause me more trouble than what it's worth." The aura of battle sent Badbh into a laughing fit as she chugged her bottle of Jonnie Walker, goading Himeros's speech. "Leave here and don't come back. You and your friends are no longer welcome. It's bad enough you have my girls spooked."

"No. We are staying. I have business with Tony." Cedric hadn't flinched and Romasanta felt pride to see the young Lord Romulus not even tense in reaction to the threat of exile.

Snorting, Himeros pushed for answers. "What do you want with a partial-blood like him? The kid knows nothing."

"Step aside, Rusty." As Cedric rose to his feet, he towered over Himeros, Tony, and the girls. "This has nothing to do with you, your girls, or your kind. If you stand in my way, it will bring unwanted attention in your direction, Himeros. I know exactly who you are."

"Hah, I haven't heard that name in centuries." Himeros took a step back, crossing his arms, desperate to hold his ground. "I'm shocked to see something like you were capable of identifying someone of my power so easily in today's time. What gave me away?"

"I am the king incubus, head of the Vampiric Order, the Hero Ilya Muromets, Bringer of Death, Slayer of Demons, and more importantly, Lord Romulus." The sound of crackling wood greeted Romasanta's ears as he smiled, proud of the pup who claimed his dominance so well in his own son's honor. "I am the all-knowing, you godling of the Greeks!"

Cedric had pulled his dominance well as the room tensed under his shadow. Romasanta's chest tingled at Lillith's mark, the bar's door opening to the whistling of the wild, snow-filled wind. The bell on the door shook violently as the blizzard rattled it and Lillith entered. Her maroon eyes were wild as she waved her arousal outward. As far as he could see, only he and Cedric felt the wave as they shuddered slightly as it washed over them. It was an intentional means of toying with them both, knowing she was doing them a favor by ridding them of the vile godling.

With each clack of her heels on the tile, Himeros flinched. He knew who she was. There was no need for horns or wings to see what stood in his bar now. If the king incubus was no threat, then the ancient queen suc-cubus should resonate with what he did know to fear. Sighing, Romasanta was thankful to be sitting far off as he watched Lillith nibble at Cedric's ear, staring in Romasanta's direction, as if hoping to arouse him. Cedric simply ignored her excessive touching, but Romasanta smirked. His yellow eyes flashed in response that she would have to try harder if she wanted the attention of her wolf. A wicked grin crawled across her face as she looked away, groping her breast with such bellicosity that Himeros could not help but watch her self-inflicted aggression.

"Well now! Since I can't get what I want from the incubus king, I shall settle for the son of Aphrodite and Ares!" Lillith's thin, tight, black dress left nothing to the imagination as she pulled herself on the bar top, leaning close to Himeros. "I don't recall ever laying with you. Let's see how much you inherited from your father, godling."

"Li-Lillith." She gripped the hair on the back of Himeros's head, sending waves of arousal through him. "This can't be."

"Did your daddy ever recover?" She shot another glance to Romasanta as she licked Himeros's neck, slid her tongue across his cheek, and kissed his temple. "Mmm, not completely I see. No worries, Cedric baby, leave this one to me."

"Enjoy your new toy, Lillith." Cedric turned away as she slid over the bar top, catching Romasanta's gaze as he watched Lillith work. "Come join us at the table, Tony."

Tony scrambled to gain distance as the office door slammed shut. Himeros's horrifying screams sent chills across him. He followed Cedric to Romasanta's booth, obedient and silent, as they gestured for him to sit. They pinned him between them, a means to imprison him long enough to explain what would be happening. Cedric had relayed the history of his trials of pain, but Tony was needed for any of them to continue the next step. Romasanta and Cedric exchanged smirks as Tony shook, his heart thudding so fast they could hear it with little effort. Fear continued waving out of the boy, his nerves sabotaging him as he sat between the two monsters.

The bar filled with the screeching and squeaking of chairs and tables being moved to the far corners and walls. Tony stared wide-eyed as he watched Morrighan and Nemaine use an unseen force to push the furniture with ease. Romasanta topped off his rocks glass once more, the commotion ripping at his sensitive ears. Badbh's eyes sparkled, her cheeks red from drinking as she placed a foot on the pool table. She gave a drunken smirk toward them as she kicked the pool table, sending it sailing through the bar top and into the display of liquor bottles. An explosion of breaking glass hammered through the place, sending Tony into a panic, as he flinched as each bottle broke. Satisfied with her ruckus, she polished off her Jonnie Walker. In one last need for destruction, the battle goddess threw the bottle at what had survived the crash, annihilating what bottles had been left intact.

Morrighan and Nemaine scoffed as they focused on the more delicate part of their duty. Consulting a massive tome, Morrighan directed Nemaine as she placed candles in different places, a particular order needed. Romasanta huffed his nose, in a failed attempt to clear the smells of the putrid candles as she lit each one. Finishing this task, Nemaine rejoined Morrighan, peering into the tome. With a playful look, Nemaine took a basket of pungent herbs and a carafe of sand, salt, and ash. She danced about the floor, from candle to candle in a ritualistic manner. Each point was rewarded with a different bundle of plants before she swirled to the next destination. The carafe poured silently as it traced her path, adding to the mesmerizing performance.

"Tony." Cedric's voice jolted both Romasanta's and Tony's attention back to him. "Let me explain what is really happening."

"O-Okay." Tony braved to look Cedric in the eye, though he was terrified.

"I apologize for the intrusion into your life, but you hold a very important key that I need to locate Merlin."

"Merlin?" Furrowing his brow, he could not piece together where Cedric was going with this information. "What do I have to do with Merlin?"

"I am afraid, more than you realize. And you even have something to do with me." Smiling, Cedric's sharp stare softened as he took on a more empathetic tone. "I hope you were paying attention to my story, because what I am about to explain might seem confusing otherwise."

"I think I can recall a good amount." The muscles in Tony's body tightened as he shifted in his seat. "Go ahead. Explain it to me, please."

"You are a blood relative to both Merlin and me."

Tony's eyes searched the air for a minute before he asked further. "Ok, and how is that possible?"

"Well, there was one element I had failed to consider in my hundred-year youth, and that was the responsibilities of the king incubus. As much as it sickens me to admit, I am responsible for replenishing the world with succubi and incubi. I took advantage of this fact, and have taken a different route than Boto. It is rare that I have to kill one of my offspring, but they are all very aware of my search for Merlin and Angeline. By some bizarre turn of fate, at some point over the hundreds of years, one of my children slept with someone from Merlin's original bloodline, or even Merlin himself, perhaps. That line moved forward for at least 200 more years before someone was born with at least some essence of holding the magic in their veins." Cedric's eyes broke away and Morrighan nodded; she and her sisters were ready to receive the blood. "You carry a strong bond and connection to Merlin. All I need is one drop of blood so that I can launch my attack on him. This keeping and torturing of Angeline has gone on too long."

"How..." Tony stopped his words, as if gathering more courage to continue digging. "How do you even know she's alive after all this time?"

"I feel her pain." Cedric's eyes dulled and his complexion paled. "Every burn, cut, broken bone, and magical torture I have felt in full force. In doing so, she has felt the love and pleasure that I can only give her, letting her know I am still here looking for her. She has had all her fingers broken, her ribs cracked, healed, and cracked again. Legs smashed with the weight of hammers and the cuttings of a dull blade that snags one's flesh in such a way that it is more like being torn open. Magic has been seeped deep within her body and soul, but with the pain going to me, Merlin has failed to cleanse me from her body or break our bond."

Cedric's story replayed across Tony's face as he stared at the desperation in the green eyes waiting for an answer. Here he had been in the company of monsters, frantic to get to Merlin, and yet they had not threatened him. Instead, with an ungodly amount of inner strength, Cedric had been patient enough to tell the story of how he came to this very point in his life to need someone like him to help. This man had slain creatures Tony had never heard of and then faced a lifetime of taking on the pain of his soulmate's torture. Saying no would make him the monster in the room.

Tony swallowed, his words stammering, but he answered as firmly as he could, "My blood is yours."

Morrighan gripped his hand and a knife ripped across it. Tony flinched as she squeezed it tight and poured his blood into the copper goblet below it. Romasanta took another deep inhale, confirming to himself it was indeed Merlin's bloodline. Being so close to it, he could now smell the faint itch of magic there. Perhaps Cedric's nose had been able to seek it out easier, but it had been a long time since he had aimed to seek out magic wielders.

Romasanta's eyes followed Morrighan as she stepped with great caution over the pattern on the tiled floor. The other sisters had taken their spots, and the air thickened as Morrighan reached her place. All facing the center where the goblet had been placed, they hummed a melody he had not heard since the time of his sister's reign as a shaman. It was an ancient song to call forth powerful magic and spirits. They swayed as they hummed ever louder; the air contorting and making the hairs at the nape of Romasanta's neck stand on end. Droplets of blood floated up and out of the goblet, and soon a line pulled upward. A spiral design in blood floated between the chanting witch-daughters as their voices were lost in the vibration of the magic humming in the air. Like a coin, the spiral started to spin until all that could be seen was a wobbling orb of crimson. Light exploded from it, stinging Romasanta's sensitive eyes.

Cedric whistled, breaking him from his stun, and Romasanta followed him through the searing white light.

Romasanta found himself alone on a shore riddled with seaweed. A heavy sigh hit him as he looked down at his clawed hands. It seems no matter what, he was cursed to the werewolf form inside sanctioned places like Avalon and the Black Forest. He snorted. The air was musky with salt and decay as he worked his way up the shore to the sand hills. Black rocks glittered with dew from the fog lying thick across the beach. Nearing the crest of the massive hill, the walls of Avalon's fortress were so close they shocked him. Magic made the air dense, and it took him a while to adjust his nose to weed out the details.

Movement caught his eye, a flash of red. Looking over his shoulder, it was a relief to see Cedric had made it through, after all. Nodding, he began trying to pull in more information as he sniffed and snorted at the air. Breaking the code, his mind slammed him with the information he had been trying to obtain. The fur on his neck and shoulders ruffled excitedly as his ears pricked forward. Some place close to where they stood was an opening that was giving out a hint of the damp mildew of the inner castle. He worked his way closer to the source, not knowing if they would find a window, door, or even a hole in the wall.

"What is the full story behind you agreeing to chase Merlin?" Cedric had chosen a lousy time to start a heart-to-heart talk. "What history do you have with the old wizard, besides the fact he cursed you? I assume you had something he wanted."

"More than you would want to know," Romasanta snarled, glowering at Cedric in hopes of ending the conversation. "Let's just say he is to blame for my form and my heartache. He is a greedy man and deserves what is coming to him. I pray to the Ancient Ones that I am the one who rightfully serves him with the punishment that he has been avoiding."

"I see this is the sort of story that dates farther back than any man who was capable of writing his own history to paper." Cedric realized that he would get nothing from Romasanta until after Merlin was gone. "I just wanted to know that this was not one of your backdoor deals, again."

Huffing, he smirked at Cedric from over his shoulder. "Fortunate for you, this is a personal reason that requires my direct dealings to satisfy the wants and needs I feel. Perhaps later on in life, I will reveal my story to you, but not today, pup."

The physical condition of the castle was in extreme disrepair. All the wards and magic in the world can only do so much without someone to maintain the tangible item they were designed to defend. Looking at one another, they were relieved to have struck such a lucky find. The crevice was massive; the stone wall had crumbled outward. Clawing away more bricks, they widened the gap so they could squeeze inside. Entering the rotting hallway, there were very few remnants of the furniture and tapestries that used to decorate the halls. Instead, piles of trash and dust lined the floors at their feet. With one last nod to one another, they took off in opposite directions. Romasanta's first focus was to find the library of Avalon.

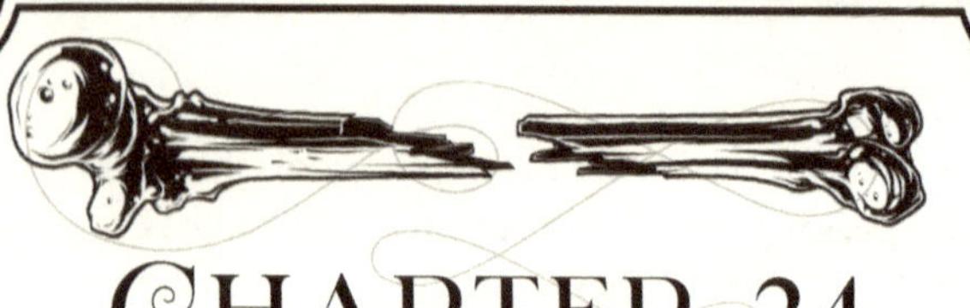

CHAPTER 24

RESTORATION

The sound of his claws echoed through the hallways as he raced to the scent matching the pages in the pouch at his waist. His nose twitched, his feet sliding on the damp moss-covered floors. At first, he had not seen any doors, but as he scrambled back to the peak of the scent, one pushed out of the stone walls. Light emitted from the pages in his satchel as he entered through the door. Stepping into the darkness, he could smell leather, ink, and parchment; this was indeed the library. As his golden eyes brought the darkness to light, he caught a glimpse of a podium holding a massive tome. This was the book controlling who could enter this place. Returning the pages inside its cover should restore the witch-daughters to their rightful access to Avalon.

Slowly, and cautious of his surroundings, he approached the library's centerpiece. Its leather cover angled awkwardly as he opened it. The bind had once held thousands of pages; all but one golden page had been ripped out. On it, a single name was written: *Merlyn Kronus Frych. Romasanta* gripped the page and ripped it out, crushing it in his palm as he growled.

A wind howled through the library, breaking his angry thoughts. He scrambled to pull the pages Morrighan had given him out of the pouch. Gale-force winds screamed through the library as he pinned his ears flat. His claws fumbled to unfold the aged parchment as it flailed about in the ruckus. The paper hit the back cover of the book with a bang as he slammed it there. A flash of gold reunited them to the binding and a long list of names reappeared across the paper as if freshly written. As the last corner revived itself and attached again, the wind stopped.

Torches and fire pit tables came to life, with flames whooshing outward from where he stood at the podium. There were more than just the sisters' names on this list. A smile came across his face as he saw that they were aiming to reestablish Avalon as a sanctuary for those bearing the curse of magic. Despite most of the surviving bloodlines being watered down, lost in generations of skipped ancestors, there were signs of a reemergence. It would take a lot of time to undo the damage Merlin had done to the magic users of the past. Regardless, this new wave of magic wielders would need a haven where they could learn to correctly use their abilities. Something the Lykaons had failed to do, let alone respect others that they practiced their art on.

His ears pricked forward as he looked over the massive canyons of the library in its new, warm glow. There would be no time to search the books, not with the fight taking place elsewhere. As he stepped away from the podium, his foot knocked into the ball of paper holding Merlin's signature. Chills snaked across him, his fur ruffled with thoughts flashing through his mind. Picking it up, he placed it in his satchel, knowing the page could never be destroyed; at least not yet. Instead, like the stone, he would guard it until a means to rid the world of it revealed itself.

Looking back at the podium, he knew if something like the book could be created, it could be destroyed. Nothing in the world was permanent, just resilient. Though he felt immortal, deep down he knew he could be killed if the enemy he faced was strong enough. All he could see was the dragon Aitvaras and how Fenrir had made him feel. In that moment, that memory Fenrir shared with him, he knew a dragon would be capable of ending his life. Once he held the stone, he would be facing the queen and king of dragons. This time, without the security of Fenrir's guidance when the battle starts.

A raven cawed, making him jerk as it floated to the floor, bursting into an explosion of feathers to reveal Badbh.

"Nemaine has managed to hit her mark and Morrighan managed to obtain the Amulet of Avalon! It seems we have him in a panic and the pages have allowed us through the doors without alarming him." A great big smile was across her face, her eyes sparkling inside her raven's mask. "But Cedric will need your help. I fear he might kill Merli—"

There was no time to waste. Romasanta leaped into full stride. The signature with *Kronus* sent his heart pounding against his chest as he burst into the hallway. He knew very little about who or what Merlin was inside his, or its, human body, but his instincts rattled his core. They would not live through this if Merlin, Kronus, was killed. He took a hard turn, his massive body banging into the stone wall as his claws struggled to grip the slippery stone floor under him. The smell of Merlin and Cedric was growing. The double doors at the end of the hallway motivated him to run faster.

A loud sucking sound popped in the air and the burning of his scar told him Gaea's law was at work. Smashing through the doors, he saw Merlin casting spells between him and the portal that had ripped into existence. Gritting his teeth, he rushed past Cedric. The cracking of ribs echoed in his skull as he slammed into Merlin's side. The wizard spun, losing his focus on keeping himself from being pulled in. The wizard's blue eyes met the searing amber of Romasanta's. As Merlin faded into the portal, Romasanta saw Merlin whisper who had sent him to his punishment, *Romasanta.*

"You ok?" Cedric joined Romasanta where the wizard and portal had disappeared. "I know it doesn't fix things but—"

Huffing, he turned away from Cedric, walking away feeling unsatisfied. "You're the only one who knows the truth about my curse and Merlin's involvement. Let's keep it that way."

The magic in Avalon shifted, and looking down at his clawed hand, he was relieved to be able to shift back into a man. It was unclear if Merlin's magic had forced him to be the wolf or if the girls had started to work their spells on the place. Closing his hand into a firm fist, he walked out the door. Cedric would be busy seeking out Angeline, but he wanted to go back to the library in hopes of finding answers. He didn't make it to the corner before the library door presented itself to him. He pushed open the doorway. The library was still lit with a warm and welcoming ambiance. Much to his surprise, the three witch-daughters were huddled around the podium, discussing what they intended to do with Avalon. They paused, facing him as he stood there, confused as to why he had sought out the library. Morrighan and Nemaine looked at Badbh, assuming she was the reason for his unexpected visit.

"What can we do for you, Romasanta?" Badbh smiled warmly. "We were trying to figure out what all we needed to do with the sanctuary, but perhaps your problem is easier to solve."

He furrowed his brow, looking over the mountains of book-filled shelves. "How do you go about looking for books in a place like this?"

"It is intimidating to look at." Morrighan waved a hand to tables with books piled on them. "But Avalon's library will bring the books to you without you having to climb a shelf. It's a blessing since all you need to do is sit and read at a table and the piles shift to match and find anything on the topic your heart desires to read about."

He started for a table when Nemaine scoffed, "You're not going to sit there naked and read, are you?"

"Yes." A devilish smile crossed his face as he looked back at her. "I'm not a magician. Clothes don't survive a shift, and I have no time to be bashful."

Badbh laughed as she patted her sister's back. "If only there were more men like him."

"You would prefer the world to be naked, Badbh?" She shuffled out of Badbh's reach, scowling at her. "Please get your friend some clothes."

"Fine." Badbh shifted into a raven, flying off from the group.

"You don't have to worry about the stone." Morrighan lifted an eyebrow as he sat at a table, befuddled at the giant pile of books on it. "It just might take me a while to break these bindings he's placed on it."

"I trust that you will cleanse the gem and hand it to me," he mumbled. He pulled a large book from the center of the pile, a few sliding off the top of the pile as he tugged it free. "But I have other things to research and this is a place I haven't had access to before."

Shrugging to one another, Morrighan and Nemaine went back to discussing how to best recover the missing pages of the Book of Bloodlines. Flipping through the pages of the book he chose, he grew frustrated. The language in the book was nothing like any he had known. He paused as he saw an image that caught his attention. A mountain with a peculiar symbol that reminded him somewhat of the Illuminati symbol on its top. Even more intriguing were the two dragons crawling around the base, one depicted as a female and the other a male.

Morrighan was right, the books on the table would give him what he wanted, but what good did it do him if he couldn't read them? The ink swirled across the parchment and looked more like a child's drawing in his eyes. He glanced at the bickering sisters at the podium and sighed. There was too much pride in him to ask for help, at least for today. Glowering down at the image, his heart ached as he rubbed the scar on his chest. This had to be the mountain and dragons from Fenrir's warning, a king and queen of sorts. Was the eye-like symbol referring to the Eye of Gaea? Could it all be written here in this book?

Warm fingers grazed his shoulder, and he flinched. Badbh had returned with clothes, placing them on the table next to him. Taking a moment, he rubbed his face, wary still from everything they had accomplished far too easily. She snorted at the idea she had startled him, sitting in the chair beside his own. Looking over at the book he had opened, she hummed as her eyes scanned the image and writing.

"Why on earth would you be interested in seeing the Oracle?" She twisted her lips to the side. "I don't even know if she's still alive. No one's been there in ages."

Pulling his hands away from the book, he looked at Badbh in bewilderment. "The Oracle?"

"Yeah, on Mount Olympus with her two obnoxious guardian dragons." Tapping the page, he looked at the writing, which still looked like doodles to him. "Typhon and Delphyne, the father and mother of dragons. Thanks to those two love birds we got a whole shitload of monsters invading the world at one point. Made for some epic battles."

"Is there a chance she's still on Mount Olympus?" He grabbed the clothes, making space for Badbh to read further as he dressed himself. "Or has that sanctuary fallen?"

"Oh, it's long gone." She nodded as she flipped a few pages. "But that's the myth side of this. Here, right here, it says that the Oracle, the priestess of Delphi, could be found on Mount Parnassus beneath the Castalian Spring. It says Delphyne, a daughter of Gaea, is the protector of this place."

"The dragon is a daughter of Gaea?" He paled as he zipped his pants. "Then what connection does the Oracle have to Gaea?"

"It doesn't say in this book. You'll have to dig through them and hope one of them might say something." Standing, she patted him on the back. "You know, if you sign your name in the book over there, you can read these just fine."

"I thought that was for magical bloodlines only." He glared at the book for a moment. "But you also said it allows passage for relatives as well?"

216

"Exactly. It recognizes that not all relatives will inherit magic." Rubbing the back of her neck, Badbh watched her sisters head to a table to start their own research. "We think he was using the pages to take out the competition, though. Using their blood signatures to trace them and their families down. I would imagine working the magic backward would give him someone of that bloodline and not always the person who signed the book."

The muscles in Romasanta's chest tightened as he recalled the night he came across Merlin for the first time. "What if a relative once signed the book and their page is missing?"

"We are trying to resolve that..." Her voice trailed off as she crossed her arms. "Are you from a magical bloodline? Who in your family would have signed the tome?"

The pounding in his ears grew loud as the question echoed ever louder in his mind. Swallowing, he forced out the truth he had been hiding. "Artemis of the Apollo bloodline."

Badbh pulled her mask off, a shocked look across her pale, scar-riddled face. "And may I ask in what way are you related to the Master Shamanka of Avalon?"

Romasanta flinched at the title his sister had earned here. He stood in front of Badbh, needing to make a decision about whether to hold his tongue any longer. Clenching his fists and furrowing his brow, he stared down at the stone floor as he waged war within himself. He had wondered how Merlin was able to keep his search ongoing for his sister's bloodline. Not even Romasanta knew where she had gone to hone her skills so quickly in the days of their youth until Badbh had uttered the title to him. There was too much at stake for him to keep his past, his connections, silent. They had all proven themselves trustworthy and the next phase of this journey would need their aid, their knowledge, and their resources to accomplish.

His eyes connected with Badbh's, a fiery flare of gold in them, as he relieved himself of his ultimate secret. "I am her twin brother. At birth, I was named Apollo."

The bronze-and-silver mask clattered against the floor like gunfire. Morrighan and Nemaine were startled from their books, the sound still echoing through the library. Badbh covered her mouth, a look of grief across her face as tears welled up in her eyes. He watched in confusion as she motioned for her sisters to come over, and they did so. Before him, Badbh pulled her emotions into check as she kneeled before him. The two sisters looked at her and then at him with an equal sense of loss as to what was happening.

"My sisters..." Badbh's voice was a whisper as she spoke. "We have been in the company of Apollo this whole time. This man, this wolf, is the cursed twin brother of Master Shamanka Artemis."

Nemaine and Morrighan fell in line at either side of her, also bowing their respects to him.

"Dear Apollo, do you not realize how important it is that we have found you?" Morrighan gave him a momentous expression as she continued to explain. "You are the rightful heir of Avalon."

"Heir?" He couldn't slow his racing heart and it took all his strength to swallow his anxious waves down. "It should go to someone other than me. I despise magic..."

The three girls looked at one another and Morrighan answered, "But the heir must be of your bloodline. Avalon was nothing more than a proving ground until Artemis took it over. It was she who created the library itself, Apoll—"

Raising a hand, he stopped her a moment. "Please, no more of that name. I abandoned it long ago and for good reasons. If someone of my bloodline needs to take hold, then I shall seek a more suitable protector. Just make sure Merlin has not set traps involving the process. He was unforgiving in his quest to gain my sister's power."

They stood, nodding in agreement.

Badbh rubbed her jaw, a smirk on her lips again. "This whole time. But whatever happened to that curse of the werewolves? Did someone heal you?"

Romasanta looked down at his hands as the faces of all he had ravaged with them flooded his mind. "If you must know, it was Fenrir. He healed me of the curse by making me heir to his demonic powers. Since the day he left me alone inside this body, I have not spread the curse."

CHAPTER 25

ALL SECRETS REVEALED

A few months passed after they sent Merlin into the mysterious void. No one knew if it was a recoil by Gaea's law or a delay in ripping his name from the book. Either way, Romasanta had settled for waiting until the damage done to Avalon and the stone could be repaired to do anything further. They were all focusing on first fixing what they knew how to fix before chasing down a wizard who may or may not have died. The first order of business was the stone and its safety. After that, they would establish Avalon for its resources and repurpose it as their new war front. Romasanta preferred the Black Forest for the peaceful, secretive sanctuary, and hated meeting at the Lykaon castle to talk about their battle plans in the past. He and Fenrir had created the sanctuary spell for Daphne's safety and protection, not to be a center of operations for vengeance.

Despite the anger waving through him for revealing his true name, a name he hadn't spoken since he left to be a farmer, a great weight had been lifted from his soul. His steps were lighter, his shoulders less tense, and his desire for drink had eased. He still went to the bar where Tony worked, a place where they had all started to indulge in the idea of running into one another without a reason or need. Himeros was long gone, and the deed had been handed over to Tony and Cedric to run the place as they saw fit.

The Lion's Den was an appropriate name for the bar and its new cast of regulars. It humored him to see the relief Tony's face held when he walked in, as if the idea of being left alone with his workers and customers was a threat without him or Cedric near. There had been a few times when he came to the booth, stuttering apologetically for some assistance with aggressive halflings. Nothing brought Romasanta more pleasure than being asked to take back the dominance in the room. To him, it was a game and a chance to relieve aggression he no longer could unleash as he had in the past.

The bell of the door rang and he glanced over his shoulder to see Cedric and Angeline already at the bar top. Tony was doing routine cleaning and his eye sparkled to see the Thursday regulars were all there. Without a word, he pulled out two rocks glasses and dropped ice into them.

"You'll never catch me actually walking in, you know?" Cedric smirked.

Tony paused, smiling as he nodded in agreement and poured vodka into the glasses. "Here you go. Same as always I see."

"I owe you the world, Tony." Romasanta watched as Cedric raised his glass to Tony, his left hand no longer missing any fingers, once more adorned with a gold wedding ring. "How's business?"

"Booming since Rusty left." Tony sighed, turning to Angeline, and waved. "And how are you doing today, Angeline?"

"Perfect." She stared down at her glass. "Still strange to see the world is so different."

Cedric eyed her from the corner of his eye before pouting his disapproval. "She cut her hair, but I'm hoping she'll let it grow back."

"I like it!" Tony gave her a sincere smile. "Well, I am just happy to meet the girl I've heard so much about."

Angeline laughed, shaking her head disapprovingly. "I still don't believe he spent months here telling you about our life together in such horrible detail."

Romasanta sighed as he listened to it all. His thoughts were working themselves into a tangled mess over the fact she would have to take over Avalon. That place held no affectionate memories for her, but ages of torture. That was something that could wait for her to rebuild who she was again. The look in Angeline's eyes reminded Romasanta of when he struggled with who he was; a wolf or a man. For her, it was hard to say what those inner forces were, perhaps they were more severe than his. Was it a force of the past versus the new world? Maybe the idea she had become something inhuman, something he also struggled to settle in his own heart.

Once more, the bell announced a new customer, and to everyone's surprise, it was Morrighan. "Good evening!"

"Oh! Hi, I haven't seen you or your sisters since, well, *that* day," Tony fumbled and managed to rectify his initial intent. "Can I get you something? It's on the house."

"No, thank you." She winked as she continued past them. "I am here to talk with Romasanta."

Leaning back in the booth, he watched as her hand hit the table in front of him. Her fingers unfolded and the red glow reflected his yellow eyes in it. Romasanta picked up the stone; the familiar warmth pulsed through it as he inspected it. When she had taken it from Merlin, it had a purple sheen and looked like an oval jewel. Here in his hand was the exact cursed stone that had destroyed his life so long ago.

"How did you get it restored this far?" Morrighan crossed her arms as Romasanta looked up at her. "I haven't seen it like this since I last touched the damn thing."

"Magic is a master of illusion, Romasanta," she huffed, scowling down at him as she questioned him. "And when were you going to tell me it was really the Eye of Gaea?"

He flinched, his eyes growing sharp as he answered. "I didn't think that was something anyone would understand. Then again, you and your sisters have been on this earth long enough to know something. There is so much I haven't told anyone. Nyctimus might know some of it, but he was there for a lot of it. Then again, I never told him or Rhea much and they still suffered."

"What are you planning to do with that stone and its power?" She was tensing as she prepared herself for an answer. "Did you have a use for it this whole time?"

Romasanta looked at Cedric and Angeline, then turned back to Morrighan, furrowing his brow. "It is my duty to take it back to Gaea so that Daphne can be freed from the laurel tree. So much has gone wrong. You want someone with my bloodline? Well, that girl is the heiress of my sister's power, a sorceress. But I will choose when to drop the weight of Avalon on her shoulders."

Shocked, Morrighan looked at Angeline, whose vacant stare lost itself in a full glass of vodka. "Artemis's heiress…"

"She is broken." His words stung, and gripping the stone tight in his hand, frustration bit at him. "I cannot let that task be known to her until

I know she has found herself again. Those eyes remind me of the centuries of hardships I undertook alone. She is fortunate to have someone at her side, and even more so, someone who fared his troubles better than I did in my past. He knows when her feelings start to cut her, he can feel them as if they are his own. Until she finds her place in this world, she is not fit to take over Avalon."

Sighing, Morrighan dropped her arms. "You are right. What do you intend on doing then from here?"

"Fenrir said to go see the Oracle, and I can't do it alone." Staring down at the stone, he huffed as he made a final judgment call. "It's time that all my secrets are revealed. Let's call a meeting for tonight so that I may share my story and see who will be facing the king and queen of dragons at Mount Parnassus with me."

TO BE CONTINUED...

READY FOR BOOK THREE?

THE ORACLE:
KEEPER OF GAEA'S GATE
IS WAITING FOR YOU.

If you enjoyed the book, or something really nagged you about the story, I encourage you to speak your mind about my book in the form of a review. Readers depend on them to know whether they will like the story and characters within the pages.

Where can you leave the review? There are a lot of places! Amazon and GoodReads are great places to leave them, but feel free to visit your favorite online venues and leave them there. Whether it's a one-liner that sums up how you feel, an in-depth review breaking down the book and characters, or a spoiler warning of a rant to follow—

ALL ARE ENCOURAGED.

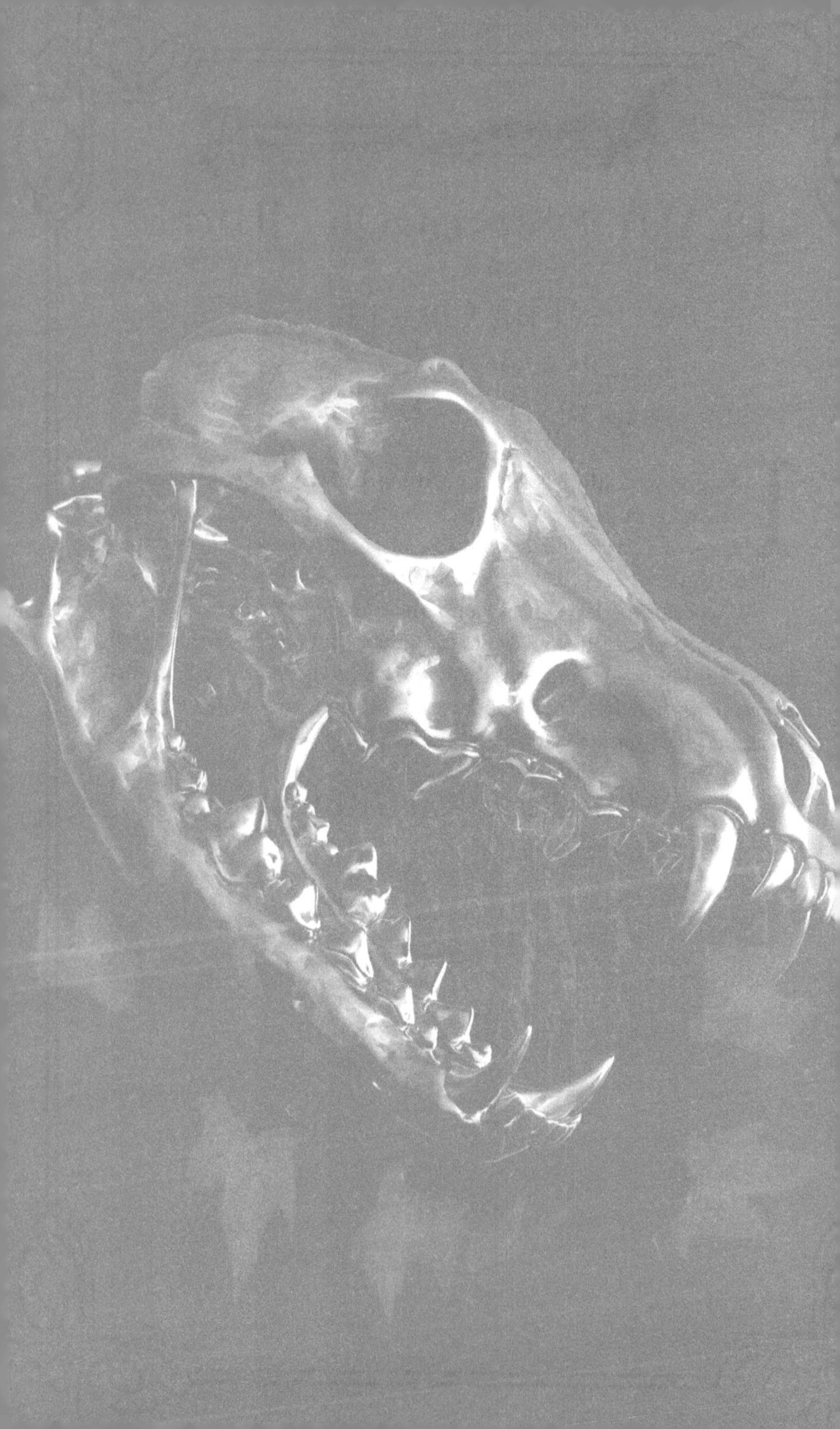

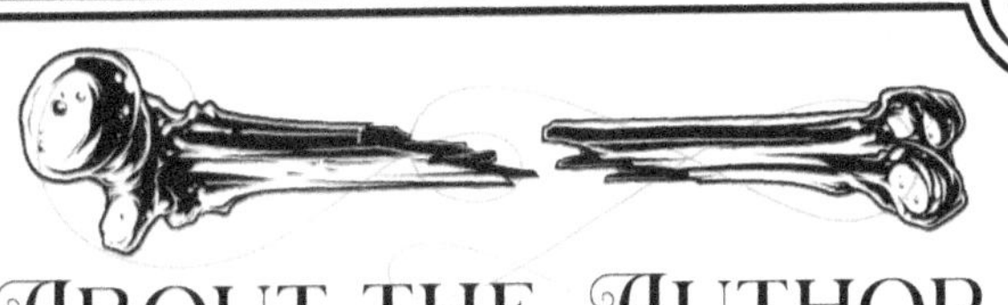

ABOUT THE AUTHOR

Valerie Willis is the Chief Operating Officer for 4 Horsemen Publications, Inc., an expert digital typesetter, and a fantasy romance author based out of Central Florida. When writing, she loves crafting novels with elements inspired by mythology, legends, folklore, fairy tales, and history. As COO, she oversees the design of all books including covers, typesets, and author branding where she pulls in creative print design while making versatile eBooks.

You can find her hosting workshops or attending as a guest speaker at many events (MegaCon, DragonCon, OCLS Writers Conference, Florida Writers Conference, SavvyAuthors, Women in Publishing Summit, etc.). She's been on panels with best-selling authors from Peter David to Delilah Dawson sharing her expertise in writing, research, worldbuilding, character development, book design, reader immersion, and more. You can also find her co-hosting on the Drinking with Authors Podcast speaking with Jonathan Maberry, Heather Graham, Charles Gannon, and many more on their own journeys as an author! Or talking about the spooky stuff over on Eerie Travels with topics such as big foots, mermaids, and even Bloody Mary!

Her award-winning dark fantasy paranormal romance, *The Cedric Series*, is a blend of genres that appeals to a wide range of readers who describe it as "dramatic, lustful, and fantasy fulfilling." The motto here is: "No immortal is beyond the ailments of man" that includes powerful creatures, demons, witches, and deities! Many of the monsters are derived from Medieval Bestiaries adding a fun flavor of new yet deeply-rooted assortment such as Coin Iotair, Shag Foal, Cynocephali, and more.

Like many authors, her writing journey started in grade school and carried her through high school. Many who grew up with her talk often of the traveling binders that were often kept safe in their lockers. This was the precursor to the now complete young adult dark urban fantasy of the *Tattooed Angels Trilogy* starting with *Rebirth*. This alternative historic piece about immortals and a failed reincarnation Hotan covers a wide variety of life lessons such as whether to follow your own lifepath or the one chosen for you, breaking toxic traditions, and the obligations of cleaning up our family's mistakes and destruction. Inspired by her own life tribulations, it has been the beacon to keep her moving toward the world of books and writing even now.

For readers of fantasy MM romance, check out her pen name V.C. Willis with the Traibon Family Saga starting with books *The Prince's Priest* and *The Priest's Assassin*. If you are looking for steamy paranormal erotica, chase down Urban Legends and modern retellings of fairy tales with Honey Cummings. Many have found themselves laughing out loud and fanning themselves while reading *Sleeping with Sasquatch* and *Wanton Woman in White*.

In 2021, she left her day job to join 4 Horsemen Publications, Inc. full time to bring over a decade of typesetting skills and industry knowledge to the table. Nothing is more rewarding for her than making fellow author's dreams come to life in physical format so they may share them with readers. Designing and writing books has been a longtime passion since childhood of hers and she continues to inspire and encourage authors around the world whenever possible, indulging whenever she can to chat about the books folks are reading and writing.

Keep in touch and keep reading!

www.WillisAuthor.com

linktr.ee/WillisAuthor

More Books by Valerie Willis

Cedric: The Demonic Knight
Romasanta: Father of Werewolves
The Oracle: Keeper of the Gaea's Gate
Artemis: Eye of Gaea
King Incubus: A New Reign
Queen Succubus: Holder of the Crown

Val's House of Musings: A Mixed Genre Short Story Collection

Rebirth
Judgment
Death

Writer's Bane: Research 101
Writer's Bane: Formatting

ANTHOLOGIES & COLLECTIONS

A World of Their Own
Work of Hearts Magazine Release
How I Met My Other: True Stories, True Love
It Was Always You: A Thrill of the Heart Anthology

Demonic Wildlife: A Fantastically Funny Adventure
Demonic Household: See Owner's Manual
Demonic Carnival: First Ticket's Free

The Hunted—Thrill of the Hunt 3
Urban Legends Reimagined—Thrill of the Hunt 4
Buried Alive—Thrill of the Hunt 5

PUBLIC DOMAIN REMAKES

Bulfinch's Mythology with Illustrations
Book of Werewolves
The Fairy Faith of Celtic Countries

Writing MM Romance as VC Willis

The Prince's Priest
The Priest's Assassin
The Assassin's Saint

The Champion's Lord: YONDER webnovel
Champion's Love: KU short story

WRITING AS HONEY CUMMINGS

Sleeping with Sasquatch
Cuddling with Chupacabra
Naked with New Jersey Devil
The Erotic Cryptid Collection

Laying with the Lady in Blue
Wanton Woman in White
Beating it with Bloody Mary
The Erotic Ghosts Collection

Beau and Professor Bestialora
The Goat's Gruff
Goldie and Her Three Beards
Pied Piper's Pipe
Princess Pea's Bed
Pinocchio and the Blow Up Doll
Jack's Beanstalk
Pulling Rapunzel's Hair
The Urban Erotica Fairy Tale
Collection

Curses & Crushes: KU short story

Queen's Incubus: YONDER webnovel

BOOK CLUB DISCUSSION QUESTIONS

1. How does Romasanta change over the course of the book?

2. What mythology did you identify?

3. What historical references were made?

4. Fenrir shares Romasanta's body with him. How did Romasanta feel when Fenrir "disappeared" and what do you believe happened to him?

5. How do you feel about Artemis's involvement in Romasanta's life?

6. Compare his relationships with Daphne, Lillith, and Rhea.

7. Did each serve a purpose in his life?

8. Could he traverse those parts of his life without them?

9. Which relationship do you feel is the strongest?

10. How did this book change your perspective from the first book, *Cedric the Demonic Knight?*

11. How many times did Romasanta lose himself to being an animal? Do you feel he was justified?

12. Nyctimus seems rather distant as a companion and friend. Why do you think he chose to be?

13. What was the most heart-wrenching moment for Romasanta in your opinion?

14. On that note, at what moment was he most blissful or content?

15. What inner fears do you think Romasanta fought with the most?

16. How significant was Romasanta's role in guiding Cedric's story and choices in life?

17. Who do you feel had the right to carry the Romulus heirloom, Boreas's silver sword? Romasanta or Cedric?

18. Why do you think the Battle Goddess Badbh likes Romasanta so much?

19. How many recognizable werewolf mythology and superstitions could you identify?

20. Apollo is most known for being a God in Greek Mythology. How much did you discover about him?

21. Lykaon history and mythology has inspired many pop culture movies on werewolves. How did the author portray them here? Why do you think she took this perspective?

22. How important was Romasanta's role in gaining access to Avalon?

23. In the scene where Romasanta returns to see Daphne, what was the significance in Lillith's own actions?

More books from 4 Horsemen Publications

Fantasy, SciFi, & Paranormal Romance

Amanda Fasciano
Waking Up Dead
Dead Vessel
The Dead Show
Dead Revelations
Dead Carnage
Dead Woods

Beau Lake
The Beast Beside Me
The Beast Within Me
Taming the Beast: Novella
The Beast After Me
Charming the Beast
The Beast Like Me

Chelsea Burton Dunn
By Moonlight
Moonbound
Bloodthirsty

D. Lambert
Rydan
Celebrant
Northlander
Esparan
King
Traitor
His Last Name

J.M. Paquette
Klauden's Ring
Solyn's Body
The Inbetween
Hannah's Heart
Call Me Forth
Invite Me In

Keep Me Close
Heart of Stone

Kait Disney-Leugers
Antique Magic
Blood Magic
Heart Magic

Lyra R. Saenz
Prelude
Sonata
Scherzo
Falsetto in the Woods: Novella
The Devil's Trill
Ragtime Swing
Midnight Cumbia
Sea Song De La Corsaire

Paige Lavoie
I'm in Love with Mothman
I'm Engaged to Mothman
Dear Galaxy

Robert J. Lewis
Shadow Guardian and the Three Bears
Shadow Guardian and the Big Bad Wolf
Shadow Guardian and the Boys That Went Woof

T.S. Simons
Project Hemisphere
The Space Between
Infinity
Circle of Protections
Sessrúmnir
The 45th Parallel

Discover more at
4HorsemenPublications.com